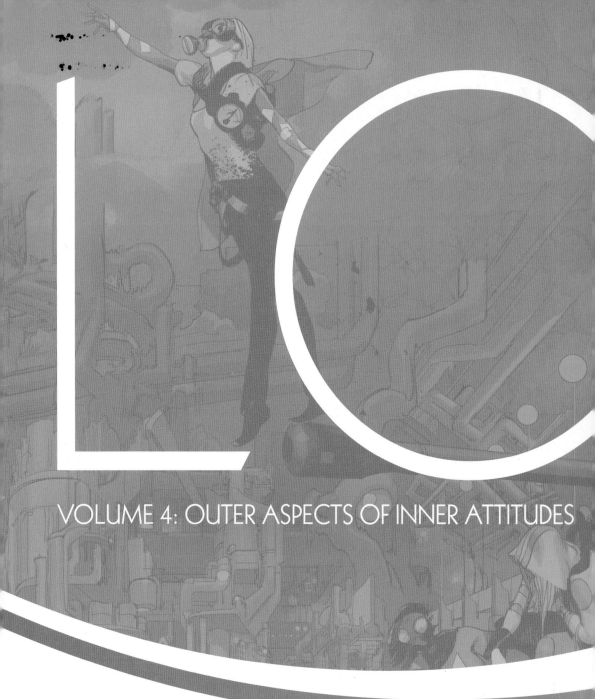

LO
VOLUME 4: OUTER ASPECTS OF INNER ATTITUDES

IMAGE COMICS, INC

Robert Kirkman: Chief Operating Officer / Erik Larsen: Chief Financial Officer / Todd McFarlane: President
Marc Silvestri: Chief Executive Officer / Jim Valentino: Vice President / Eric Stephenson: Publisher
Corey Murphy: Director of Sales / Jeff Boison: Director of Publishing Planning & Book Trade Sales
Chris Ross: Director of Digital Sales / Jeff Stang: Director of Specialty Sales / Kat Salazar: Director of PR & Marketing Branwyn
Bigglestone: Controller / Kali Dugan: Senior Accounting Manager / Sue Korpela: Accounting & HR Manager
Drew Gill: Art Director / Heather Doornink: Production Director / Leigh Thomas: Print Manager / Tricia Ramos: Traffic Manager
Briah Skelly: Publicist / Aly Hoffman: Events & Conventions Coordinator / Sasha Head: Sales & Marketing Production Designer
David Brothers: Branding Manager / Melissa Gifford: Content Manager / Drew Fitzgerald: Publicity Assistant
Vincent Kukua: Production Artist / Erika Schnatz: Production Artist / Ryan Brewer: Production Artist
Shanna Matuszak: Production Artist / Carey Hall: Production Artist / Esther Kim: Direct Market Sales Representative
Emilio Bautista: Digital Sales Representative / Leanna Caunter: Accounting Analyst
Chloe Ramos-Peterson: Library Market Sales Representative / Marla Eizik: Administrative Assistant
IMAGECOMICS.COM

GIANT
GENERATOR

JEFF POWELL
Collection Design

ISBN 978-1-5343-0229-7

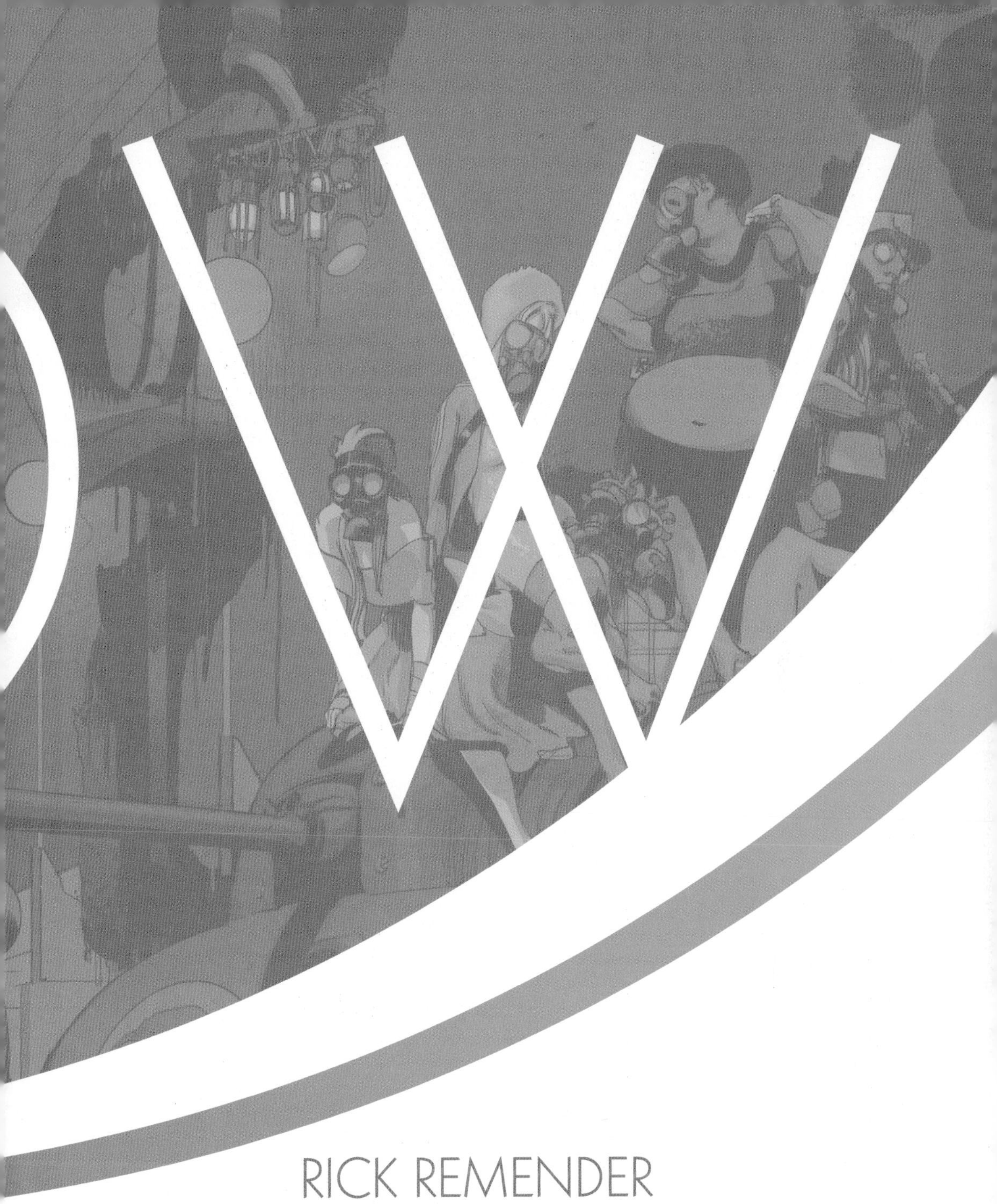

RICK REMENDER
writer

GREG TOCCHINI
artist, story (#16)

DAVE McCAIG
colors

RUS WOOTON
letterer

SEBASTIAN GIRNER
editor

Created by Rick Remender & Greg Tocchini

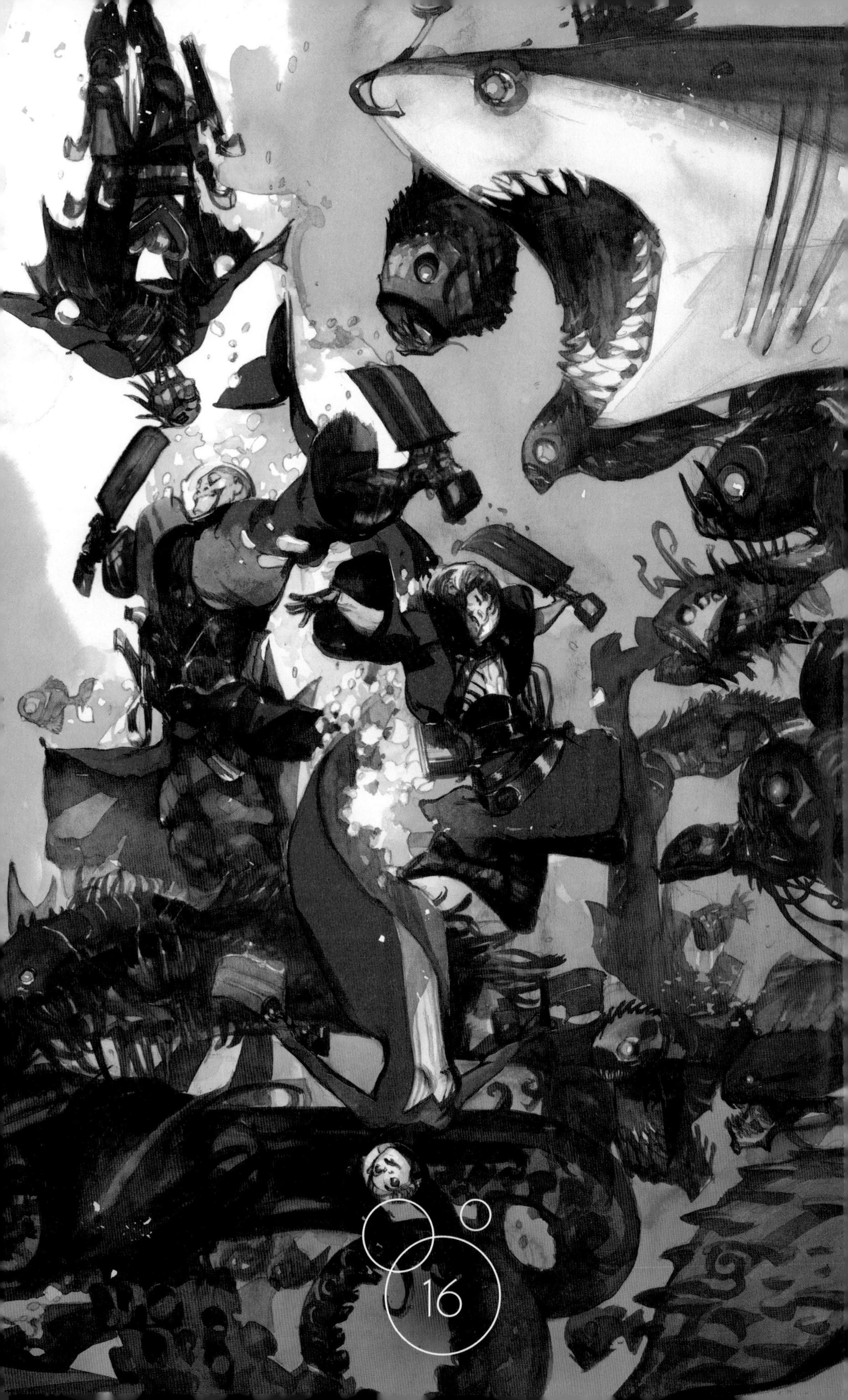

16

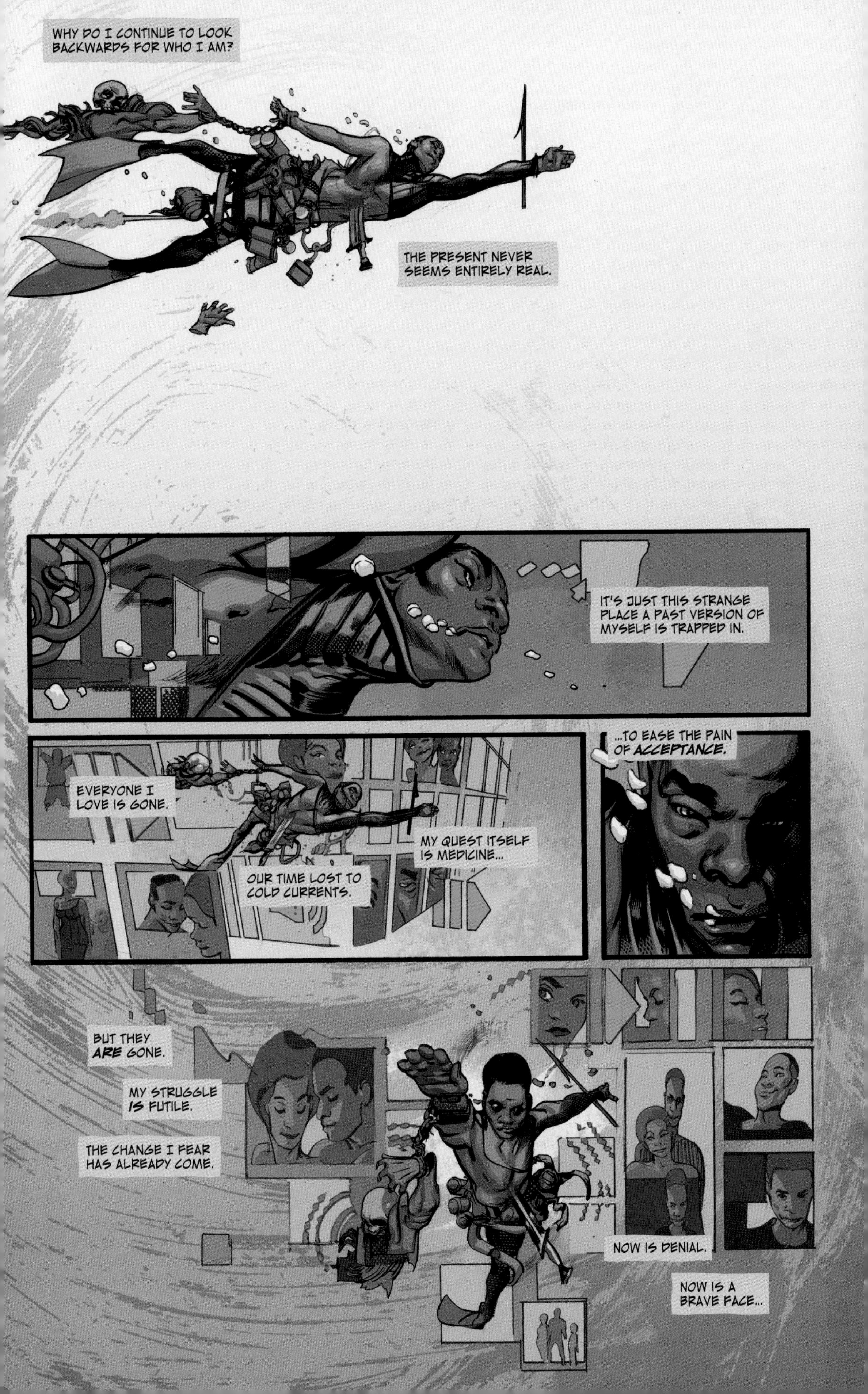
WHY DO I CONTINUE TO LOOK BACKWARDS FOR WHO I AM?
THE PRESENT NEVER SEEMS ENTIRELY REAL.
IT'S JUST THIS STRANGE PLACE A PAST VERSION OF MYSELF IS TRAPPED IN.
EVERYONE I LOVE IS GONE.
OUR TIME LOST TO COLD CURRENTS.
MY QUEST ITSELF IS MEDICINE...
...TO EASE THE PAIN OF ACCEPTANCE.
BUT THEY ARE GONE.
MY STRUGGLE IS FUTILE.
THE CHANGE I FEAR HAS ALREADY COME.
NOW IS DENIAL.
NOW IS A BRAVE FACE...

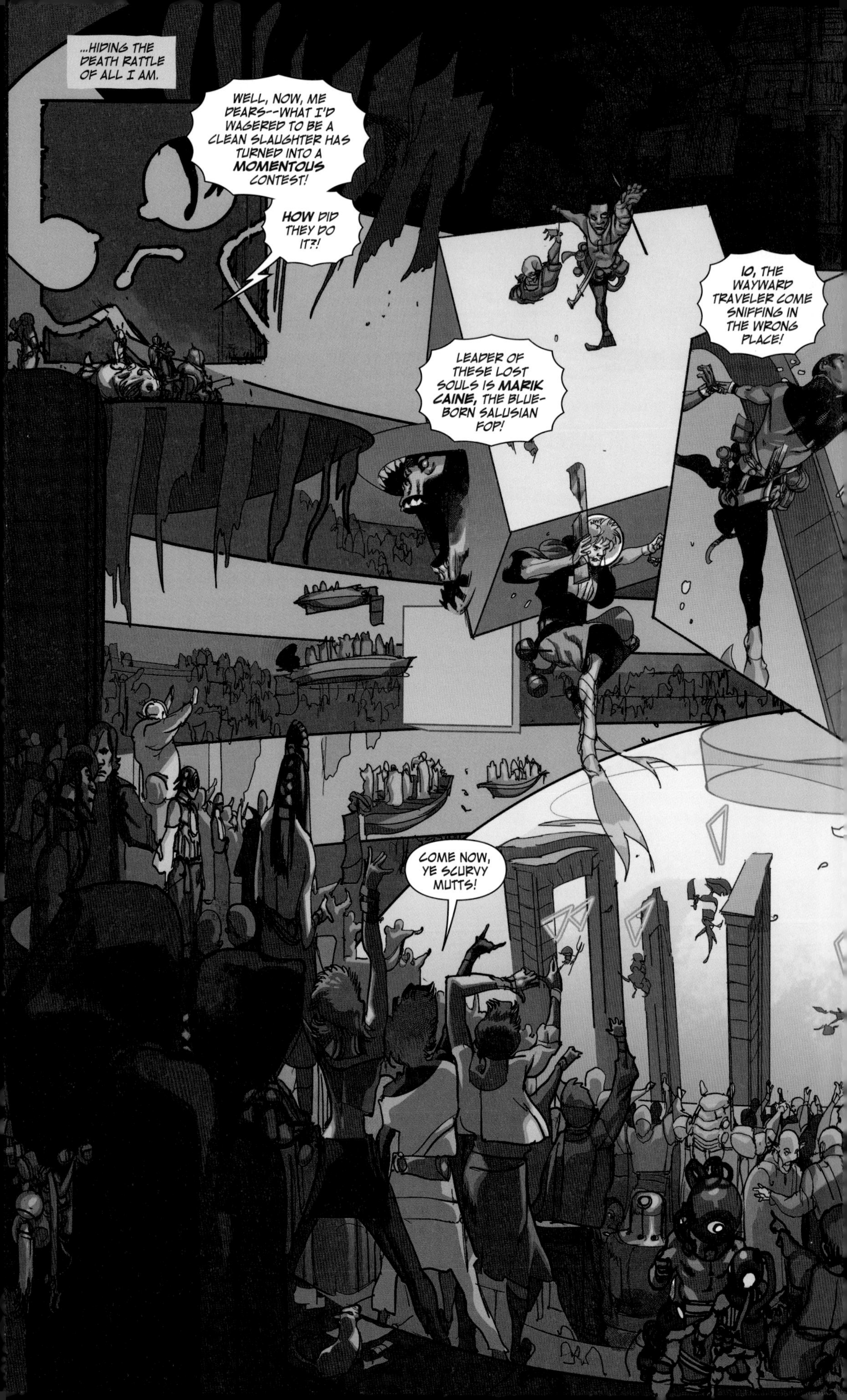
...HIDING THE DEATH RATTLE OF ALL I AM.
WELL, NOW, ME DEARS--WHAT I'D WAGERED TO BE A CLEAN SLAUGHTER HAS TURNED INTO A MOMENTOUS CONTEST!
HOW DID THEY DO IT?!
IO, THE WAYWARD TRAVELER COME SNIFFING IN THE WRONG PLACE!
LEADER OF THESE LOST SOULS IS MARIK CAINE, THE BLUE-BORN SALUSIAN FOP!
COME NOW, YE SCURVY MUTTS!

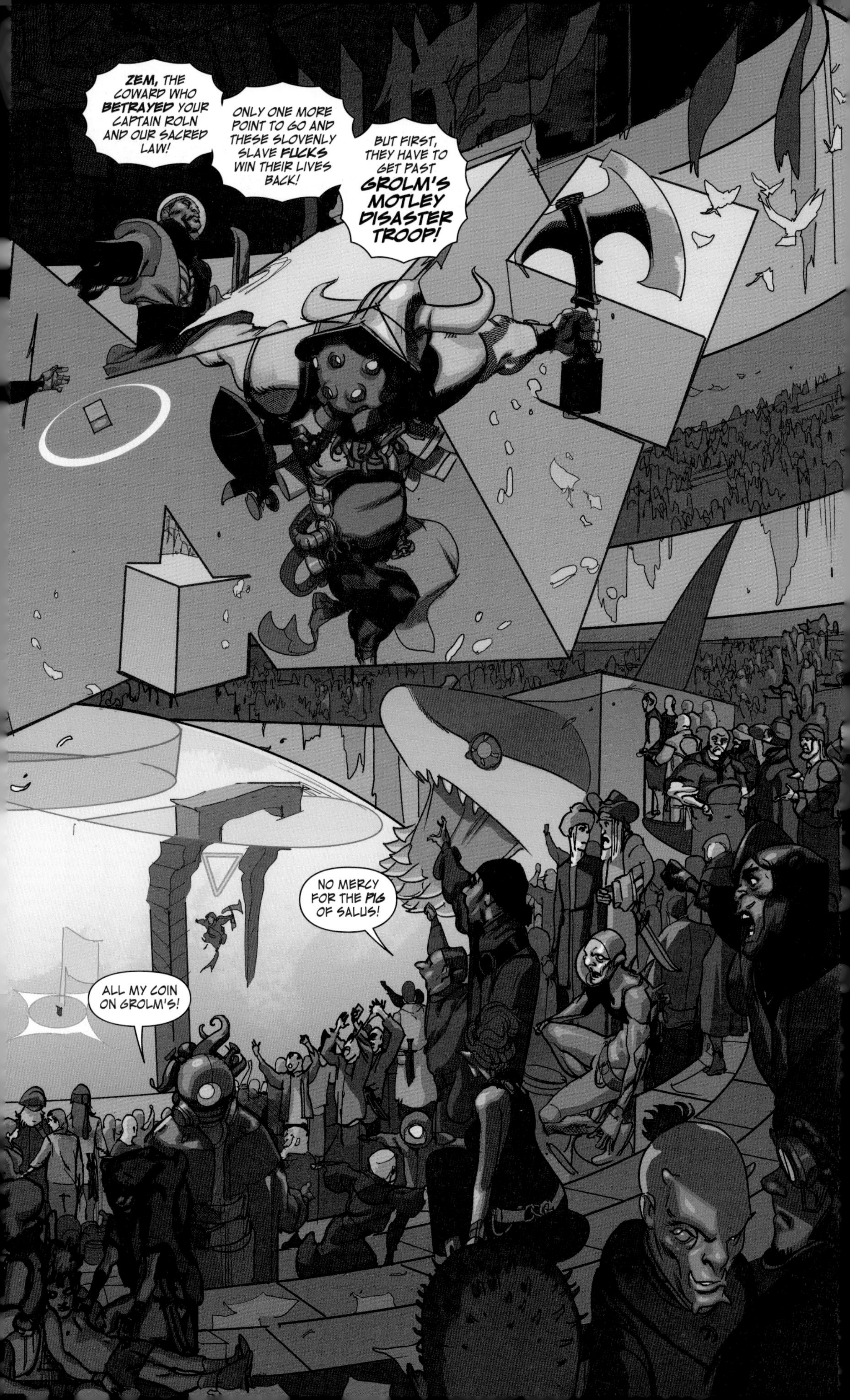
ZEM, THE COWARD WHO BETRAYED YOUR CAPTAIN ROLN AND OUR SACRED LAW!
ONLY ONE MORE POINT TO GO AND THESE SLOVENLY SLAVE FUCKS WIN THEIR LIVES BACK!
BUT FIRST, THEY HAVE TO GET PAST GROLM'S MOTLEY DISASTER TROOP!
NO MERCY FOR THE PIG OF SALUS!
ALL MY COIN ON GROLM'S!

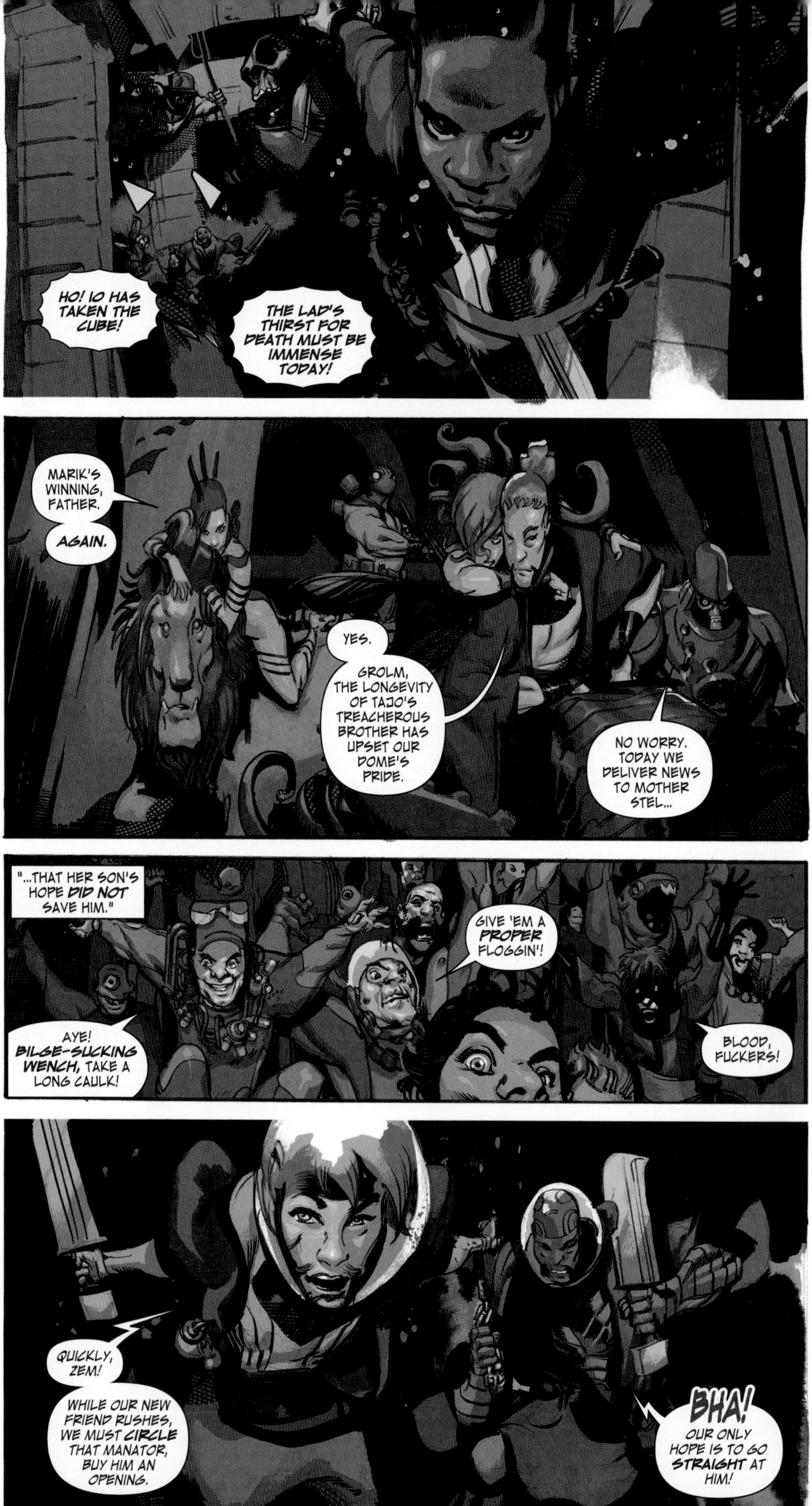
HO! IO HAS TAKEN THE CUBE!
THE LAD'S THIRST FOR DEATH MUST BE IMMENSE TODAY!
MARIK'S WINNING, FATHER.
AGAIN.
YES.
GROLM, THE LONGEVITY OF TAJO'S TREACHEROUS BROTHER HAS UPSET OUR DOME'S PRIDE.
NO WORRY. TODAY WE DELIVER NEWS TO MOTHER STEL...
"...THAT HER SON'S HOPE DID NOT SAVE HIM."
GIVE 'EM A PROPER FLOGGIN'!
AYE! BILGE-SUCKING WENCH, TAKE A LONG CAULK!
BLOOD, FUCKERS!
QUICKLY, ZEM!
WHILE OUR NEW FRIEND RUSHES, WE MUST CIRCLE THAT MANATOR, BUY HIM AN OPENING.
BHA!
OUR ONLY HOPE IS TO GO STRAIGHT AT HIM!

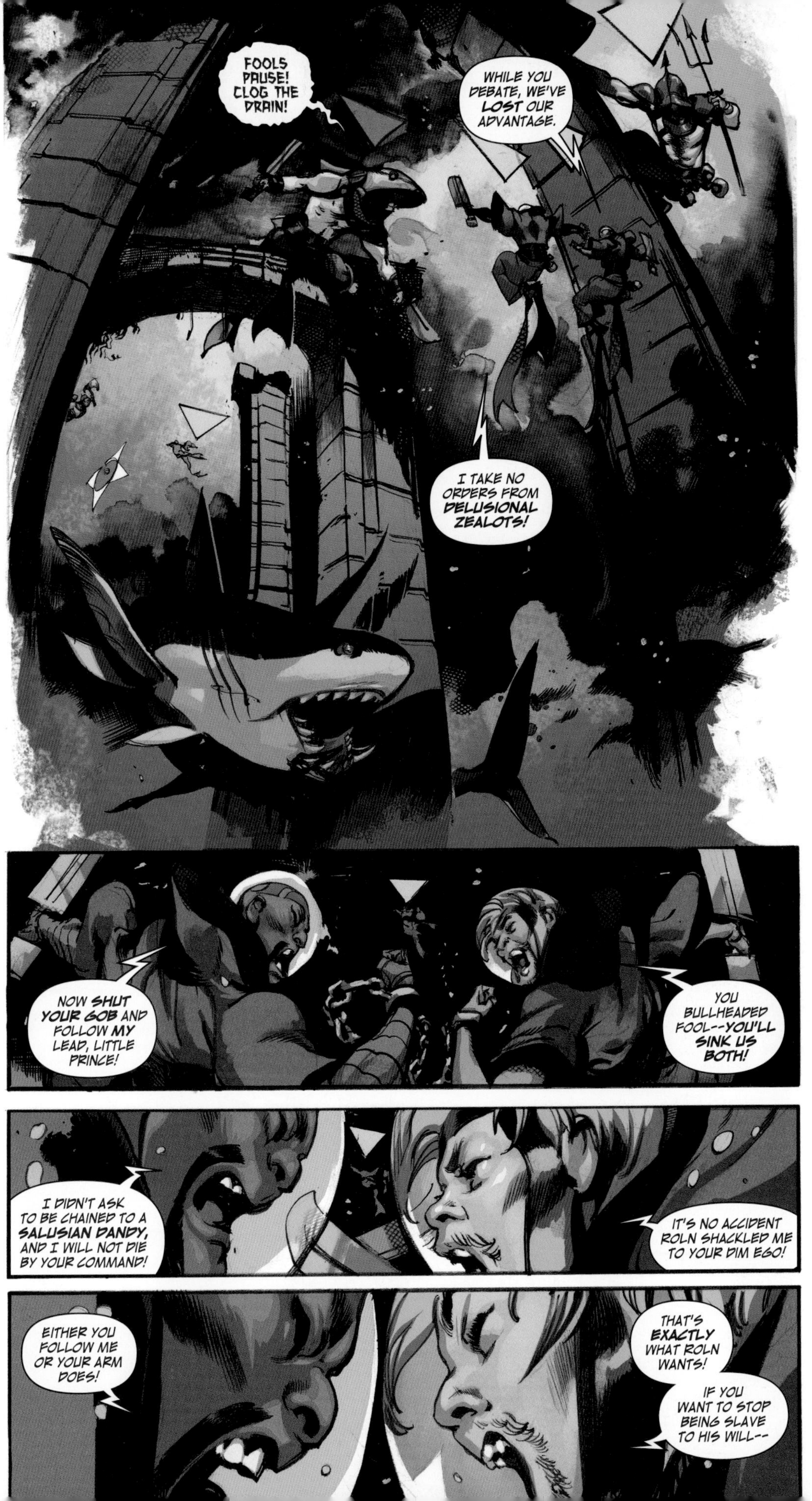
FOOLS PAUSE! CLOG THE DRAIN!
WHILE YOU DEBATE, WE'VE LOST OUR ADVANTAGE.
I TAKE NO ORDERS FROM DELUSIONAL ZEALOTS!
NOW SHUT YOUR GOB AND FOLLOW MY LEAD, LITTLE PRINCE!
YOU BULLHEADED FOOL--YOU'LL SINK US BOTH!
I DIDN'T ASK TO BE CHAINED TO A SALUSIAN DANDY, AND I WILL NOT DIE BY YOUR COMMAND!
IT'S NO ACCIDENT ROLN SHACKLED ME TO YOUR DIM EGO!
EITHER YOU FOLLOW ME OR YOUR ARM DOES!
THAT'S EXACTLY WHAT ROLN WANTS!
IF YOU WANT TO STOP BEING SLAVE TO HIS WILL--

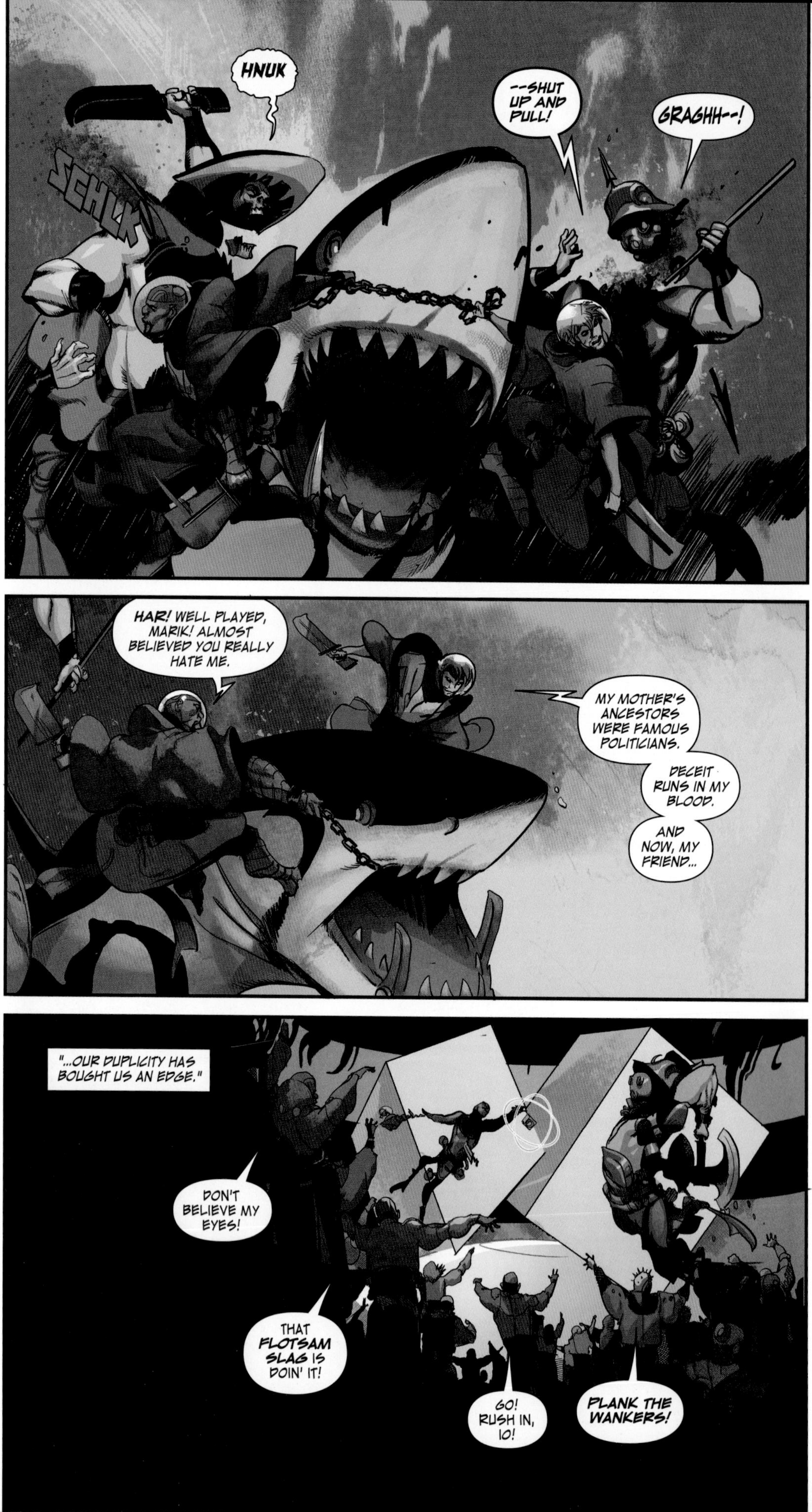
HNUK
SCHLK
--SHUT UP AND PULL!
GRAGHH--!
HAR! WELL PLAYED, MARIK! ALMOST BELIEVED YOU REALLY HATE ME.
MY MOTHER'S ANCESTORS WERE FAMOUS POLITICIANS.
DECEIT RUNS IN MY BLOOD.
AND NOW, MY FRIEND...
"...OUR DUPLICITY HAS BOUGHT US AN EDGE."
DON'T BELIEVE MY EYES!
THAT FLOTSAM SLAG IS DOIN' IT!
GO! RUSH IN, IO!
PLANK THE WANKERS!

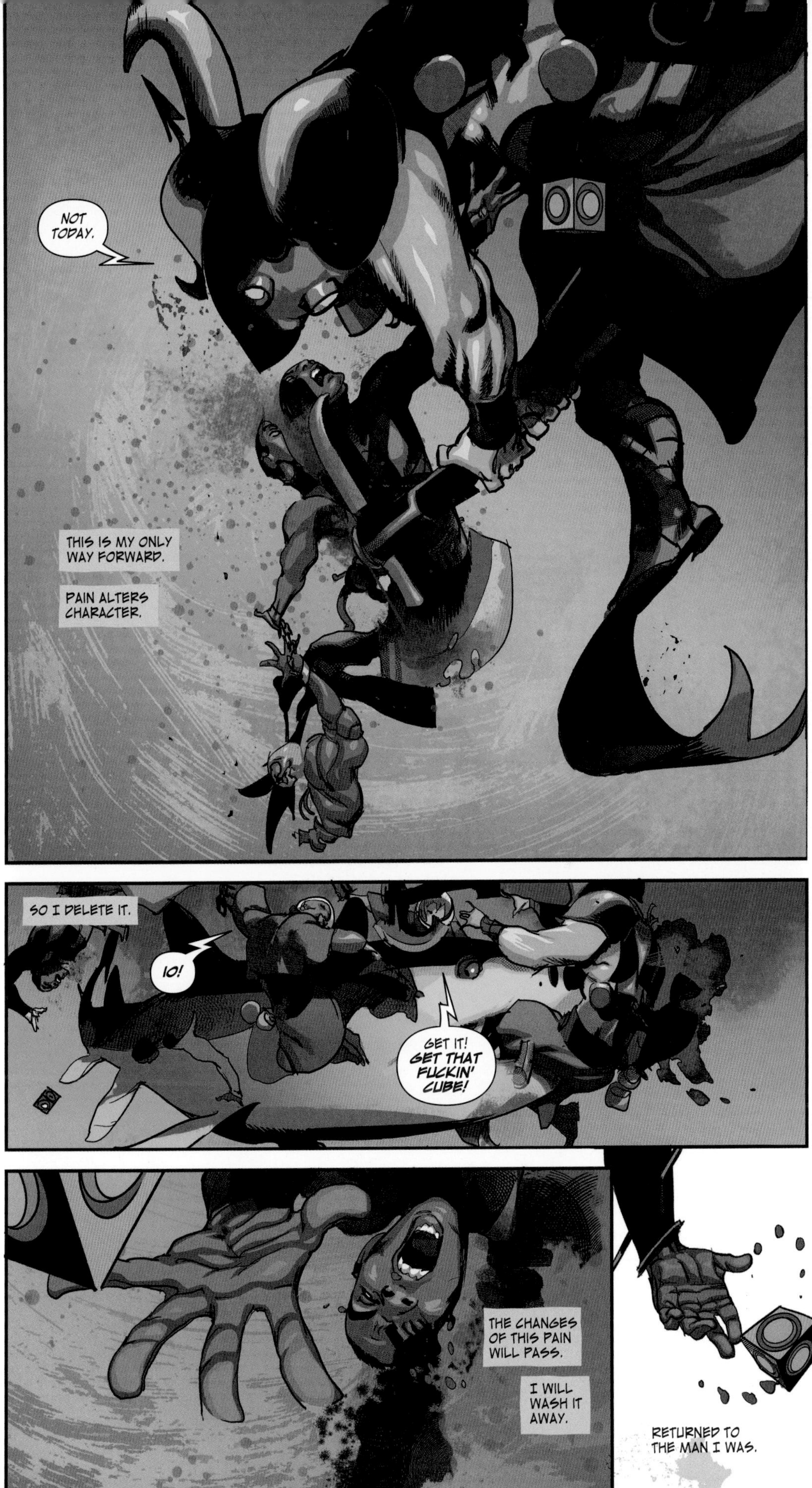
NOT TODAY.
THIS IS MY ONLY WAY FORWARD.
PAIN ALTERS CHARACTER.
SO I DELETE IT.
IO!
GET IT! GET THAT FUCKIN' CUBE!
THE CHANGES OF THIS PAIN WILL PASS.
I WILL WASH IT AWAY.
RETURNED TO THE MAN I WAS.

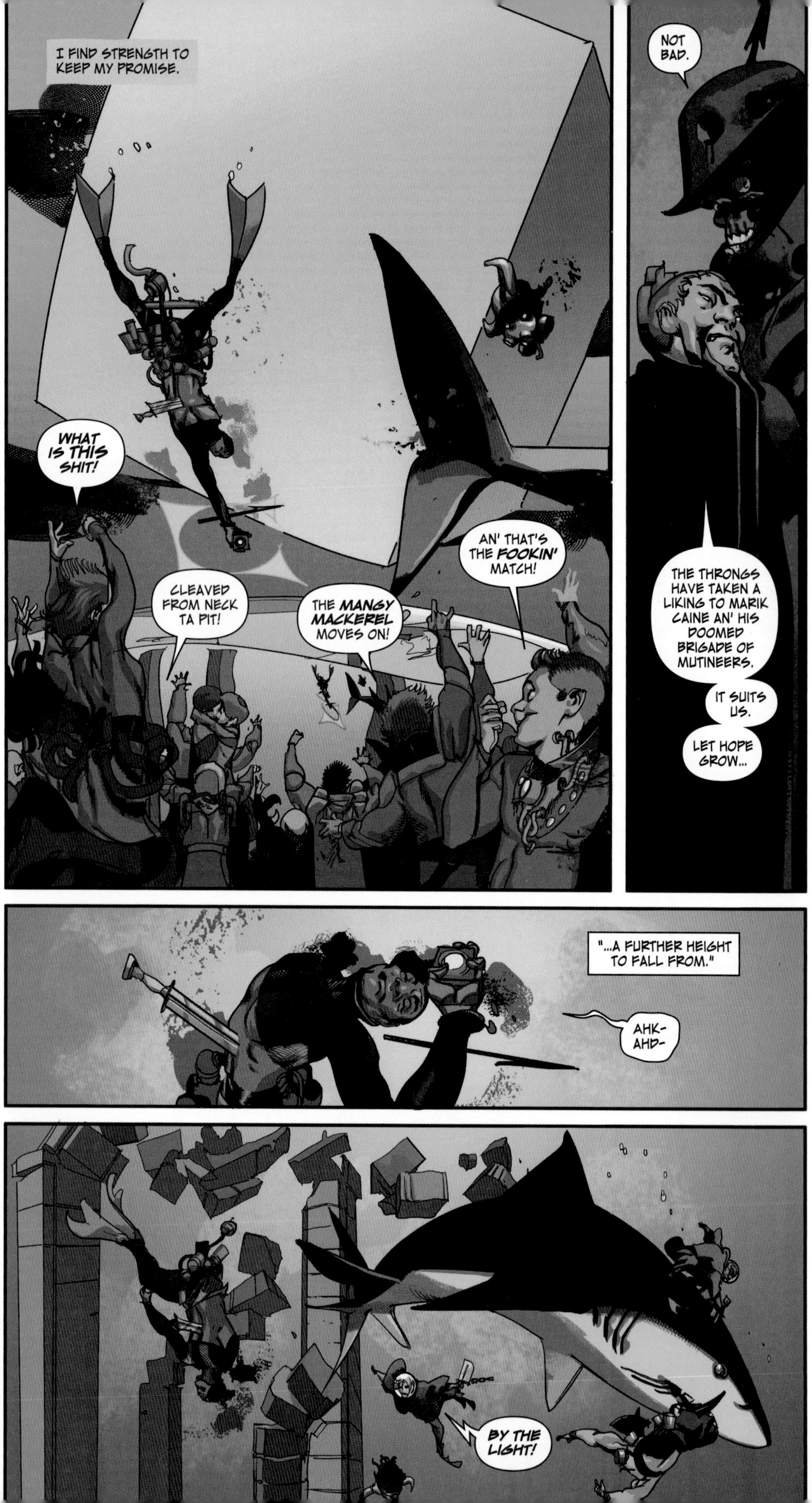
I FIND STRENGTH TO KEEP MY PROMISE.
WHAT IS THIS SHIT!
CLEAVED FROM NECK TA PIT!
THE MANGY MACKEREL MOVES ON!
AN' THAT'S THE FOOKIN' MATCH!
NOT BAD.
THE THRONGS HAVE TAKEN A LIKING TO MARIK CAINE AN' HIS DOOMED BRIGADE OF MUTINEERS.
IT SUITS US.
LET HOPE GROW...
"...A FURTHER HEIGHT TO FALL FROM."
AHK-AHD-
BY THE LIGHT!

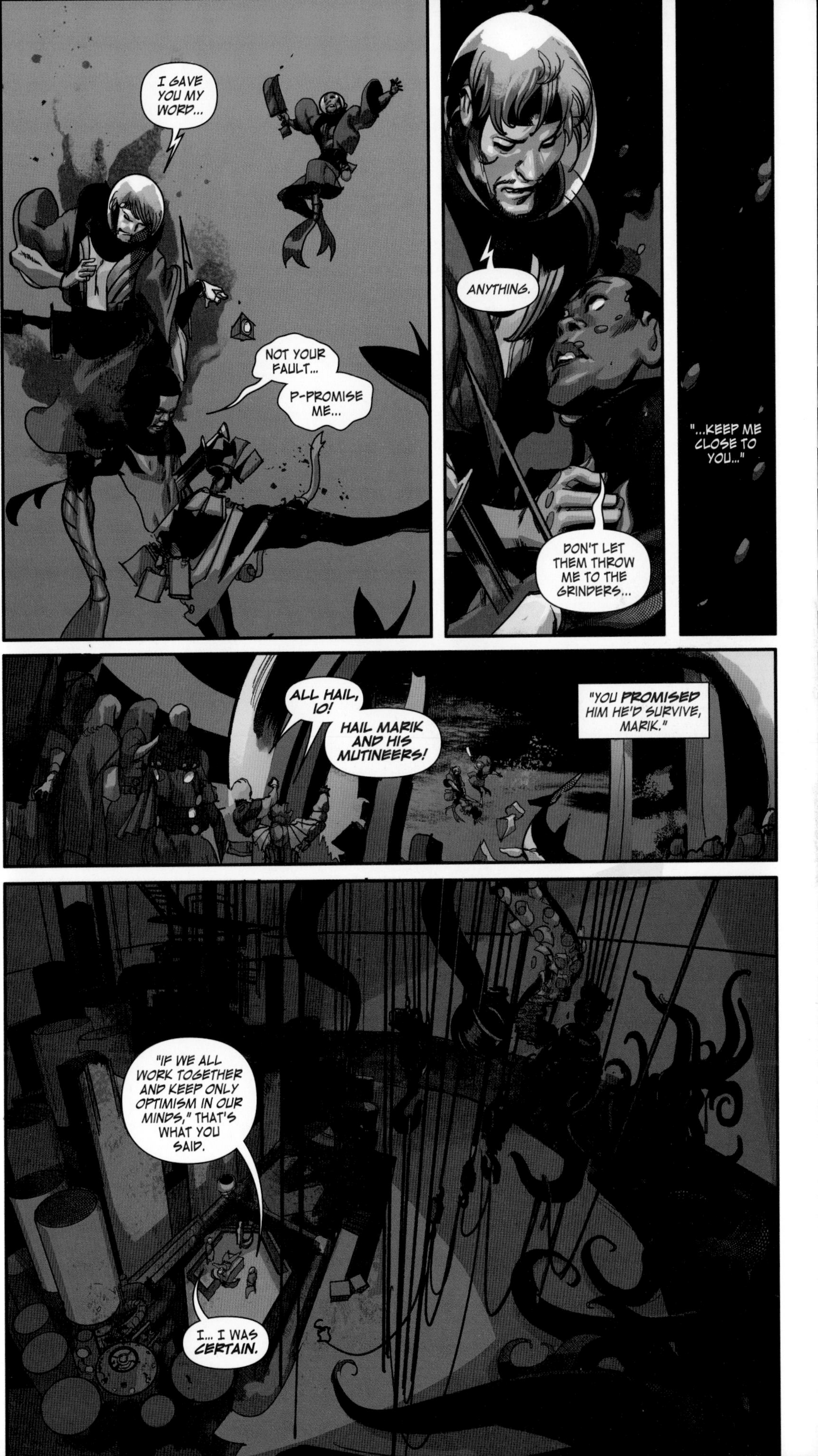
I GAVE YOU MY WORD...
NOT YOUR FAULT...
P-PROMISE ME...
ANYTHING.
DON'T LET THEM THROW ME TO THE GRINDERS...
"...KEEP ME CLOSE TO YOU..."
ALL HAIL, IO!
HAIL MARIK AND HIS MUTINEERS!
"YOU **PROMISED** HIM HE'D SURVIVE, MARIK."
"IF WE ALL WORK TOGETHER AND KEEP ONLY OPTIMISM IN OUR MINDS," THAT'S WHAT YOU SAID.
I... I WAS ***CERTAIN.***

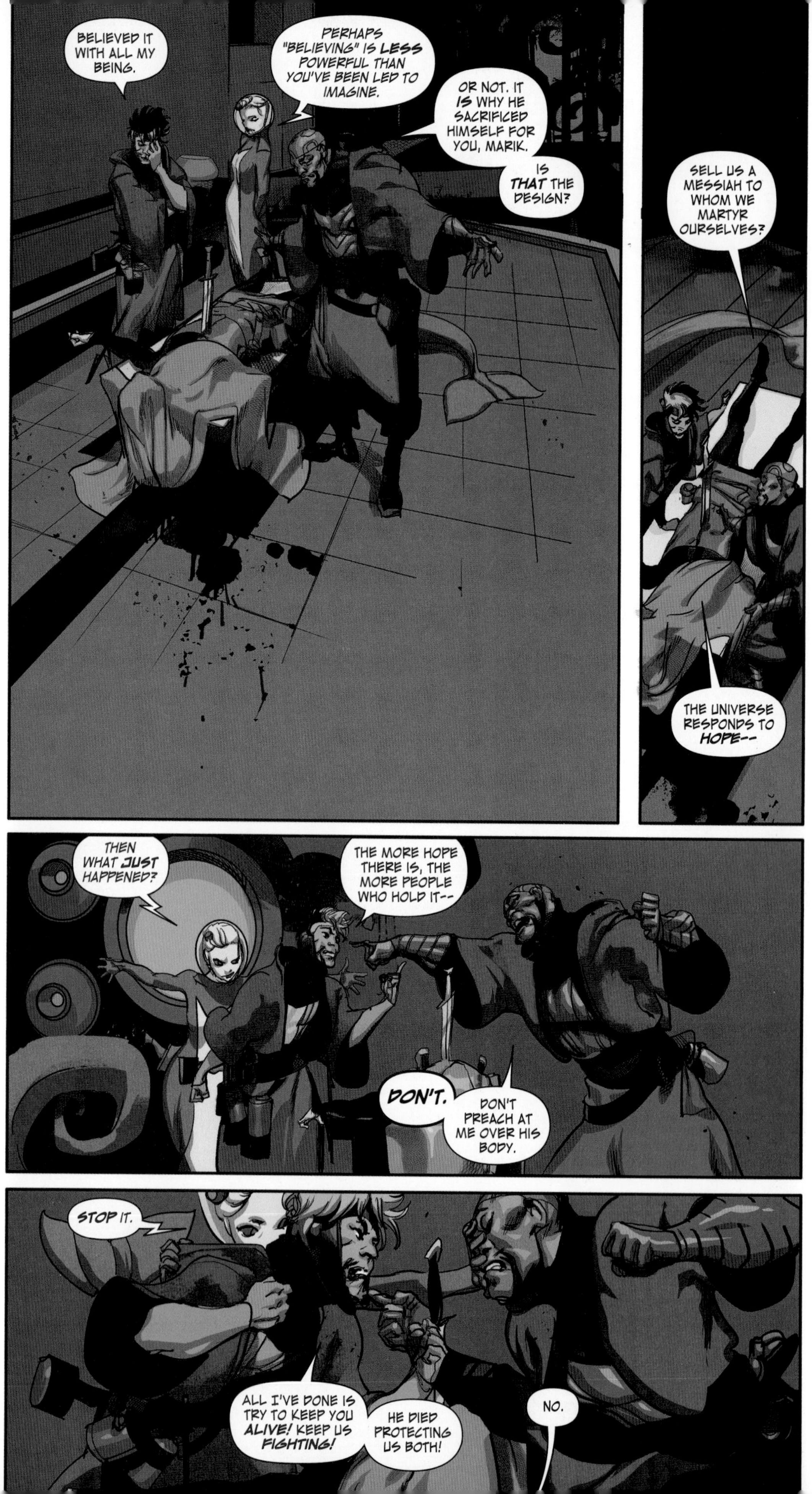
BELIEVED IT WITH ALL MY BEING.
PERHAPS "BELIEVING" IS LESS POWERFUL THAN YOU'VE BEEN LED TO IMAGINE.
OR NOT. IT IS WHY HE SACRIFICED HIMSELF FOR YOU, MARIK.
IS THAT THE DESIGN?
SELL US A MESSIAH TO WHOM WE MARTYR OURSELVES?
THE UNIVERSE RESPONDS TO HOPE--
THEN WHAT JUST HAPPENED?
THE MORE HOPE THERE IS, THE MORE PEOPLE WHO HOLD IT--
DON'T.
DON'T PREACH AT ME OVER HIS BODY.
STOP IT.
ALL I'VE DONE IS TRY TO KEEP YOU ALIVE! KEEP US FIGHTING!
HE DIED PROTECTING US BOTH!
NO.

I MOSTLY DID IT FOR YOU, MARIK.

HOW...?

DON'T LET THIS DETRACT FROM MARIK'S QUANTUMOLOGY.

I DOUBTED IT MYSELF, BUT THE MATH ADDS UP.

QUANTUM MECHANICS STATES THAT PARTICLES DO NOT HAVE DEFINED LOCATIONS UNTIL THEY ARE OBSERVED.

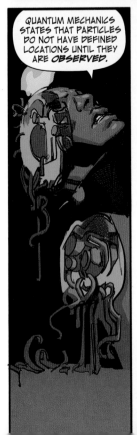

SCHLKK

WHAT YOU HOLD IN YOUR MIND DOES AFFECT WHAT YOU OBSERVE.

SO, IN THAT SENSE, YOUR MOTHER IS RIGHT.

THOUGH IT IS NOT AS MUCH A RELIGION AS A UNIVERSAL PRINCIPLE.

WH-WHAT ARE YOU?

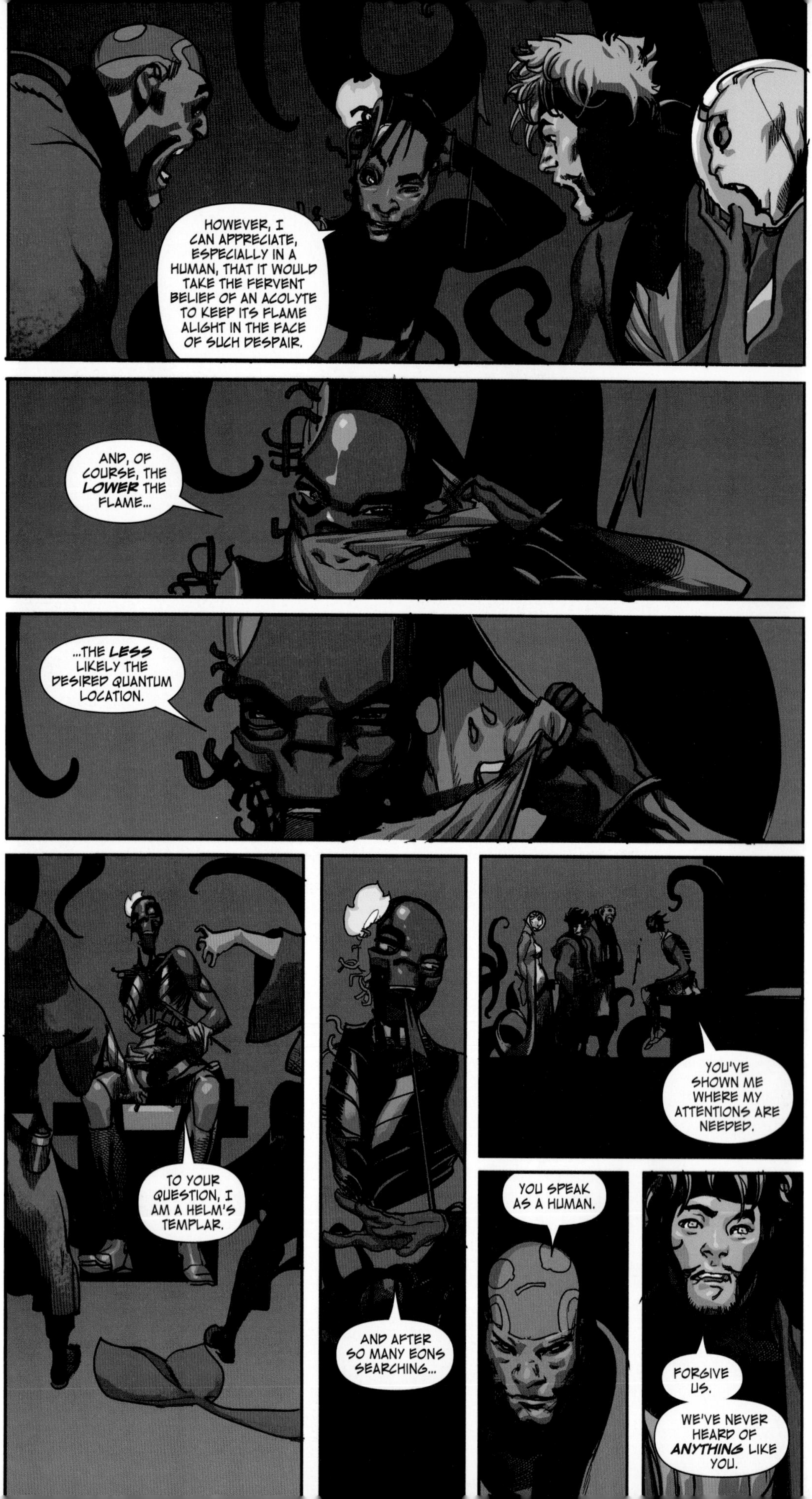
HOWEVER, I CAN APPRECIATE, ESPECIALLY IN A HUMAN, THAT IT WOULD TAKE THE FERVENT BELIEF OF AN ACOLYTE TO KEEP ITS FLAME ALIGHT IN THE FACE OF SUCH DESPAIR.
AND, OF COURSE, THE LOWER THE FLAME...
...THE LESS LIKELY THE DESIRED QUANTUM LOCATION.
TO YOUR QUESTION, I AM A HELM'S TEMPLAR.
AND AFTER SO MANY EONS SEARCHING...
YOU'VE SHOWN ME WHERE MY ATTENTIONS ARE NEEDED.
YOU SPEAK AS A HUMAN.
FORGIVE US.
WE'VE NEVER HEARD OF ANYTHING LIKE YOU.

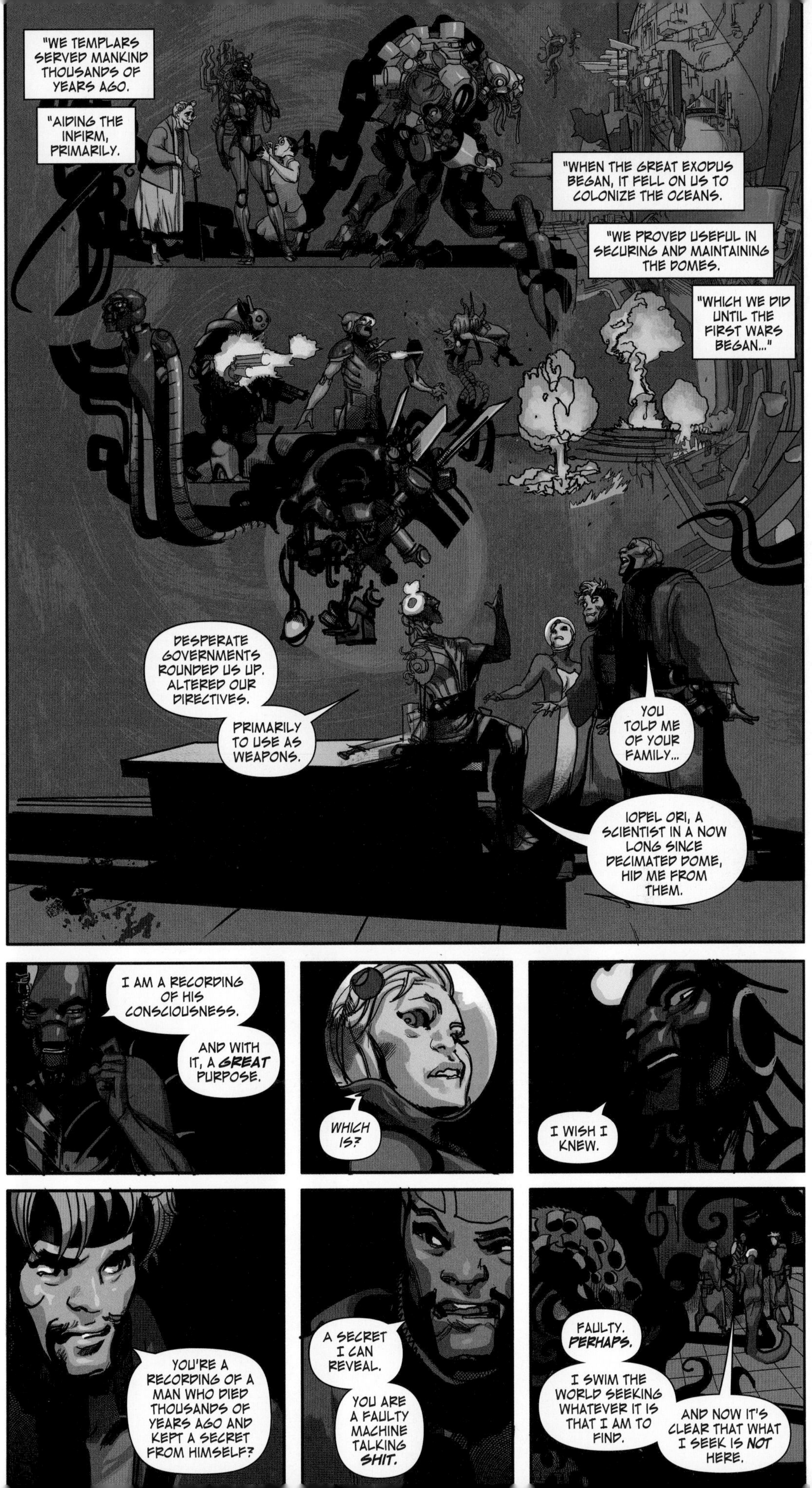
"WE TEMPLARS SERVED MANKIND THOUSANDS OF YEARS AGO.
"AIDING THE INFIRM, PRIMARILY.
"WHEN THE GREAT EXODUS BEGAN, IT FELL ON US TO COLONIZE THE OCEANS.
"WE PROVED USEFUL IN SECURING AND MAINTAINING THE DOMES.
"WHICH WE DID UNTIL THE FIRST WARS BEGAN..."
DESPERATE GOVERNMENTS ROUNDED US UP. ALTERED OUR DIRECTIVES.
PRIMARILY TO USE AS WEAPONS.
YOU TOLD ME OF YOUR FAMILY...
IOPEL ORI, A SCIENTIST IN A NOW LONG SINCE DECIMATED DOME, HID ME FROM THEM.
I AM A RECORDING OF HIS CONSCIOUSNESS.
AND WITH IT, A **GREAT** PURPOSE.
WHICH IS?
I WISH I KNEW.
YOU'RE A RECORDING OF A MAN WHO DIED THOUSANDS OF YEARS AGO AND KEPT A SECRET FROM HIMSELF?
A SECRET I CAN REVEAL.
YOU ARE A FAULTY MACHINE TALKING **SHIT.**
FAULTY. **PERHAPS.**
I SWIM THE WORLD SEEKING WHATEVER IT IS THAT I AM TO FIND.
AND NOW IT'S CLEAR THAT WHAT I SEEK IS **NOT** HERE.

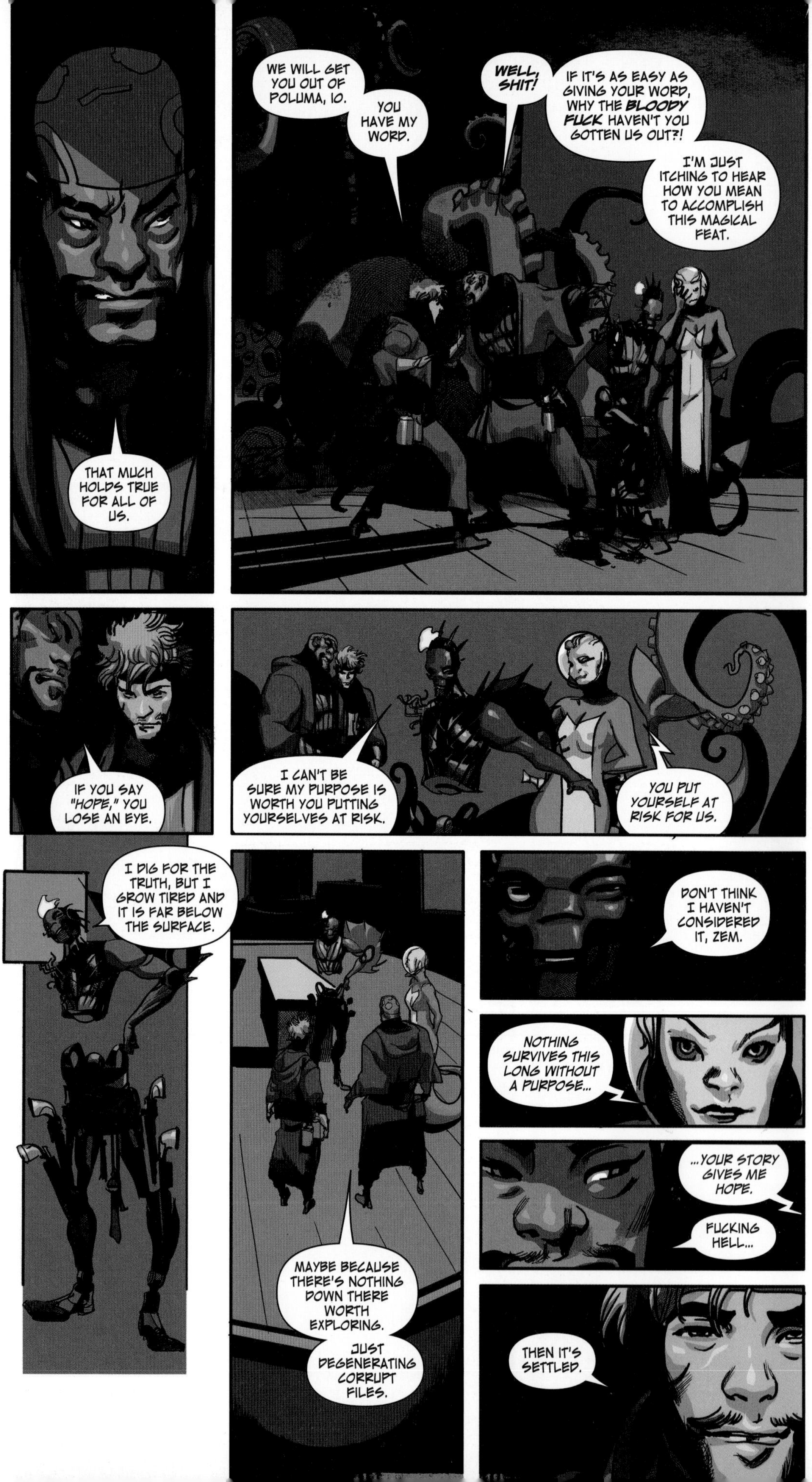
WE WILL GET YOU OUT OF POLUMA, IO.
YOU HAVE MY WORD.
WELL, SHIT!
IF IT'S AS EASY AS GIVING YOUR WORD, WHY THE BLOODY FUCK HAVEN'T YOU GOTTEN US OUT?!
I'M JUST ITCHING TO HEAR HOW YOU MEAN TO ACCOMPLISH THIS MAGICAL FEAT.
THAT MUCH HOLDS TRUE FOR ALL OF US.
IF YOU SAY "HOPE," YOU LOSE AN EYE.
I CAN'T BE SURE MY PURPOSE IS WORTH YOU PUTTING YOURSELVES AT RISK.
YOU PUT YOURSELF AT RISK FOR US.
I DIG FOR THE TRUTH, BUT I GROW TIRED AND IT IS FAR BELOW THE SURFACE.
MAYBE BECAUSE THERE'S NOTHING DOWN THERE WORTH EXPLORING.
JUST DEGENERATING CORRUPT FILES.
DON'T THINK I HAVEN'T CONSIDERED IT, ZEM.
NOTHING SURVIVES THIS LONG WITHOUT A PURPOSE...
...YOUR STORY GIVES ME HOPE.
FUCKING HELL...
THEN IT'S SETTLED.

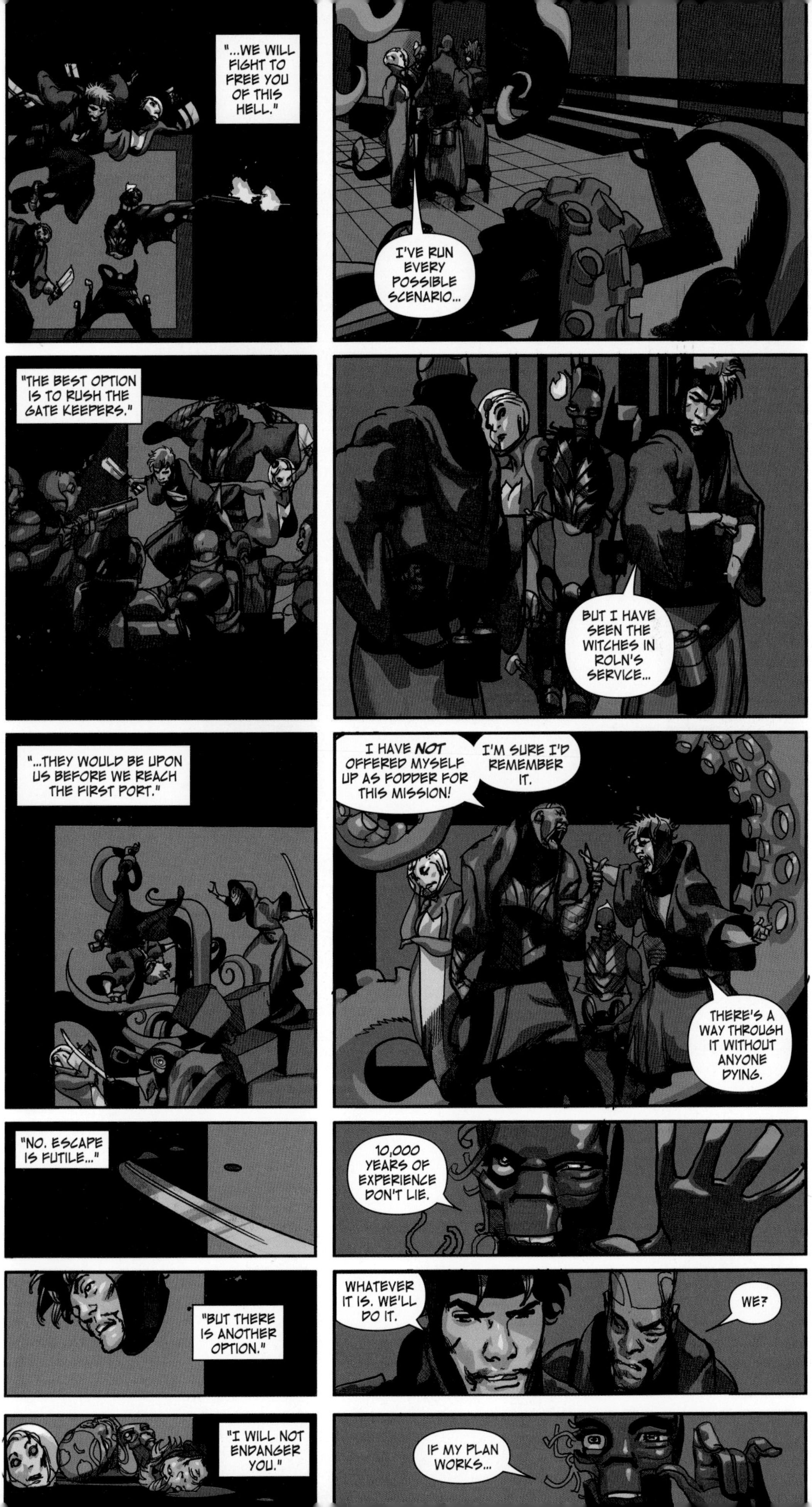
"...WE WILL FIGHT TO FREE YOU OF THIS HELL."
I'VE RUN EVERY POSSIBLE SCENARIO...
"THE BEST OPTION IS TO RUSH THE GATE KEEPERS."
BUT I HAVE SEEN THE WITCHES IN ROLN'S SERVICE...
"...THEY WOULD BE UPON US BEFORE WE REACH THE FIRST PORT."
I HAVE NOT OFFERED MYSELF UP AS FODDER FOR THIS MISSION!
I'M SURE I'D REMEMBER IT.
THERE'S A WAY THROUGH IT WITHOUT ANYONE DYING.
"NO. ESCAPE IS FUTILE..."
10,000 YEARS OF EXPERIENCE DON'T LIE.
"BUT THERE IS ANOTHER OPTION."
WHATEVER IT IS, WE'LL DO IT.
WE?
"I WILL NOT ENDANGER YOU."
IF MY PLAN WORKS...

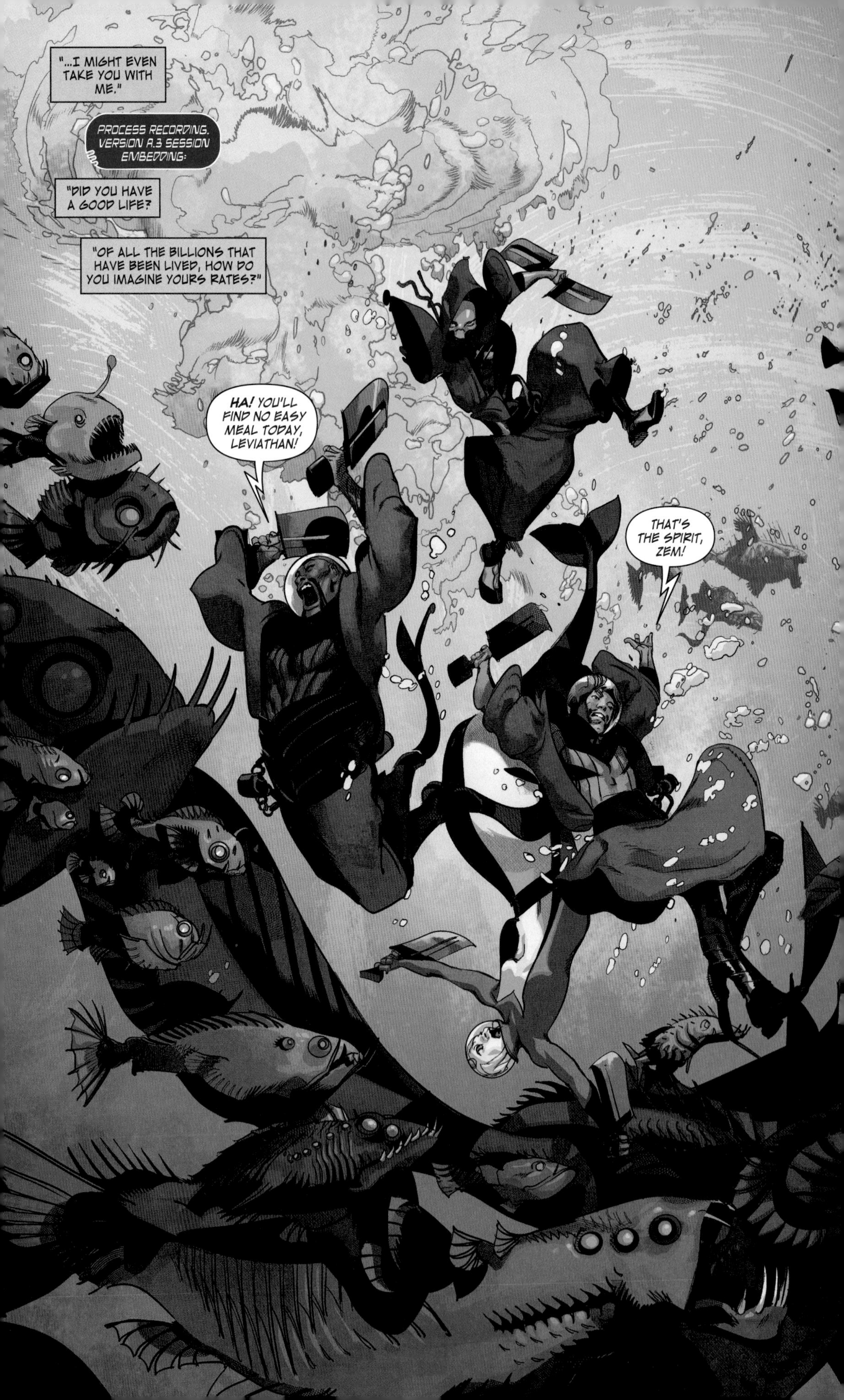
"...I MIGHT EVEN TAKE YOU WITH ME."
PROCESS RECORDING. VERSION A.3 SESSION EMBEDDING:
"DID YOU HAVE A GOOD LIFE?
"OF ALL THE BILLIONS THAT HAVE BEEN LIVED, HOW DO YOU IMAGINE YOURS RATES?"
HA! YOU'LL FIND NO EASY MEAL TODAY, LEVIATHAN!
THAT'S THE SPIRIT, ZEM!

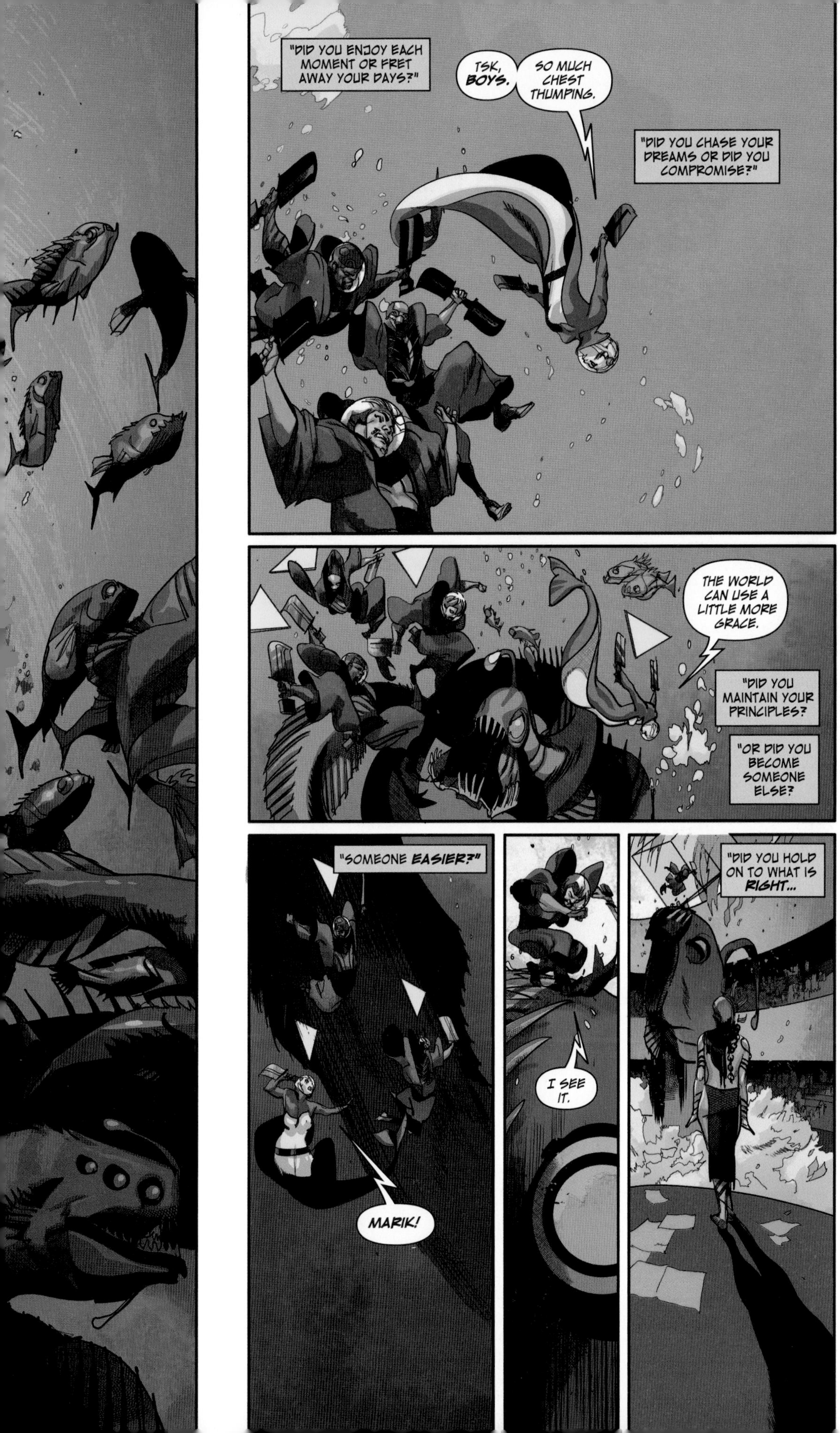

"DID YOU ENJOY EACH MOMENT OR FRET AWAY YOUR DAYS?"
TSK, BOYS.
SO MUCH CHEST THUMPING.
"DID YOU CHASE YOUR DREAMS OR DID YOU COMPROMISE?"
THE WORLD CAN USE A LITTLE MORE GRACE.
"DID YOU MAINTAIN YOUR PRINCIPLES?
"OR DID YOU BECOME SOMEONE ELSE?
"SOMEONE EASIER?"
MARIK!
I SEE IT.
"DID YOU HOLD ON TO WHAT IS RIGHT...

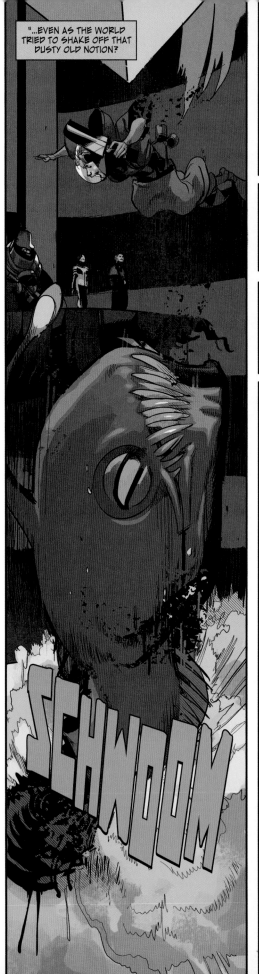

"...EVEN AS THE WORLD TRIED TO SHAKE OFF THAT DUSTY OLD NOTION?

SCHWOOM

"DID YOU RESIST THE HOPELESS-NESS AROUND YOU?

"MOST IMPORTANTLY...

"...DID YOU INSPIRE OTHERS TO?"

KRRSHHH

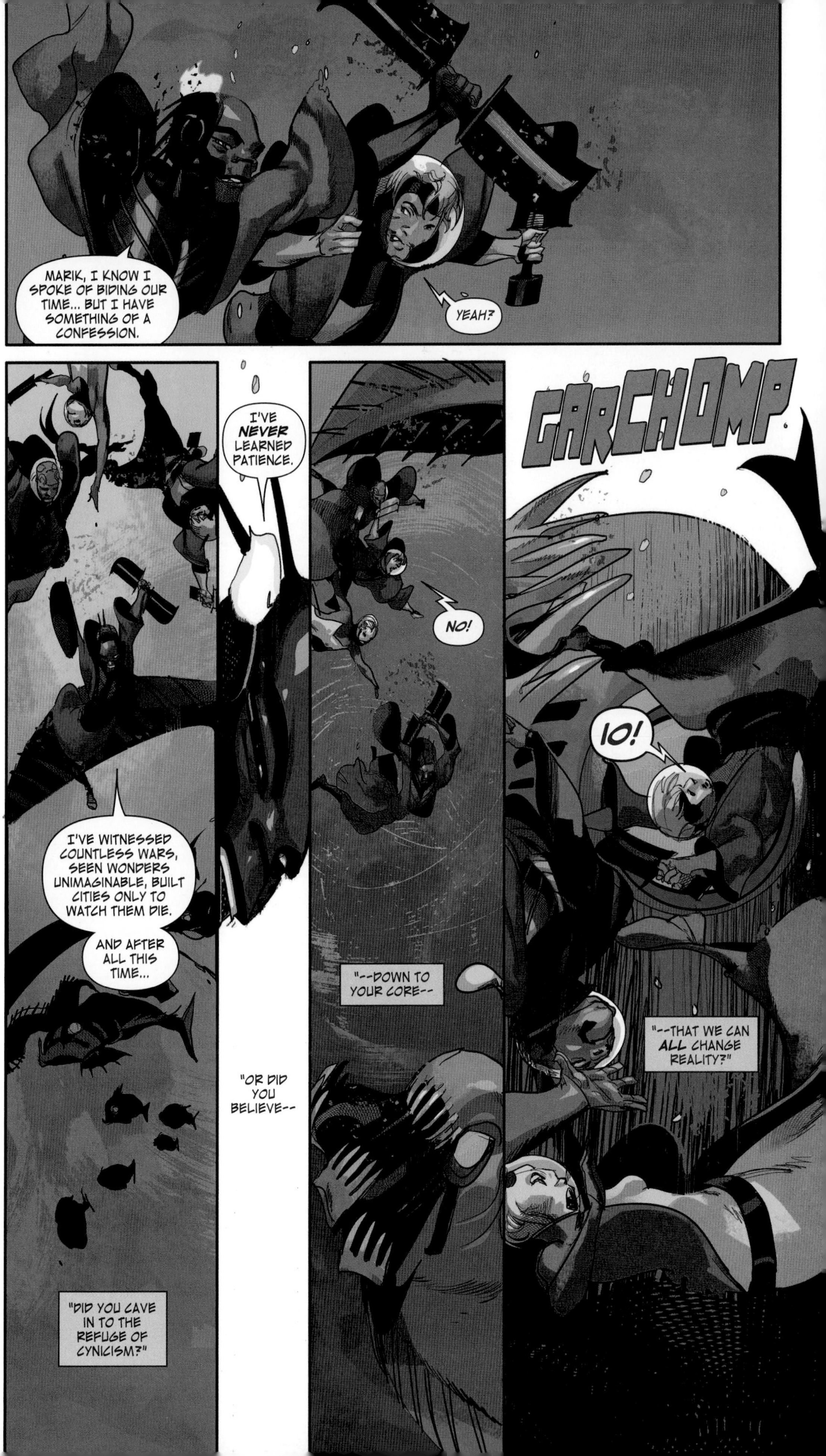

MARIK, I KNOW I SPOKE OF BIDING OUR TIME... BUT I HAVE SOMETHING OF A CONFESSION.
YEAH?
I'VE NEVER LEARNED PATIENCE.
I'VE WITNESSED COUNTLESS WARS, SEEN WONDERS UNIMAGINABLE, BUILT CITIES ONLY TO WATCH THEM DIE.
AND AFTER ALL THIS TIME...
"DID YOU CAVE IN TO THE REFUGE OF CYNICISM?"
"OR DID YOU BELIEVE--
NO!
"--DOWN TO YOUR CORE--
GARCHOMP
IO!
"--THAT WE CAN ALL CHANGE REALITY?"

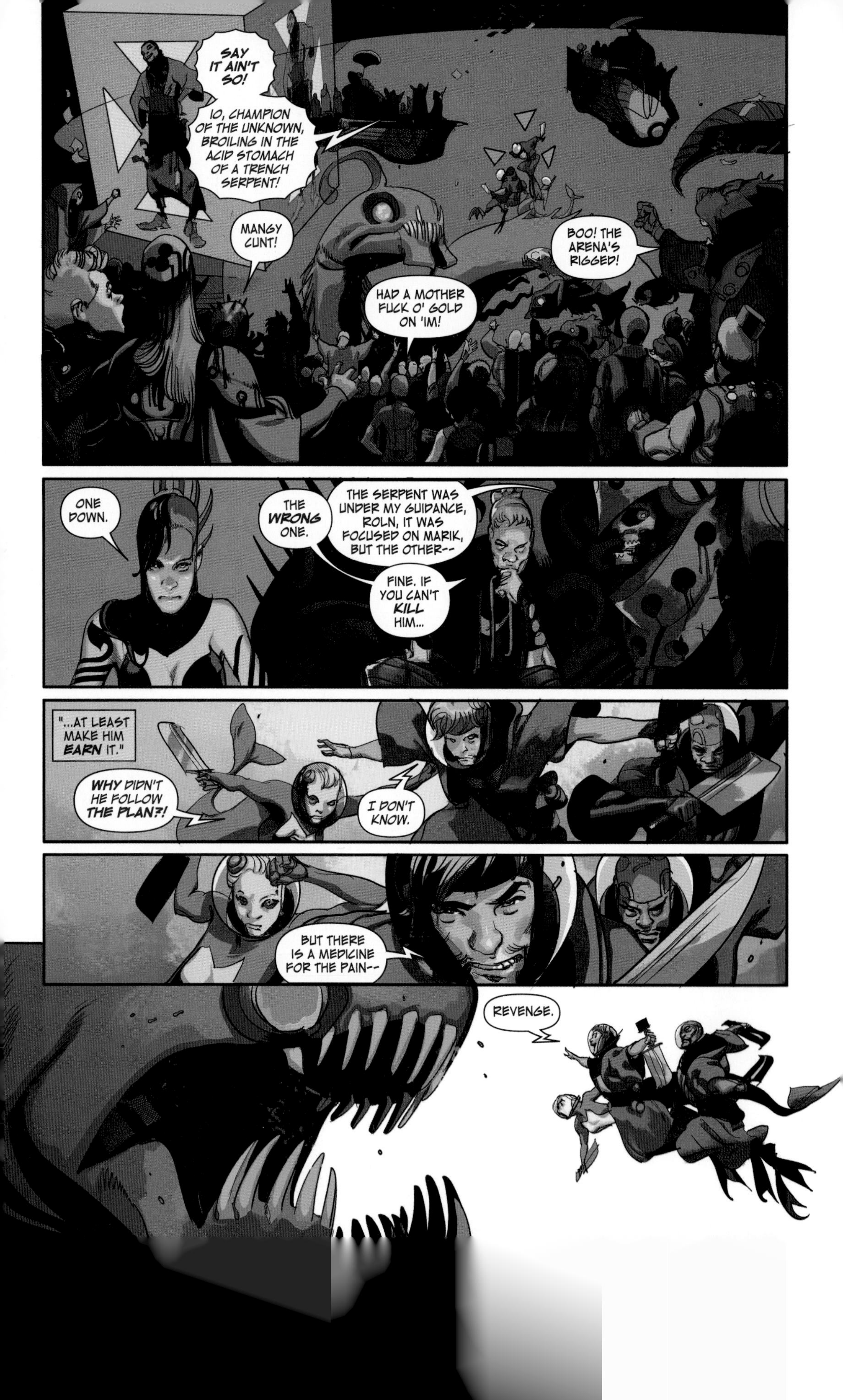
SAY IT AIN'T SO!
IO, CHAMPION OF THE UNKNOWN, BROILING IN THE ACID STOMACH OF A TRENCH SERPENT!
MANGY CUNT!
HAD A MOTHER FUCK O' GOLD ON 'IM!
BOO! THE ARENA'S RIGGED!
ONE DOWN.
THE WRONG ONE.
THE SERPENT WAS UNDER MY GUIDANCE, ROLN, IT WAS FOCUSED ON MARIK, BUT THE OTHER--
FINE. IF YOU CAN'T KILL HIM...
"...AT LEAST MAKE HIM EARN IT."
WHY DIDN'T HE FOLLOW THE PLAN?!
I DON'T KNOW.
BUT THERE IS A MEDICINE FOR THE PAIN--
REVENGE.

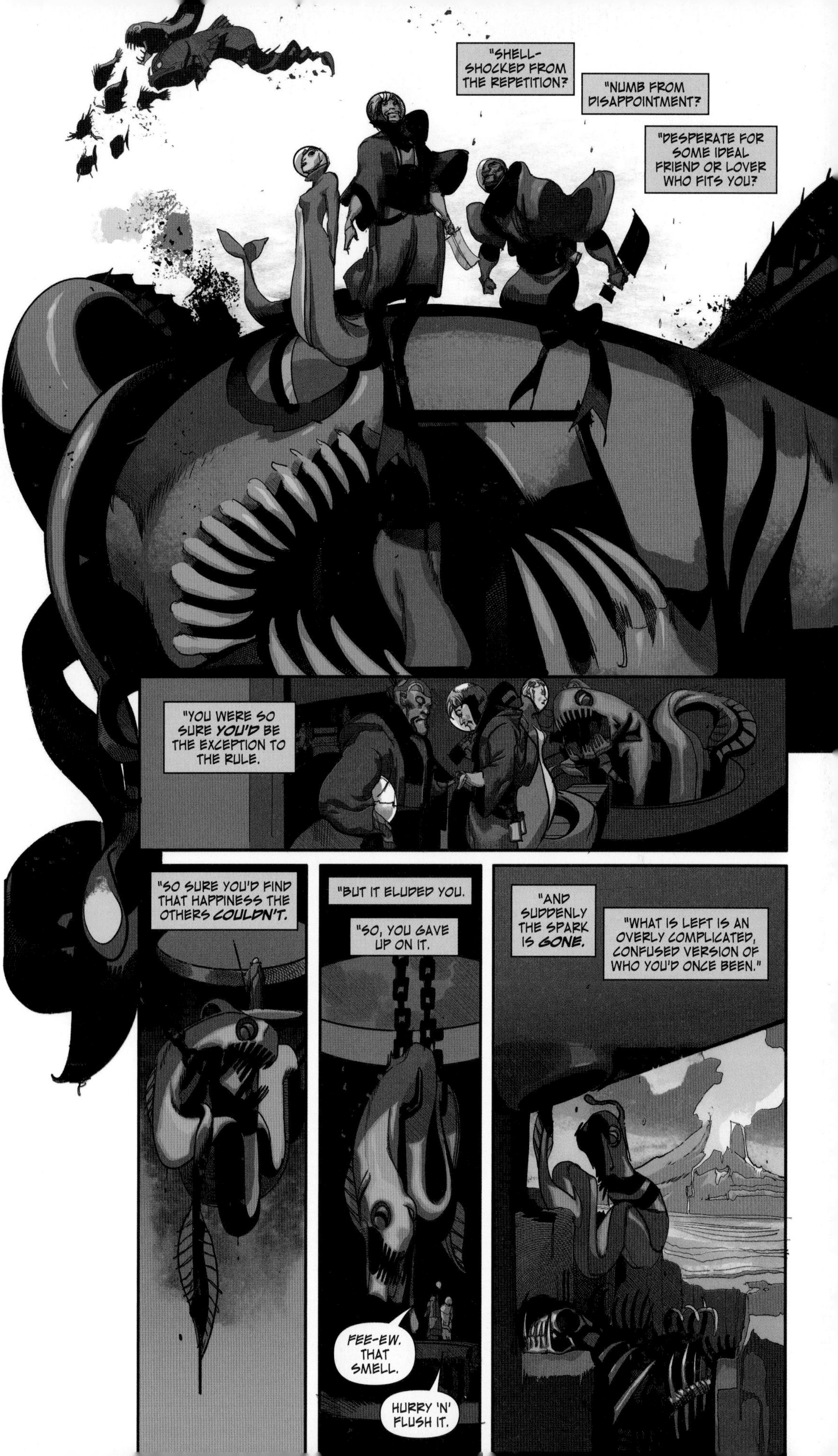
"SHELL-SHOCKED FROM THE REPETITION?
"NUMB FROM DISAPPOINTMENT?
"DESPERATE FOR SOME IDEAL FRIEND OR LOVER WHO FITS YOU?
"YOU WERE SO SURE YOU'D BE THE EXCEPTION TO THE RULE.
"SO SURE YOU'D FIND THAT HAPPINESS THE OTHERS COULDN'T.
"BUT IT ELUDED YOU.
"SO, YOU GAVE UP ON IT.
FEE-EW. THAT SMELL.
HURRY 'N' FLUSH IT.
"AND SUDDENLY THE SPARK IS GONE.
"WHAT IS LEFT IS AN OVERLY COMPLICATED, CONFUSED VERSION OF WHO YOU'D ONCE BEEN."

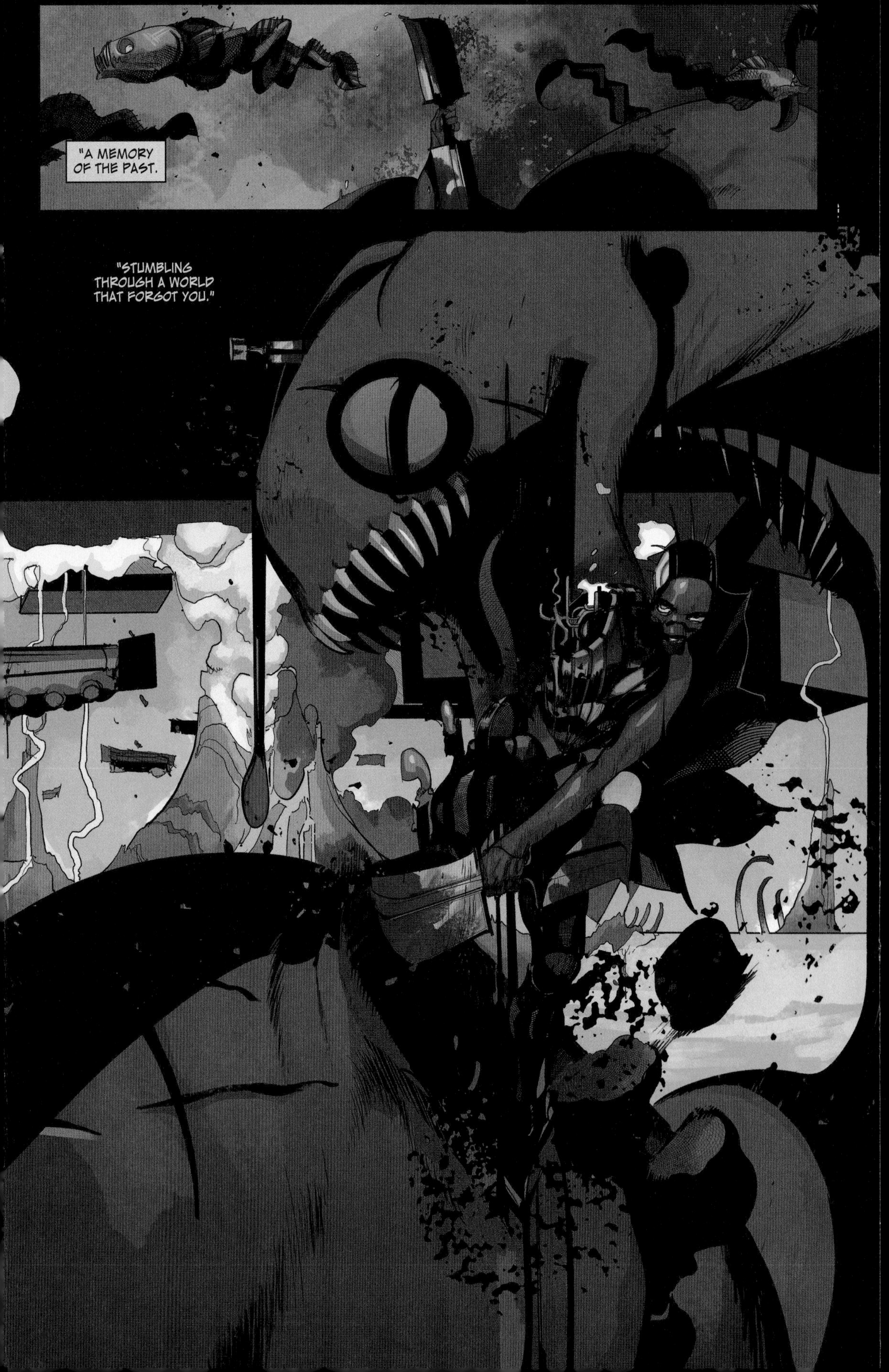
"A MEMORY
OF THE PAST.
"STUMBLING
THROUGH A WORLD
THAT FORGOT YOU."

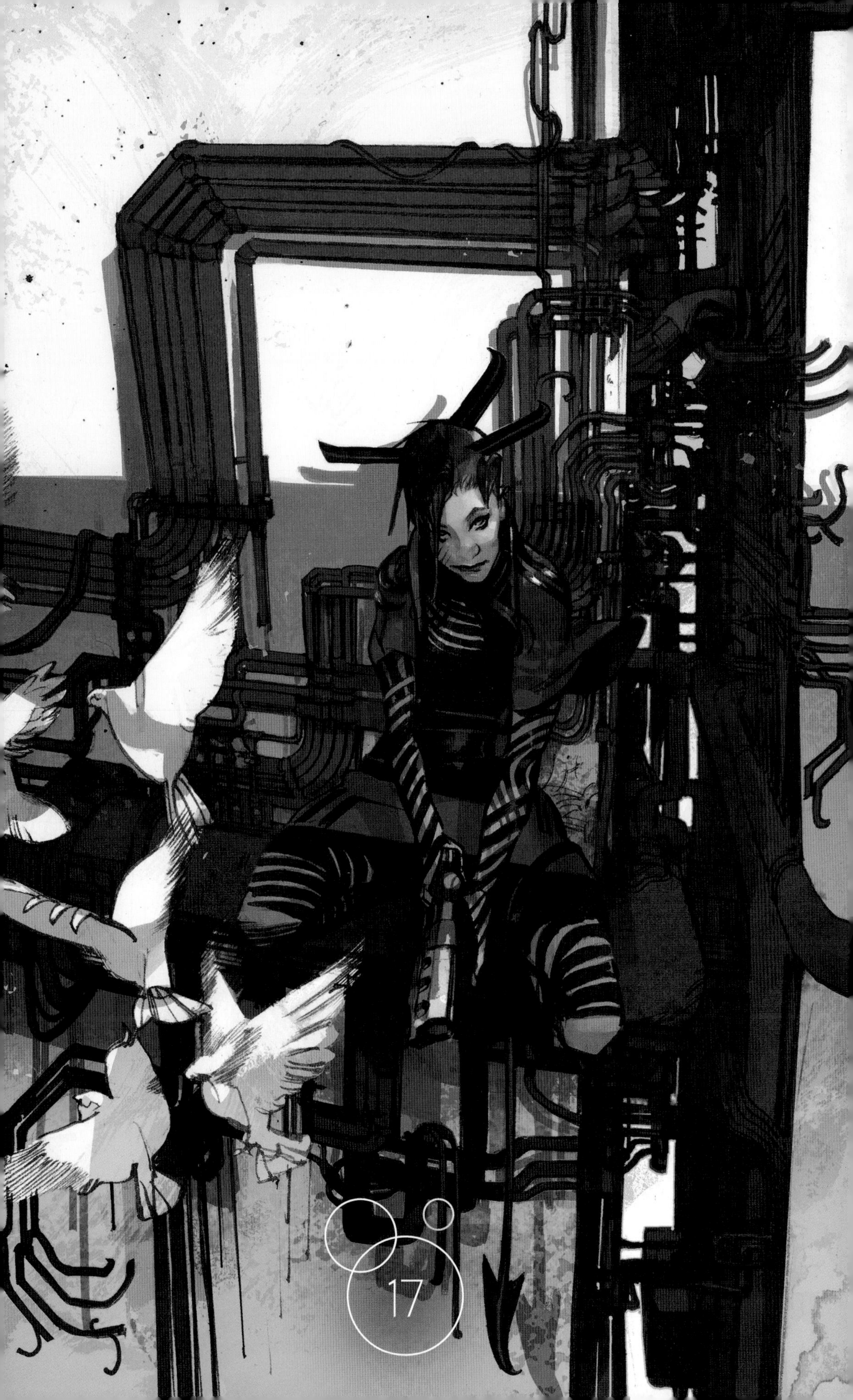

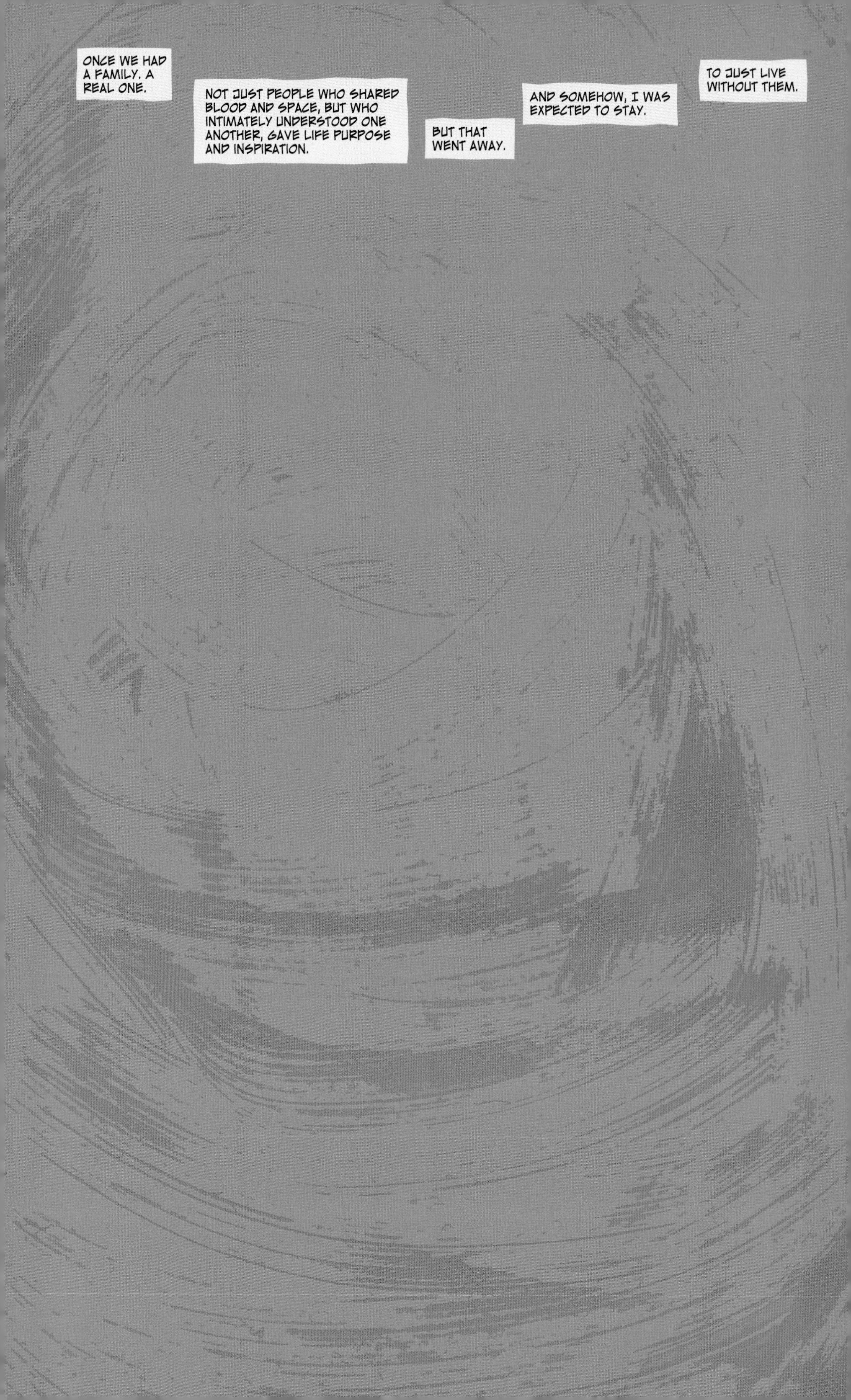
ONCE WE HAD A FAMILY. A REAL ONE.
NOT JUST PEOPLE WHO SHARED BLOOD AND SPACE, BUT WHO INTIMATELY UNDERSTOOD ONE ANOTHER, GAVE LIFE PURPOSE AND INSPIRATION.
BUT THAT WENT AWAY.
AND SOMEHOW, I WAS EXPECTED TO STAY.
TO JUST LIVE WITHOUT THEM.

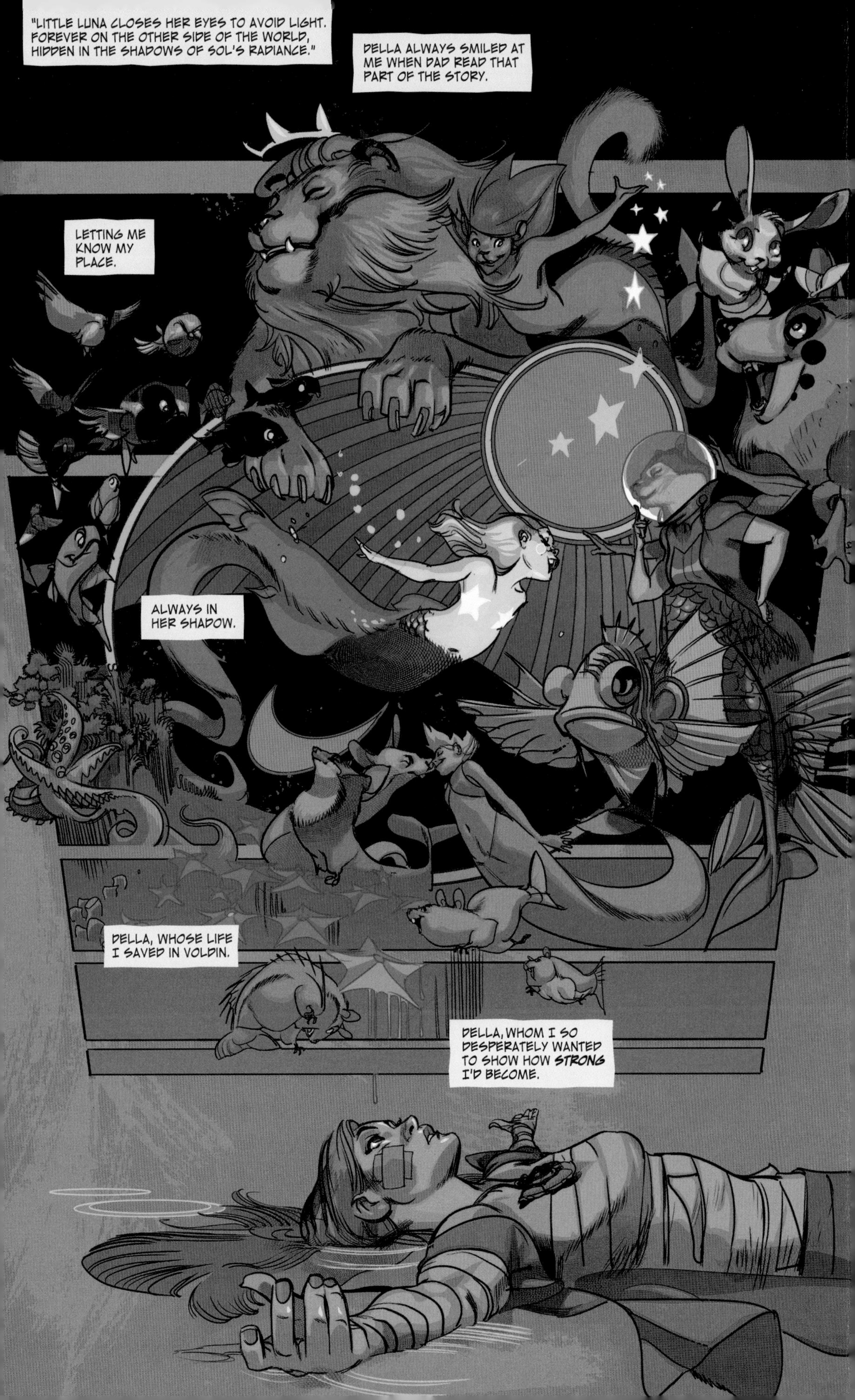
"LITTLE LUNA CLOSES HER EYES TO AVOID LIGHT. FOREVER ON THE OTHER SIDE OF THE WORLD, HIDDEN IN THE SHADOWS OF SOL'S RADIANCE."
DELLA ALWAYS SMILED AT ME WHEN DAD READ THAT PART OF THE STORY.
LETTING ME KNOW MY PLACE.
ALWAYS IN HER SHADOW.
DELLA, WHOSE LIFE I SAVED IN VOLDIN.
DELLA, WHOM I SO DESPERATELY WANTED TO SHOW HOW **STRONG** I'D BECOME.

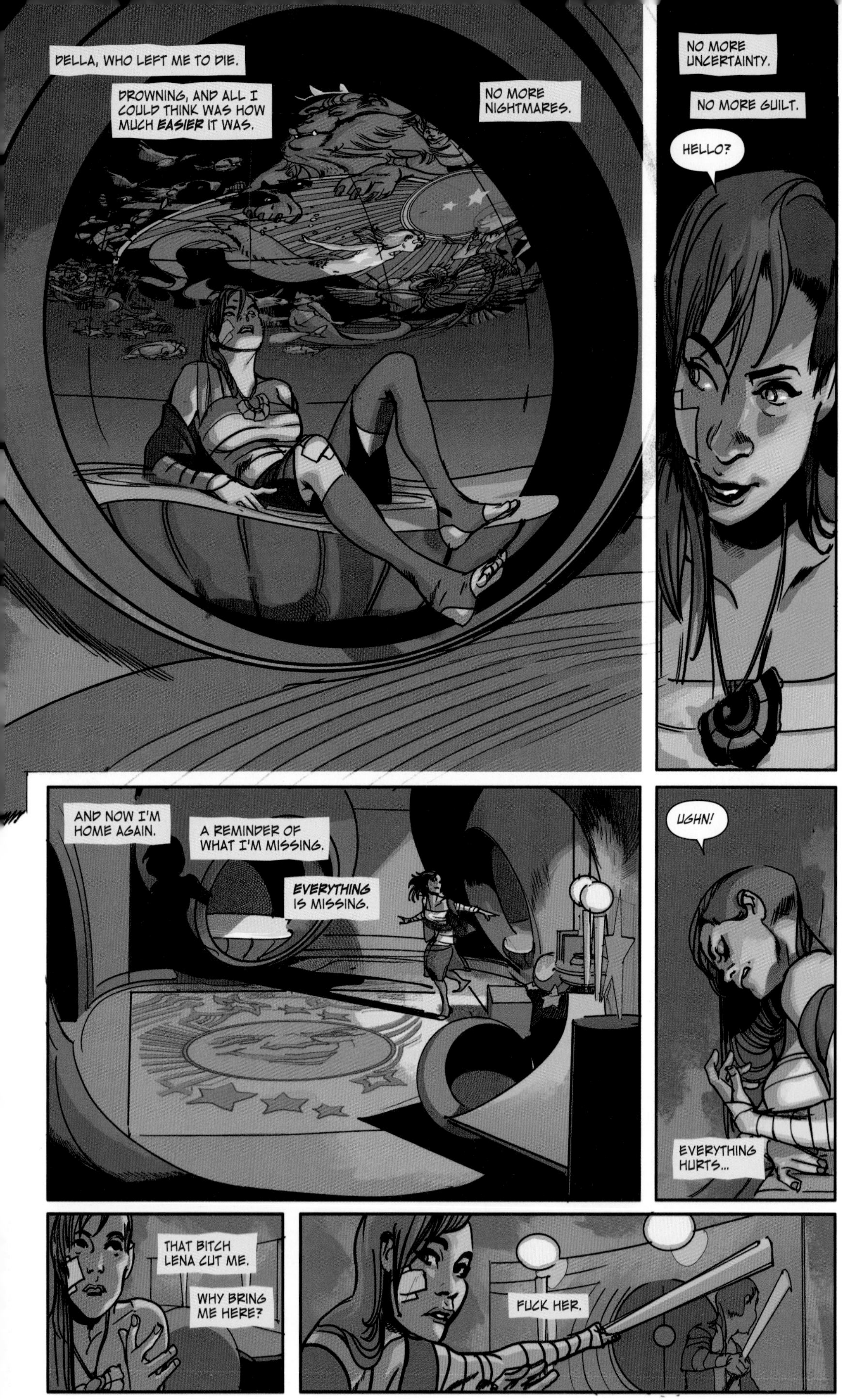

DELLA, WHO LEFT ME TO DIE.
DROWNING, AND ALL I COULD THINK WAS HOW MUCH EASIER IT WAS.
NO MORE NIGHTMARES.
NO MORE UNCERTAINTY.
NO MORE GUILT.
HELLO?
AND NOW I'M HOME AGAIN.
A REMINDER OF WHAT I'M MISSING.
EVERYTHING IS MISSING.
UGHN!
EVERYTHING HURTS...
THAT BITCH LENA CUT ME.
WHY BRING ME HERE?
FUCK HER.

MOM'S DEAD GARDEN.
STOMACH LOCKS UP
WITH MEMORIES.

FAMILY
PHOTOS
STILL UP.

AS A GIRL, I'D
STARE AT THEM
AND GET SO
FUCKING SAD.

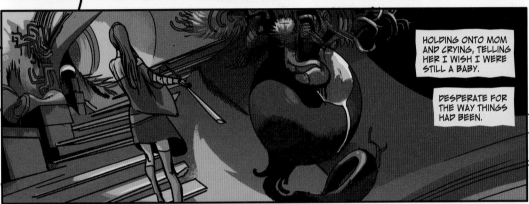

HOLDING ONTO MOM
AND CRYING, TELLING
HER I WISH I WERE
STILL A BABY.

DESPERATE FOR
THE WAY THINGS
HAD BEEN.

THE WORLD
HIJACKS US
WITH THE
TRUTH.

ALL THE PROTECTIVE
ILLUSIONS OUR PARENTS
PERPETUATE VANISH.

REALITY ENCIRCLES
US LIKE EELS...

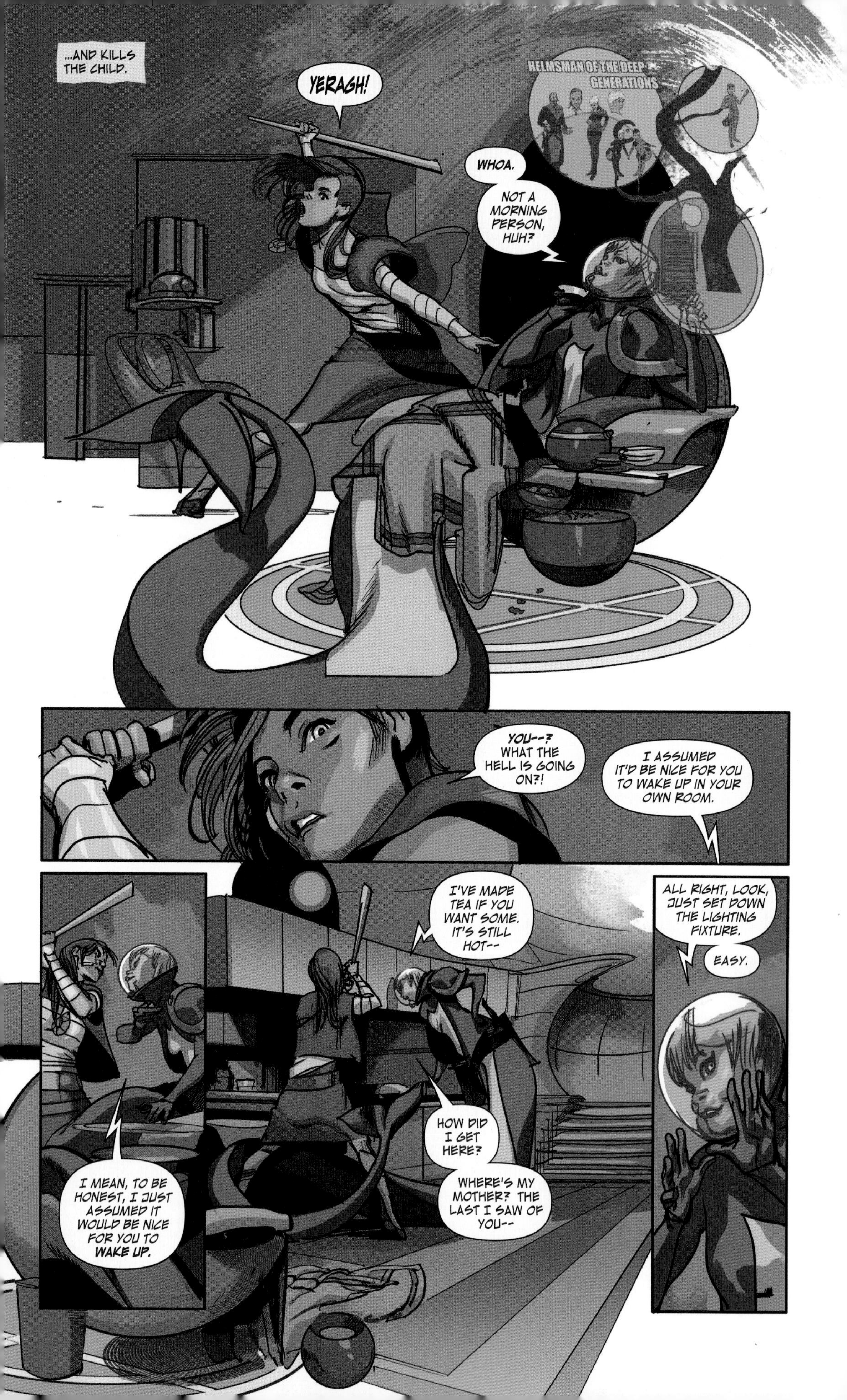
...AND KILLS THE CHILD.
YERAGH!
HELMSMAN OF THE DEEP GENERATIONS
WHOA.
NOT A MORNING PERSON, HUH?
YOU--? WHAT THE HELL IS GOING ON?!
I ASSUMED IT'D BE NICE FOR YOU TO WAKE UP IN YOUR OWN ROOM.
I MEAN, TO BE HONEST, I JUST ASSUMED IT WOULD BE NICE FOR YOU TO WAKE UP.
I'VE MADE TEA IF YOU WANT SOME. IT'S STILL HOT--
HOW DID I GET HERE?
WHERE'S MY MOTHER? THE LAST I SAW OF YOU--
ALL RIGHT, LOOK, JUST SET DOWN THE LIGHTING FIXTURE.
EASY.

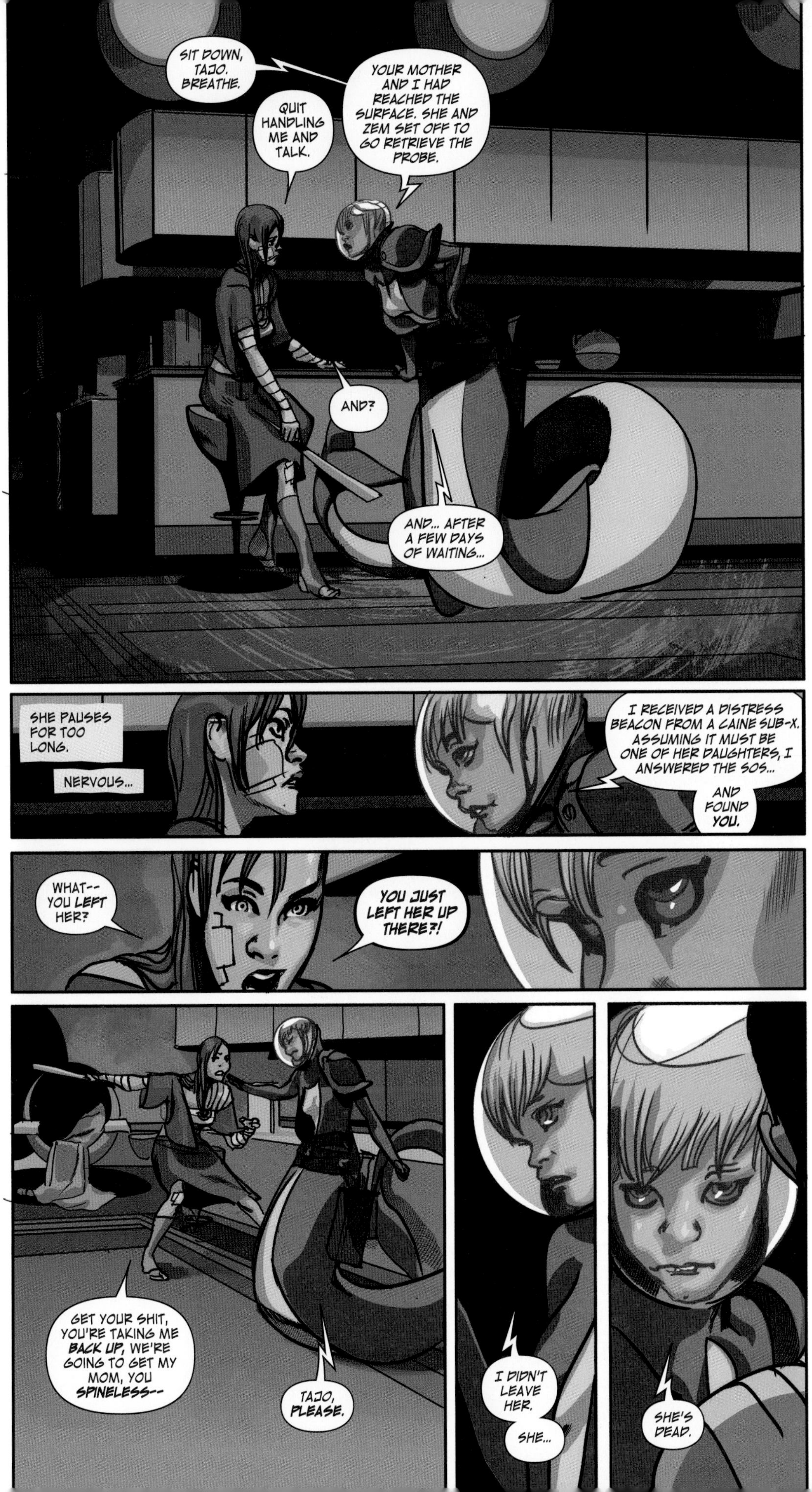
SIT DOWN, TAJO. BREATHE.
YOUR MOTHER AND I HAD REACHED THE SURFACE. SHE AND ZEM SET OFF TO GO RETRIEVE THE PROBE.
QUIT HANDLING ME AND TALK.
AND?
AND... AFTER A FEW DAYS OF WAITING...
SHE PAUSES FOR TOO LONG.
NERVOUS...
I RECEIVED A DISTRESS BEACON FROM A CAINE SUB-X. ASSUMING IT MUST BE ONE OF HER DAUGHTERS, I ANSWERED THE SOS...
AND FOUND YOU.
WHAT-- YOU LEFT HER?
YOU JUST LEFT HER UP THERE?!
GET YOUR SHIT, YOU'RE TAKING ME BACK UP, WE'RE GOING TO GET MY MOM, YOU SPINELESS--
TAJO, PLEASE.
I DIDN'T LEAVE HER.
SHE...
SHE'S DEAD.

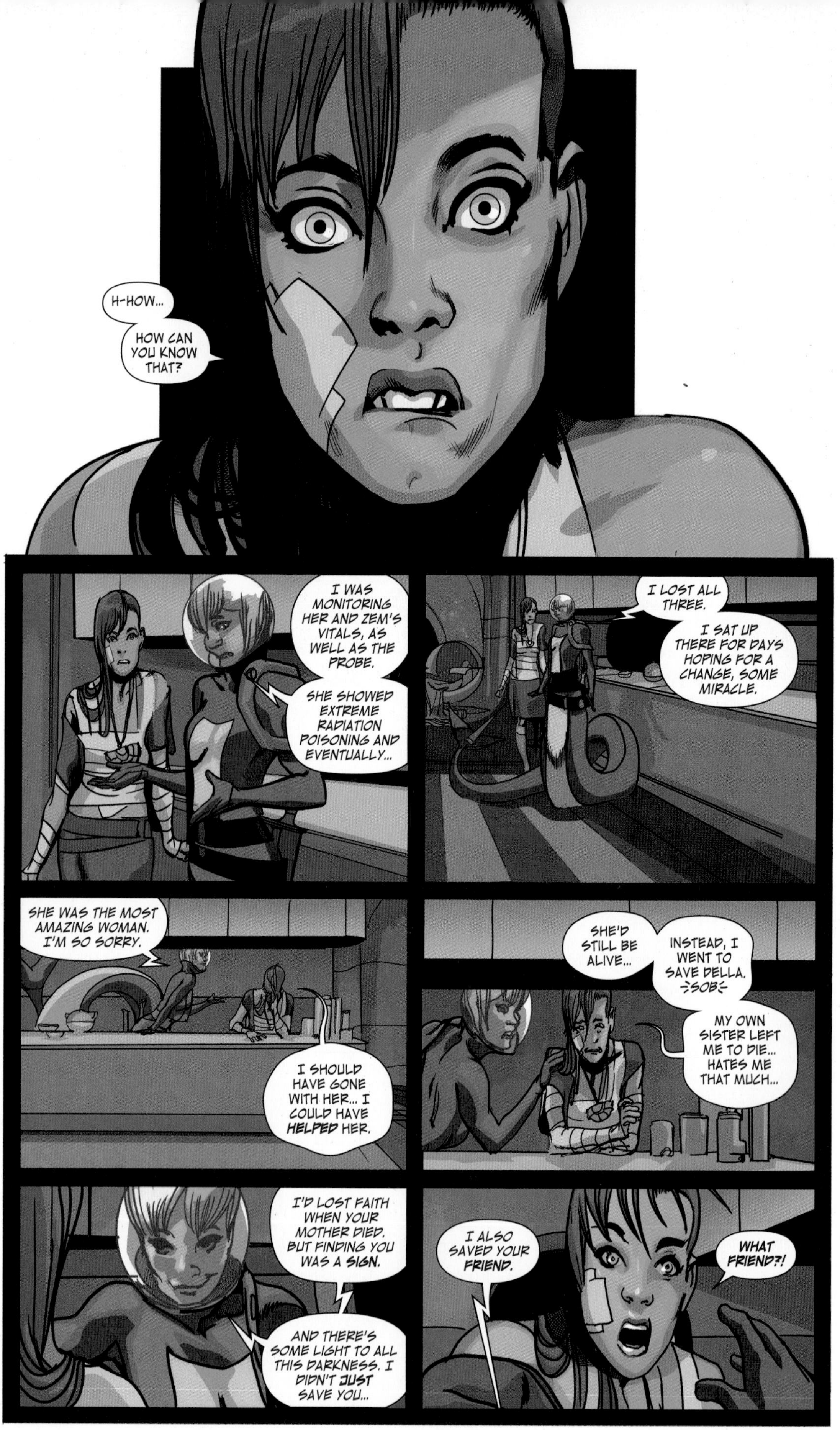
H-HOW...
HOW CAN YOU KNOW THAT?
I WAS MONITORING HER AND ZEM'S VITALS, AS WELL AS THE PROBE.
SHE SHOWED EXTREME RADIATION POISONING AND EVENTUALLY...
I LOST ALL THREE.
I SAT UP THERE FOR DAYS HOPING FOR A CHANGE, SOME MIRACLE.
SHE WAS THE MOST AMAZING WOMAN. I'M SO SORRY.
I SHOULD HAVE GONE WITH HER... I COULD HAVE HELPED HER.
SHE'D STILL BE ALIVE...
INSTEAD, I WENT TO SAVE DELLA. SOB
MY OWN SISTER LEFT ME TO DIE... HATES ME THAT MUCH...
I'D LOST FAITH WHEN YOUR MOTHER DIED. BUT FINDING YOU WAS A SIGN.
AND THERE'S SOME LIGHT TO ALL THIS DARKNESS. I DIDN'T JUST SAVE YOU...
I ALSO SAVED YOUR FRIEND.
WHAT FRIEND?!

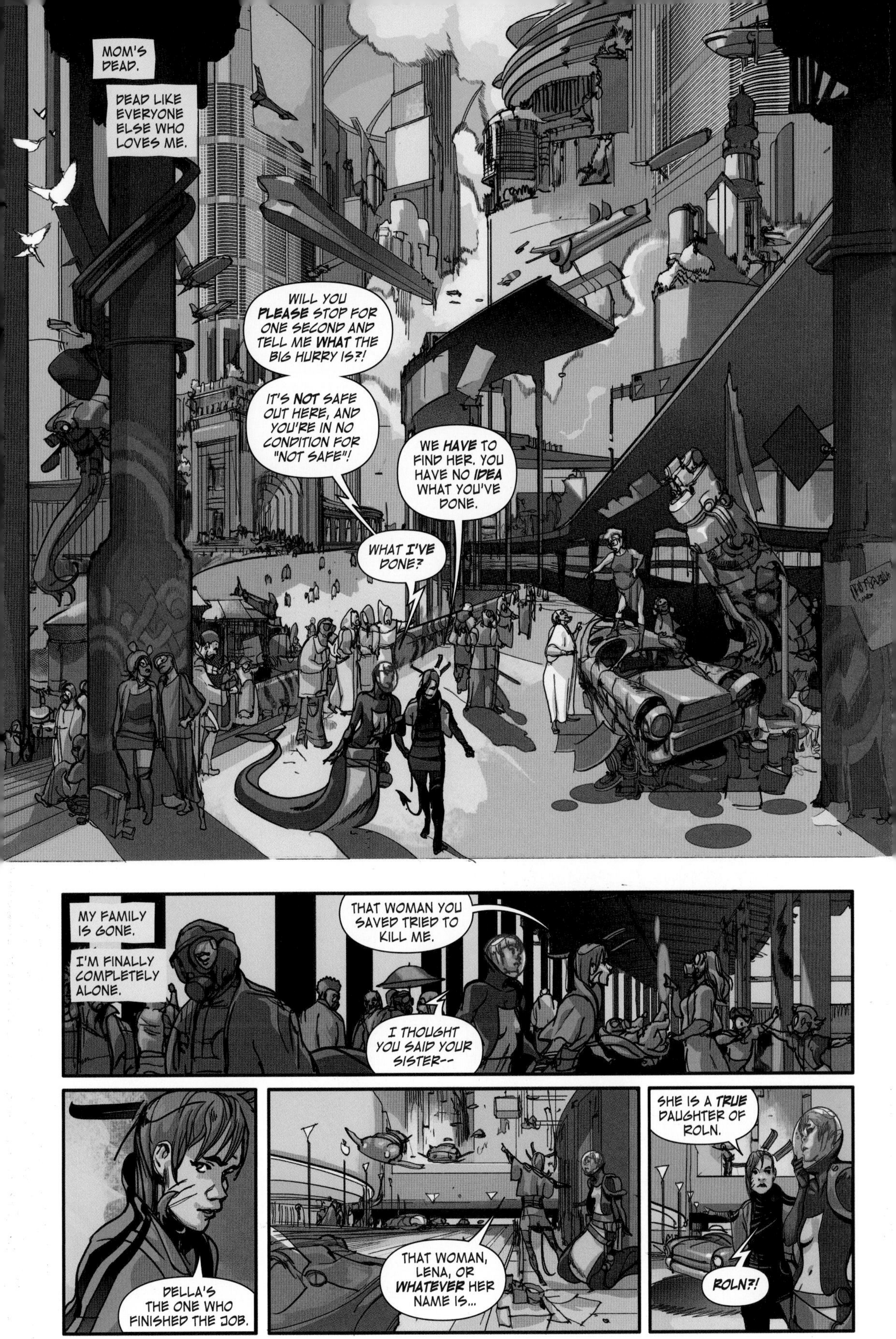
MOM'S DEAD.
DEAD LIKE EVERYONE ELSE WHO LOVES ME.
WILL YOU PLEASE STOP FOR ONE SECOND AND TELL ME WHAT THE BIG HURRY IS?!
IT'S NOT SAFE OUT HERE, AND YOU'RE IN NO CONDITION FOR "NOT SAFE"!
WE HAVE TO FIND HER. YOU HAVE NO IDEA WHAT YOU'VE DONE.
WHAT I'VE DONE?
MY FAMILY IS GONE.
I'M FINALLY COMPLETELY ALONE.
THAT WOMAN YOU SAVED TRIED TO KILL ME.
I THOUGHT YOU SAID YOUR SISTER--
DELLA'S THE ONE WHO FINISHED THE JOB.
THAT WOMAN, LENA, OR WHATEVER HER NAME IS...
SHE IS A TRUE DAUGHTER OF ROLN.
ROLN?!

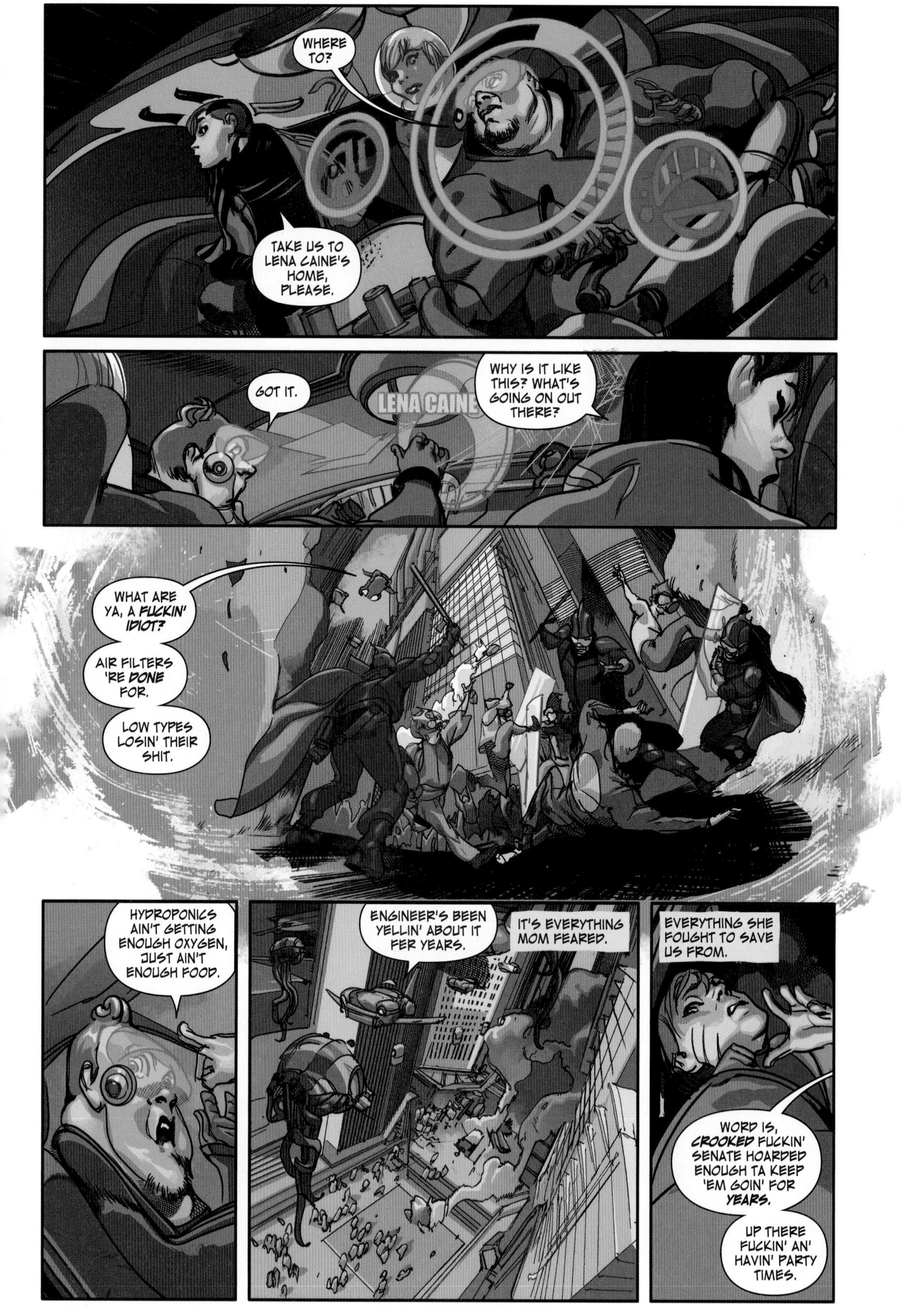
WHERE TO?
TAKE US TO LENA CAINE'S HOME, PLEASE.
GOT IT.
LENA CAINE
WHY IS IT LIKE THIS? WHAT'S GOING ON OUT THERE?
WHAT ARE YA, A *FUCKIN'* *IDIOT?*
AIR FILTERS 'RE *DONE* FOR.
LOW TYPES LOSIN' THEIR SHIT.
HYDROPONICS AIN'T GETTING ENOUGH OXYGEN, JUST AIN'T ENOUGH FOOD.
ENGINEER'S BEEN YELLIN' ABOUT IT FER YEARS.
IT'S EVERYTHING MOM FEARED.
EVERYTHING SHE FOUGHT TO SAVE US FROM.
WORD IS, *CROOKED* FUCKIN' SENATE HOARDED ENOUGH TA KEEP 'EM GOIN' FOR *YEARS.*
UP THERE FUCKIN' AN' HAVIN' PARTY TIMES.

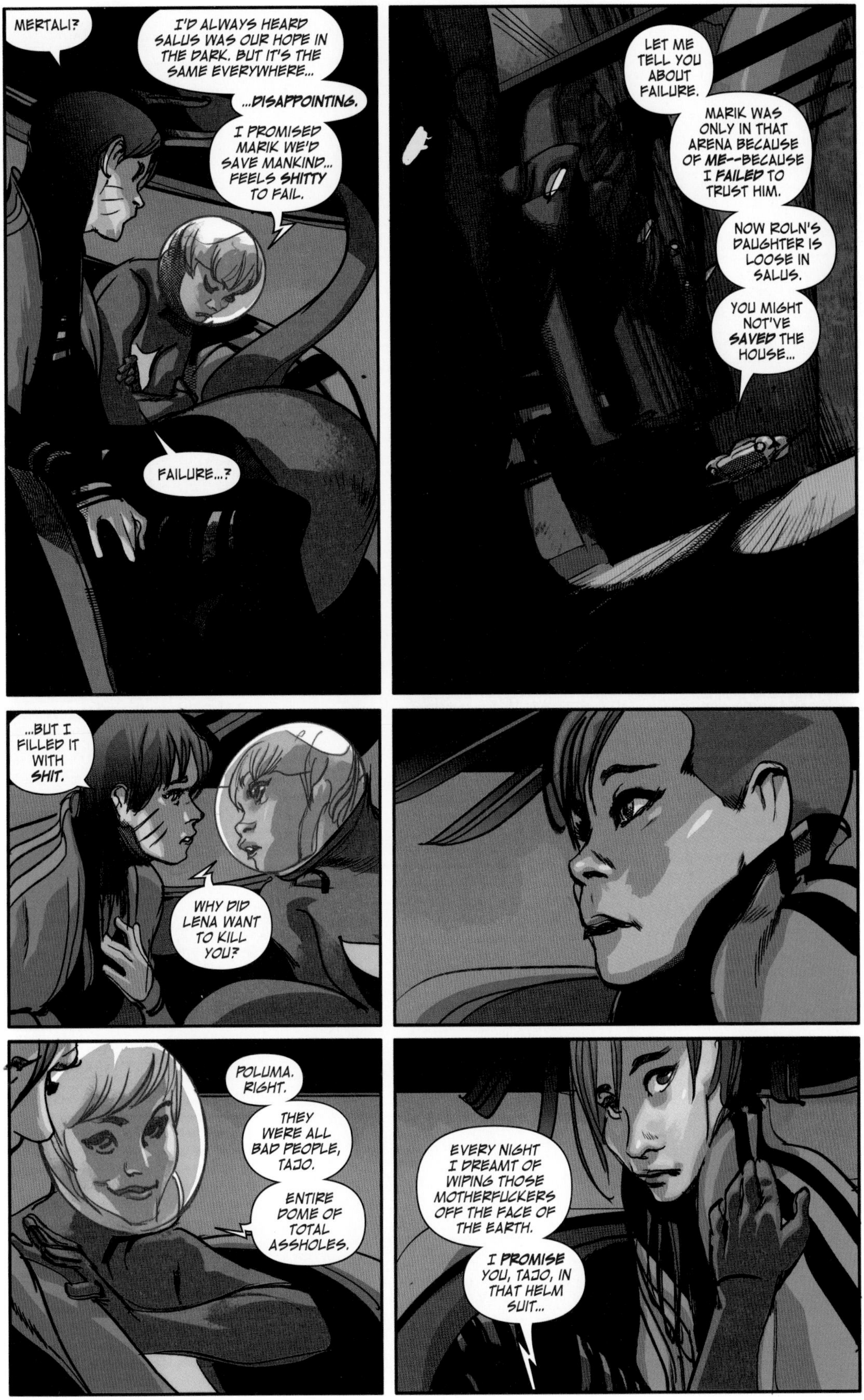
MERTALI?
I'D ALWAYS HEARD SALUS WAS OUR HOPE IN THE DARK. BUT IT'S THE SAME EVERYWHERE...
...DISAPPOINTING.
I PROMISED MARIK WE'D SAVE MANKIND... FEELS SHITTY TO FAIL.
FAILURE...?
LET ME TELL YOU ABOUT FAILURE.
MARIK WAS ONLY IN THAT ARENA BECAUSE OF ME--BECAUSE I FAILED TO TRUST HIM.
NOW ROLN'S DAUGHTER IS LOOSE IN SALUS.
YOU MIGHT NOT'VE SAVED THE HOUSE...
...BUT I FILLED IT WITH SHIT.
WHY DID LENA WANT TO KILL YOU?
POLUMA. RIGHT.
THEY WERE ALL BAD PEOPLE, TAJO.
ENTIRE DOME OF TOTAL ASSHOLES.
EVERY NIGHT I DREAMT OF WIPING THOSE MOTHERFUCKERS OFF THE FACE OF THE EARTH.
I PROMISE YOU, TAJO, IN THAT HELM SUIT...

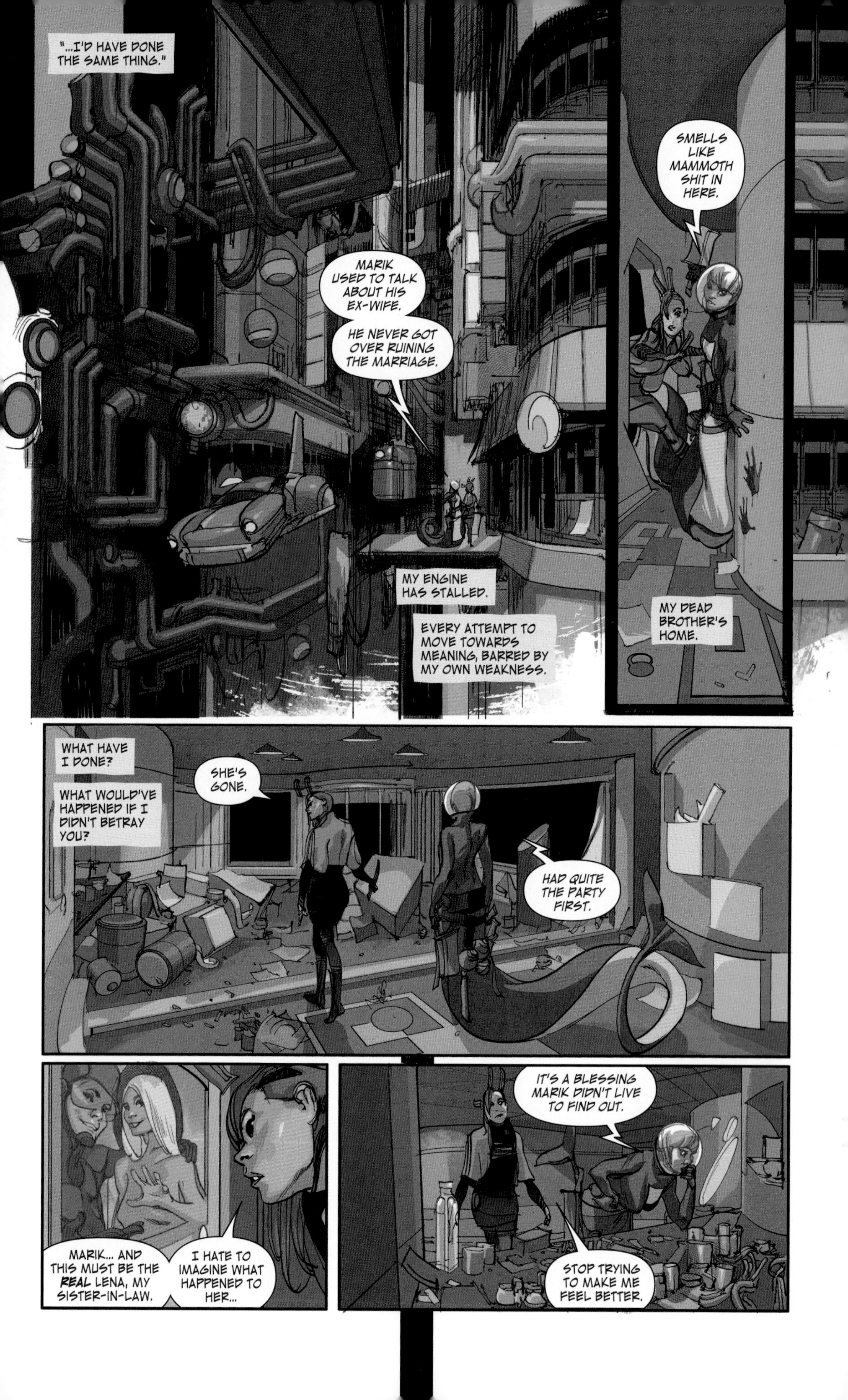
"...I'D HAVE DONE THE SAME THING."
MARIK USED TO TALK ABOUT HIS EX-WIFE.
HE NEVER GOT OVER RUINING THE MARRIAGE.
MY ENGINE HAS STALLED.
EVERY ATTEMPT TO MOVE TOWARDS MEANING, BARRED BY MY OWN WEAKNESS.
SMELLS LIKE MAMMOTH SHIT IN HERE.
MY DEAD BROTHER'S HOME.
WHAT HAVE I DONE?
WHAT WOULD'VE HAPPENED IF I DIDN'T BETRAY YOU?
SHE'S GONE.
HAD QUITE THE PARTY FIRST.
MARIK... AND THIS MUST BE THE REAL LENA, MY SISTER-IN-LAW.
I HATE TO IMAGINE WHAT HAPPENED TO HER...
IT'S A BLESSING MARIK DIDN'T LIVE TO FIND OUT.
STOP TRYING TO MAKE ME FEEL BETTER.

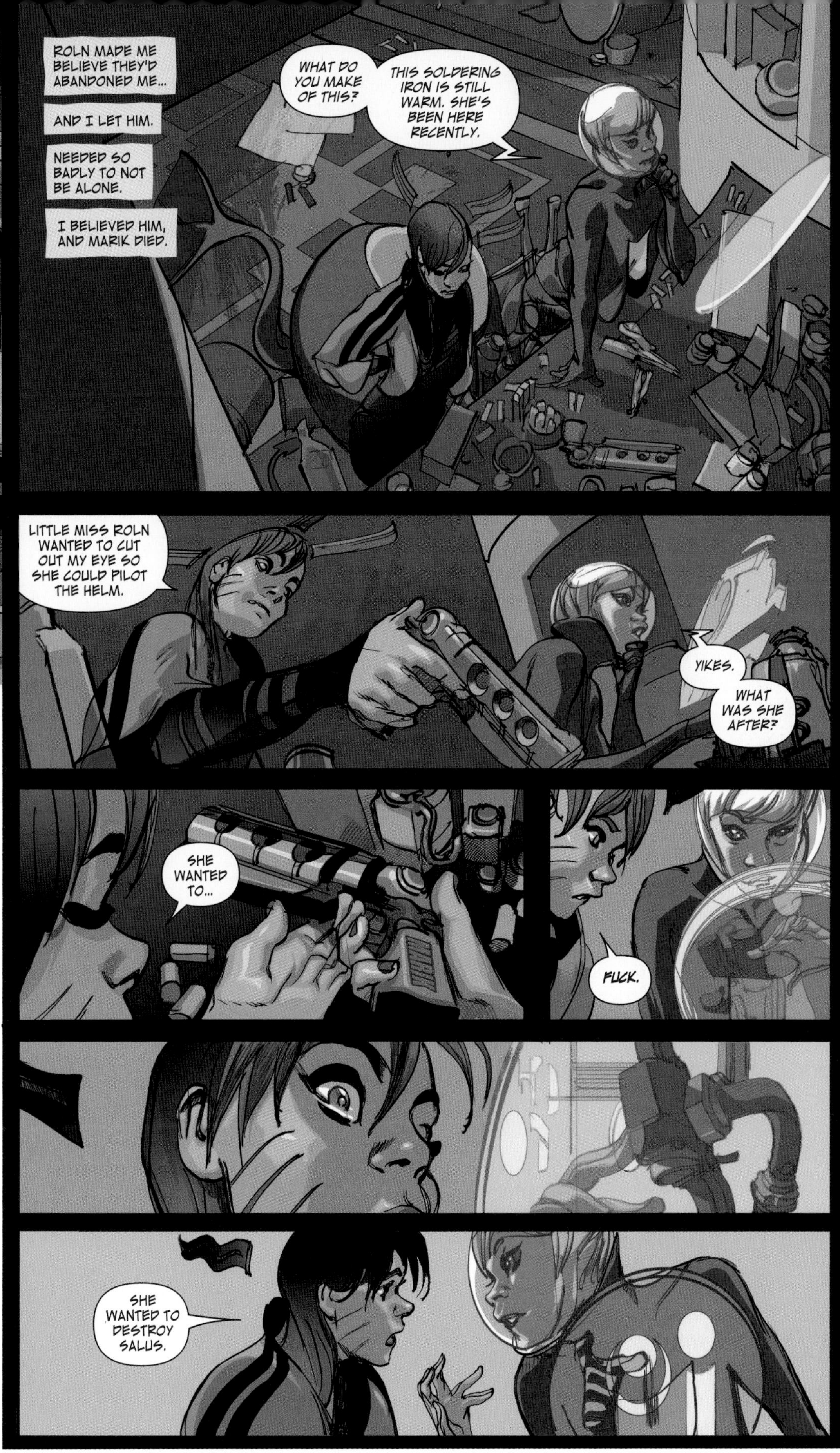
ROLN MADE ME BELIEVE THEY'D ABANDONED ME...
AND I LET HIM.
NEEDED SO BADLY TO NOT BE ALONE.
I BELIEVED HIM, AND MARIK DIED.
WHAT DO YOU MAKE OF THIS?
THIS SOLDERING IRON IS STILL WARM. SHE'S BEEN HERE RECENTLY.
LITTLE MISS ROLN WANTED TO CUT OUT MY EYE SO SHE COULD PILOT THE HELM.
YIKES.
WHAT WAS SHE AFTER?
SHE WANTED TO...
FUCK.
SHE WANTED TO DESTROY SALUS.

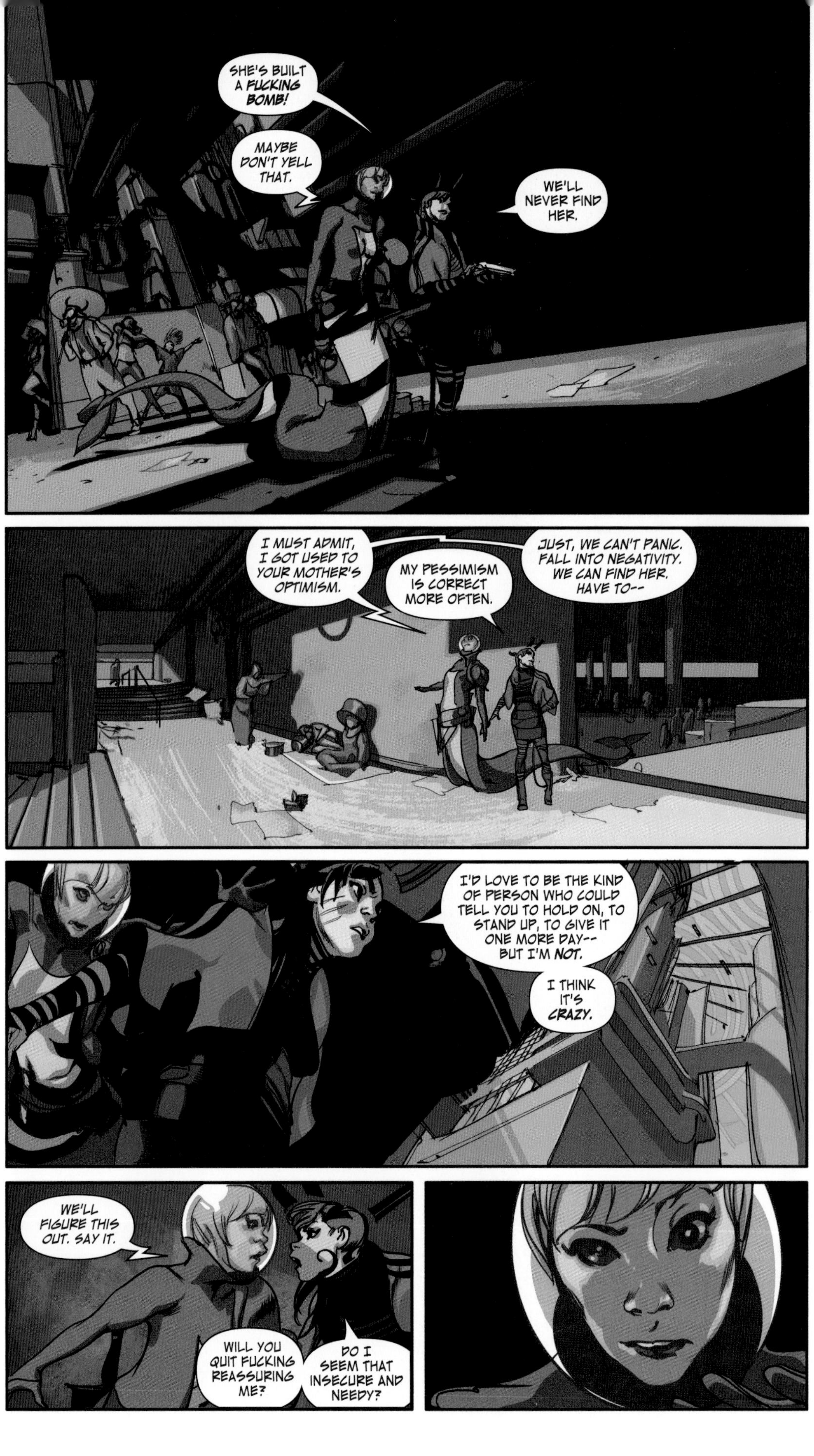
SHE'S BUILT A FUCKING BOMB!
MAYBE DON'T YELL THAT.
WE'LL NEVER FIND HER.
I MUST ADMIT, I GOT USED TO YOUR MOTHER'S OPTIMISM.
MY PESSIMISM IS CORRECT MORE OFTEN.
JUST, WE CAN'T PANIC. FALL INTO NEGATIVITY. WE CAN FIND HER. HAVE TO--
I'D LOVE TO BE THE KIND OF PERSON WHO COULD TELL YOU TO HOLD ON, TO STAND UP, TO GIVE IT ONE MORE DAY-- BUT I'M NOT.
I THINK IT'S CRAZY.
WE'LL FIGURE THIS OUT. SAY IT.
WILL YOU QUIT FUCKING REASSURING ME?
DO I SEEM THAT INSECURE AND NEEDY?

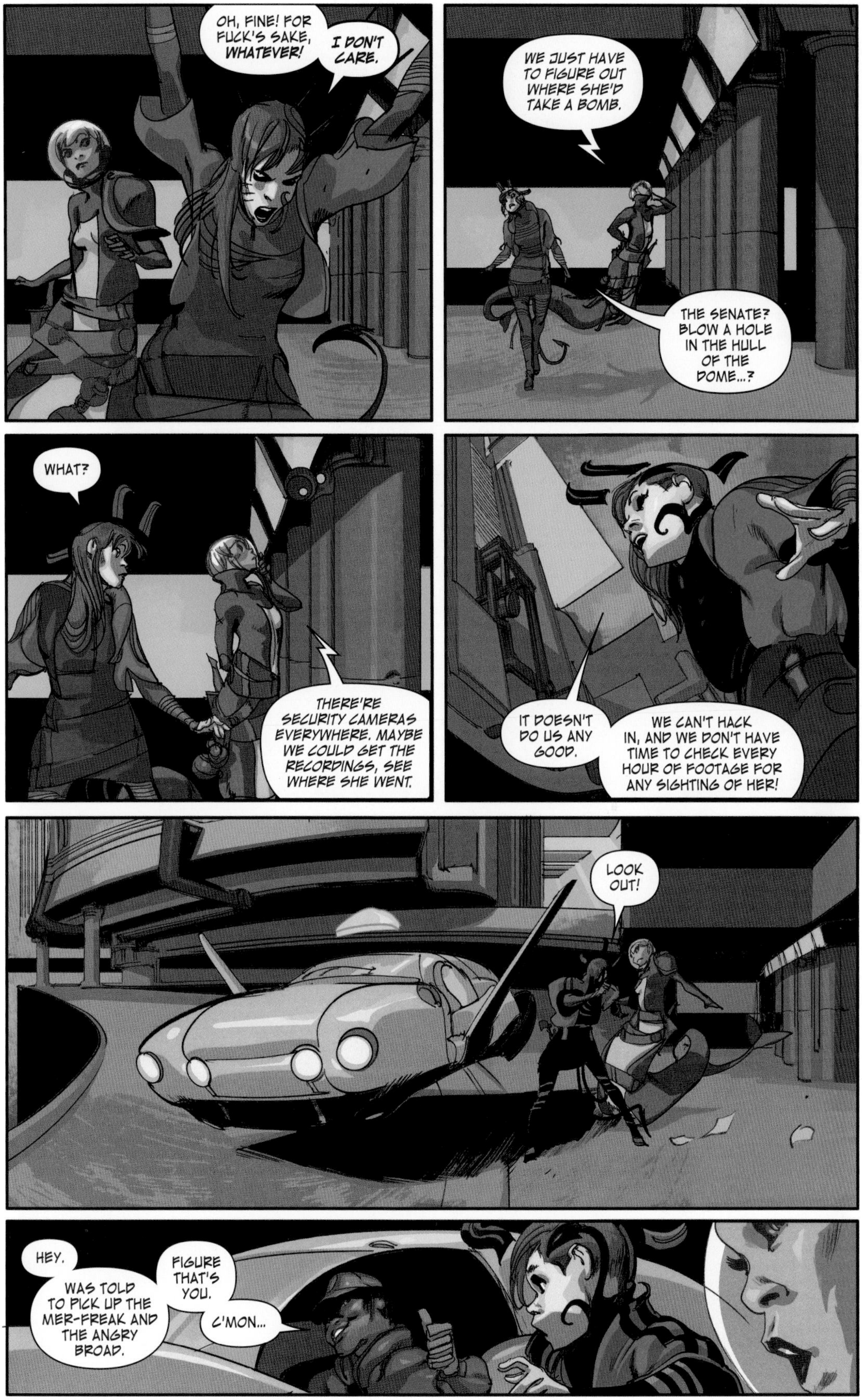
OH, FINE! FOR FUCK'S SAKE, WHATEVER!
I DON'T CARE.
WE JUST HAVE TO FIGURE OUT WHERE SHE'D TAKE A BOMB.
THE SENATE? BLOW A HOLE IN THE HULL OF THE DOME...?
WHAT?
THERE'RE SECURITY CAMERAS EVERYWHERE. MAYBE WE COULD GET THE RECORDINGS, SEE WHERE SHE WENT.
IT DOESN'T DO US ANY GOOD.
WE CAN'T HACK IN, AND WE DON'T HAVE TIME TO CHECK EVERY HOUR OF FOOTAGE FOR ANY SIGHTING OF HER!
LOOK OUT!
HEY.
WAS TOLD TO PICK UP THE MER-FREAK AND THE ANGRY BROAD.
FIGURE THAT'S YOU.
C'MON...

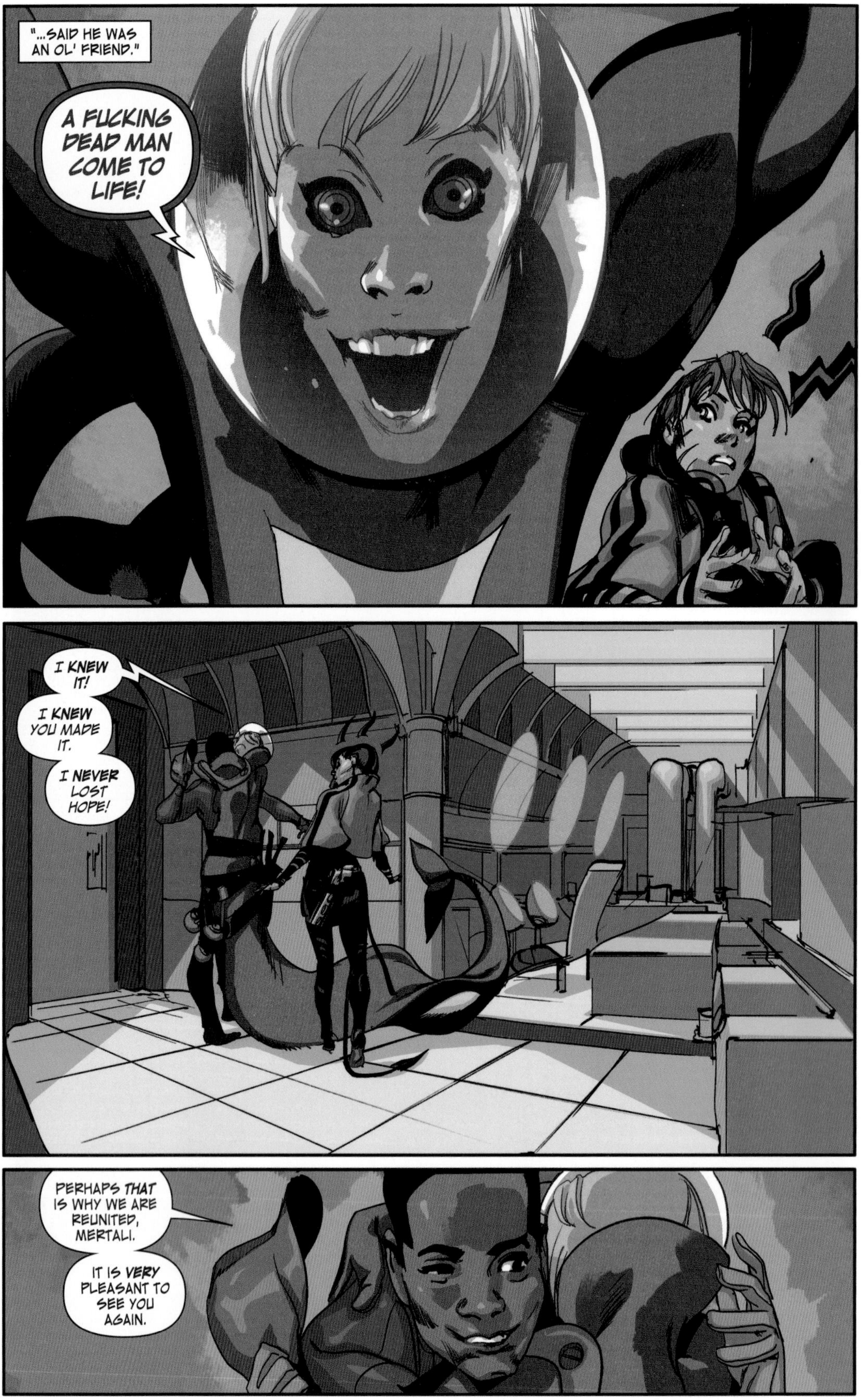
"...SAID HE WAS AN OL' FRIEND."
A FUCKING DEAD MAN COME TO LIFE!
I KNEW IT!
I KNEW YOU MADE IT.
I NEVER LOST HOPE!
PERHAPS THAT IS WHY WE ARE REUNITED, MERTALI.
IT IS VERY PLEASANT TO SEE YOU AGAIN.

"VERY PLEASANT TO SEE YOU"? YOU HEAR THIS GUY?

WE FOUGHT IN THE ARENAS TOGETHER FOR HOW LONG? AND THAT'S THE MOST EMOTION I GET OUT OF HIM.

I'LL SHOW YOU "PLEASANT," IO.

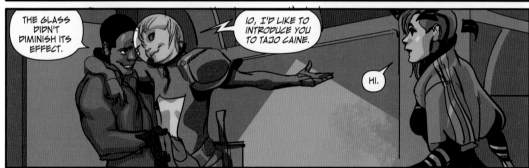

THE GLASS DIDN'T DIMINISH ITS EFFECT.

IO, I'D LIKE TO INTRODUCE YOU TO TAJO CAINE.

HI.

HEY, KID.

DO I KNOW YOU?

NO, MY DEAR, NO. BUT I KNOW YOU. YOUR BROTHER TOLD ME COUNTLESS STORIES.

WHEN I HEARD WHAT HAPPENED IN POLUMA, I ASSUMED YOU'D PERISHED WITH ROLN, BUT HERE YOU ARE.

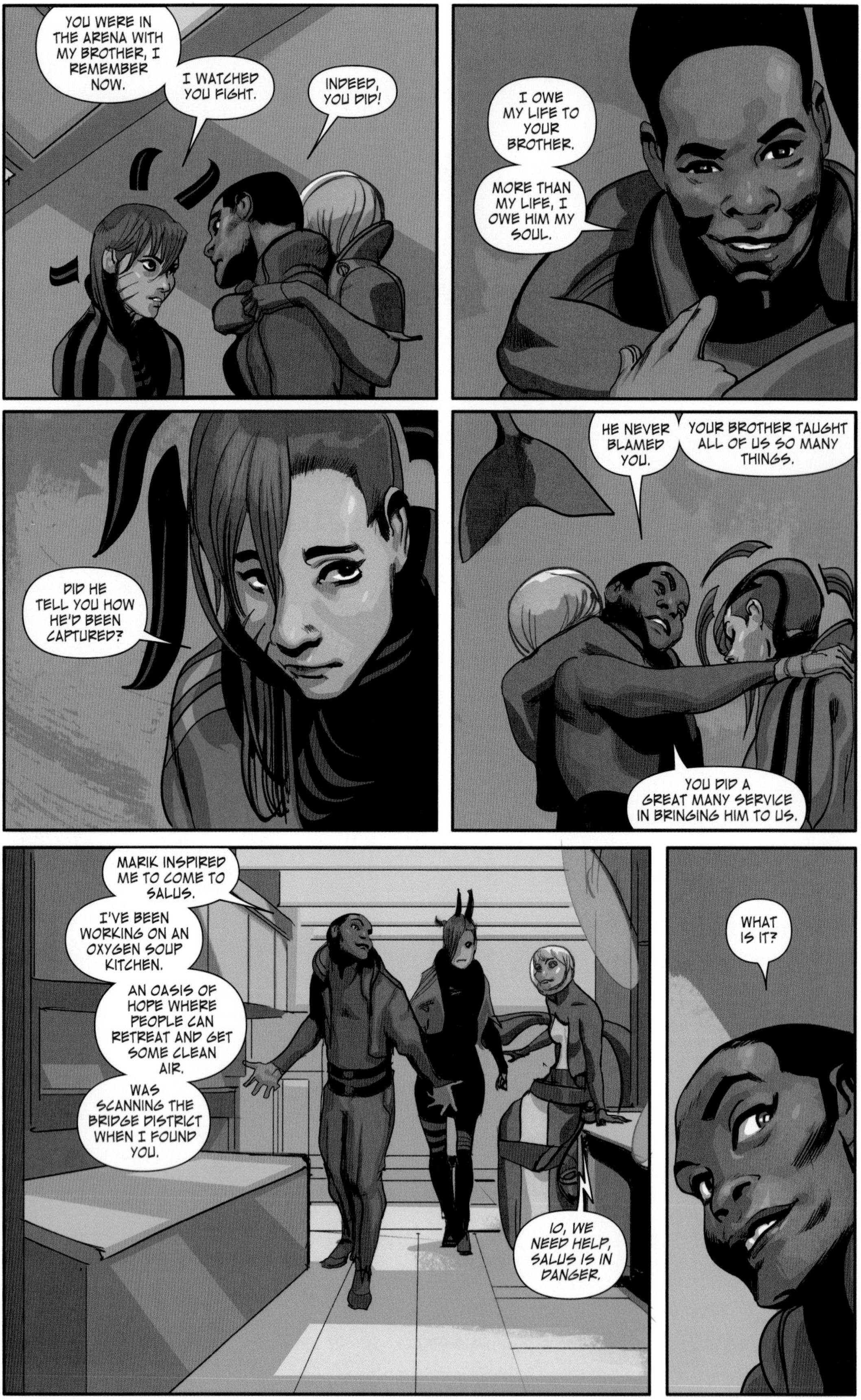
YOU WERE IN THE ARENA WITH MY BROTHER, I REMEMBER NOW.
I WATCHED YOU FIGHT.
INDEED, YOU DID!
I OWE MY LIFE TO YOUR BROTHER.
MORE THAN MY LIFE, I OWE HIM MY SOUL.
DID HE TELL YOU HOW HE'D BEEN CAPTURED?
HE NEVER BLAMED YOU.
YOUR BROTHER TAUGHT ALL OF US SO MANY THINGS.
YOU DID A GREAT MANY SERVICE IN BRINGING HIM TO US.
MARIK INSPIRED ME TO COME TO SALUS.
I'VE BEEN WORKING ON AN OXYGEN SOUP KITCHEN.
AN OASIS OF HOPE WHERE PEOPLE CAN RETREAT AND GET SOME CLEAN AIR.
WAS SCANNING THE BRIDGE DISTRICT WHEN I FOUND YOU.
IO, WE NEED HELP, SALUS IS IN DANGER.
WHAT IS IT?

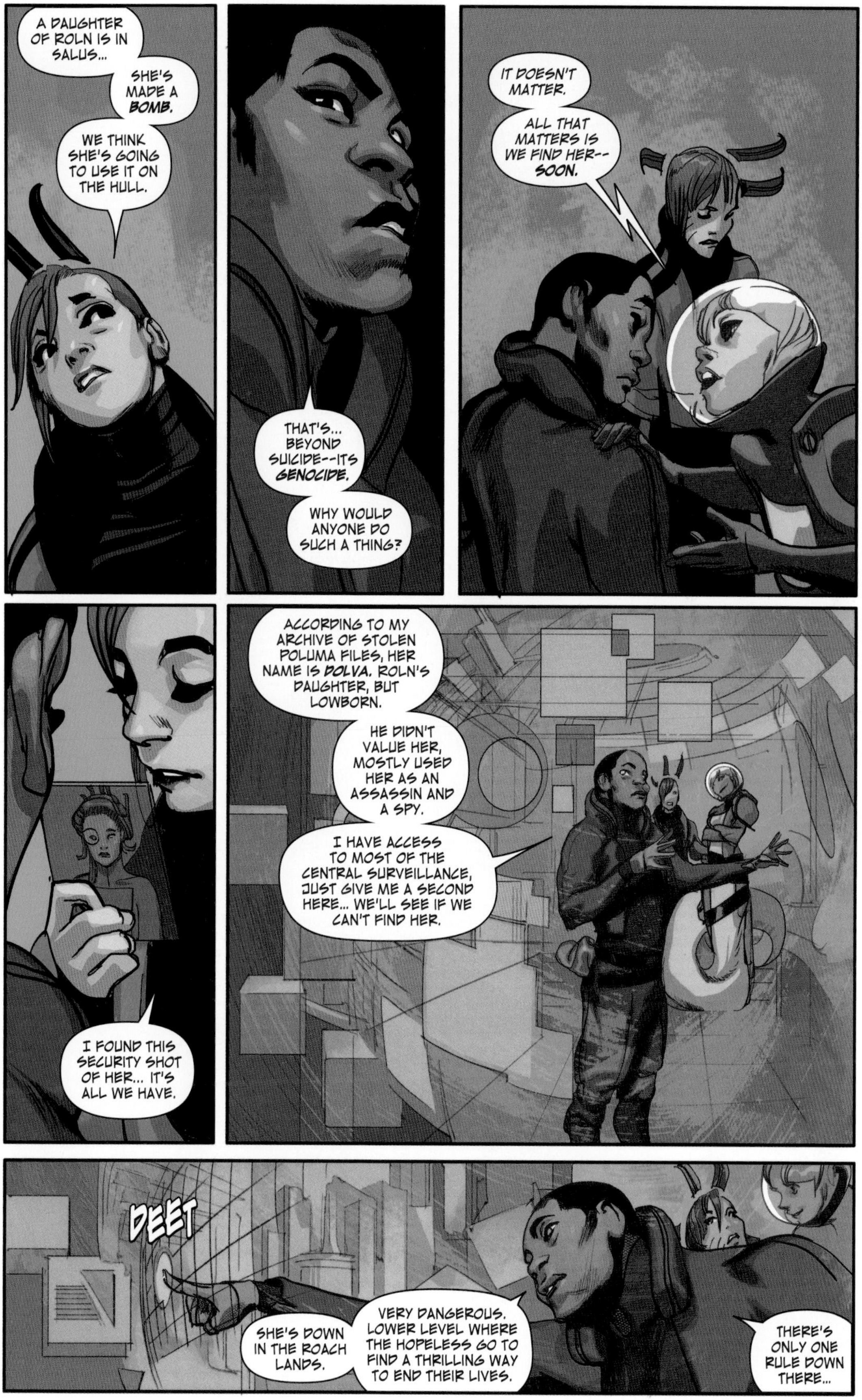
A DAUGHTER OF ROLN IS IN SALUS...
SHE'S MADE A BOMB.
WE THINK SHE'S GOING TO USE IT ON THE HULL.
THAT'S... BEYOND SUICIDE--ITS GENOCIDE.
WHY WOULD ANYONE DO SUCH A THING?
IT DOESN'T MATTER.
ALL THAT MATTERS IS WE FIND HER-- SOON.
I FOUND THIS SECURITY SHOT OF HER... IT'S ALL WE HAVE.
ACCORDING TO MY ARCHIVE OF STOLEN POLUMA FILES, HER NAME IS DOLVA. ROLN'S DAUGHTER, BUT LOWBORN.
HE DIDN'T VALUE HER, MOSTLY USED HER AS AN ASSASSIN AND A SPY.
I HAVE ACCESS TO MOST OF THE CENTRAL SURVEILLANCE, JUST GIVE ME A SECOND HERE... WE'LL SEE IF WE CAN'T FIND HER.
DEET
SHE'S DOWN IN THE ROACH LANDS.
VERY DANGEROUS. LOWER LEVEL WHERE THE HOPELESS GO TO FIND A THRILLING WAY TO END THEIR LIVES.
THERE'S ONLY ONE RULE DOWN THERE...

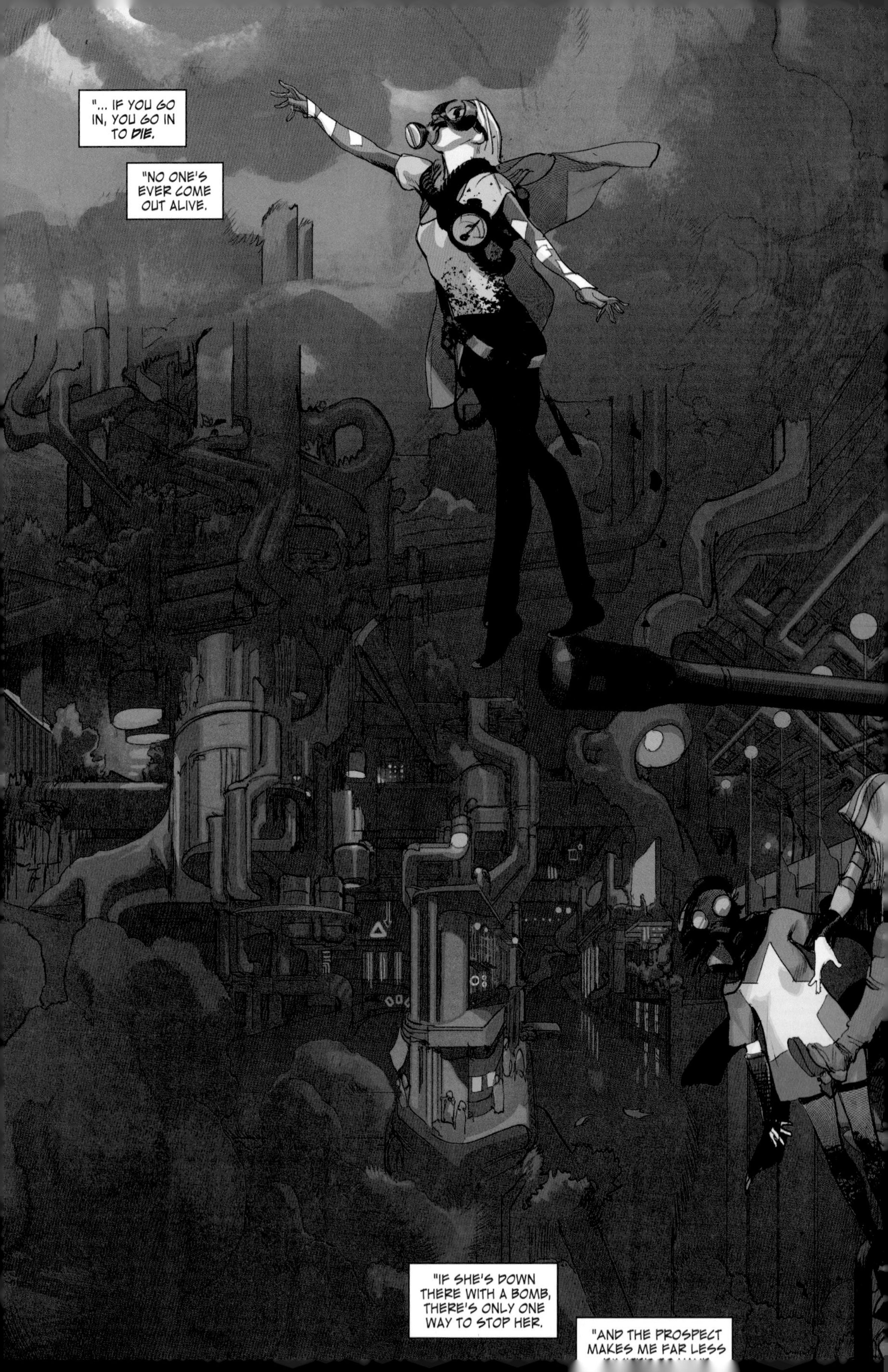
"... IF YOU GO IN, YOU GO IN TO DIE.
"NO ONE'S EVER COME OUT ALIVE.
"IF SHE'S DOWN THERE WITH A BOMB, THERE'S ONLY ONE WAY TO STOP HER.
"AND THE PROSPECT MAKES ME FAR LESS

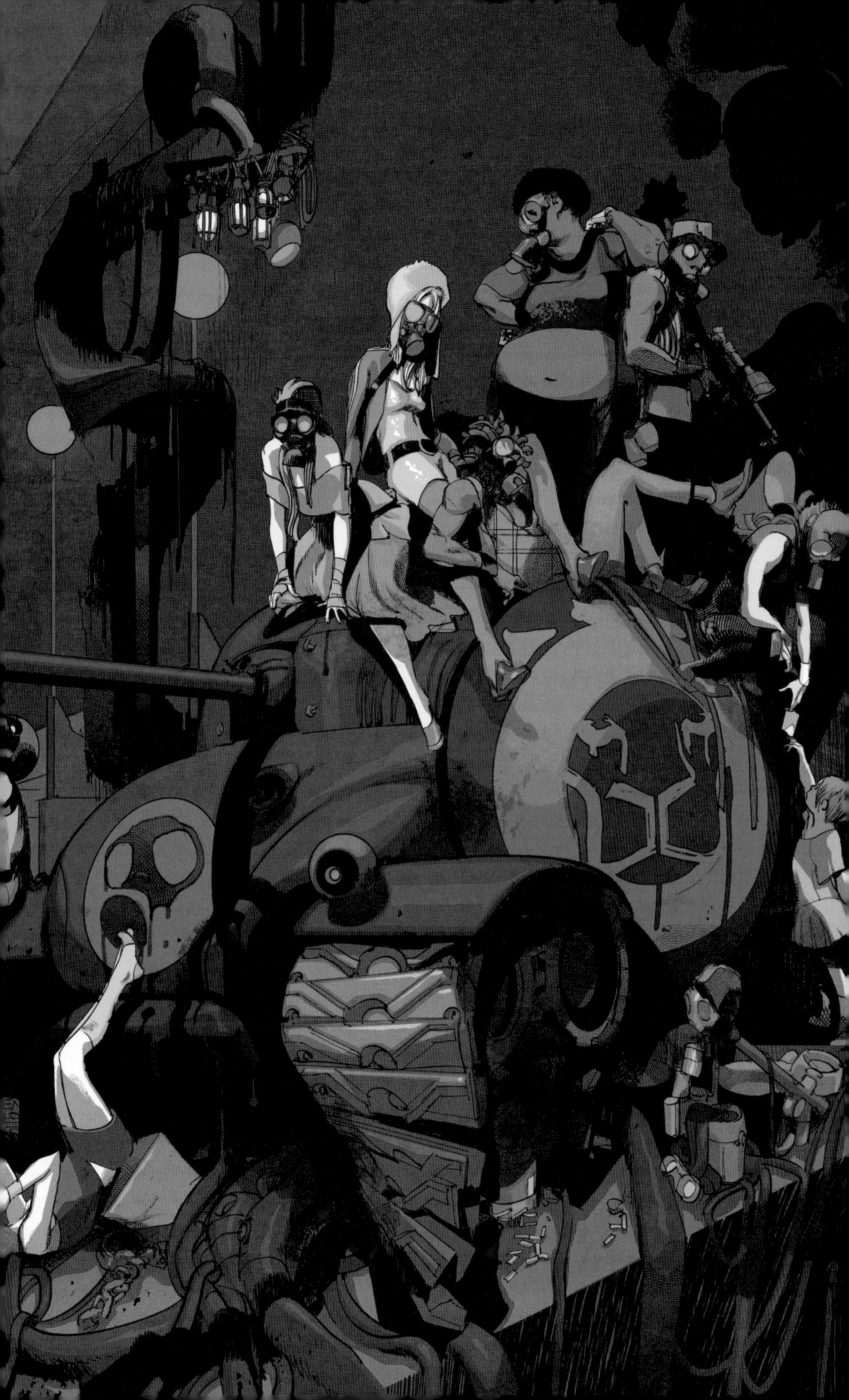

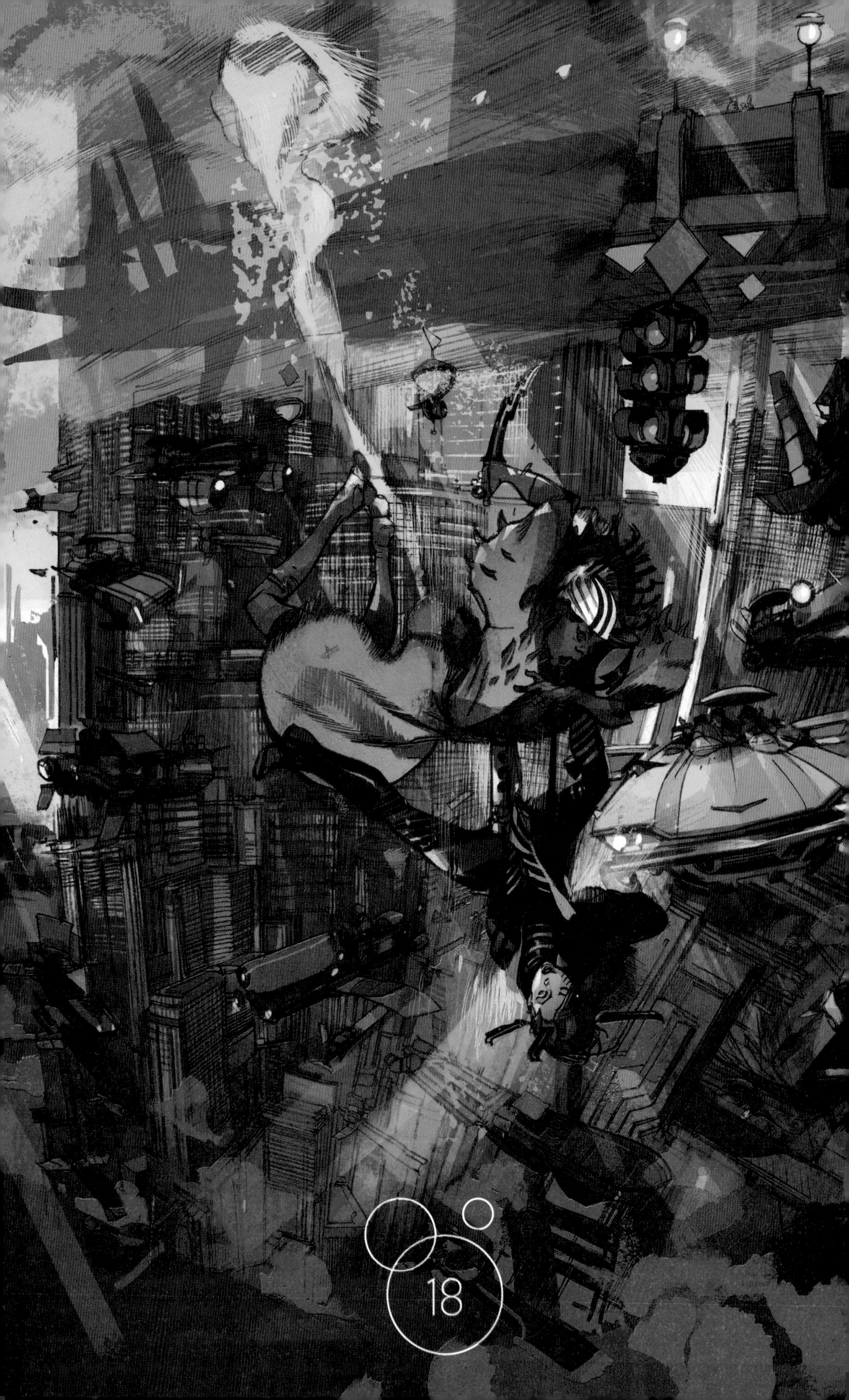

18

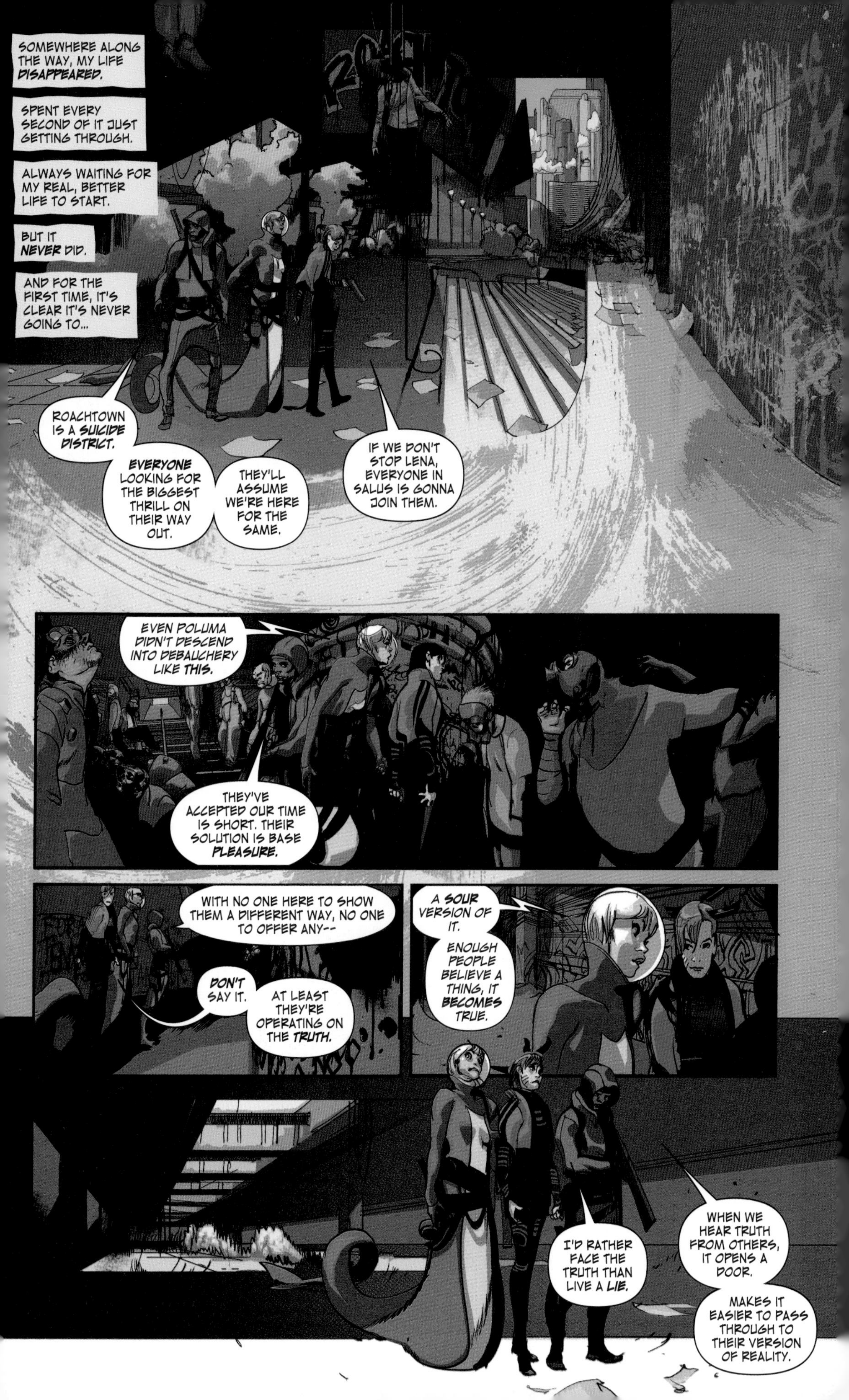

SOMEWHERE ALONG THE WAY, MY LIFE DISAPPEARED.
SPENT EVERY SECOND OF IT JUST GETTING THROUGH.
ALWAYS WAITING FOR MY REAL, BETTER LIFE TO START.
BUT IT NEVER DID.
AND FOR THE FIRST TIME, IT'S CLEAR IT'S NEVER GOING TO...
ROACHTOWN IS A SUICIDE DISTRICT.
EVERYONE LOOKING FOR THE BIGGEST THRILL ON THEIR WAY OUT.
THEY'LL ASSUME WE'RE HERE FOR THE SAME.
IF WE DON'T STOP LENA, EVERYONE IN SALUS IS GONNA JOIN THEM.
EVEN POLUMA DIDN'T DESCEND INTO DEBAUCHERY LIKE THIS.
THEY'VE ACCEPTED OUR TIME IS SHORT. THEIR SOLUTION IS BASE PLEASURE.
WITH NO ONE HERE TO SHOW THEM A DIFFERENT WAY, NO ONE TO OFFER ANY--
DON'T SAY IT.
AT LEAST THEY'RE OPERATING ON THE TRUTH.
A SOUR VERSION OF IT.
ENOUGH PEOPLE BELIEVE A THING, IT BECOMES TRUE.
I'D RATHER FACE THE TRUTH THAN LIVE A LIE.
WHEN WE HEAR TRUTH FROM OTHERS, IT OPENS A DOOR.
MAKES IT EASIER TO PASS THROUGH TO THEIR VERSION OF REALITY.

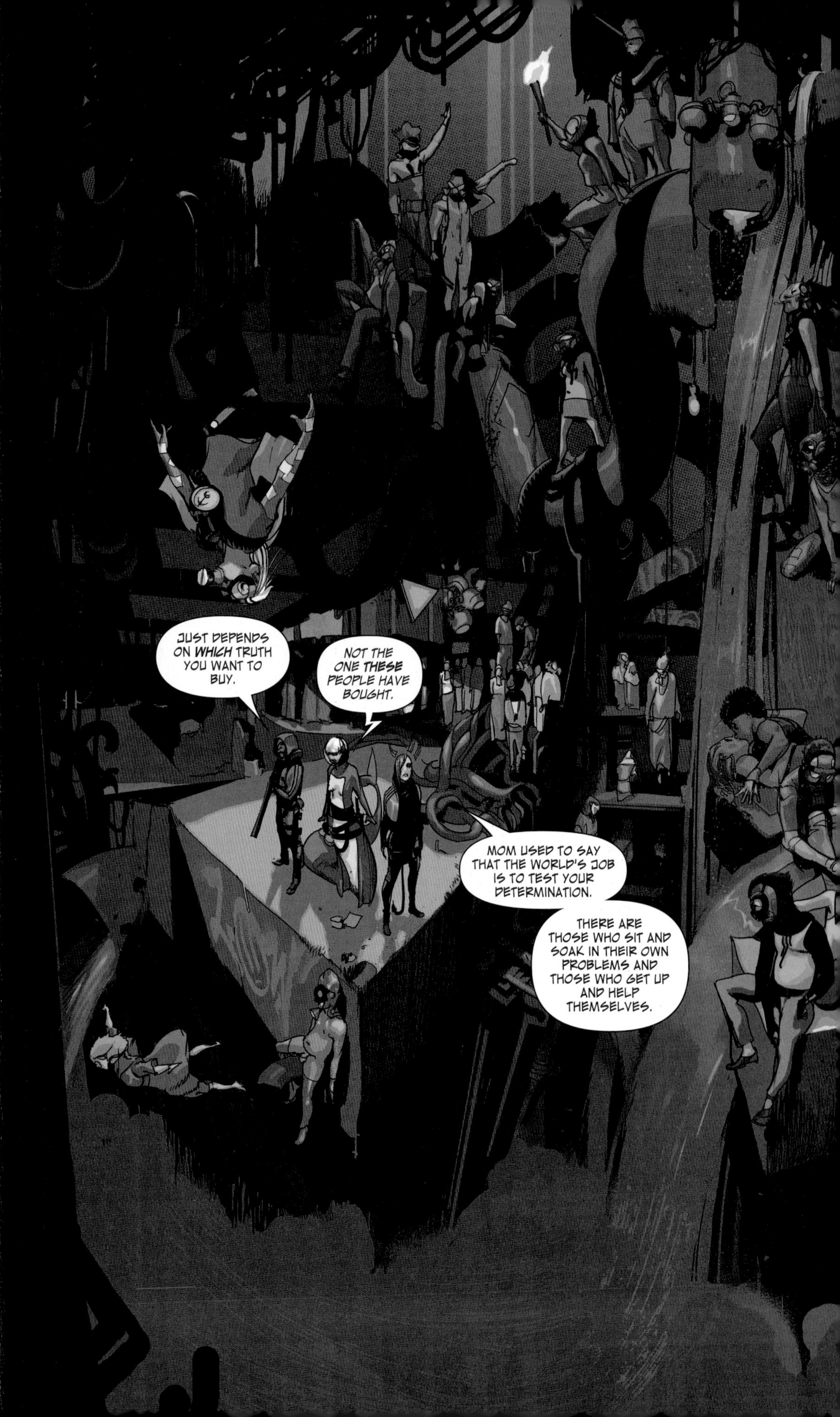
JUST DEPENDS ON *WHICH* TRUTH YOU WANT TO BUY.
NOT THE ONE **THESE** PEOPLE HAVE BOUGHT.
MOM USED TO SAY THAT THE WORLD'S JOB IS TO TEST YOUR DETERMINATION.
THERE ARE THOSE WHO SIT AND SOAK IN THEIR OWN PROBLEMS AND THOSE WHO GET UP AND HELP THEMSELVES.

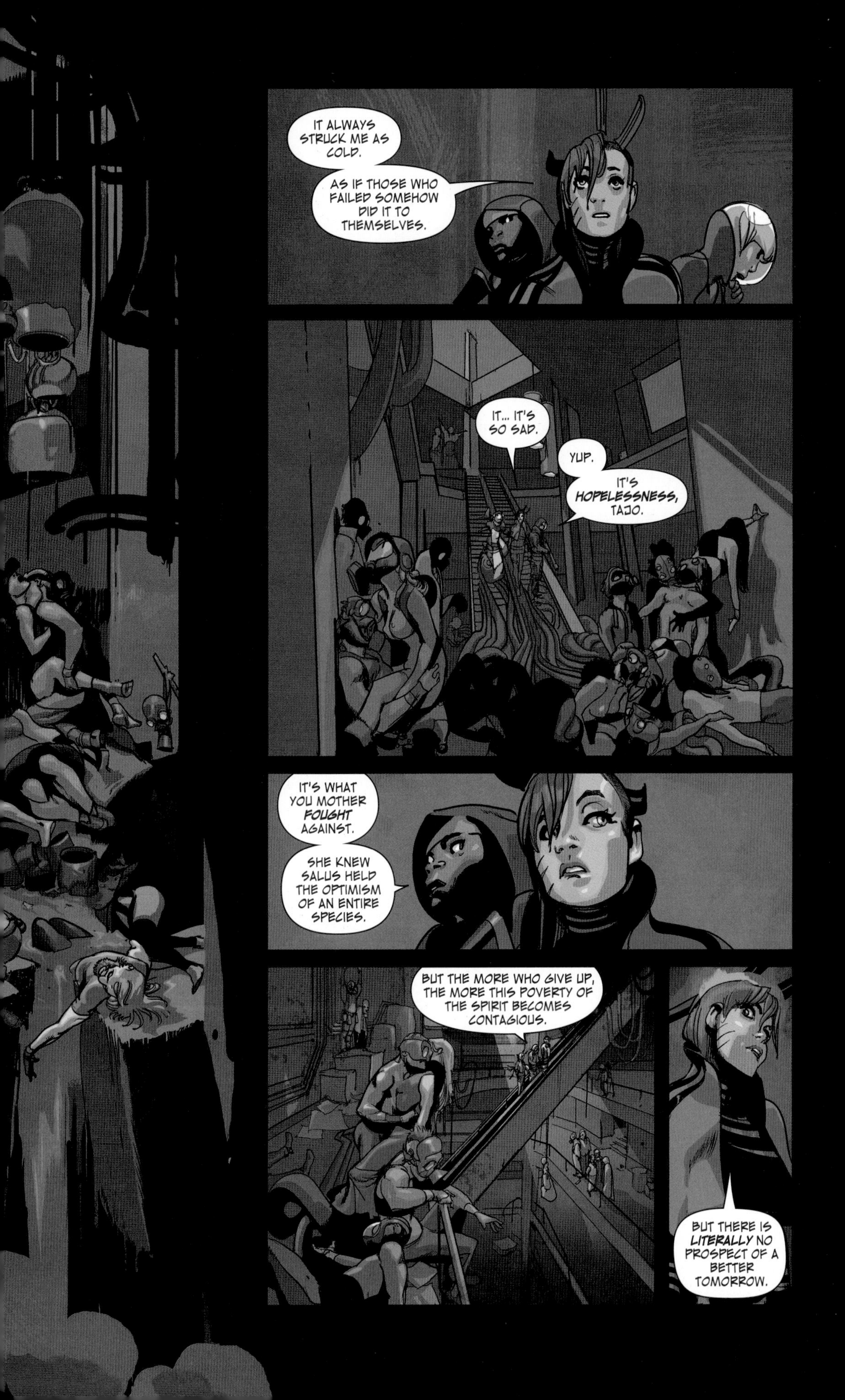
IT ALWAYS STRUCK ME AS COLD.
AS IF THOSE WHO FAILED SOMEHOW DID IT TO THEMSELVES.
IT... IT'S SO SAD.
YUP.
IT'S **HOPELESSNESS,** TAJO.
IT'S WHAT YOU MOTHER **FOUGHT** AGAINST.
SHE KNEW SALUS HELD THE OPTIMISM OF AN ENTIRE SPECIES.
BUT THE MORE WHO GIVE UP, THE MORE THIS POVERTY OF THE SPIRIT BECOMES CONTAGIOUS.
BUT THERE IS **LITERALLY** NO PROSPECT OF A BETTER TOMORROW.

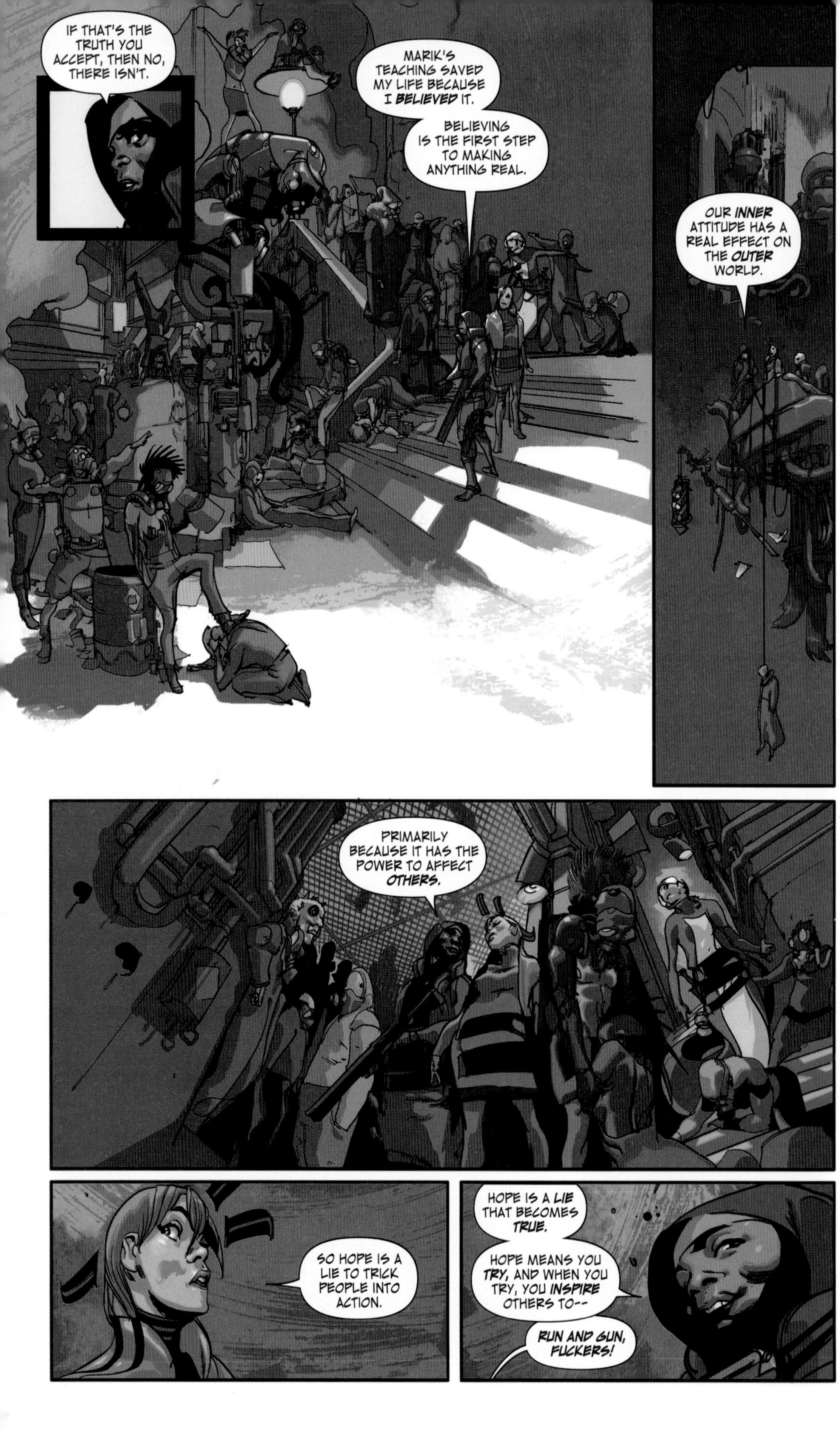
IF THAT'S THE TRUTH YOU ACCEPT, THEN NO, THERE ISN'T.
MARIK'S TEACHING SAVED MY LIFE BECAUSE I **BELIEVED** IT.
BELIEVING IS THE FIRST STEP TO MAKING ANYTHING REAL.
OUR **INNER** ATTITUDE HAS A REAL EFFECT ON THE **OUTER** WORLD.
PRIMARILY BECAUSE IT HAS THE POWER TO AFFECT **OTHERS.**
SO HOPE IS A LIE TO TRICK PEOPLE INTO ACTION.
HOPE IS A **LIE** THAT BECOMES **TRUE.**
HOPE MEANS YOU **TRY,** AND WHEN YOU TRY, YOU **INSPIRE** OTHERS TO--
RUN AND GUN, FUCKERS!

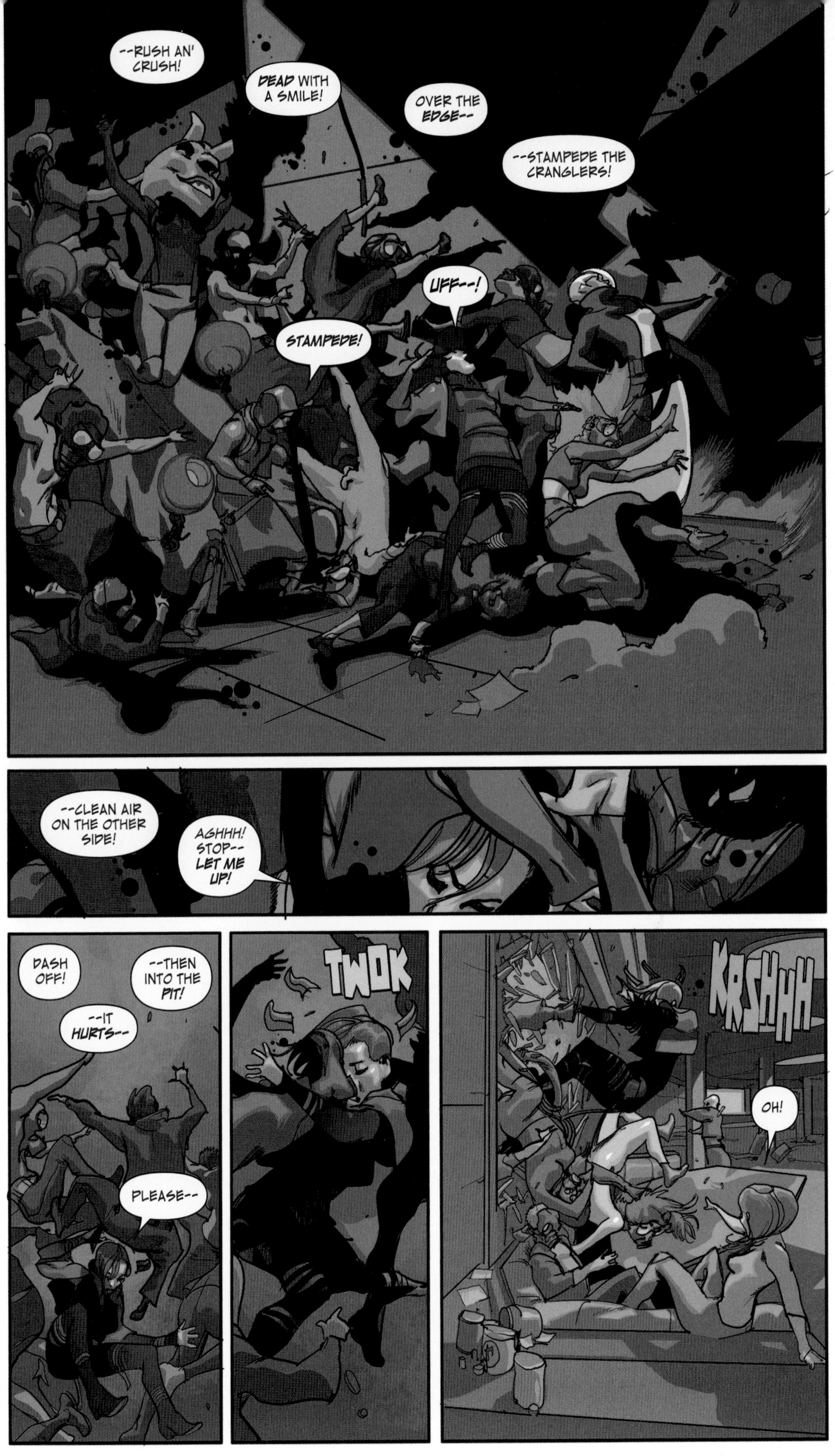
--RUSH AN' CRUSH!
DEAD WITH A SMILE!
OVER THE EDGE--
--STAMPEDE THE CRANGLERS!
UFF--!
STAMPEDE!
--CLEAN AIR ON THE OTHER SIDE!
AGHHH! STOP-- LET ME UP!
DASH OFF!
--THEN INTO THE PIT!
--IT HURTS--
PLEASE--
TWOK
KRSHHH
OH!

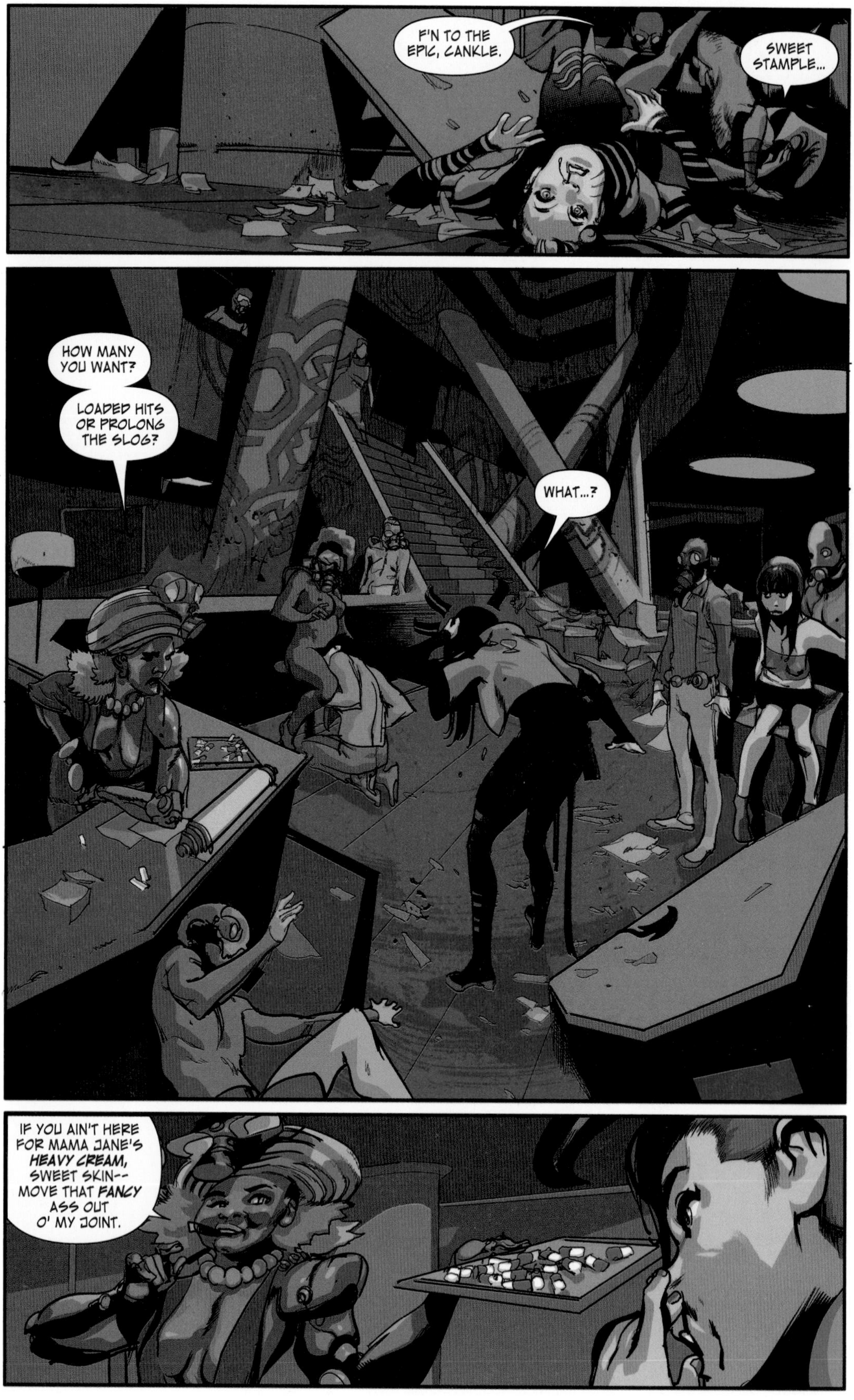

F'N TO THE EPIC, CANKLE.
SWEET STAMPLE...
HOW MANY YOU WANT?
LOADED HITS OR PROLONG THE SLOG?
WHAT...?
IF YOU AIN'T HERE FOR MAMA JANE'S HEAVY CREAM, SWEET SKIN-- MOVE THAT FANCY ASS OUT O' MY JOINT.

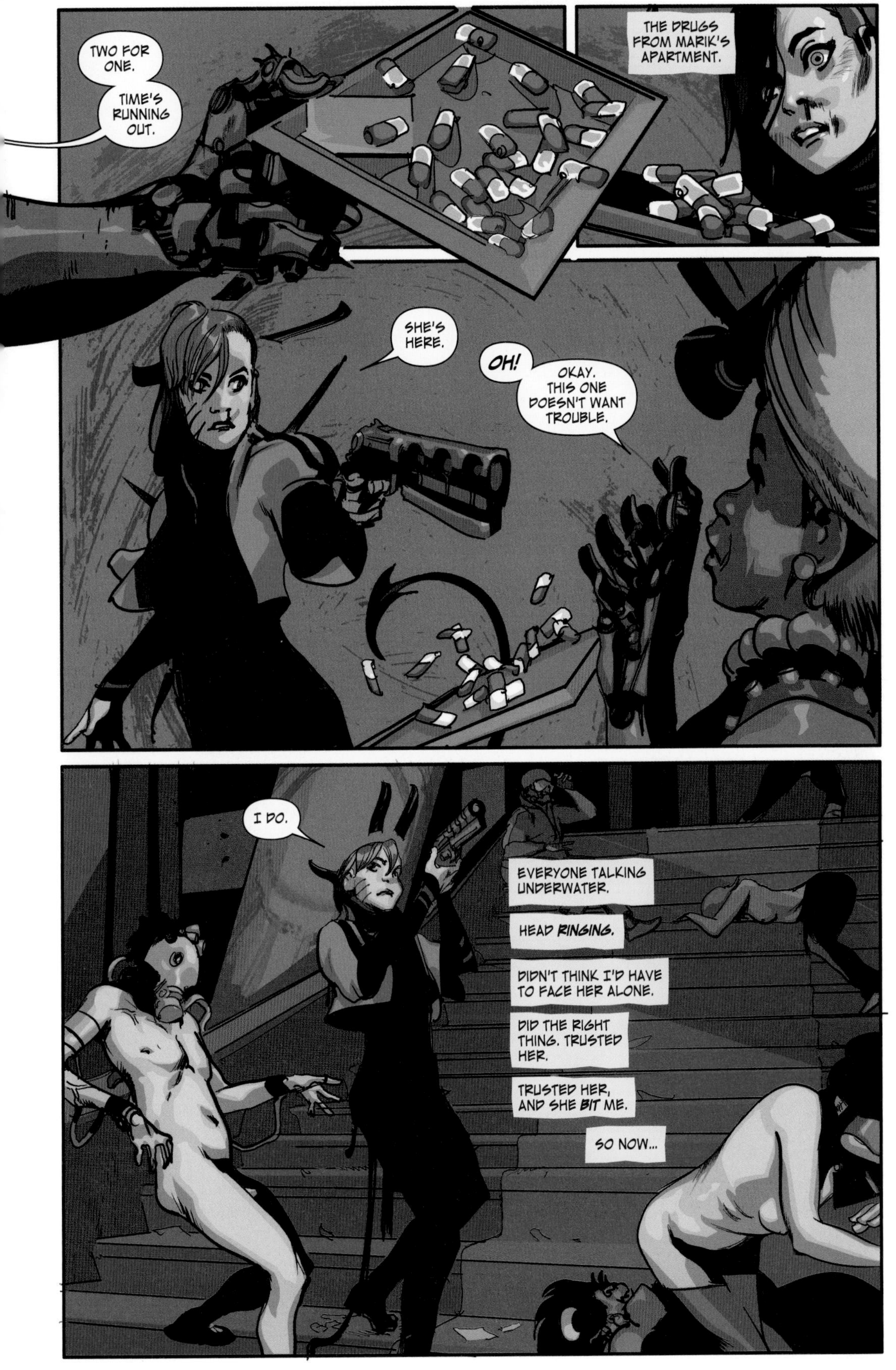
TWO FOR ONE.
TIME'S RUNNING OUT.
THE DRUGS FROM MARIK'S APARTMENT.
SHE'S HERE.
OH!
OKAY. THIS ONE DOESN'T WANT TROUBLE.
I DO.
EVERYONE TALKING UNDERWATER.
HEAD RINGING.
DIDN'T THINK I'D HAVE TO FACE HER ALONE.
DID THE RIGHT THING. TRUSTED HER.
TRUSTED HER, AND SHE BIT ME.
SO NOW...

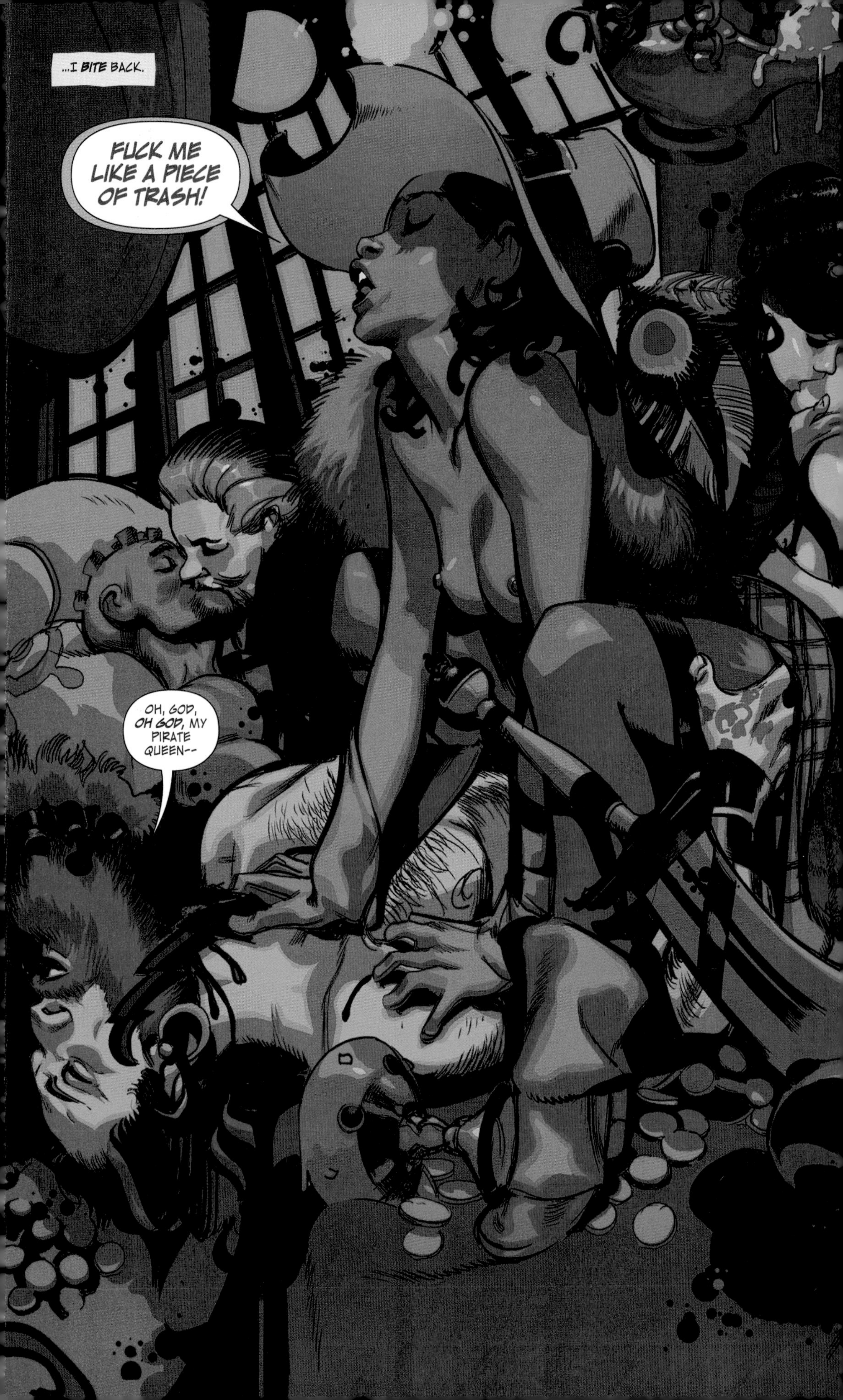
...I BITE BACK.
FUCK ME LIKE A PIECE OF TRASH!
OH, GOD, OH GOD, MY PIRATE QUEEN--

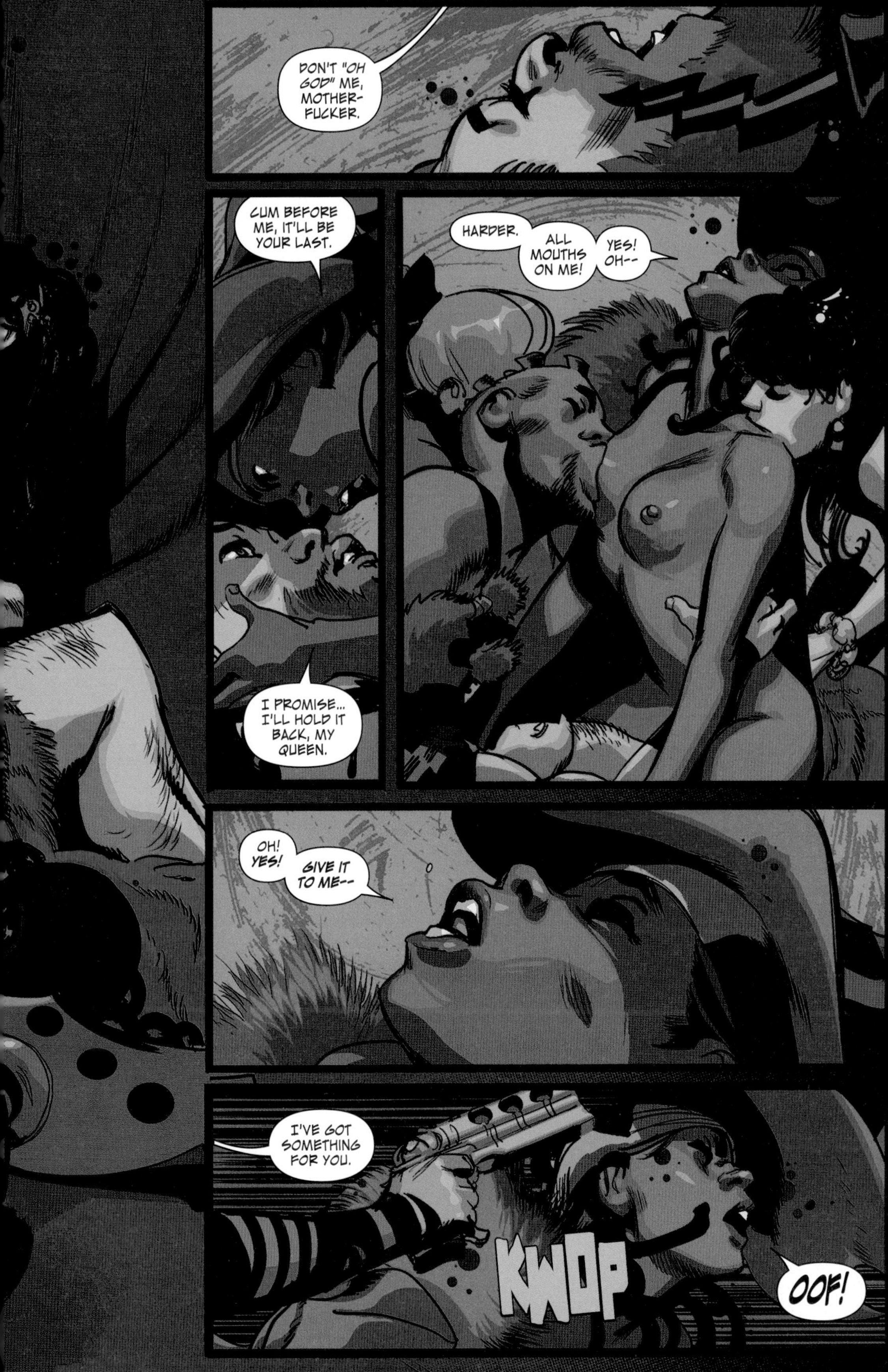

DON'T "OH GOD" ME, MOTHER-FUCKER.
CUM BEFORE ME, IT'LL BE YOUR LAST.
I PROMISE... I'LL HOLD IT BACK, MY QUEEN.
HARDER.
ALL MOUTHS ON ME!
YES! OH--
OH! YES!
GIVE IT TO ME--
I'VE GOT SOMETHING FOR YOU.
KWOP
OOF!

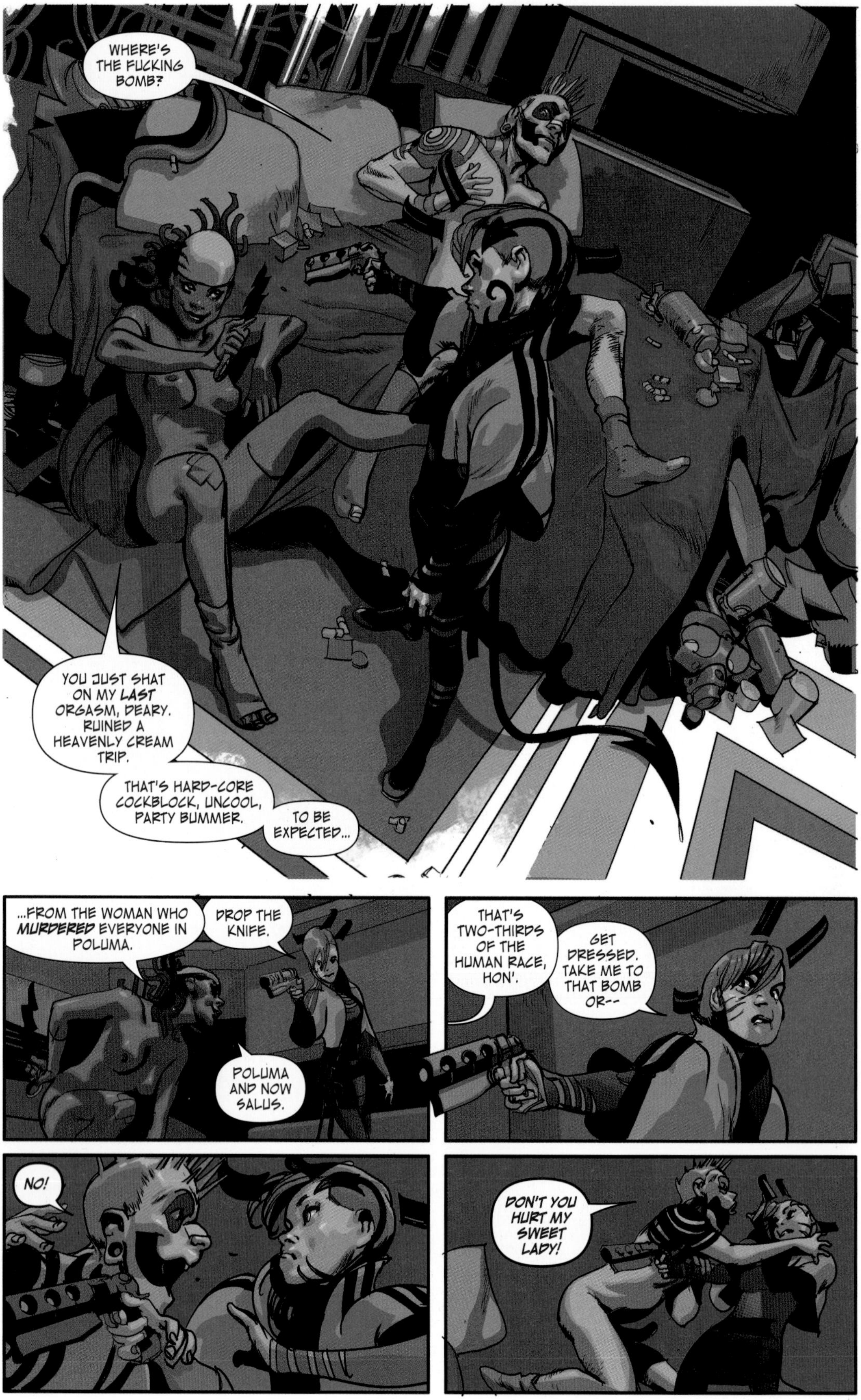
WHERE'S THE FUCKING BOMB?
YOU JUST SHAT ON MY LAST ORGASM, DEARY. RUINED A HEAVENLY CREAM TRIP.
THAT'S HARD-CORE COCKBLOCK, UNCOOL, PARTY BUMMER.
TO BE EXPECTED...
...FROM THE WOMAN WHO MURDERED EVERYONE IN POLUMA.
DROP THE KNIFE.
POLUMA AND NOW SALUS.
THAT'S TWO-THIRDS OF THE HUMAN RACE, HON'.
GET DRESSED. TAKE ME TO THAT BOMB OR--
NO!
DON'T YOU HURT MY SWEET LADY!

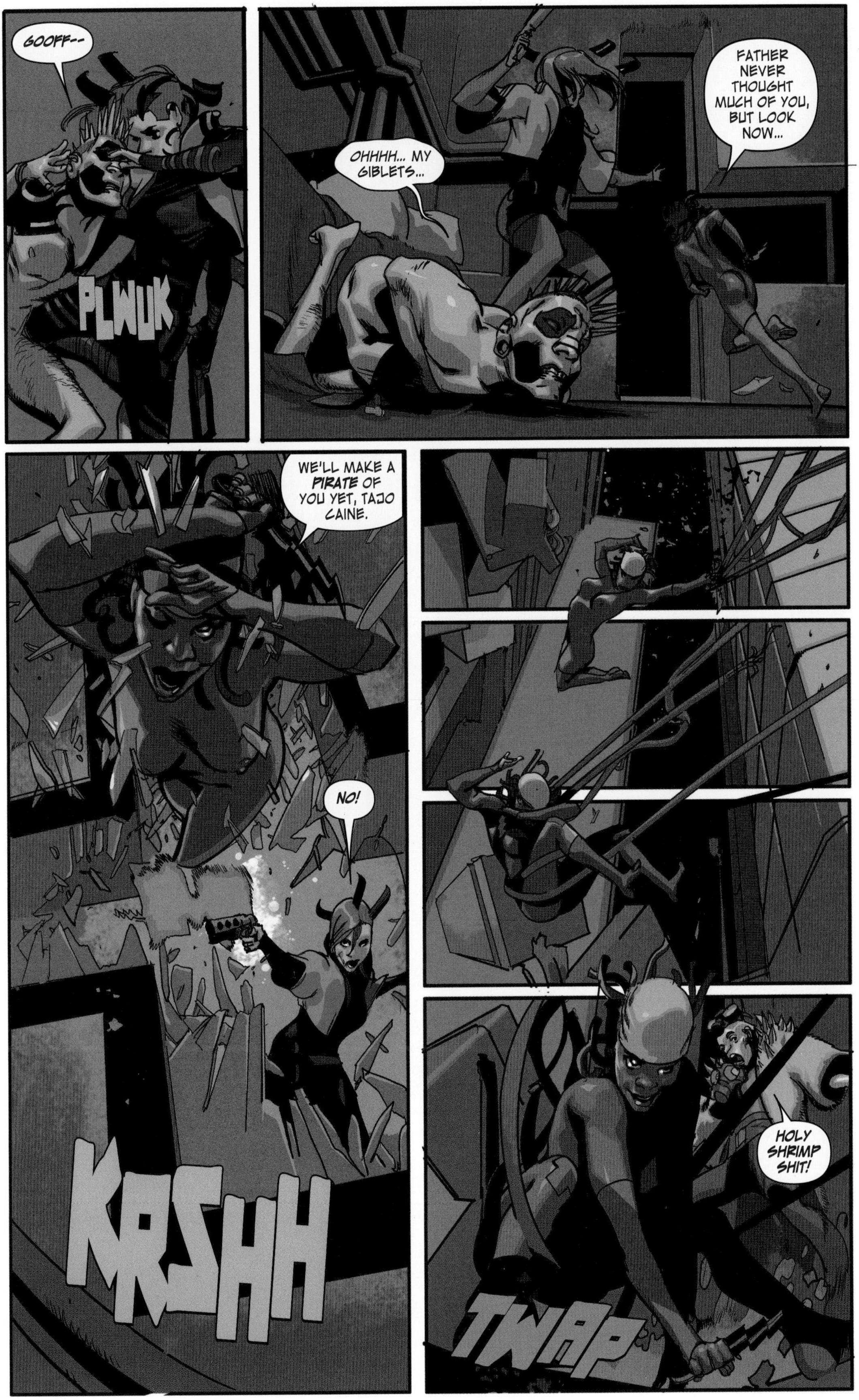
GOOFF--
PLWUK
OHHHH... MY GIBLETS...
FATHER NEVER THOUGHT MUCH OF YOU, BUT LOOK NOW...
WE'LL MAKE A PIRATE OF YOU YET, TAJO CAINE.
NO!
KRSHH
HOLY SHRIMP SHIT!
TWAP

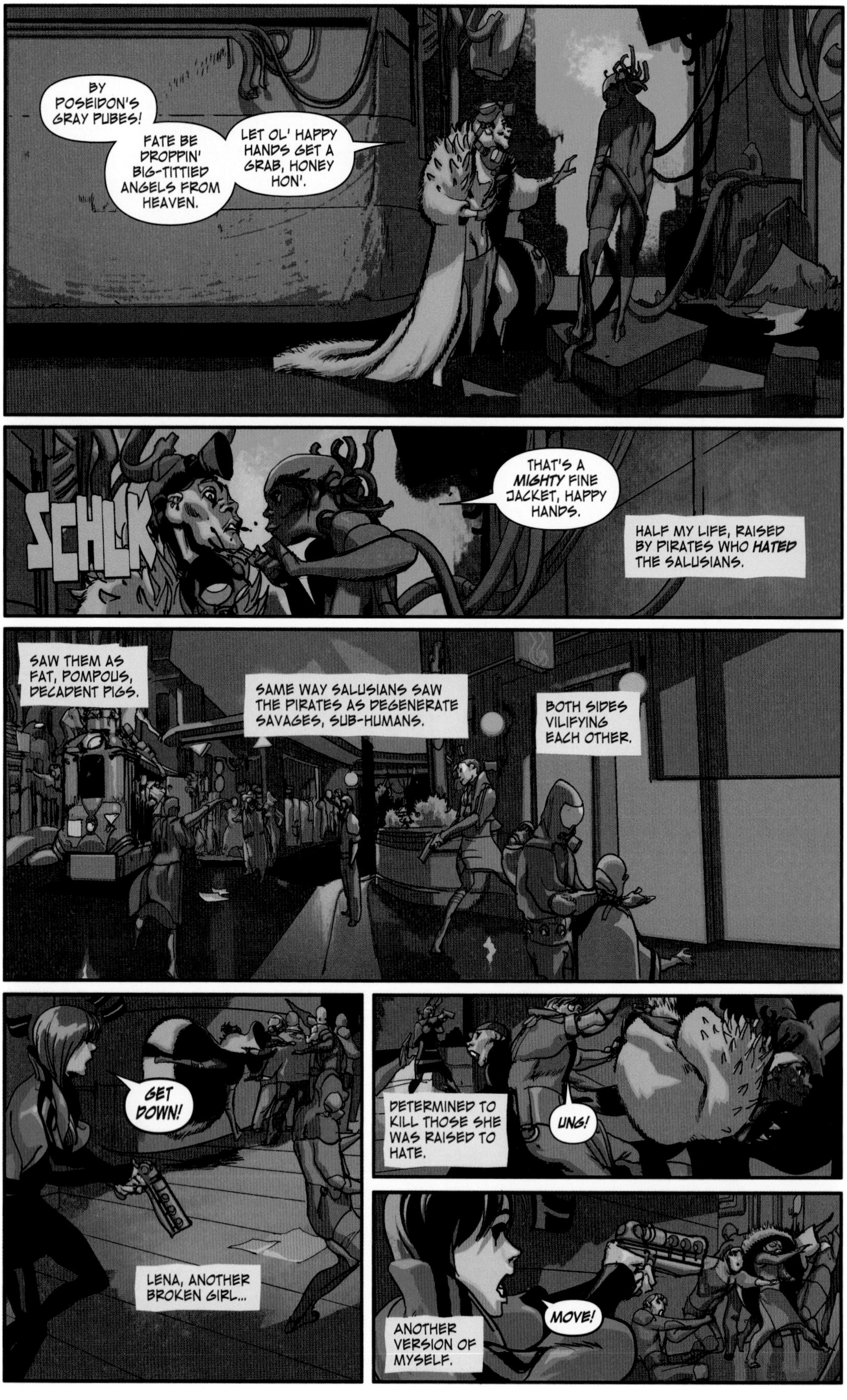

BY POSEIDON'S GRAY PUBES!
FATE BE DROPPIN' BIG-TITTIED ANGELS FROM HEAVEN.
LET OL' HAPPY HANDS GET A GRAB, HONEY HON'.
SCHLK
THAT'S A MIGHTY FINE JACKET, HAPPY HANDS.
HALF MY LIFE, RAISED BY PIRATES WHO HATED THE SALUSIANS.
SAW THEM AS FAT, POMPOUS, DECADENT PIGS.
SAME WAY SALUSIANS SAW THE PIRATES AS DEGENERATE SAVAGES, SUB-HUMANS.
BOTH SIDES VILIFYING EACH OTHER.
GET DOWN!
LENA, ANOTHER BROKEN GIRL...
DETERMINED TO KILL THOSE SHE WAS RAISED TO HATE.
UNG!
MOVE!
ANOTHER VERSION OF MYSELF.

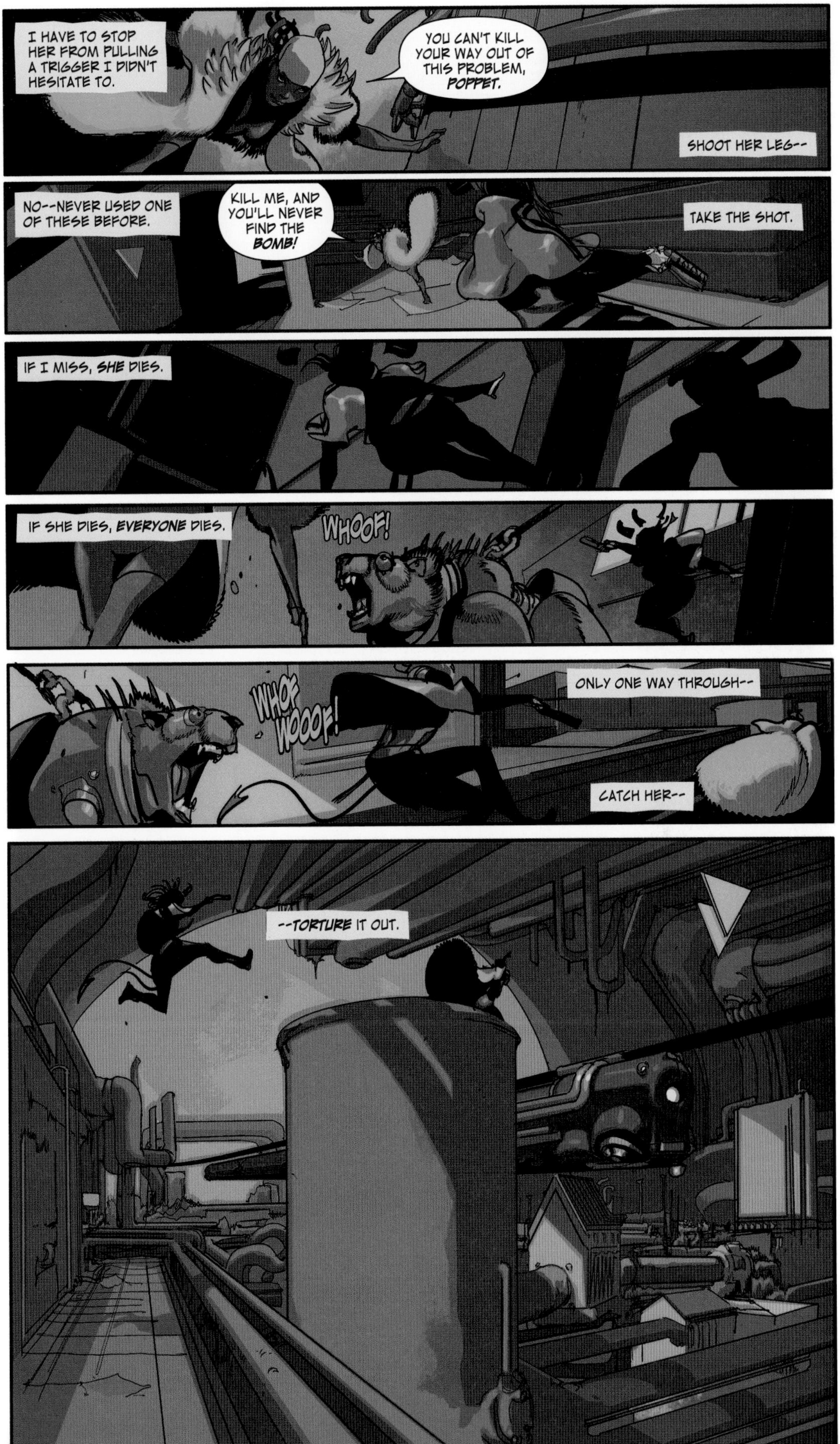
I HAVE TO STOP HER FROM PULLING A TRIGGER I DIDN'T HESITATE TO.
YOU CAN'T KILL YOUR WAY OUT OF THIS PROBLEM, POPPET.
SHOOT HER LEG--
NO--NEVER USED ONE OF THESE BEFORE.
KILL ME, AND YOU'LL NEVER FIND THE BOMB!
TAKE THE SHOT.
IF I MISS, SHE DIES.
IF SHE DIES, EVERYONE DIES.
WHOOF!
WHOF
WOOOF!
ONLY ONE WAY THROUGH--
CATCH HER--
--TORTURE IT OUT.

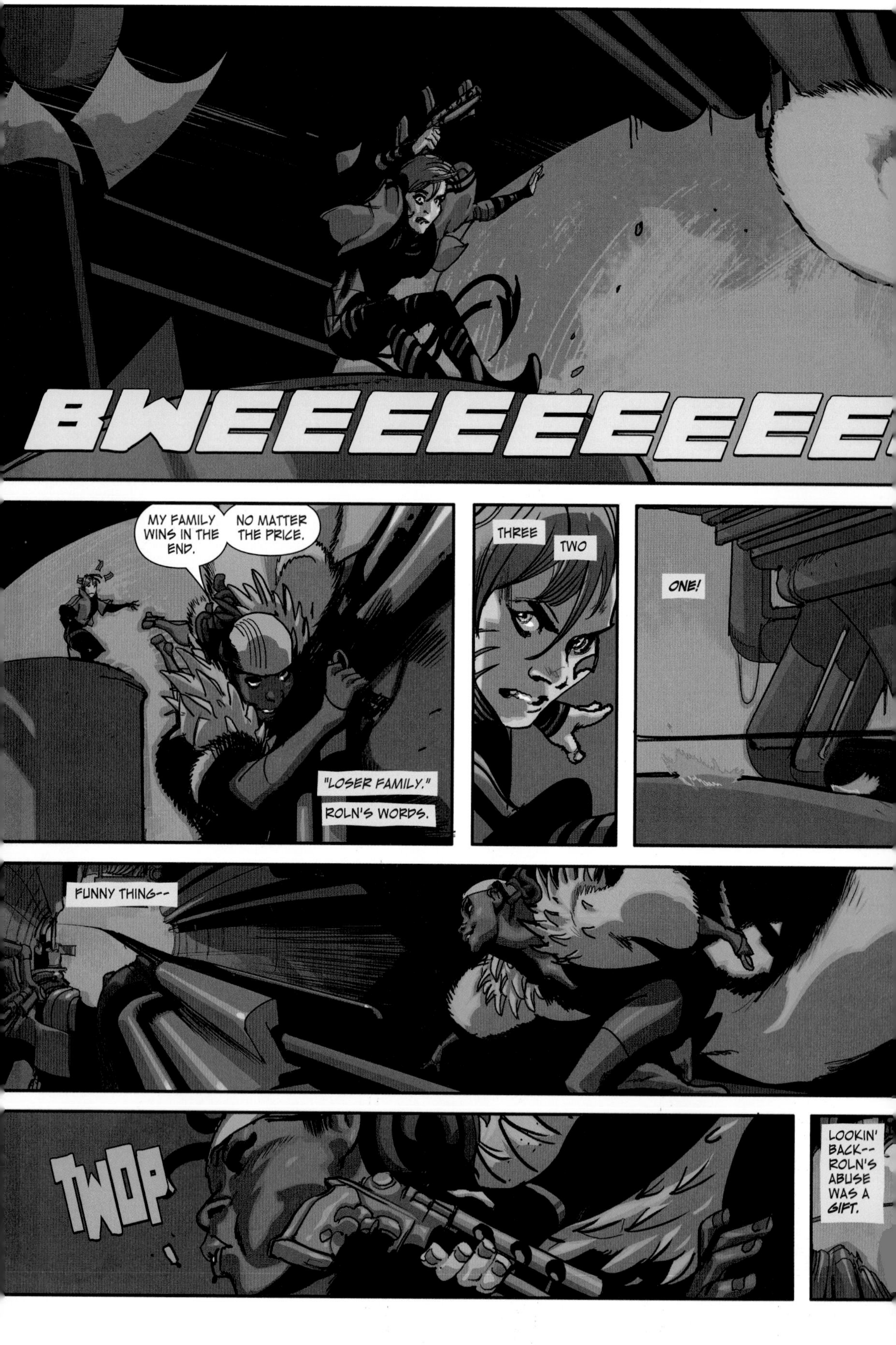
BWEEEEEEEEEE
MY FAMILY WINS IN THE END.
NO MATTER THE PRICE.
"LOSER FAMILY."
ROLN'S WORDS.
THREE
TWO
ONE!
FUNNY THING--
TWOP
LOOKIN' BACK-- ROLN'S ABUSE WAS A GIFT.

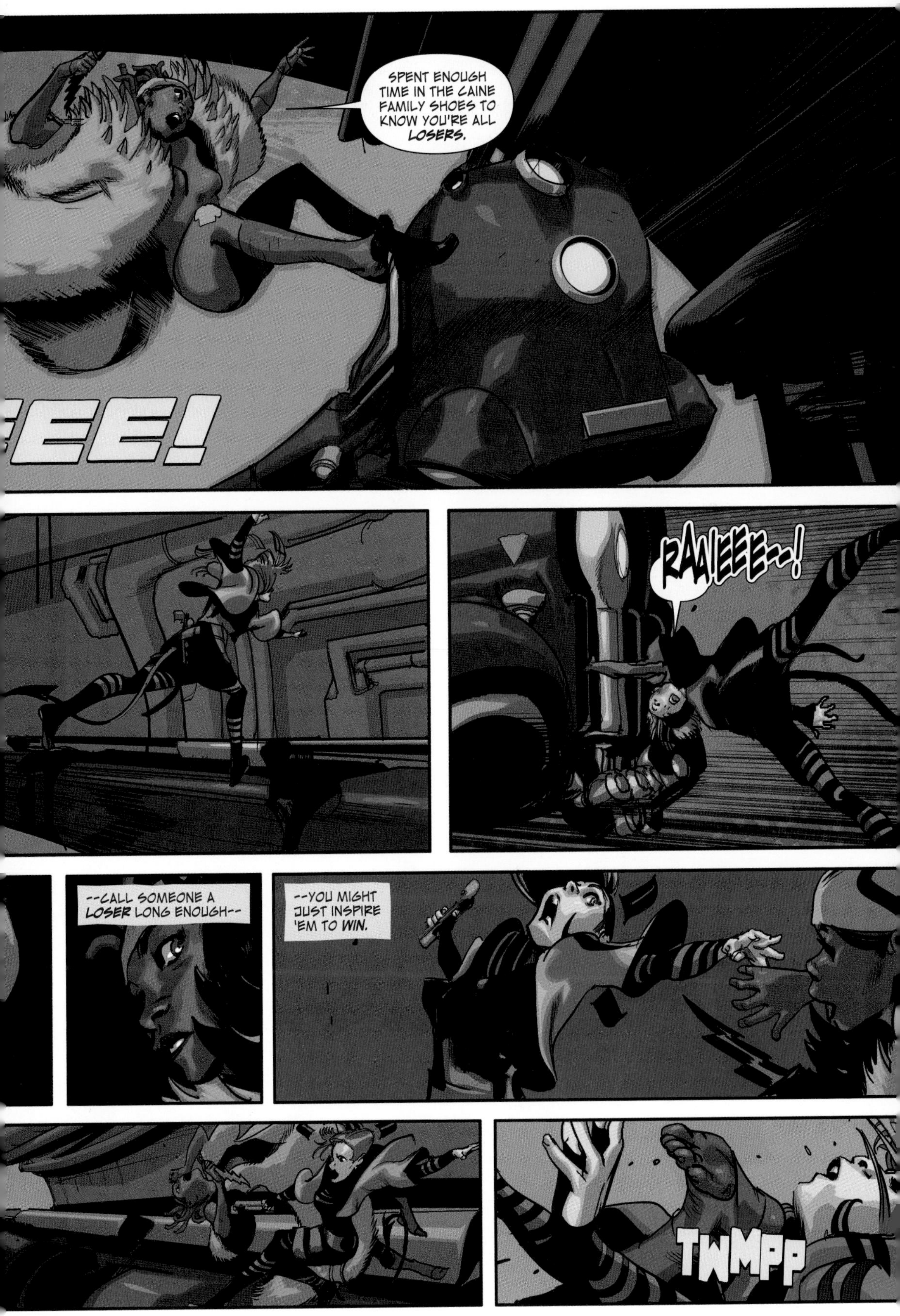
SPENT ENOUGH TIME IN THE CAINE FAMILY SHOES TO KNOW YOU'RE ALL LOSERS.
EEE!
RAAIEEE--!
--CALL SOMEONE A LOSER LONG ENOUGH--
--YOU MIGHT JUST INSPIRE 'EM TO WIN.
TWMPP

IMPRESSIVE, TAJO.

WITH A BIT ON THE LINE, YOU *FINALLY* SHOW UP.

EVERYONE IN YOUR LIFE HAD LOW EXPECTATIONS FOR YOU.

YOU USED IT TO *JUMP*.

USED IT TO *FACE* THIS MEAN BITCH WHO CUT YOU UP.

YOU USED IT TO *RISE*.

YOU DID IT JUST IN TIME--

ANOTHER JUMP.

GO.

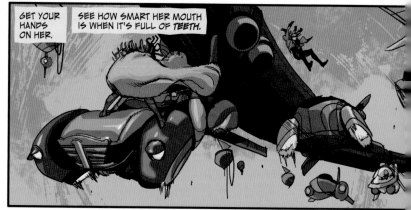

GET YOUR HANDS ON HER.

SEE HOW SMART HER MOUTH IS WHEN IT'S FULL OF *TEETH*.

ASSHOLE!

KRNCH

HOLY HELL!

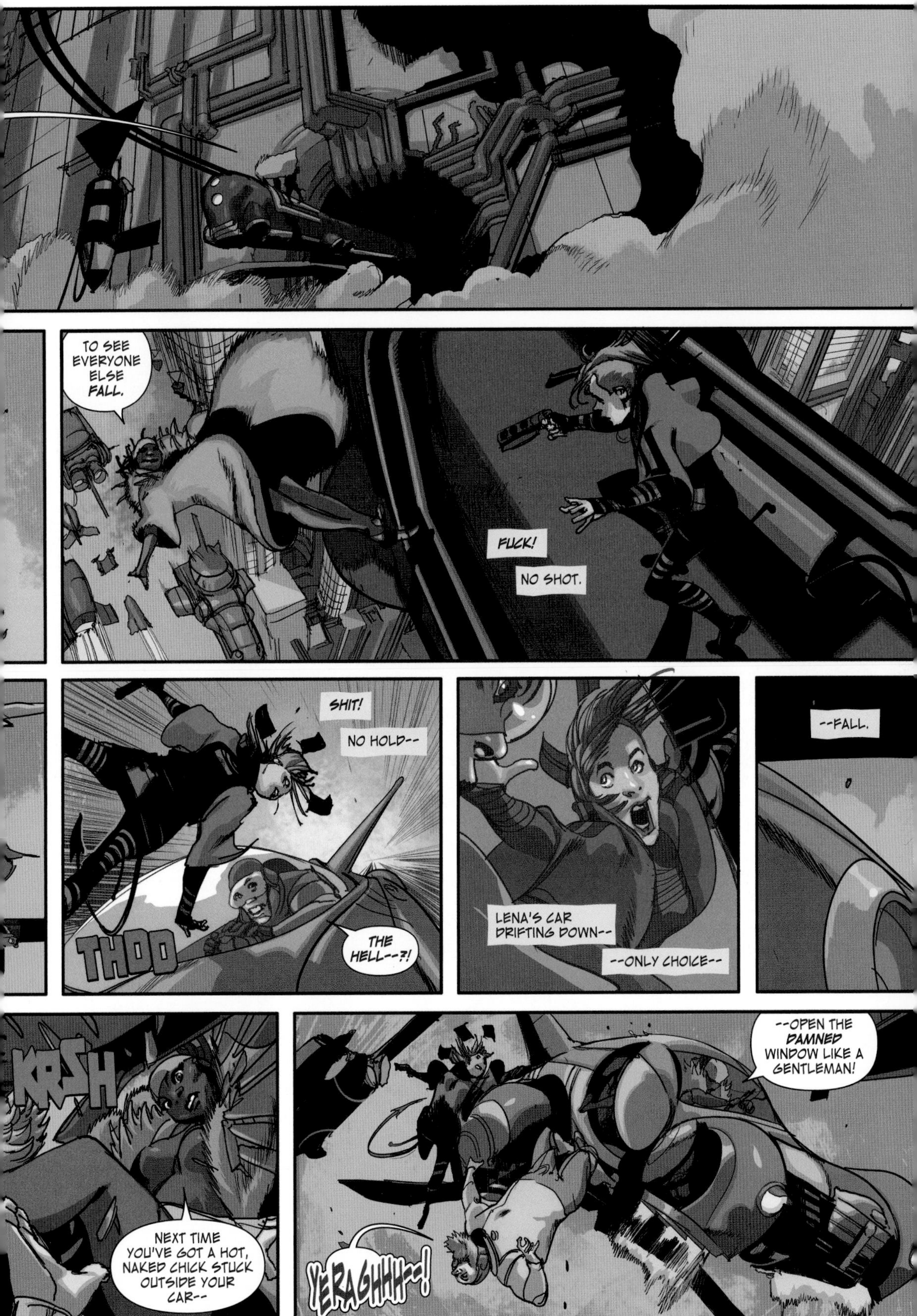
TO SEE EVERYONE ELSE FALL.
FUCK!
NO SHOT.
SHIT!
NO HOLD--
THOO
THE HELL--?!
LENA'S CAR DRIFTING DOWN--
--ONLY CHOICE--
--FALL.
KRSH
NEXT TIME YOU'VE GOT A HOT, NAKED CHICK STUCK OUTSIDE YOUR CAR--
--OPEN THE DAMNED WINDOW LIKE A GENTLEMAN!
YERAGHHH--!

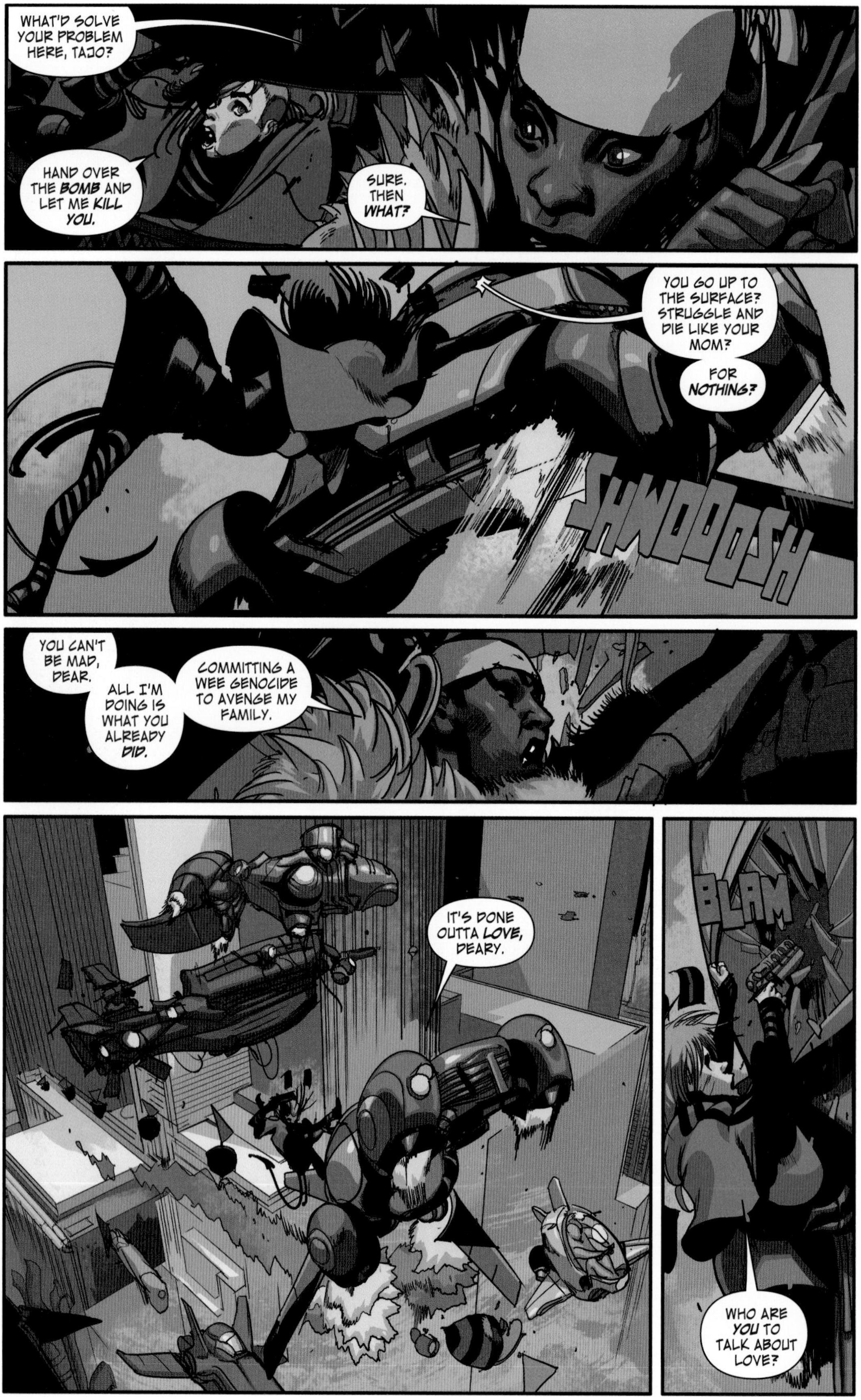
WHAT'D SOLVE YOUR PROBLEM HERE, TAJO?
HAND OVER THE BOMB AND LET ME KILL YOU.
SURE. THEN WHAT?
YOU GO UP TO THE SURFACE? STRUGGLE AND DIE LIKE YOUR MOM?
FOR NOTHING?
SHWOOOSH
YOU CAN'T BE MAD, DEAR.
ALL I'M DOING IS WHAT YOU ALREADY DID.
COMMITTING A WEE GENOCIDE TO AVENGE MY FAMILY.
IT'S DONE OUTTA LOVE, DEARY.
BLAM
WHO ARE YOU TO TALK ABOUT LOVE?

THE **REAL** QUESTION IS, WHO ARE **YOU**?

DAUGHTER TO THE MAN WHO KEPT YOU **SAFE** OR THE ONE WHO **ABANDONED** YOU?

I'M TAJO, DAUGHTER OF JOHL CAINE--

HELMSWOMAN OF SALUS!

AGHHH!

BLAMM

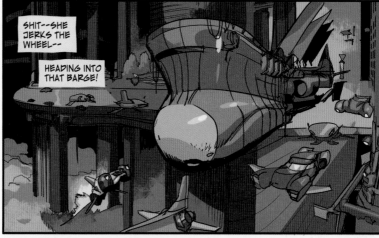

SHIT--SHE JERKS THE WHEEL--

HEADING INTO THAT BARGE!

NO.

MOVE!

YOU **BITCH**!

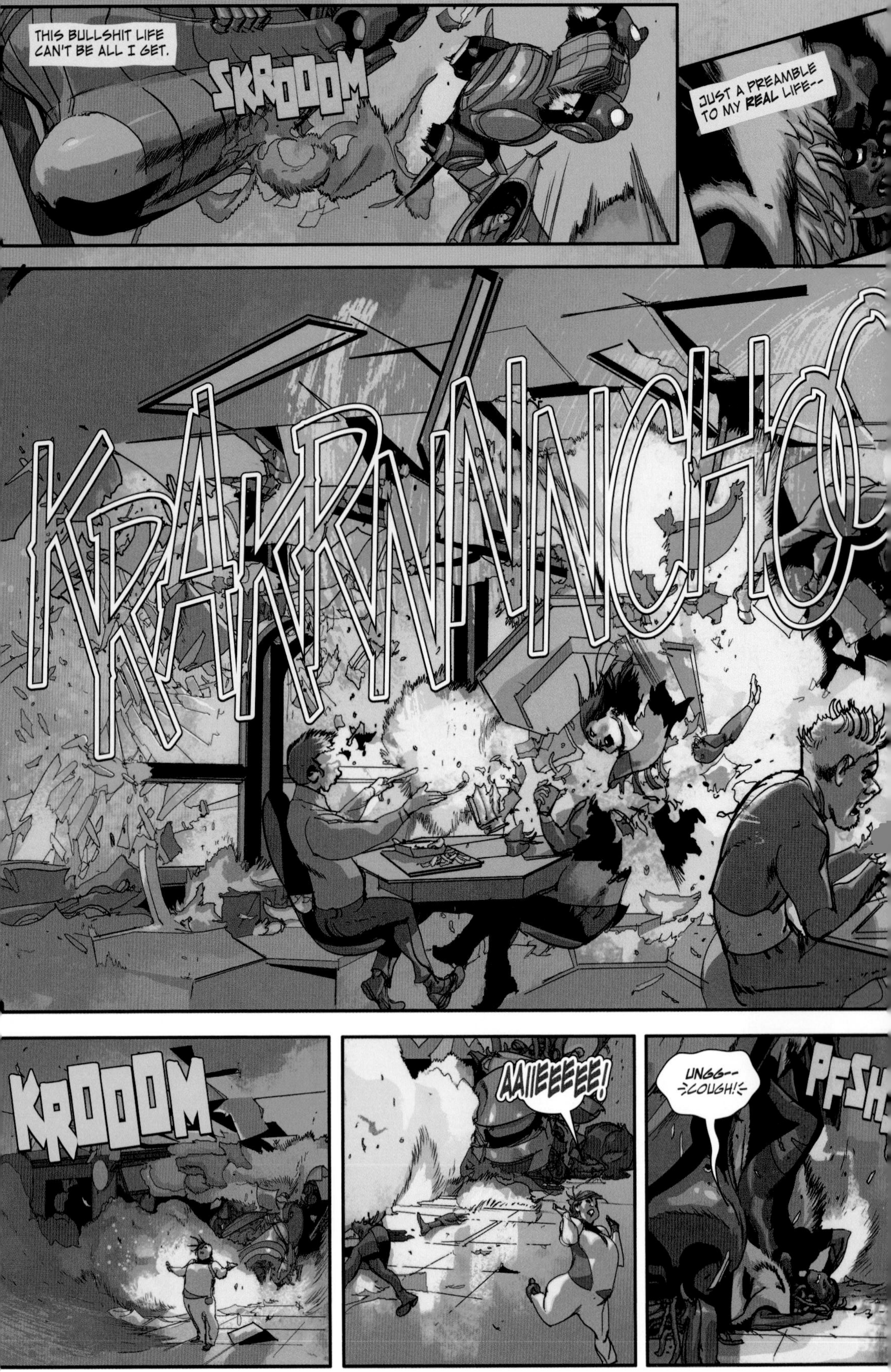
THIS BULLSHIT LIFE CAN'T BE ALL I GET.
SKROOOM
JUST A PREAMBLE TO MY REAL LIFE--
KRAKRNNNCHOO
KROOOM
AAIIEEEEE!
UNGG-- -COUGH!-
PFSH

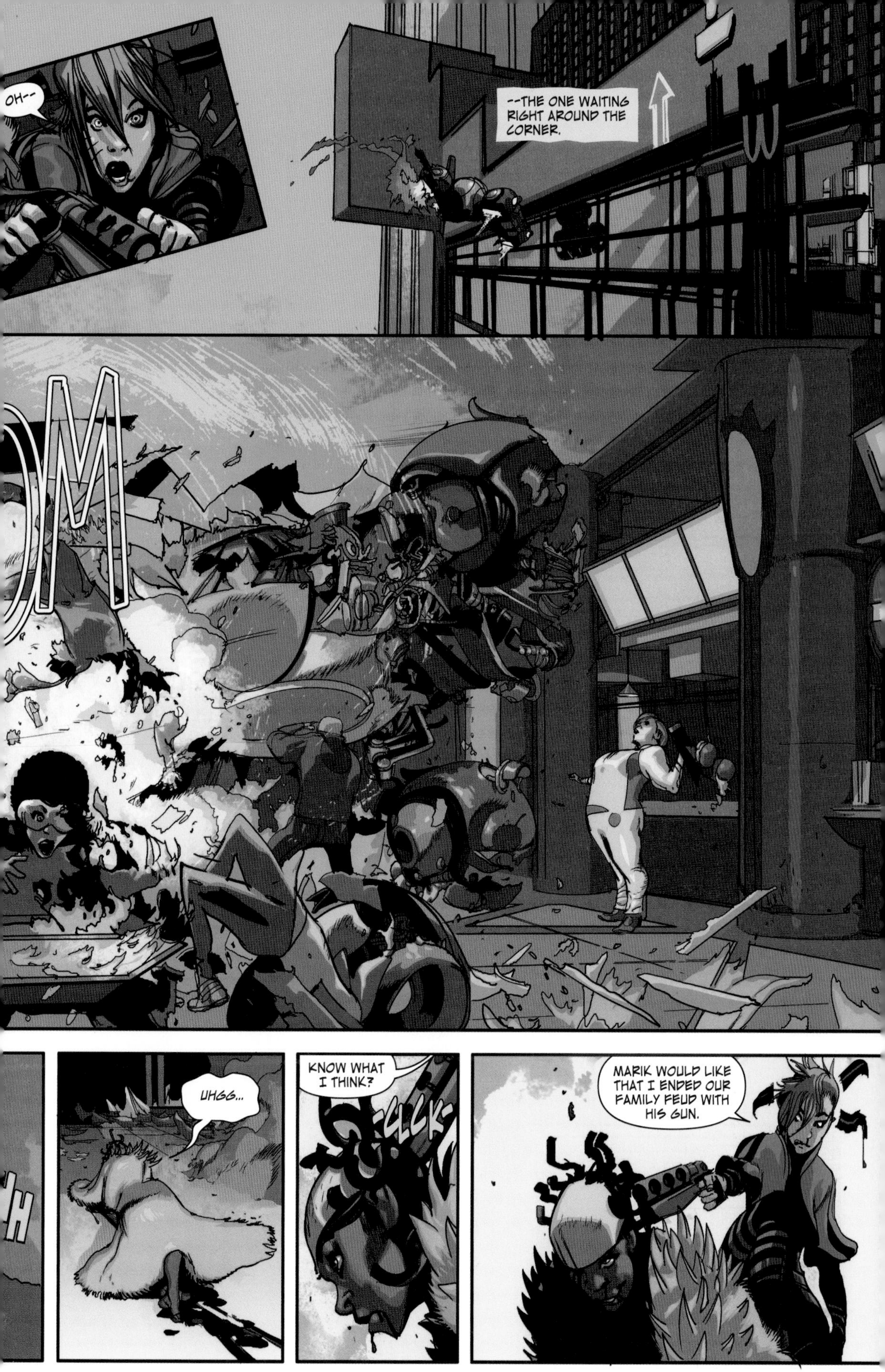
OH--
--THE ONE WAITING RIGHT AROUND THE CORNER.
UHGG...
KNOW WHAT I THINK?
MARIK WOULD LIKE THAT I ENDED OUR FAMILY FEUD WITH HIS GUN.

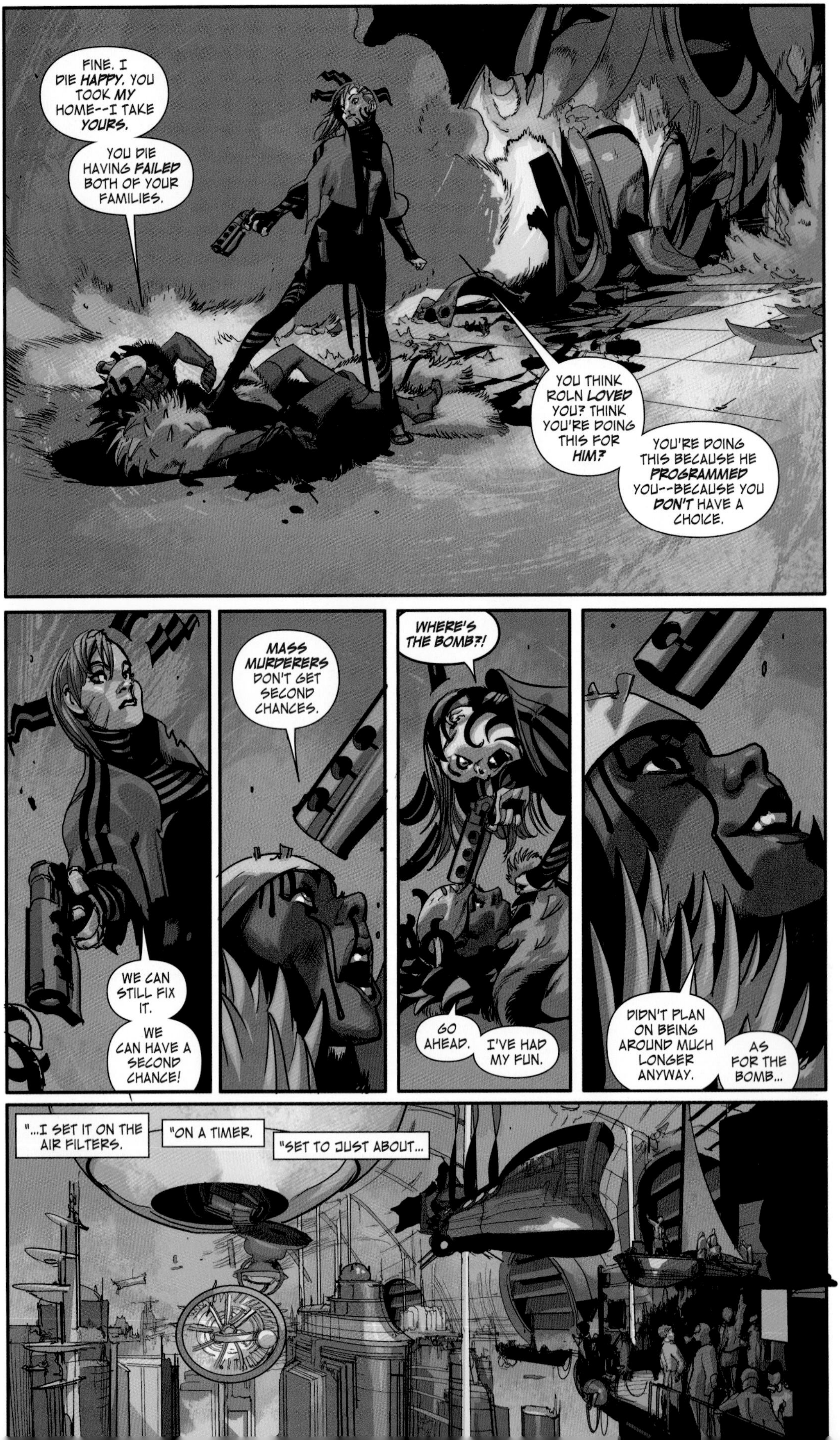
FINE. I DIE HAPPY. YOU TOOK MY HOME--I TAKE YOURS.
YOU DIE HAVING FAILED BOTH OF YOUR FAMILIES.
YOU THINK ROLN LOVED YOU? THINK YOU'RE DOING THIS FOR HIM?
YOU'RE DOING THIS BECAUSE HE PROGRAMMED YOU--BECAUSE YOU DON'T HAVE A CHOICE.
WE CAN STILL FIX IT.
WE CAN HAVE A SECOND CHANCE!
MASS MURDERERS DON'T GET SECOND CHANCES.
WHERE'S THE BOMB?!
GO AHEAD.
I'VE HAD MY FUN.
DIDN'T PLAN ON BEING AROUND MUCH LONGER ANYWAY.
AS FOR THE BOMB...
"...I SET IT ON THE AIR FILTERS.
"ON A TIMER.
"SET TO JUST ABOUT...

"...NOW."

KRAKADOOM

I ALMOST BOUGHT INTO IT.

TWOO

THE IDEA THINGS COULD GET BETTER IF WE BELIEVE.

I TRIED. BUT HERE WE ARE.

IT ALL FALLS ANYWAY.

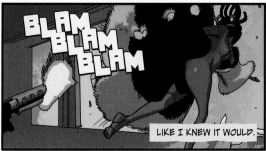

BLAM BLAM BLAM

LIKE I KNEW IT WOULD.

AND IT FEELS RIGHT.

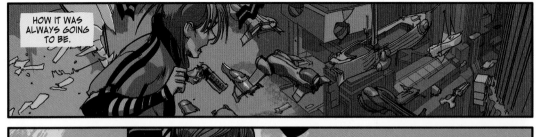

HOW IT WAS ALWAYS GOING TO BE.

AT LEAST THIS IS REAL.

AT LEAST THIS IS *HONEST*.

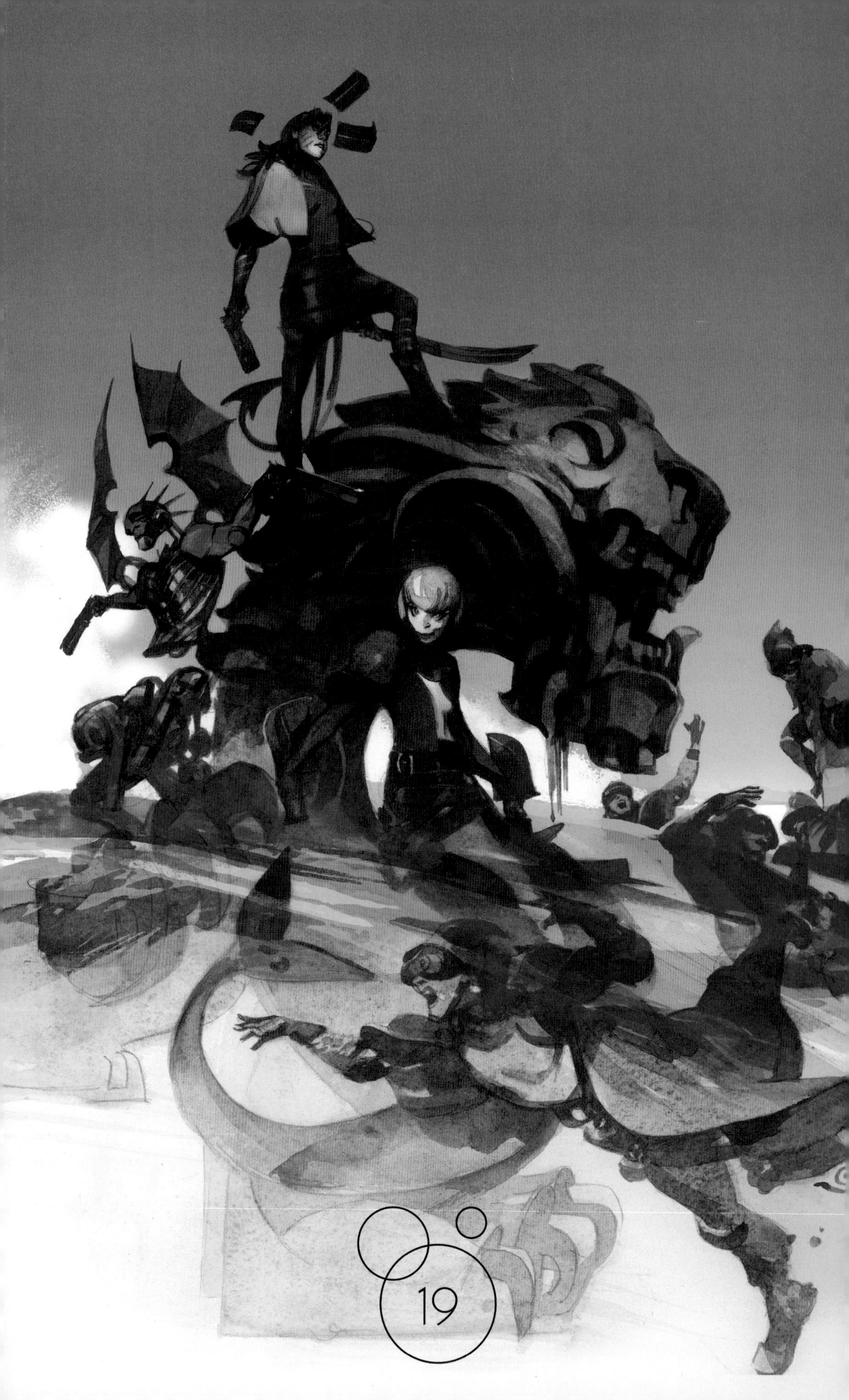

19

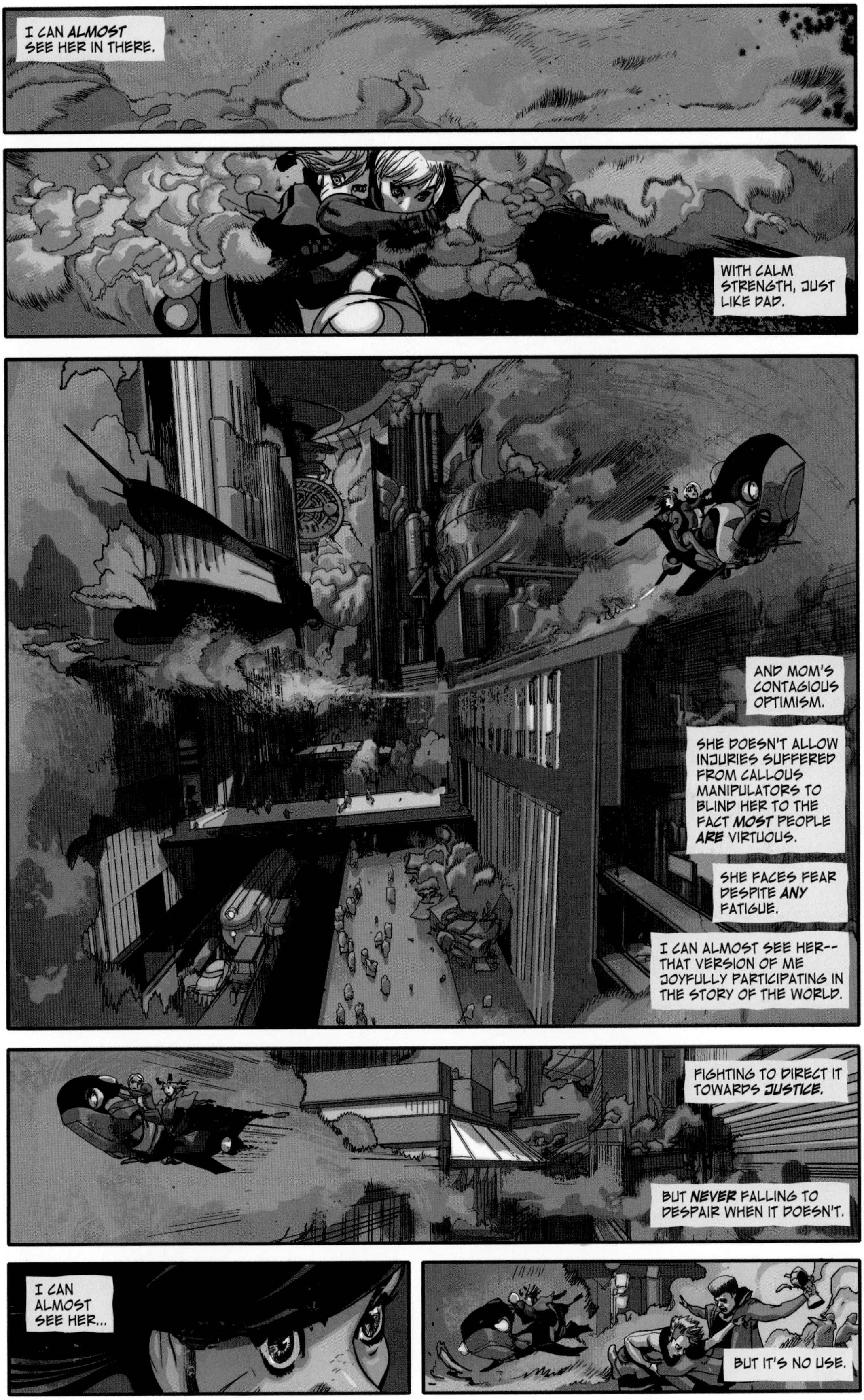
I CAN ALMOST SEE HER IN THERE.
WITH CALM STRENGTH, JUST LIKE DAD.
AND MOM'S CONTAGIOUS OPTIMISM.
SHE DOESN'T ALLOW INJURIES SUFFERED FROM CALLOUS MANIPULATORS TO BLIND HER TO THE FACT MOST PEOPLE ARE VIRTUOUS.
SHE FACES FEAR DESPITE ANY FATIGUE.
I CAN ALMOST SEE HER-- THAT VERSION OF ME JOYFULLY PARTICIPATING IN THE STORY OF THE WORLD.
FIGHTING TO DIRECT IT TOWARDS JUSTICE.
BUT NEVER FALLING TO DESPAIR WHEN IT DOESN'T.
I CAN ALMOST SEE HER...
BUT IT'S NO USE.

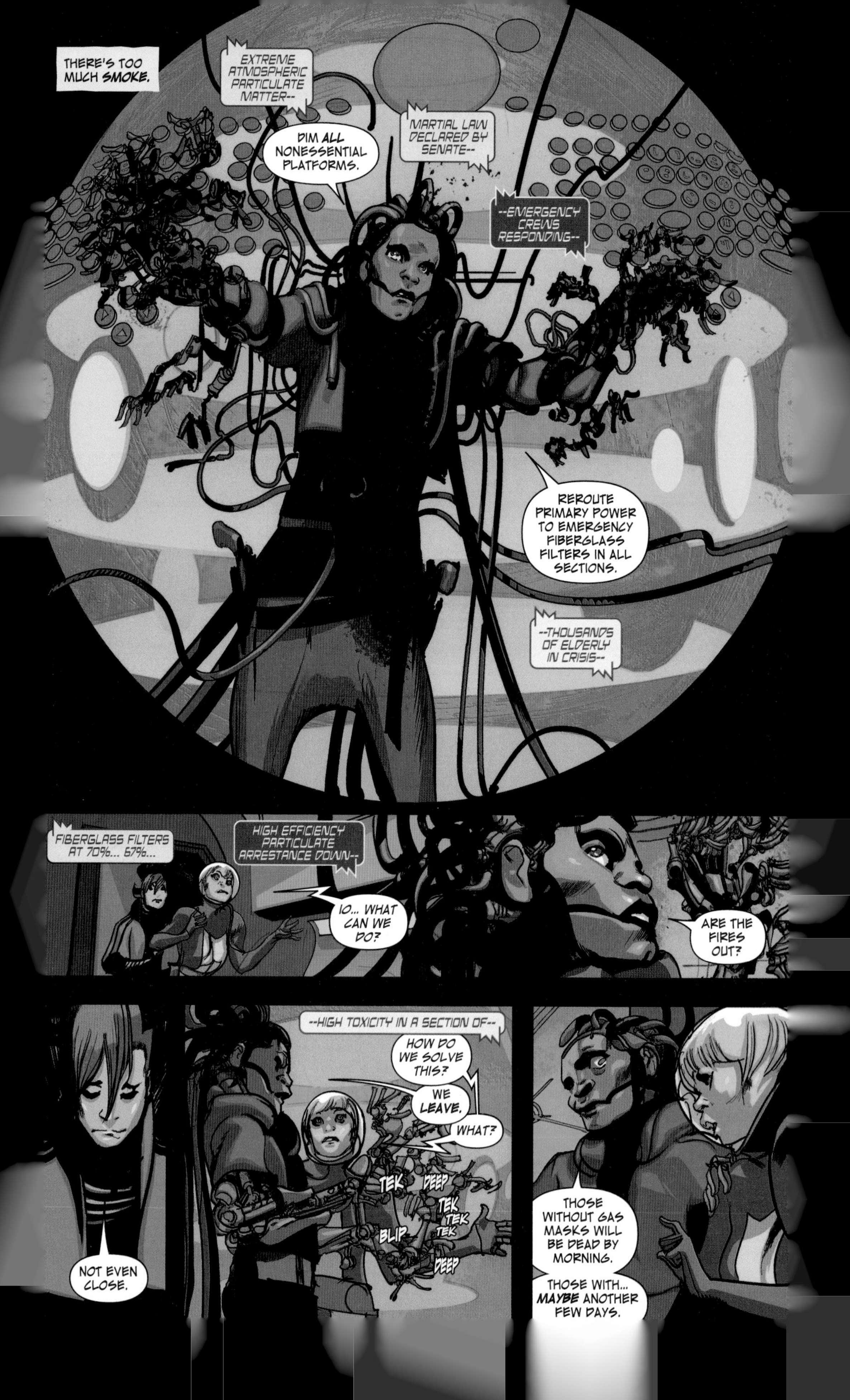
THERE'S TOO MUCH SMOKE.
EXTREME ATMOSPHERIC PARTICULATE MATTER--
DIM ALL NONESSENTIAL PLATFORMS.
MARTIAL LAW DECLARED BY SENATE--
--EMERGENCY CREWS RESPONDING--
REROUTE PRIMARY POWER TO EMERGENCY FIBERGLASS FILTERS IN ALL SECTIONS.
--THOUSANDS OF ELDERLY IN CRISIS--
FIBERGLASS FILTERS AT 70%... 67%...
HIGH EFFICIENCY PARTICULATE ARRESTANCE DOWN--
IO... WHAT CAN WE DO?
ARE THE FIRES OUT?
NOT EVEN CLOSE.
--HIGH TOXICITY IN A SECTION OF--
HOW DO WE SOLVE THIS?
WE LEAVE.
WHAT?
TEK
DEEP
TEK
TEK
TEK
BLIP
DEEP
THOSE WITHOUT GAS MASKS WILL BE DEAD BY MORNING.
THOSE WITH... MAYBE ANOTHER FEW DAYS.

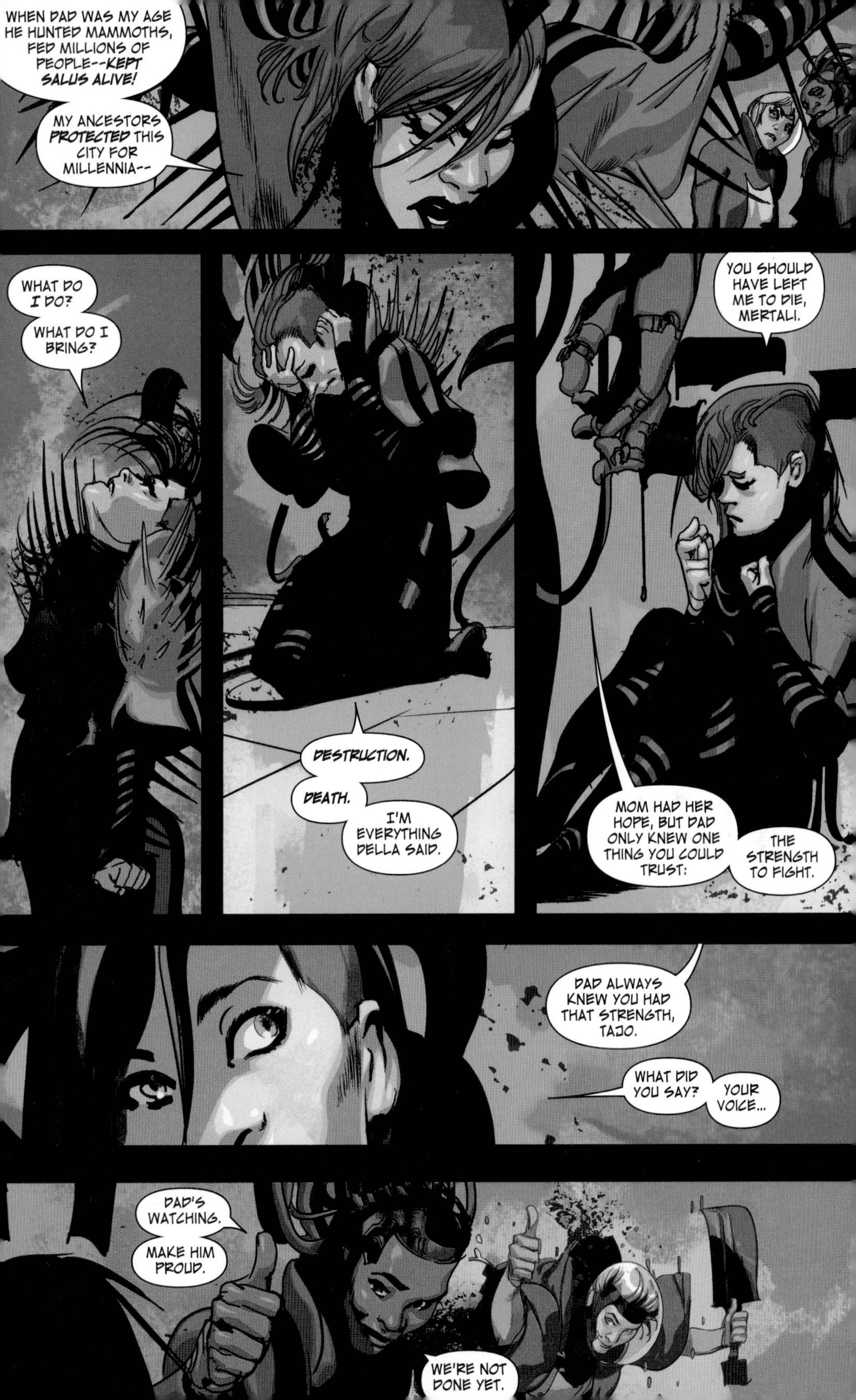
WHEN DAD WAS MY AGE HE HUNTED MAMMOTHS, FED MILLIONS OF PEOPLE--KEPT SALUS ALIVE!
MY ANCESTORS PROTECTED THIS CITY FOR MILLENNIA--
WHAT DO I DO?
WHAT DO I BRING?
DESTRUCTION.
DEATH.
I'M EVERYTHING DELLA SAID.
YOU SHOULD HAVE LEFT ME TO DIE, MERTALI.
MOM HAD HER HOPE, BUT DAD ONLY KNEW ONE THING YOU COULD TRUST:
THE STRENGTH TO FIGHT.
DAD ALWAYS KNEW YOU HAD THAT STRENGTH, TAJO.
WHAT DID YOU SAY?
YOUR VOICE...
DAD'S WATCHING.
MAKE HIM PROUD.
WE'RE NOT DONE YET.

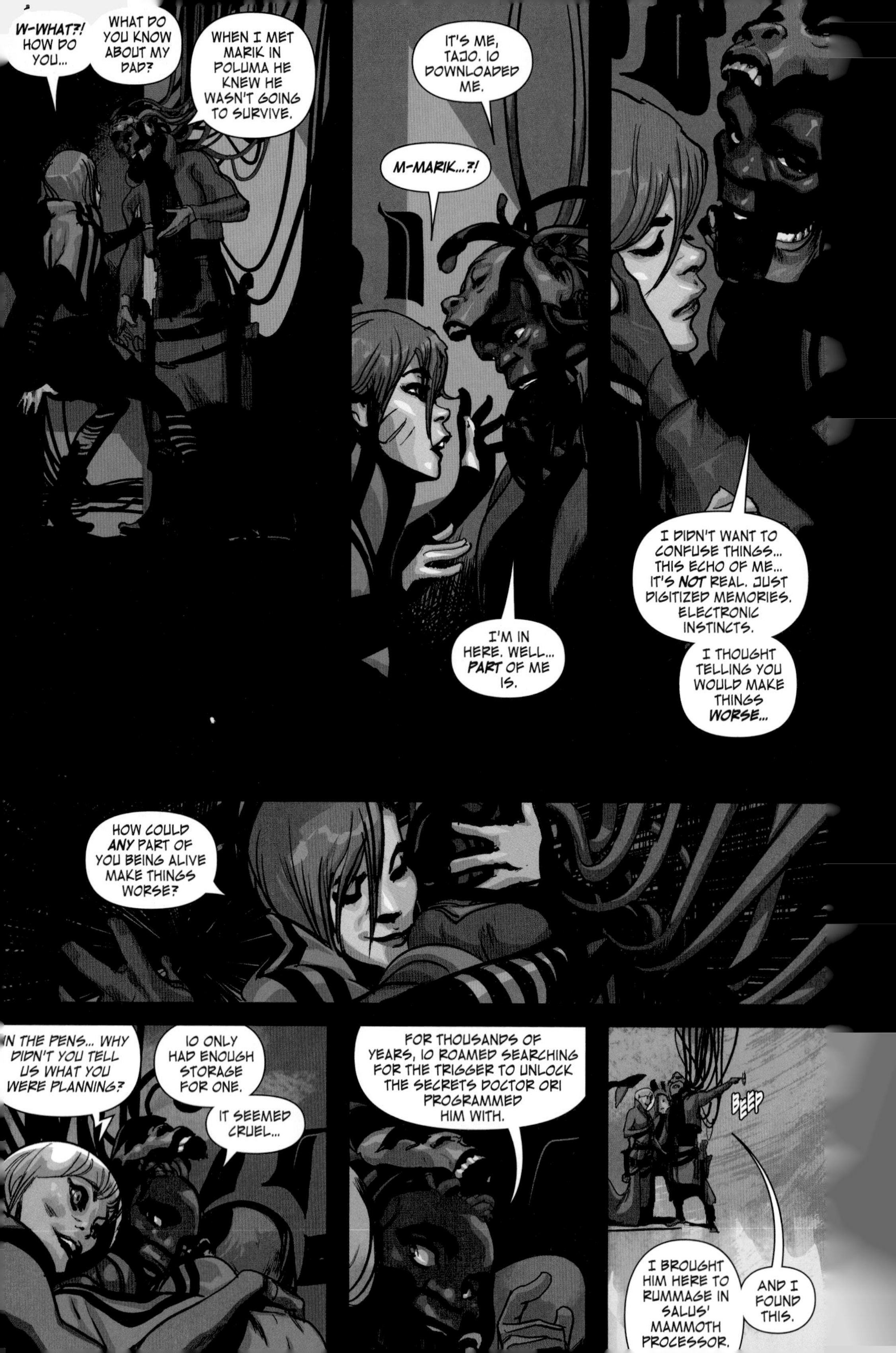
W-WHAT?! HOW DO YOU...
WHAT DO YOU KNOW ABOUT MY DAD?
WHEN I MET MARIK IN POLUMA HE KNEW HE WASN'T GOING TO SURVIVE.
IT'S ME, TAJO. IO DOWNLOADED ME.
M-MARIK...?!
I'M IN HERE. WELL... PART OF ME IS.
I DIDN'T WANT TO CONFUSE THINGS... THIS ECHO OF ME... IT'S NOT REAL. JUST DIGITIZED MEMORIES. ELECTRONIC INSTINCTS.
I THOUGHT TELLING YOU WOULD MAKE THINGS WORSE...
HOW COULD ANY PART OF YOU BEING ALIVE MAKE THINGS WORSE?
IN THE PENS... WHY DIDN'T YOU TELL US WHAT YOU WERE PLANNING?
IO ONLY HAD ENOUGH STORAGE FOR ONE.
IT SEEMED CRUEL...
FOR THOUSANDS OF YEARS, IO ROAMED SEARCHING FOR THE TRIGGER TO UNLOCK THE SECRETS DOCTOR ORI PROGRAMMED HIM WITH.
BEEP
I BROUGHT HIM HERE TO RUMMAGE IN SALUS' MAMMOTH PROCESSOR.
AND I FOUND THIS.

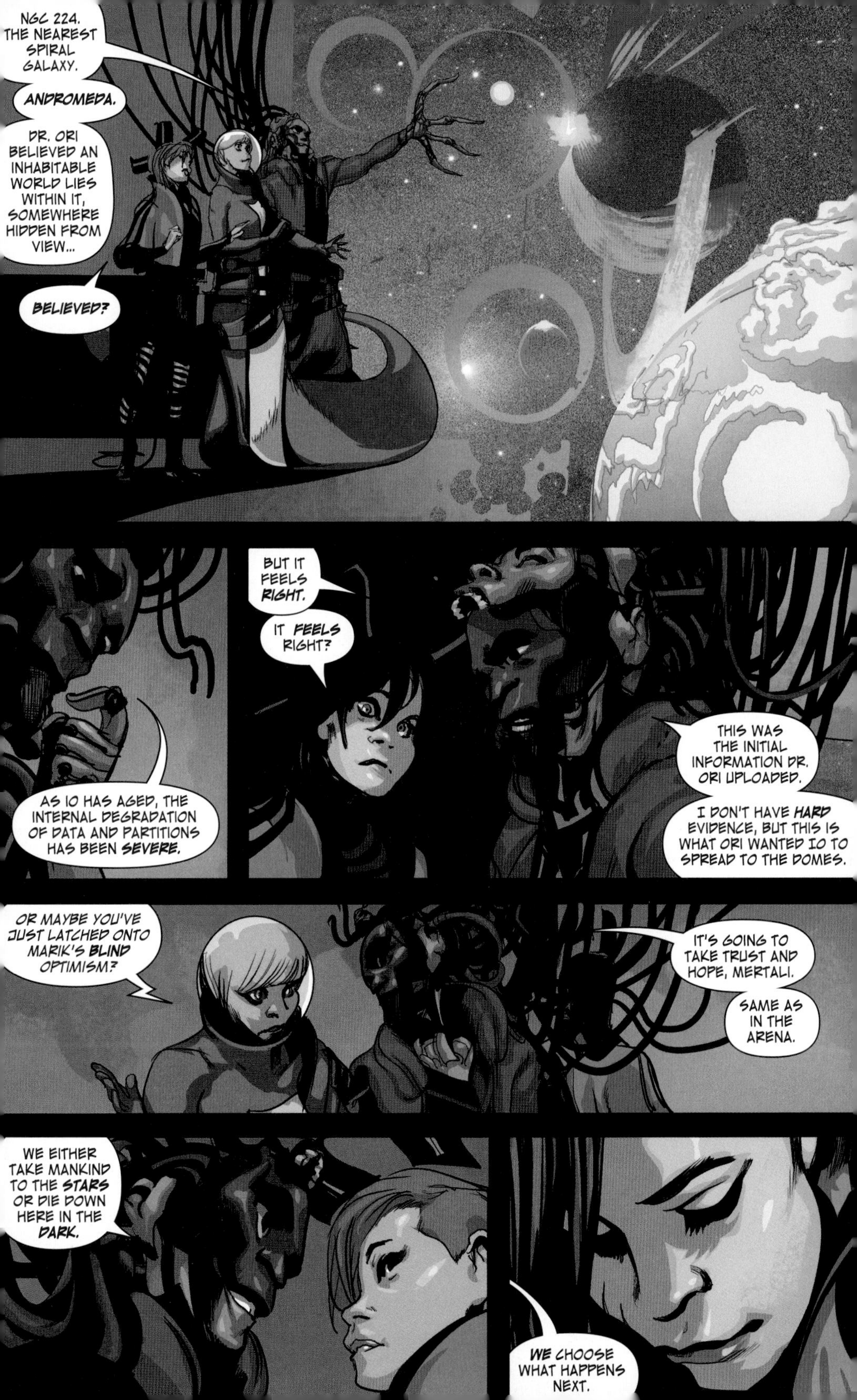
NGC 224. THE NEAREST SPIRAL GALAXY.
ANDROMEDA.
DR. ORI BELIEVED AN INHABITABLE WORLD LIES WITHIN IT, SOMEWHERE HIDDEN FROM VIEW...
BELIEVED?
AS IO HAS AGED, THE INTERNAL DEGRADATION OF DATA AND PARTITIONS HAS BEEN SEVERE.
BUT IT FEELS RIGHT.
IT FEELS RIGHT?
THIS WAS THE INITIAL INFORMATION DR. ORI UPLOADED.
I DON'T HAVE HARD EVIDENCE, BUT THIS IS WHAT ORI WANTED IO TO SPREAD TO THE DOMES.
OR MAYBE YOU'VE JUST LATCHED ONTO MARIK'S BLIND OPTIMISM?
IT'S GOING TO TAKE TRUST AND HOPE, MERTALI.
SAME AS IN THE ARENA.
WE EITHER TAKE MANKIND TO THE STARS OR DIE DOWN HERE IN THE DARK.
WE CHOOSE WHAT HAPPENS NEXT.

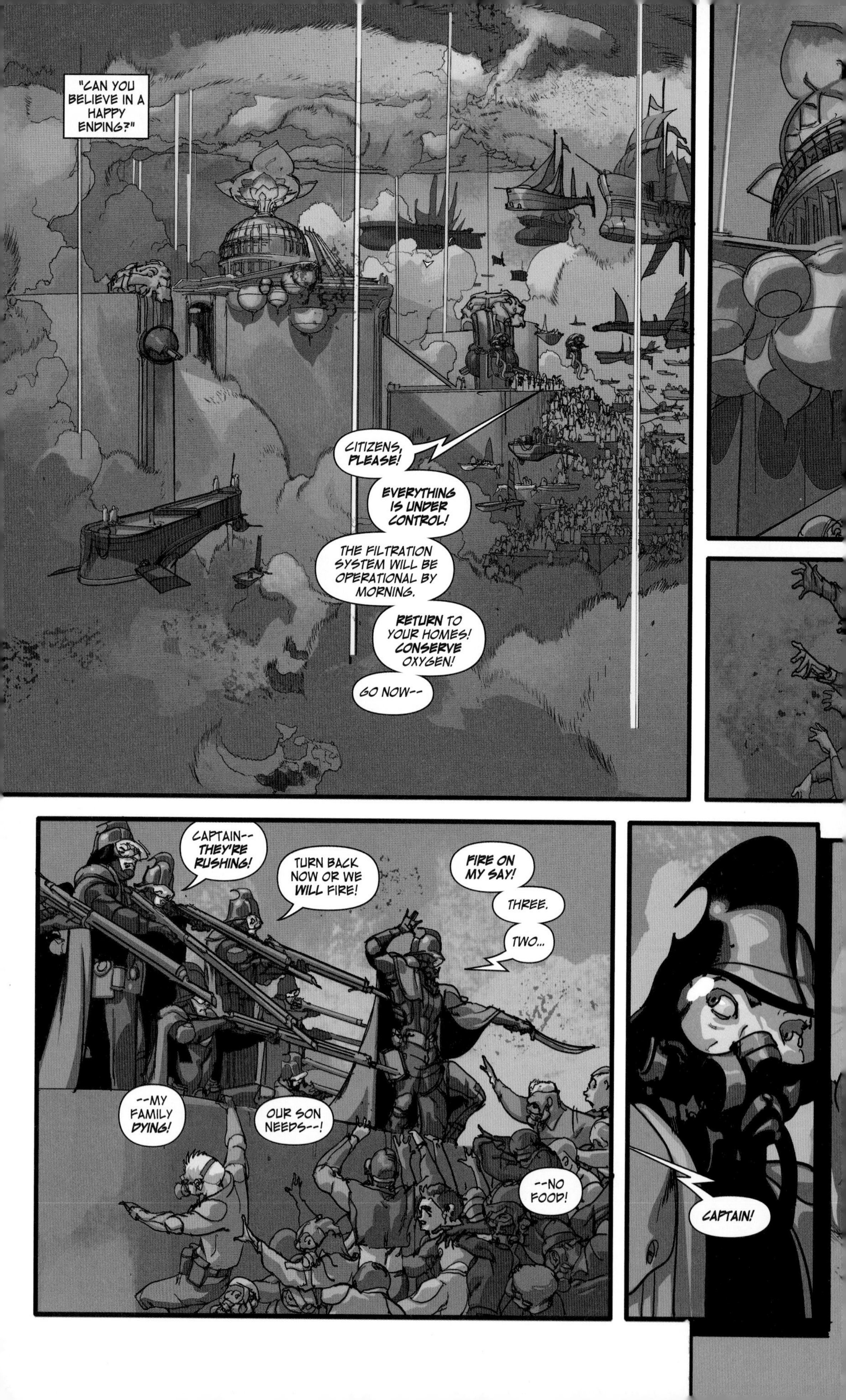
"CAN YOU BELIEVE IN A HAPPY ENDING?"
CITIZENS, PLEASE!
EVERYTHING IS UNDER CONTROL!
THE FILTRATION SYSTEM WILL BE OPERATIONAL BY MORNING.
RETURN TO YOUR HOMES! CONSERVE OXYGEN!
GO NOW--
CAPTAIN-- THEY'RE RUSHING!
TURN BACK NOW OR WE WILL FIRE!
FIRE ON MY SAY!
THREE.
TWO...
--MY FAMILY DYING!
OUR SON NEEDS--!
--NO FOOD!
CAPTAIN!

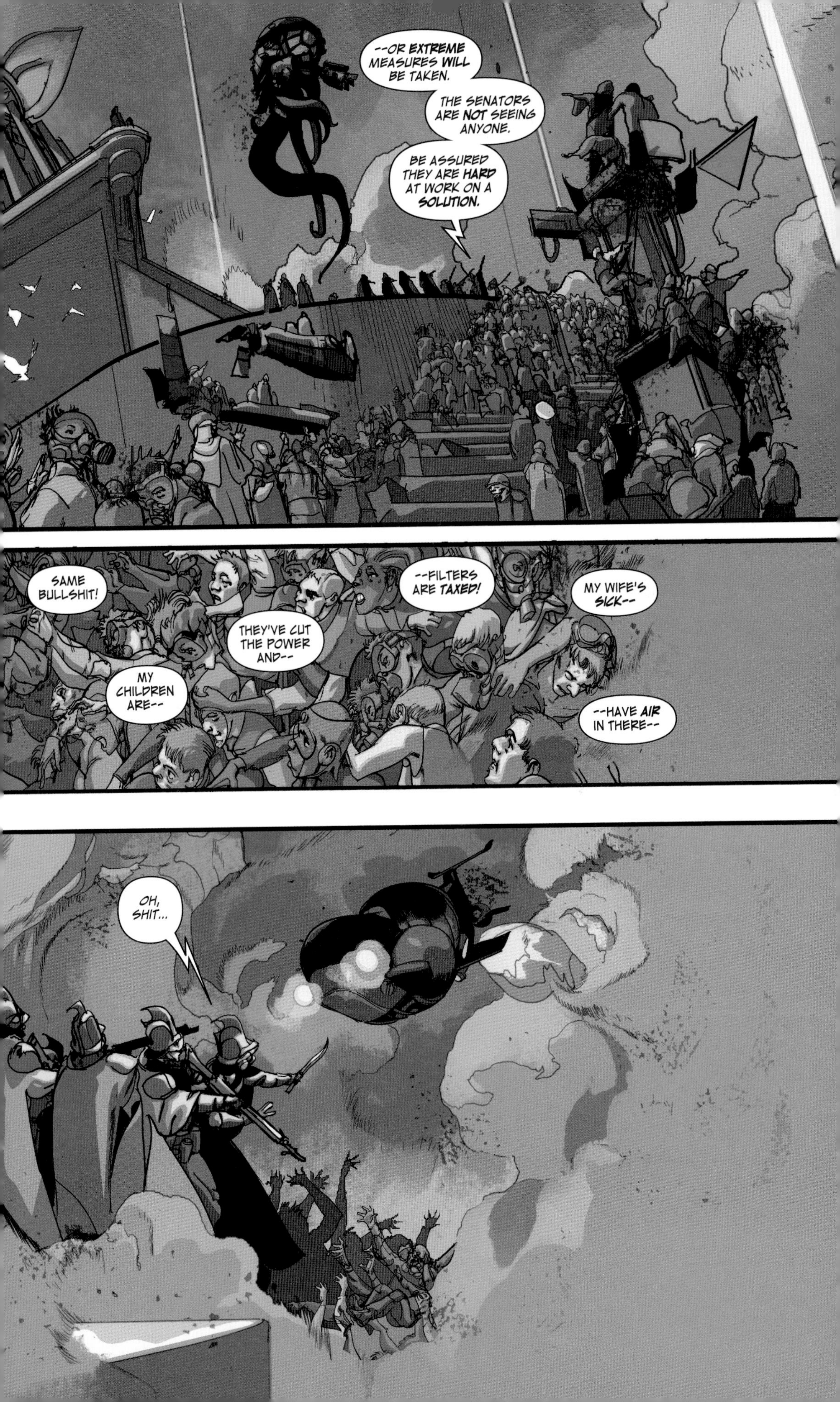
--OR EXTREME MEASURES WILL BE TAKEN.
THE SENATORS ARE NOT SEEING ANYONE.
BE ASSURED THEY ARE HARD AT WORK ON A SOLUTION.
SAME BULLSHIT!
--FILTERS ARE TAXED!
MY WIFE'S SICK--
THEY'VE CUT THE POWER AND--
MY CHILDREN ARE--
--HAVE AIR IN THERE--
OH, SHIT...

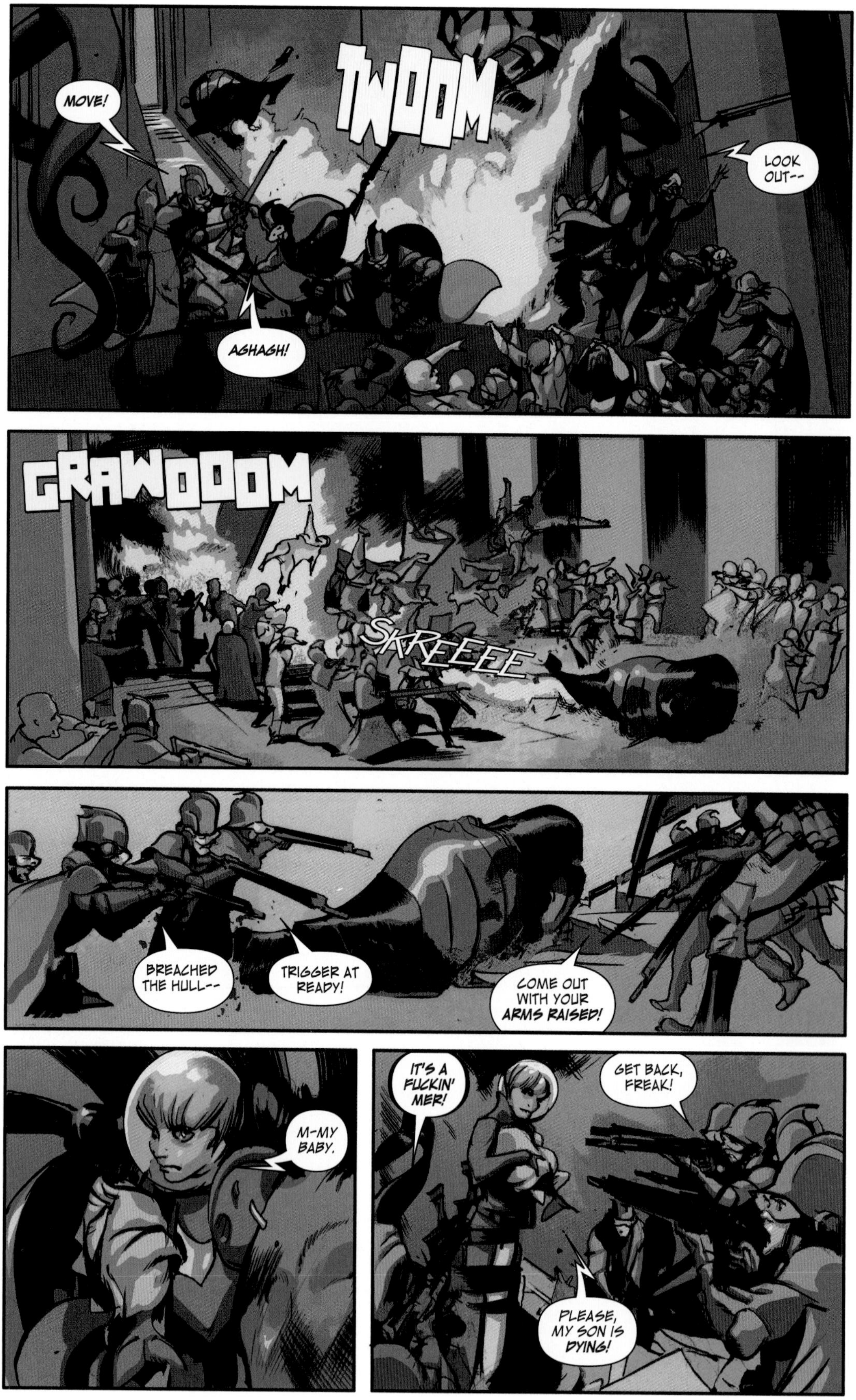
MOVE!
TWOOM
LOOK OUT--
AGHAGH!
GRAWOOOM
SKREEEEE
BREACHED THE HULL--
TRIGGER AT READY!
COME OUT WITH YOUR ARMS RAISED!
M-MY BABY.
IT'S A FUCKIN' MER!
GET BACK, FREAK!
PLEASE, MY SON IS DYING!

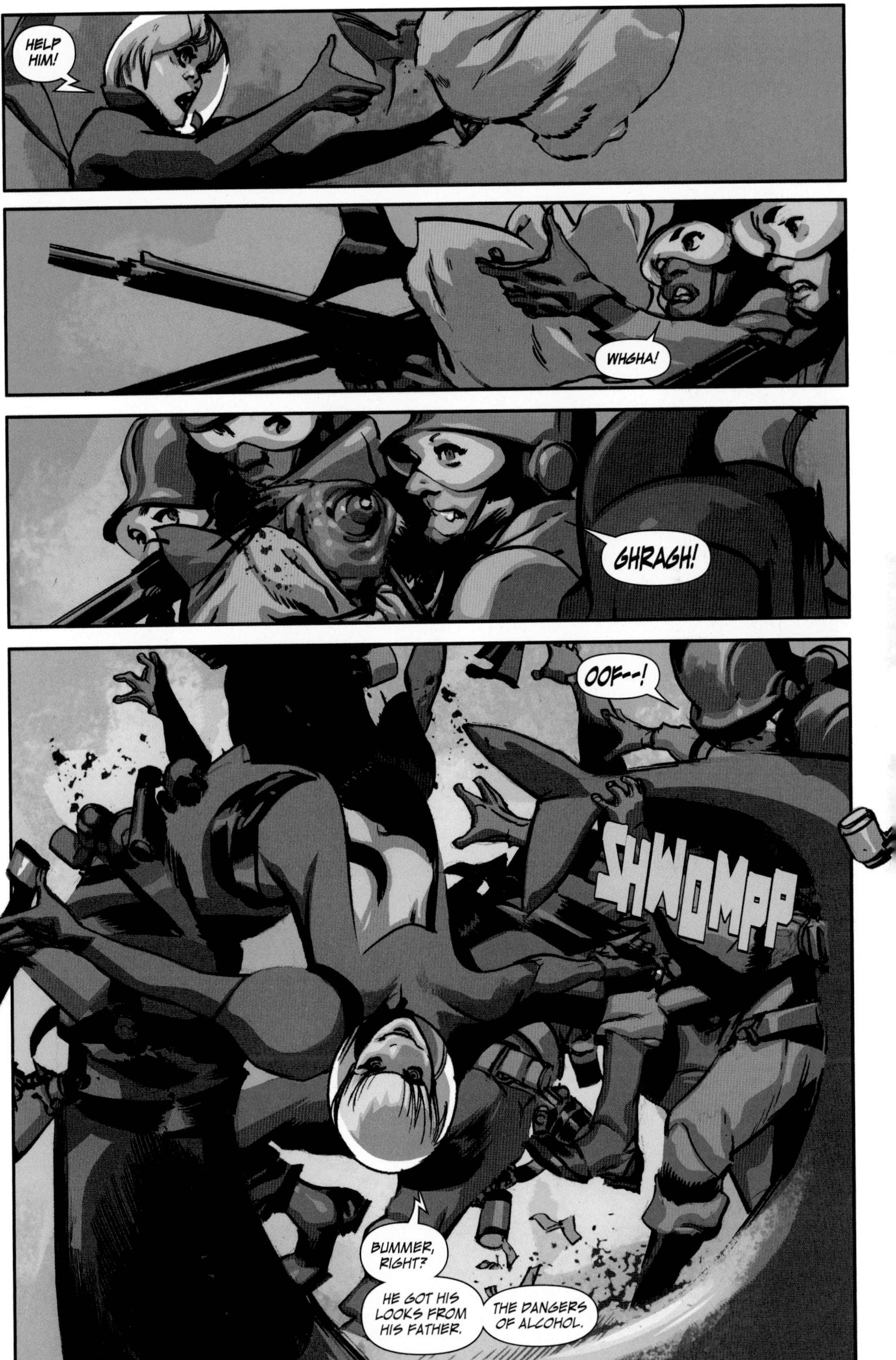
HELP HIM!
WHGHA!
GHRAGH!
OOF--!
SHWOMPP
BUMMER, RIGHT?
HE GOT HIS LOOKS FROM HIS FATHER.
THE DANGERS OF ALCOHOL.

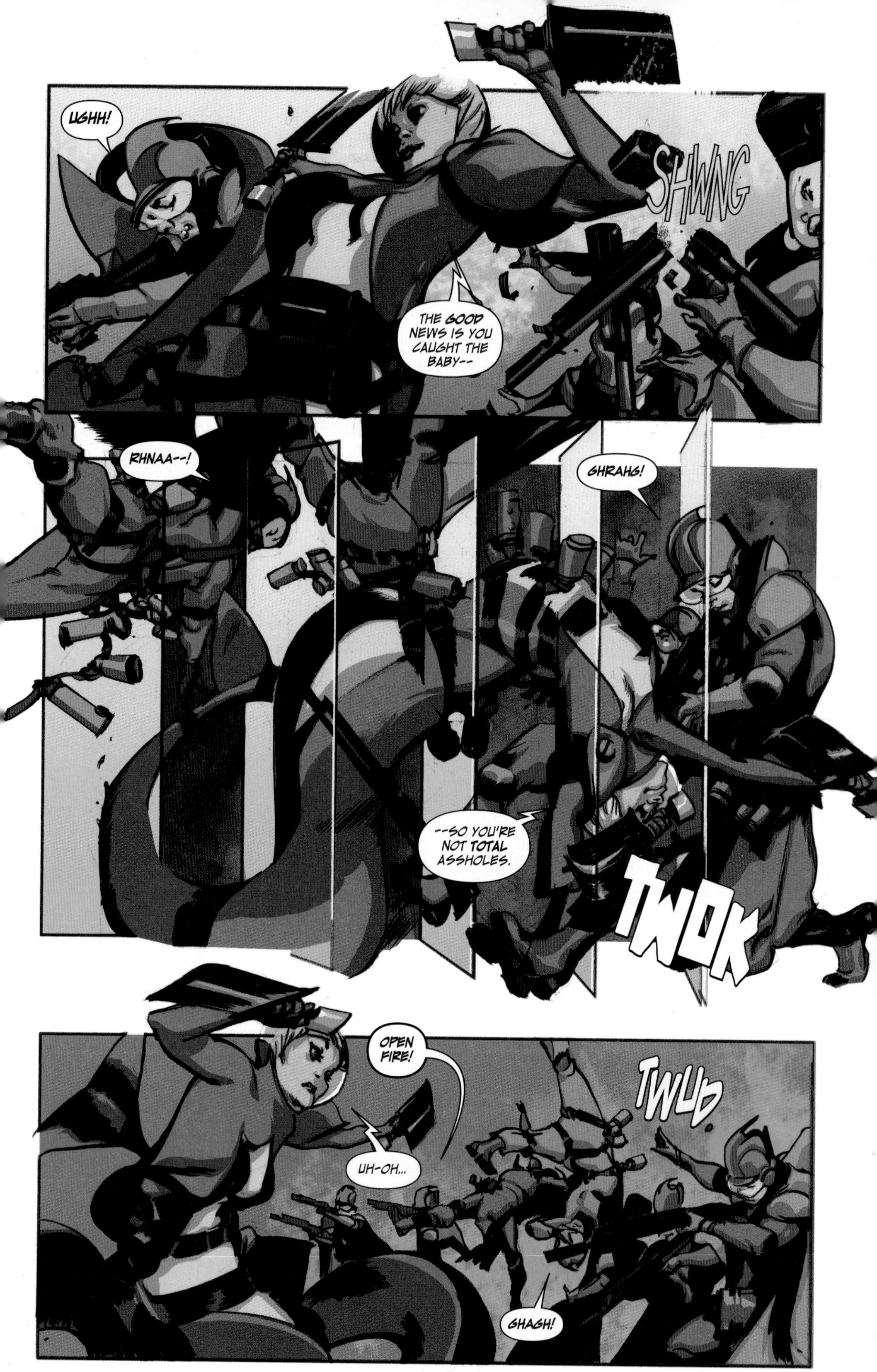
UGHH!
SHWNG
THE GOOD NEWS IS YOU CAUGHT THE BABY--
RHNAA--!
GHRAHG!
--SO YOU'RE NOT TOTAL ASSHOLES.
TWOK
OPEN FIRE!
TWUD
UH-OH...
GHAGH!

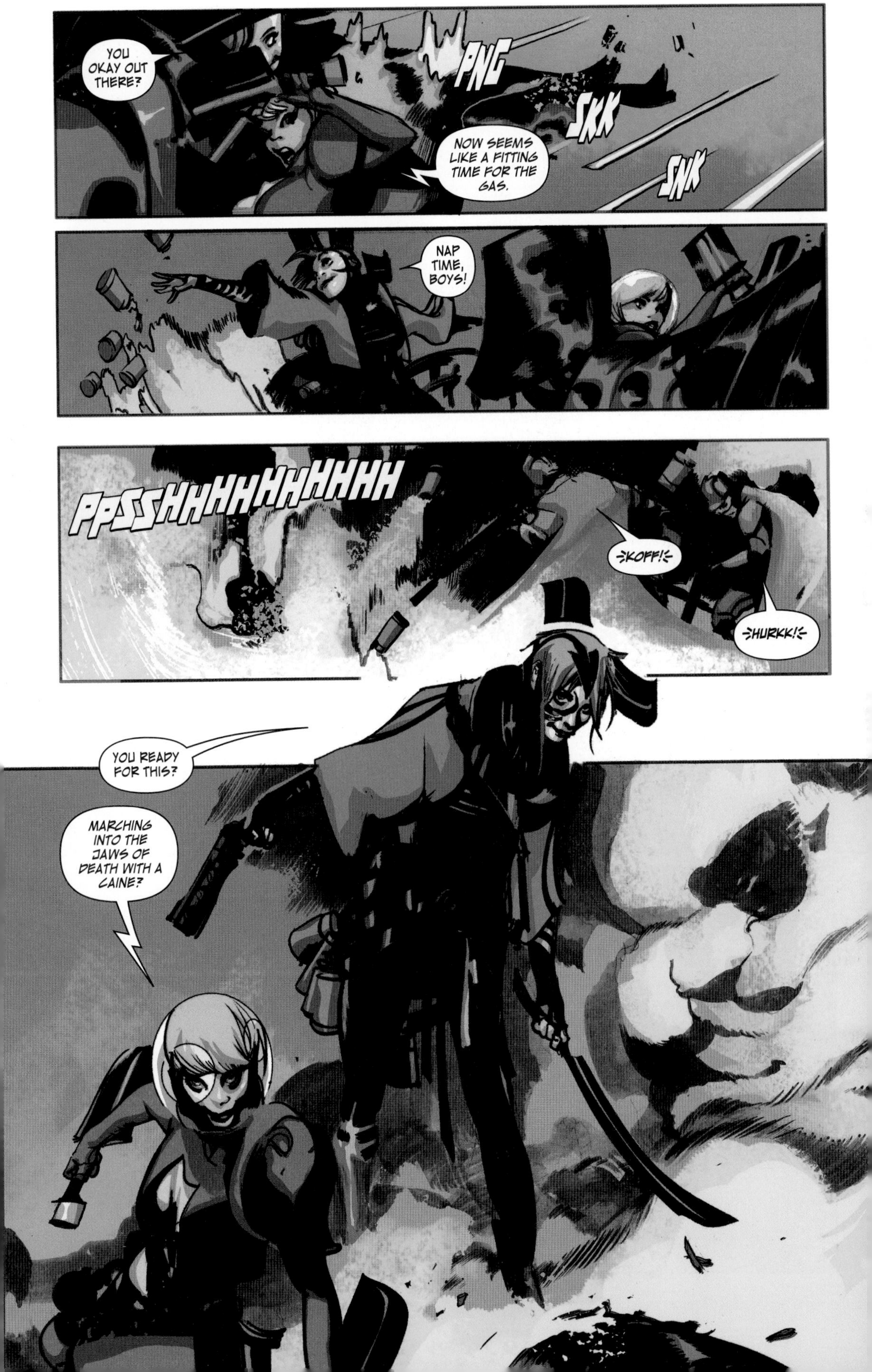
YOU OKAY OUT THERE?
PNG
SKK
NOW SEEMS LIKE A FITTING TIME FOR THE GAS.
SNK
NAP TIME, BOYS!
PPSSHHHHHHHHHHH
KOFF!
HURKK!
YOU READY FOR THIS?
MARCHING INTO THE JAWS OF DEATH WITH A CAINE?

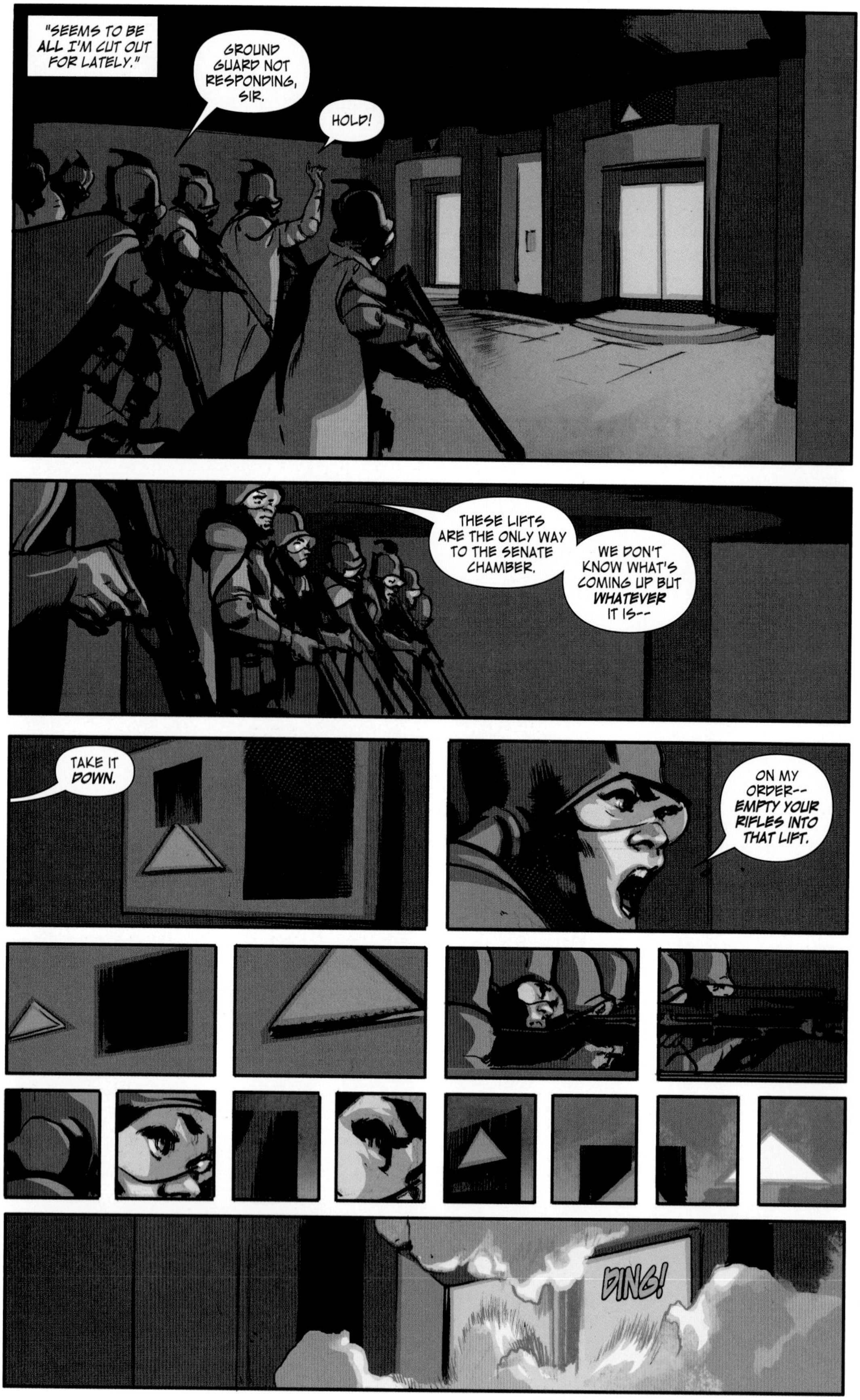
"SEEMS TO BE ALL I'M CUT OUT FOR LATELY."
GROUND GUARD NOT RESPONDING, SIR.
HOLD!
THESE LIFTS ARE THE ONLY WAY TO THE SENATE CHAMBER.
WE DON'T KNOW WHAT'S COMING UP BUT WHATEVER IT IS--
TAKE IT DOWN.
ON MY ORDER-- EMPTY YOUR RIFLES INTO THAT LIFT.
DING!

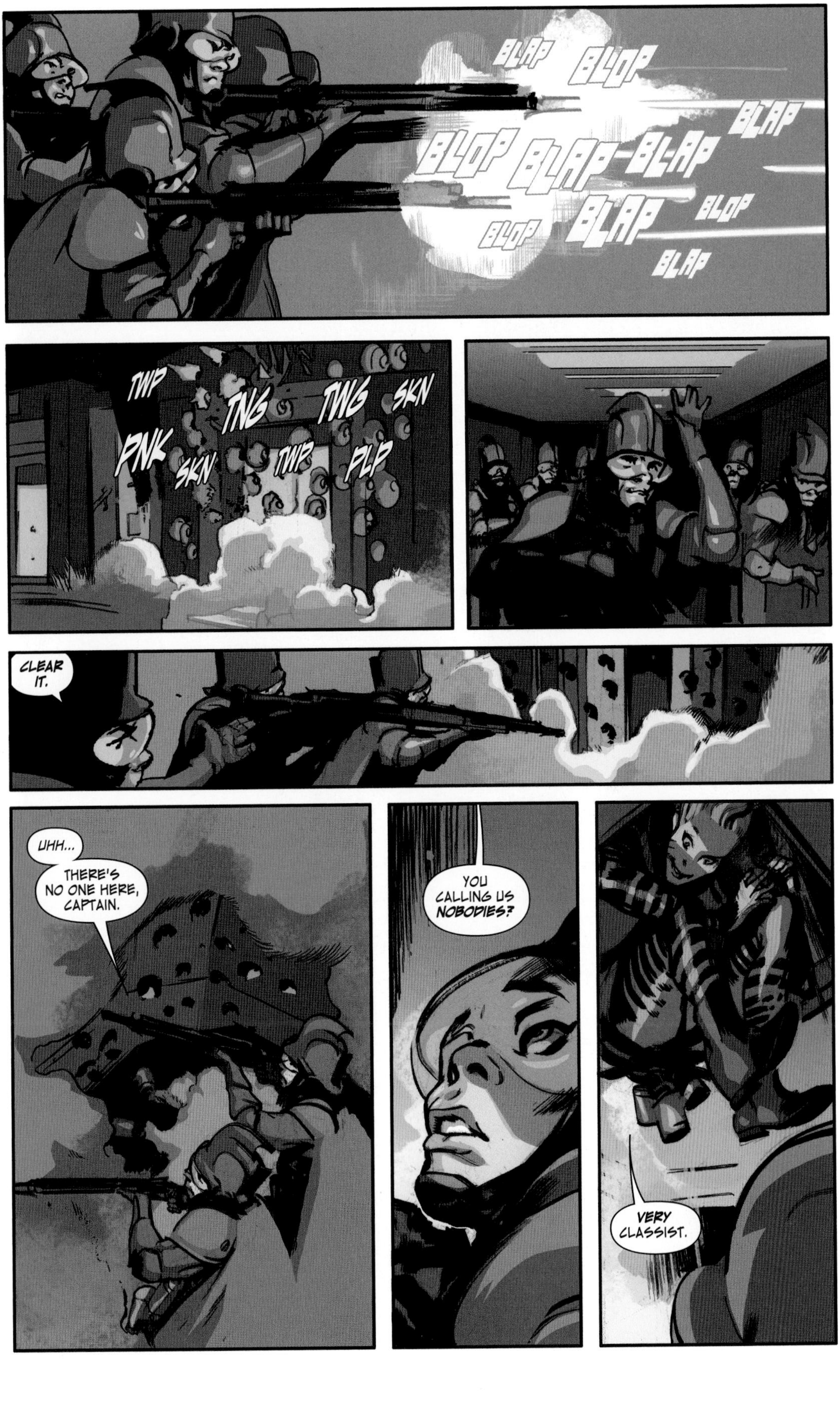
BLAP
BLOP
BLAP
BLOP
BLAP-BLAP
BLOP
BLAP
BLOP
BLAP
TWP
TNG
TWG
SKN
PNK
SKN
TWP
PLP
CLEAR IT.
UHH...
THERE'S NO ONE HERE, CAPTAIN.
YOU CALLING US NOBODIES?
VERY CLASSIST.

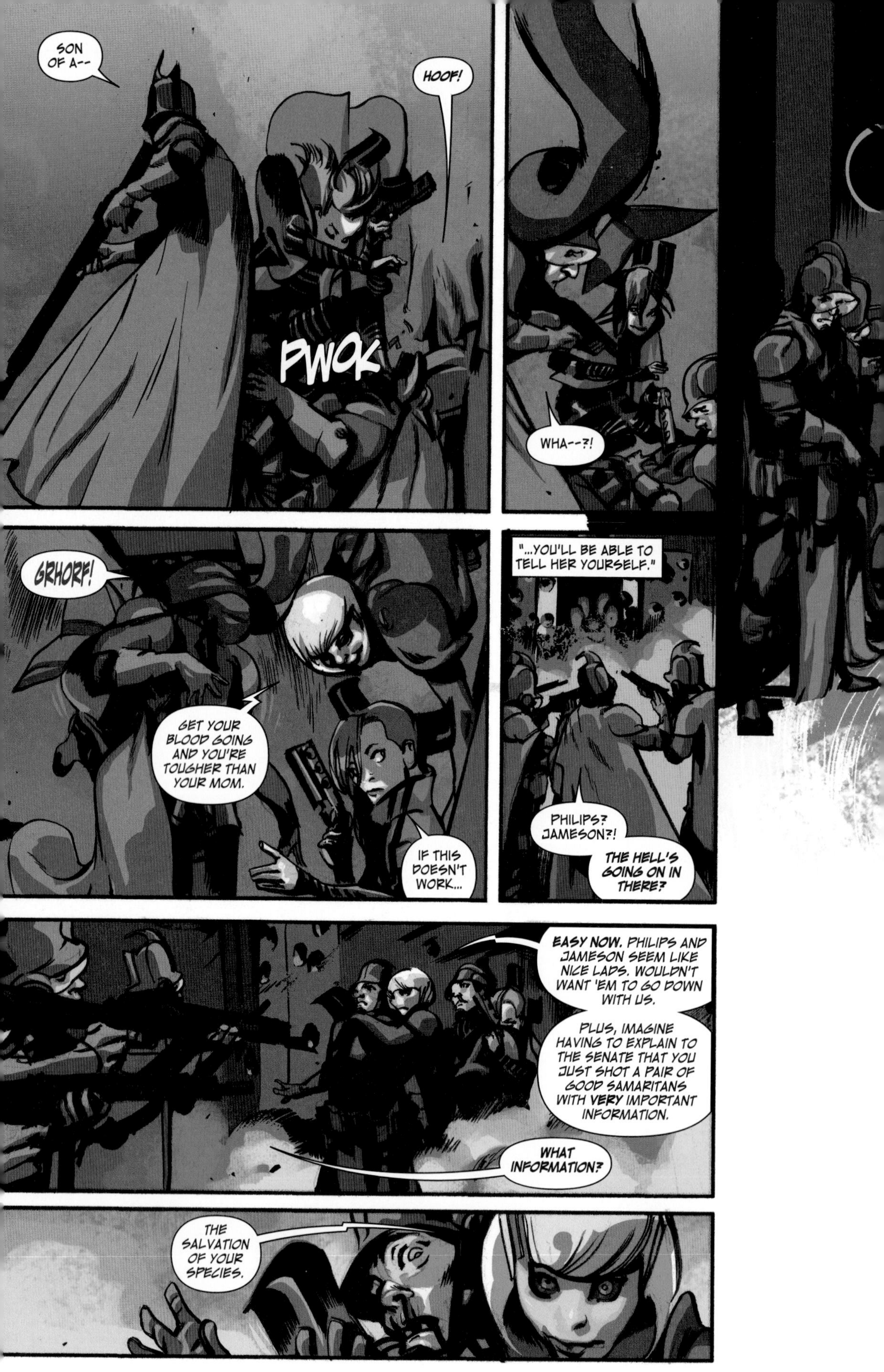
SON OF A--
HOOF!
PWOK
WHA--?!
GRHORF!
GET YOUR BLOOD GOING AND YOU'RE TOUGHER THAN YOUR MOM.
IF THIS DOESN'T WORK...
"...YOU'LL BE ABLE TO TELL HER YOURSELF."
PHILIPS? JAMESON?!
THE HELL'S GOING ON IN THERE?
EASY NOW. PHILIPS AND JAMESON SEEM LIKE NICE LADS. WOULDN'T WANT 'EM TO GO DOWN WITH US.
PLUS, IMAGINE HAVING TO EXPLAIN TO THE SENATE THAT YOU JUST SHOT A PAIR OF GOOD SAMARITANS WITH VERY IMPORTANT INFORMATION.
WHAT INFORMATION?
THE SALVATION OF YOUR SPECIES.

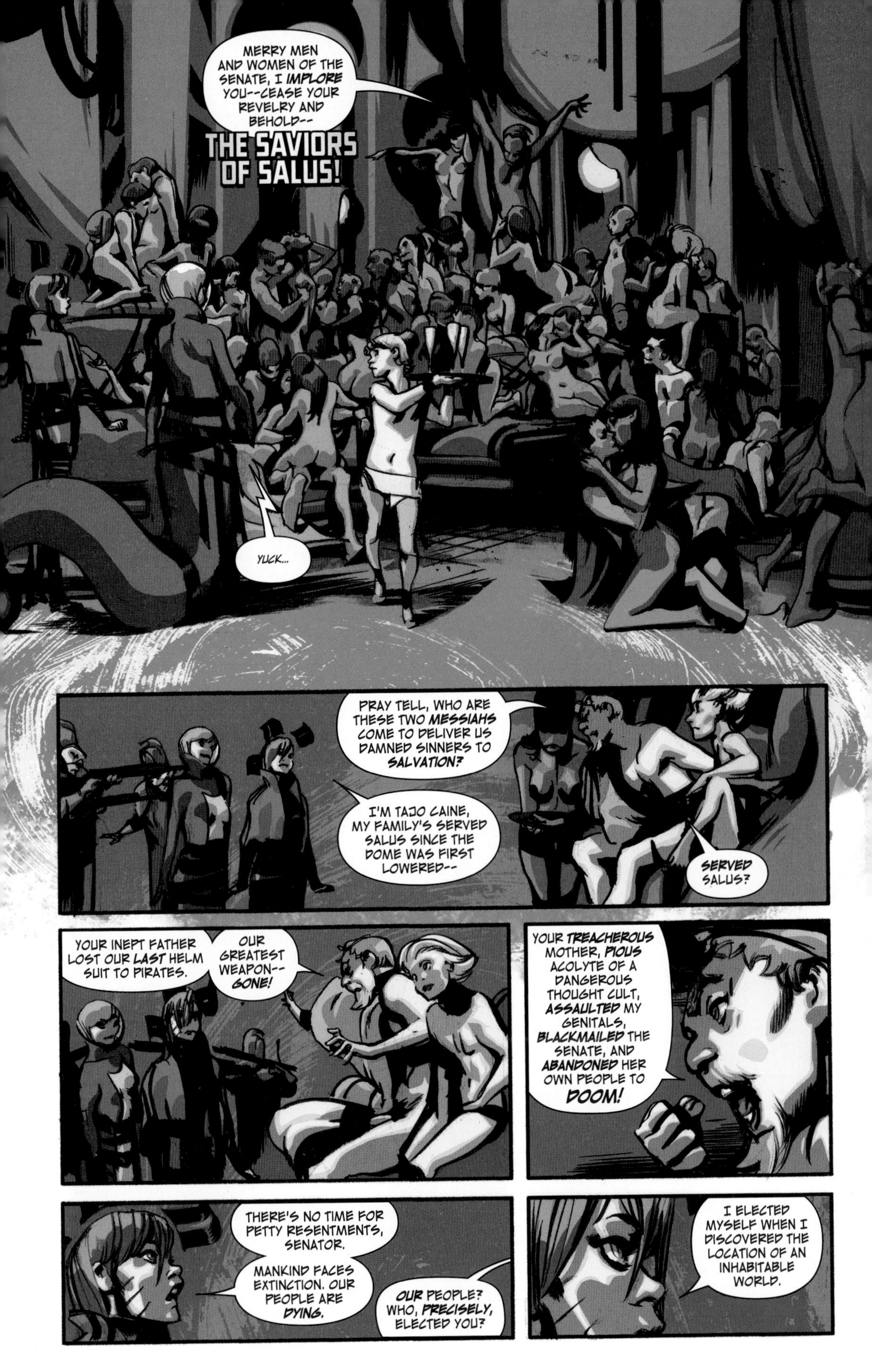
MERRY MEN AND WOMEN OF THE SENATE, I IMPLORE YOU--CEASE YOUR REVELRY AND BEHOLD--
THE SAVIORS OF SALUS!
YUCK...
PRAY TELL, WHO ARE THESE TWO MESSIAHS COME TO DELIVER US DAMNED SINNERS TO SALVATION?
I'M TAJO CAINE, MY FAMILY'S SERVED SALUS SINCE THE DOME WAS FIRST LOWERED--
SERVED SALUS?
YOUR INEPT FATHER LOST OUR LAST HELM SUIT TO PIRATES.
OUR GREATEST WEAPON--GONE!
YOUR TREACHEROUS MOTHER, PIOUS ACOLYTE OF A DANGEROUS THOUGHT CULT, ASSAULTED MY GENITALS, BLACKMAILED THE SENATE, AND ABANDONED HER OWN PEOPLE TO DOOM!
THERE'S NO TIME FOR PETTY RESENTMENTS, SENATOR.
MANKIND FACES EXTINCTION. OUR PEOPLE ARE DYING.
OUR PEOPLE? WHO, PRECISELY, ELECTED YOU?
I ELECTED MYSELF WHEN I DISCOVERED THE LOCATION OF AN INHABITABLE WORLD.

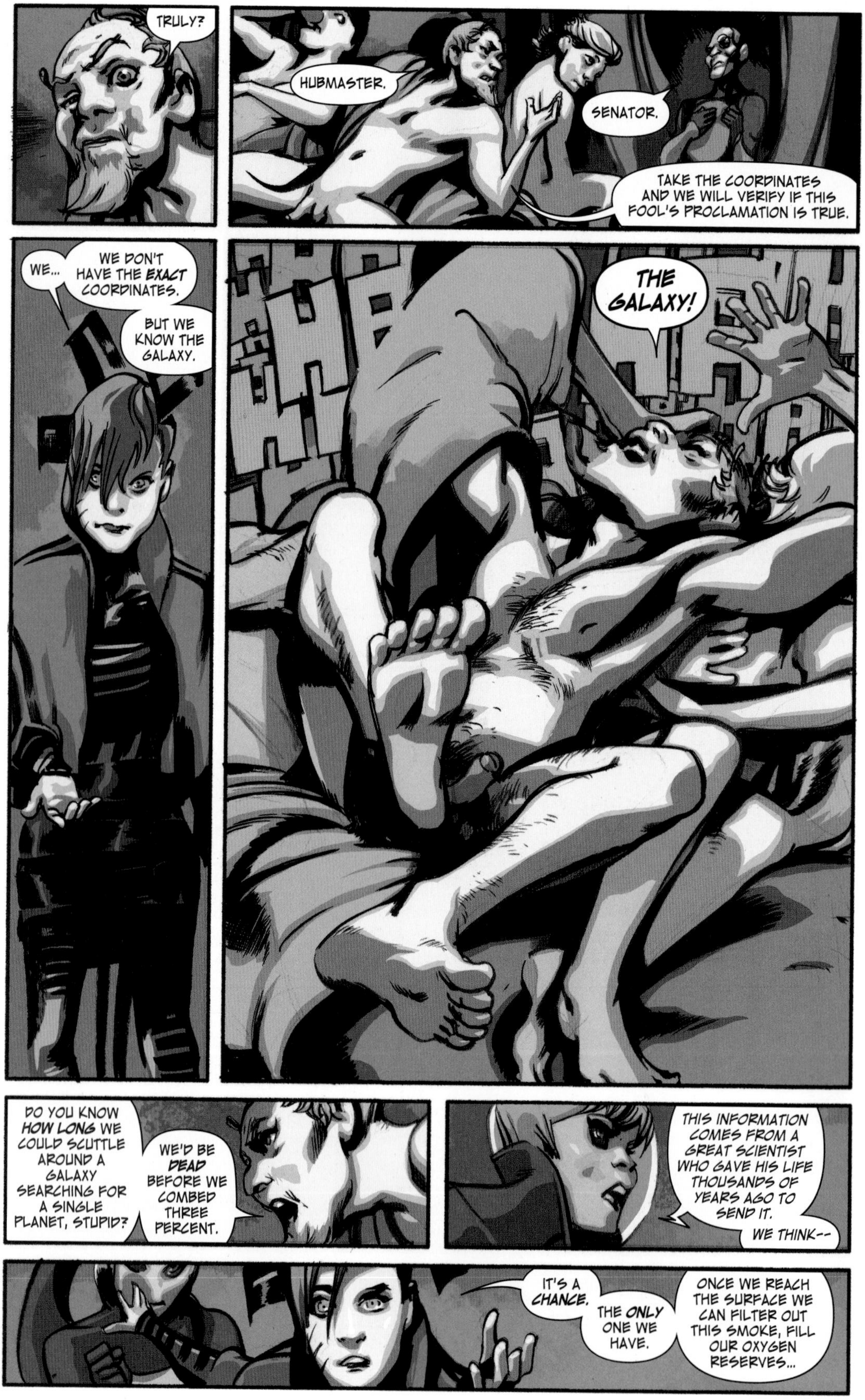
TRULY?
HUBMASTER.
SENATOR.
TAKE THE COORDINATES AND WE WILL VERIFY IF THIS FOOL'S PROCLAMATION IS TRUE.
WE...
WE DON'T HAVE THE EXACT COORDINATES.
BUT WE KNOW THE GALAXY.
THE GALAXY!
DO YOU KNOW HOW LONG WE COULD SCUTTLE AROUND A GALAXY SEARCHING FOR A SINGLE PLANET, STUPID?
WE'D BE DEAD BEFORE WE COMBED THREE PERCENT.
THIS INFORMATION COMES FROM A GREAT SCIENTIST WHO GAVE HIS LIFE THOUSANDS OF YEARS AGO TO SEND IT.
WE THINK--
IT'S A CHANCE.
THE ONLY ONE WE HAVE.
ONCE WE REACH THE SURFACE WE CAN FILTER OUT THIS SMOKE, FILL OUR OXYGEN RESERVES...

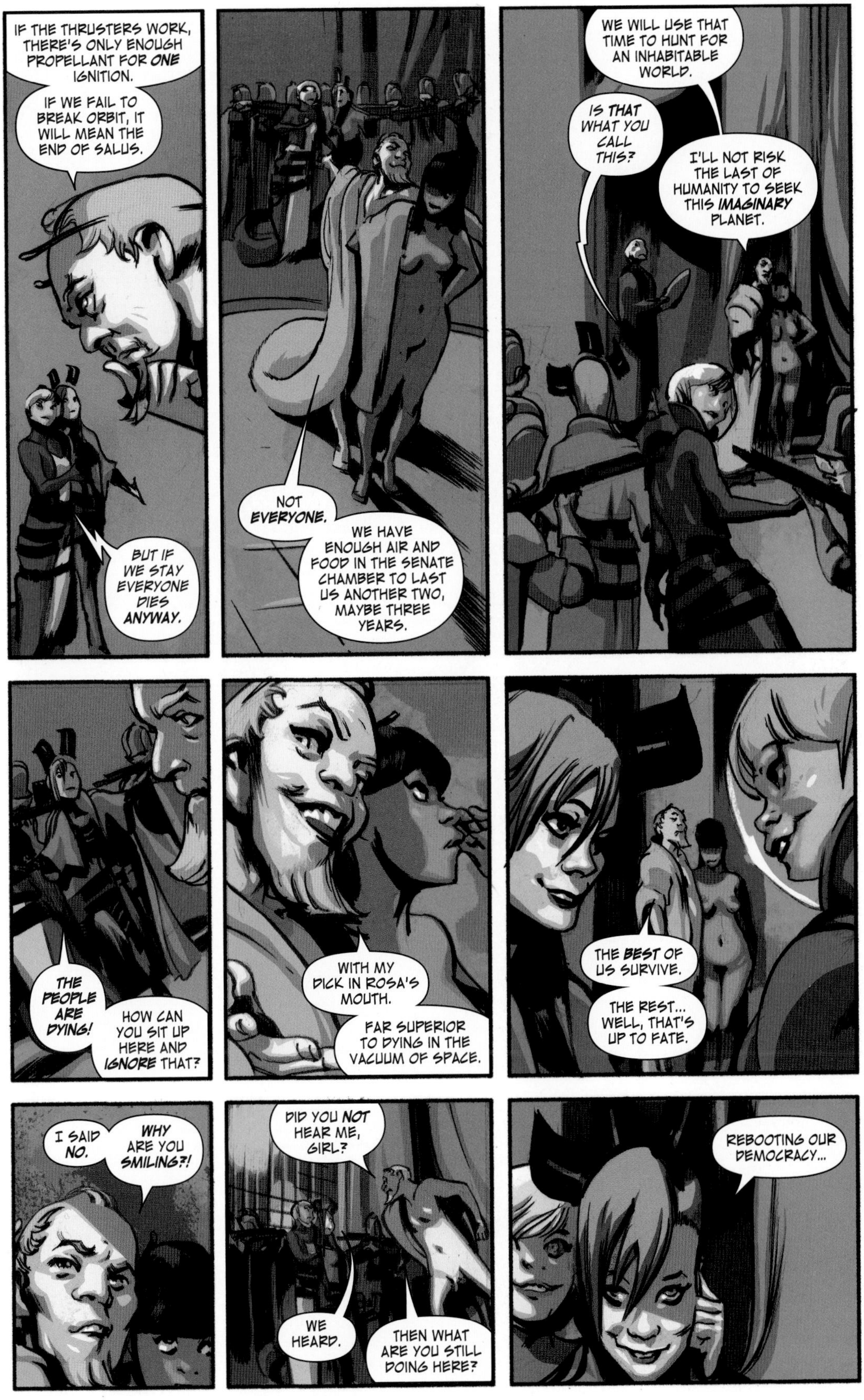
IF THE THRUSTERS WORK, THERE'S ONLY ENOUGH PROPELLANT FOR ONE IGNITION.
IF WE FAIL TO BREAK ORBIT, IT WILL MEAN THE END OF SALUS.
BUT IF WE STAY EVERYONE DIES ANYWAY.
NOT EVERYONE.
WE HAVE ENOUGH AIR AND FOOD IN THE SENATE CHAMBER TO LAST US ANOTHER TWO, MAYBE THREE YEARS.
WE WILL USE THAT TIME TO HUNT FOR AN INHABITABLE WORLD.
IS THAT WHAT YOU CALL THIS?
I'LL NOT RISK THE LAST OF HUMANITY TO SEEK THIS IMAGINARY PLANET.
THE PEOPLE ARE DYING!
HOW CAN YOU SIT UP HERE AND IGNORE THAT?
WITH MY DICK IN ROSA'S MOUTH.
FAR SUPERIOR TO DYING IN THE VACUUM OF SPACE.
THE BEST OF US SURVIVE.
THE REST... WELL, THAT'S UP TO FATE.
I SAID NO.
WHY ARE YOU SMILING?!
DID YOU NOT HEAR ME, GIRL?
WE HEARD.
THEN WHAT ARE YOU STILL DOING HERE?
REBOOTING OUR DEMOCRACY...

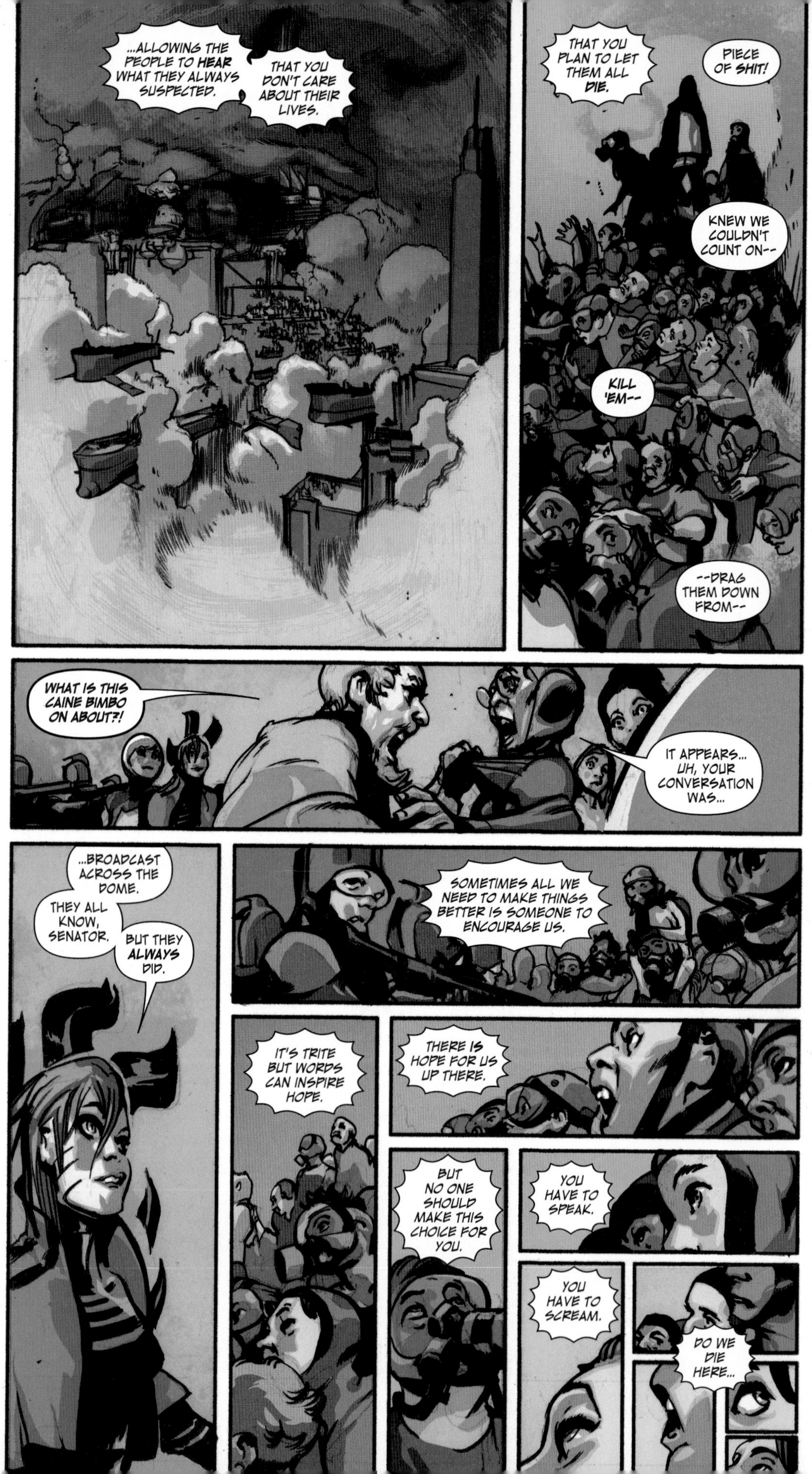
...ALLOWING THE PEOPLE TO HEAR WHAT THEY ALWAYS SUSPECTED.
THAT YOU DON'T CARE ABOUT THEIR LIVES.
THAT YOU PLAN TO LET THEM ALL DIE.
PIECE OF SHIT!
KNEW WE COULDN'T COUNT ON--
KILL 'EM--
--DRAG THEM DOWN FROM--
WHAT IS THIS CAINE BIMBO ON ABOUT?!
IT APPEARS... UH, YOUR CONVERSATION WAS...
...BROADCAST ACROSS THE DOME.
THEY ALL KNOW, SENATOR.
BUT THEY ALWAYS DID.
SOMETIMES ALL WE NEED TO MAKE THINGS BETTER IS SOMEONE TO ENCOURAGE US.
IT'S TRITE BUT WORDS CAN INSPIRE HOPE.
THERE IS HOPE FOR US UP THERE.
BUT NO ONE SHOULD MAKE THIS CHOICE FOR YOU.
YOU HAVE TO SPEAK.
YOU HAVE TO SCREAM.
DO WE DIE HERE...

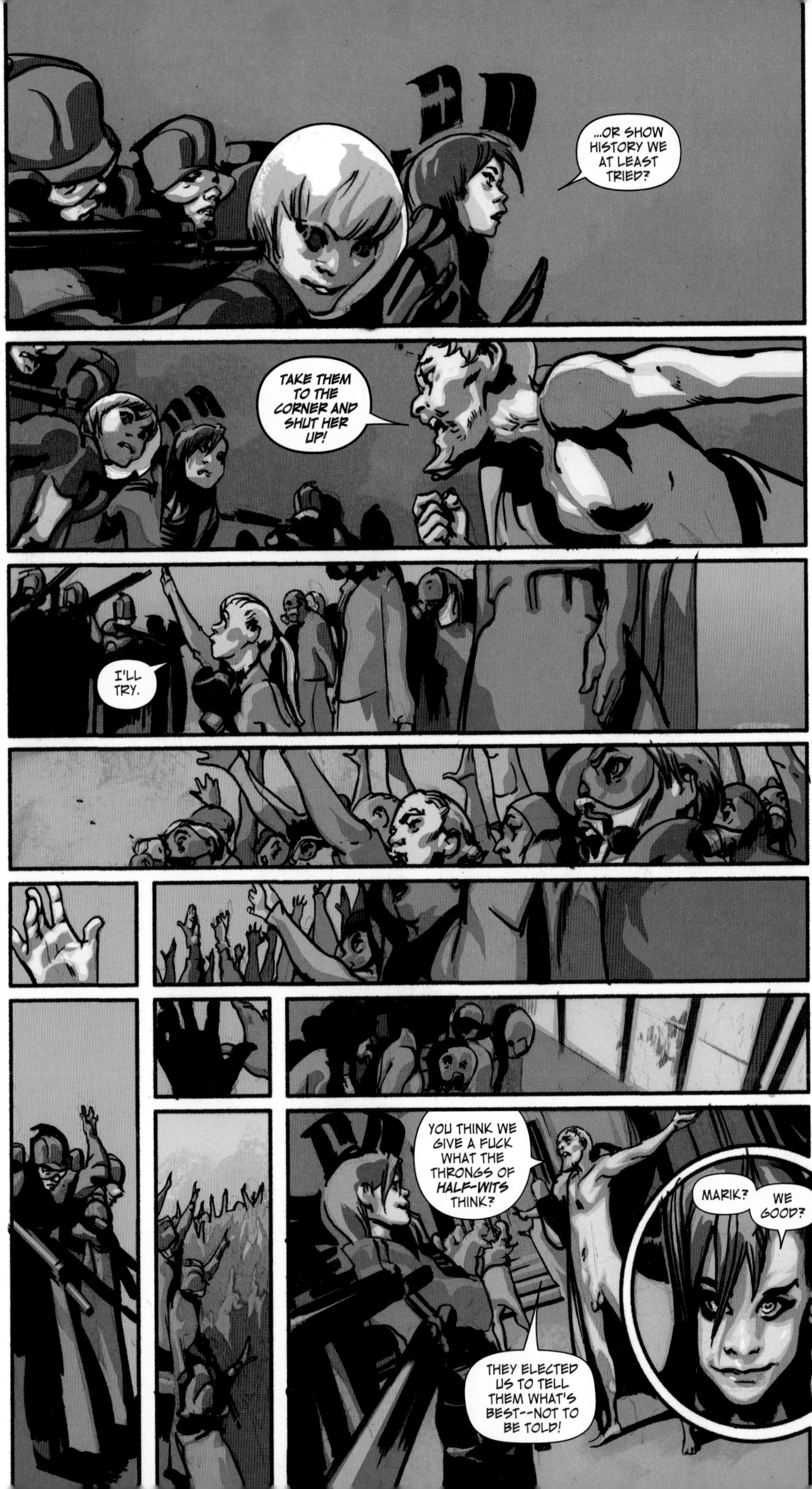
...OR SHOW HISTORY WE AT LEAST TRIED?
TAKE THEM TO THE CORNER AND SHUT HER UP!
I'LL TRY.
YOU THINK WE GIVE A FUCK WHAT THE THRONGS OF HALF-WITS THINK?
THEY ELECTED US TO TELL THEM WHAT'S BEST--NOT TO BE TOLD!
MARIK?
WE GOOD?

IF BY "GOOD" YOU MEAN DID I GET INTO THE COMMAND HUB AND INITIATE IGNITION SEQUENCE?

I DO.

IN THAT CASE--WE'RE GOOD.

ENOUGH!

KILL THEM!

WE'RE ALL IN THIS TOGETHER.

THESE PIGS WILL ONLY EVER TAKE CARE OF THEMSELVES.

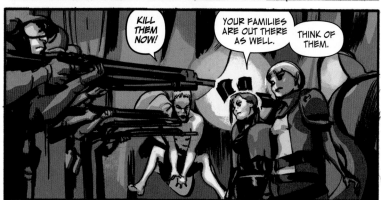

KILL THEM NOW!

YOUR FAMILIES ARE OUT THERE AS WELL.

THINK OF THEM.

WHAT ARE YOU DOING?!

THEY'RE GIVING THE POWER BACK TO THE PEOPLE, MOTHERFUCKER.

MARIK, WE'RE ALL SET ON OUR END...

...TAKE US TO THE STARS.

KLANGG

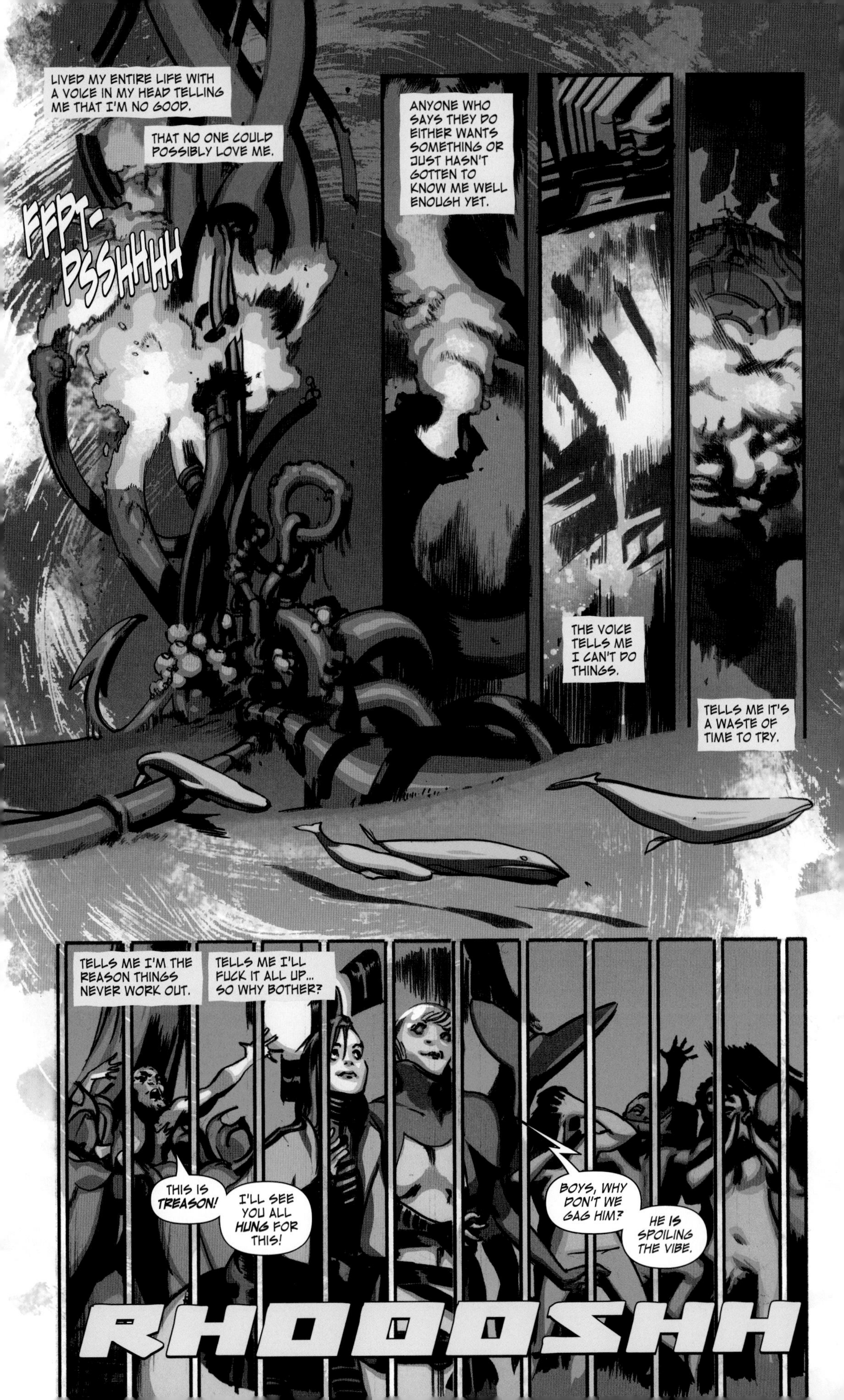

LIVED MY ENTIRE LIFE WITH A VOICE IN MY HEAD TELLING ME THAT I'M NO GOOD.
THAT NO ONE COULD POSSIBLY LOVE ME.
FFPT-PSSHHHH
ANYONE WHO SAYS THEY DO EITHER WANTS SOMETHING OR JUST HASN'T GOTTEN TO KNOW ME WELL ENOUGH YET.
THE VOICE TELLS ME I CAN'T DO THINGS.
TELLS ME IT'S A WASTE OF TIME TO TRY.
TELLS ME I'M THE REASON THINGS NEVER WORK OUT.
TELLS ME I'LL FUCK IT ALL UP... SO WHY BOTHER?
THIS IS *TREASON!*
I'LL SEE YOU ALL *HUNG* FOR THIS!
BOYS, WHY DON'T WE GAG HIM?
HE *IS* SPOILING THE VIBE.
RHOOOSHH

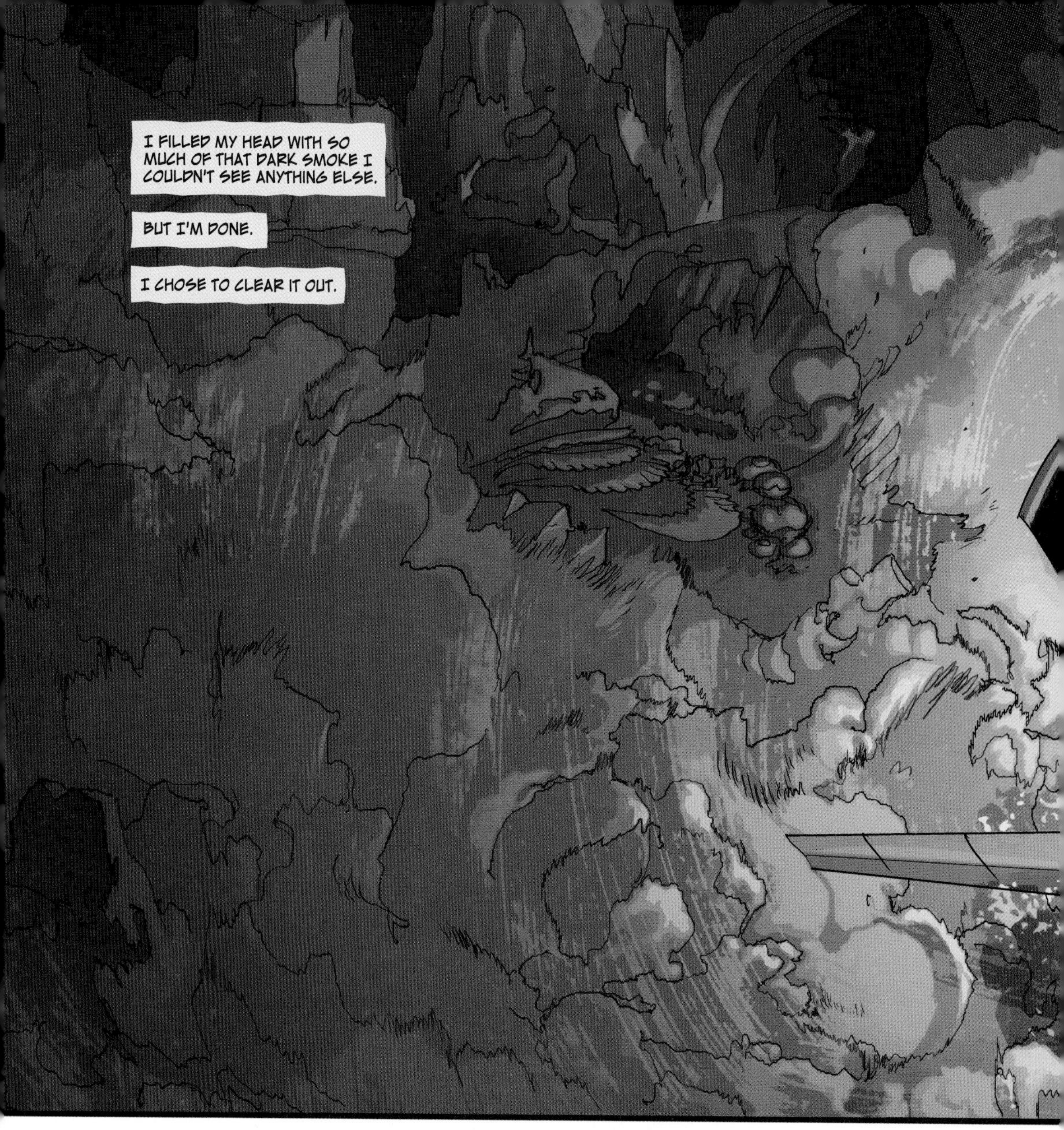
I FILLED MY HEAD WITH SO MUCH OF THAT DARK SMOKE I COULDN'T SEE ANYTHING ELSE.
BUT I'M DONE.
I CHOSE TO CLEAR IT OUT.

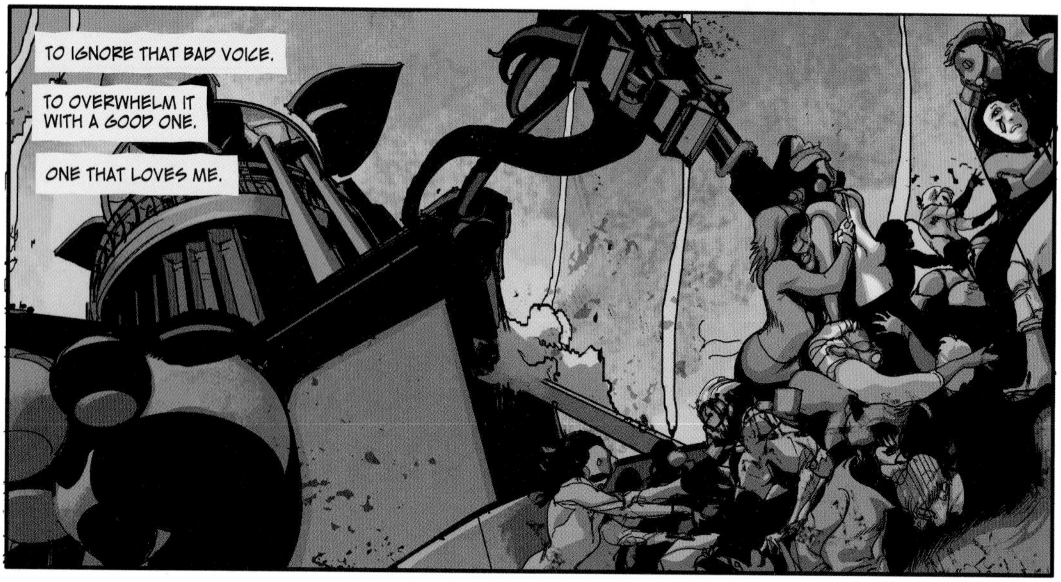
TO IGNORE THAT BAD VOICE.
TO OVERWHELM IT WITH A GOOD ONE.
ONE THAT LOVES ME.

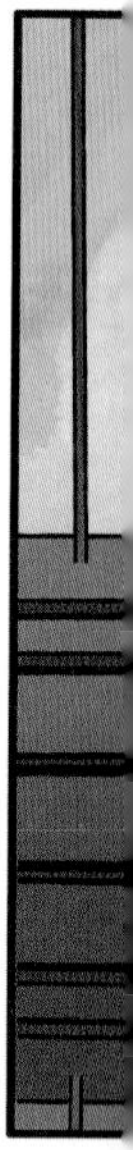

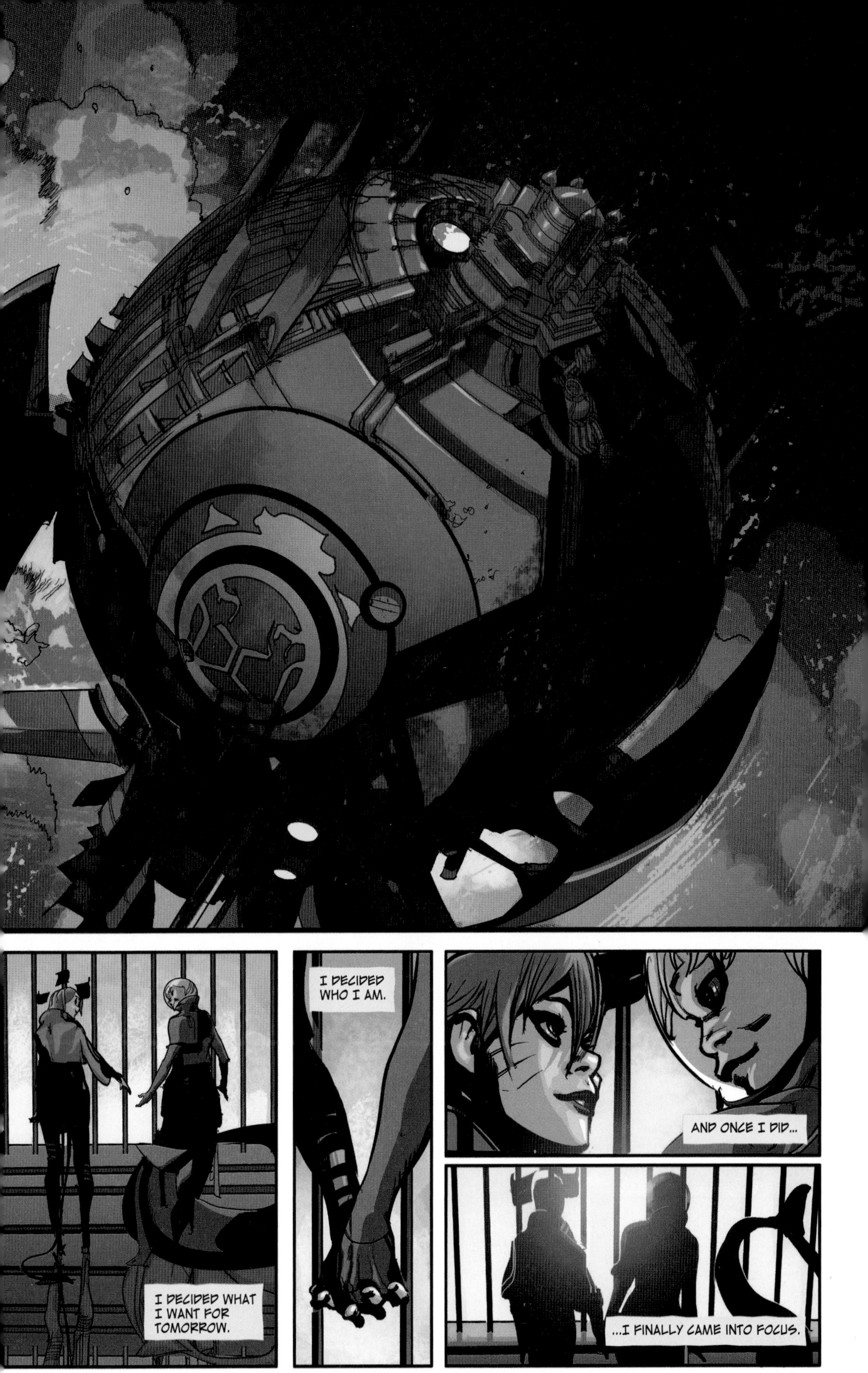
I DECIDED WHAT I WANT FOR TOMORROW.
I DECIDED WHO I AM.
AND ONCE I DID...
...I FINALLY CAME INTO FOCUS.

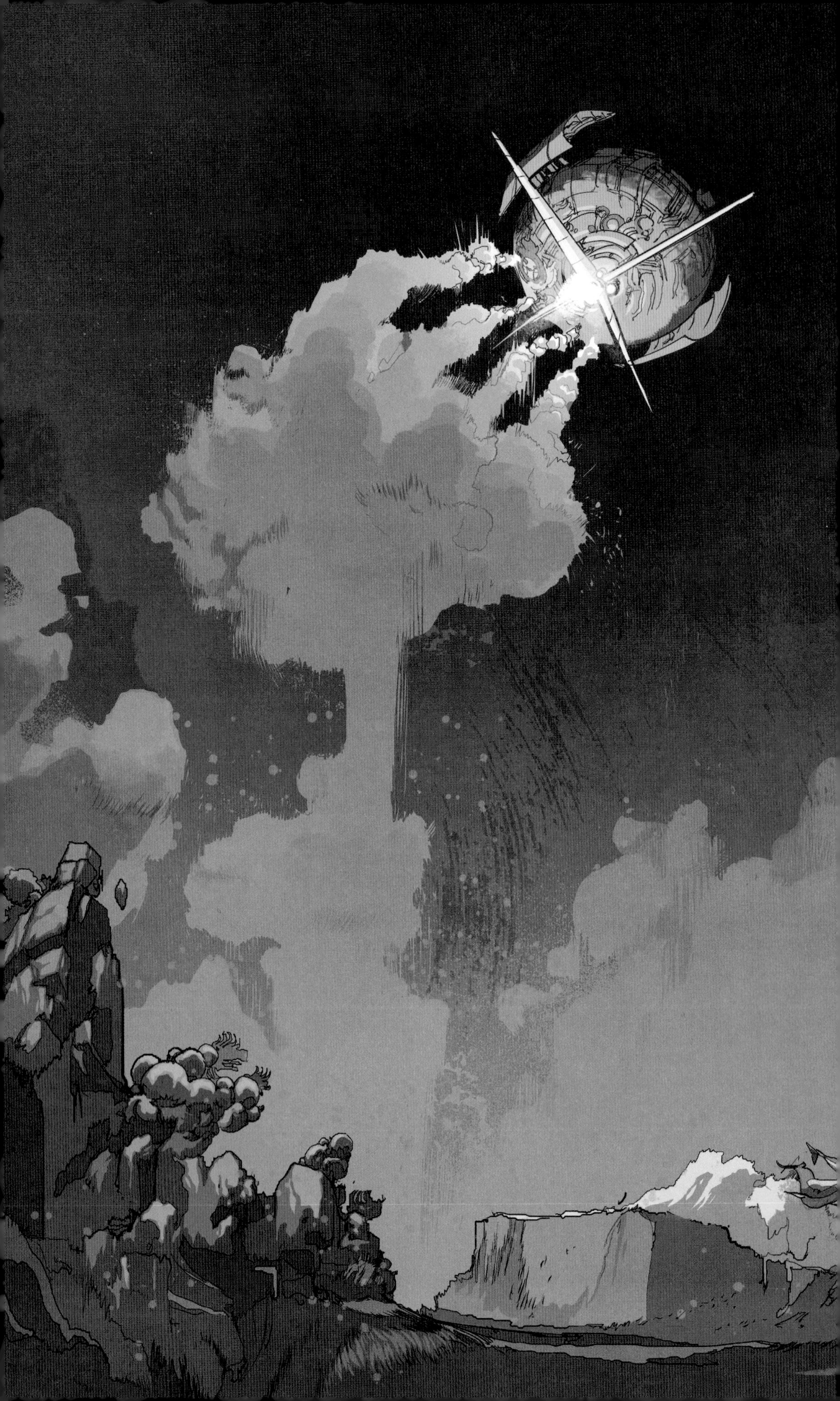

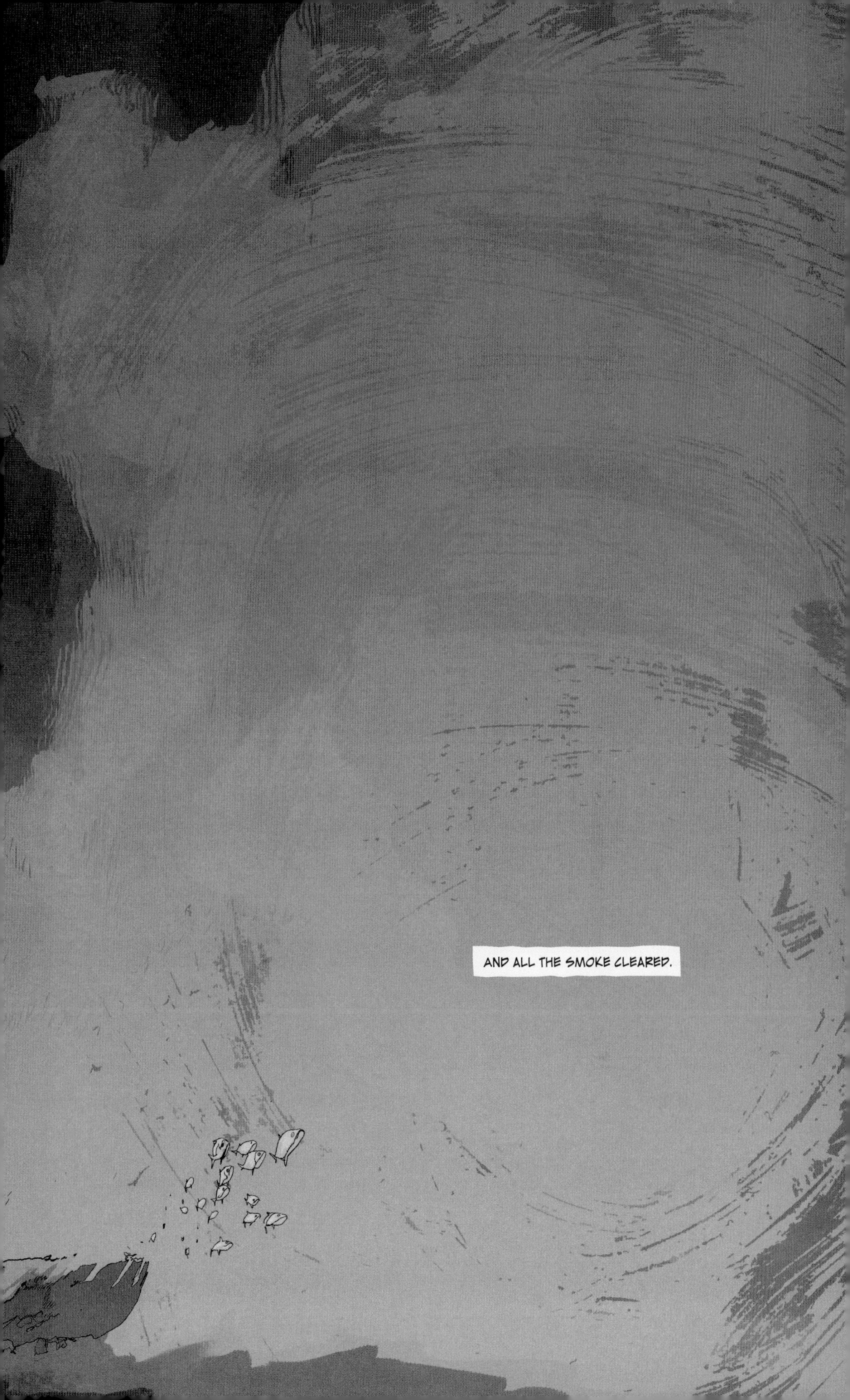
AND ALL THE SMOKE CLEARED.

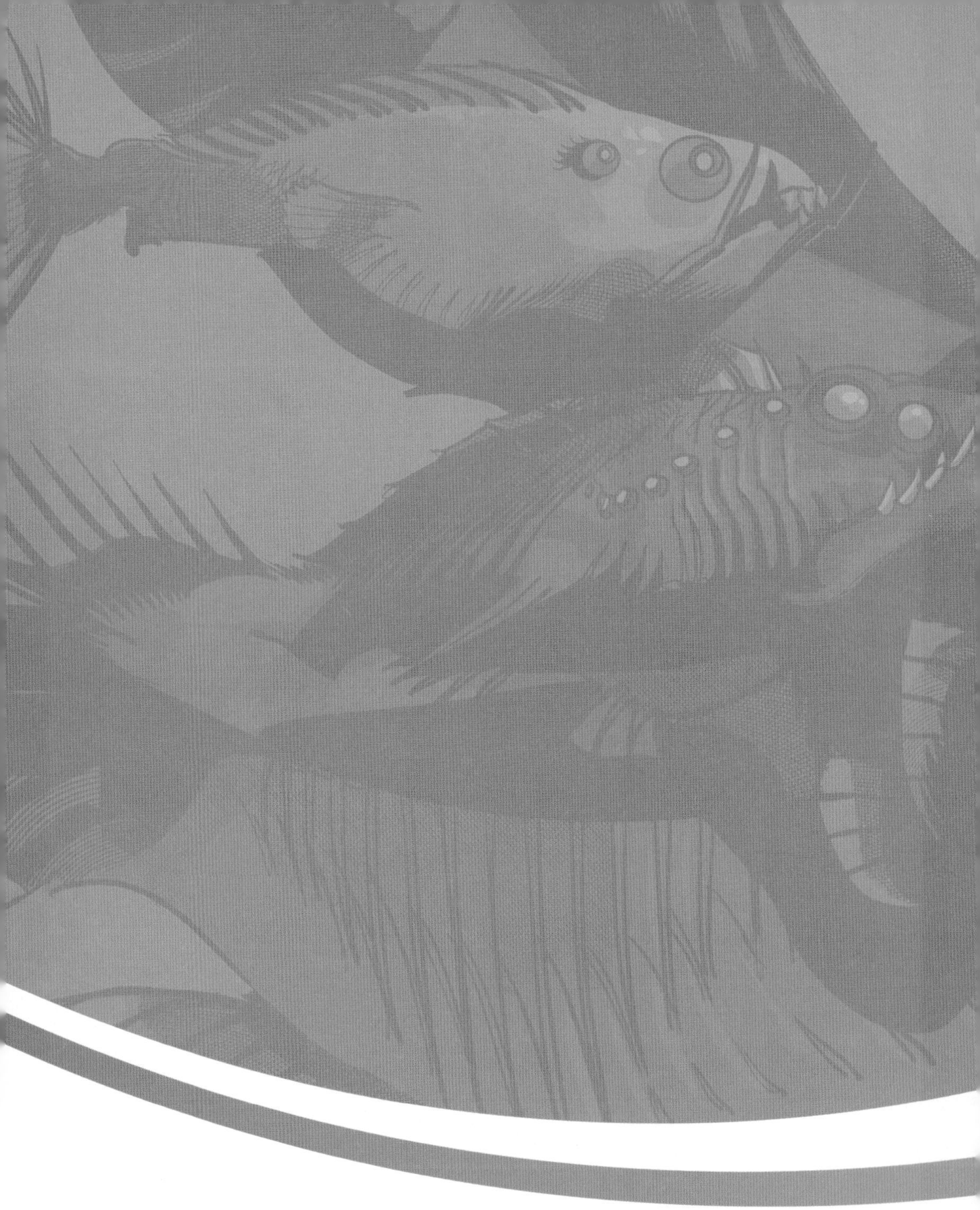

VARIANT COVER
GALLERY

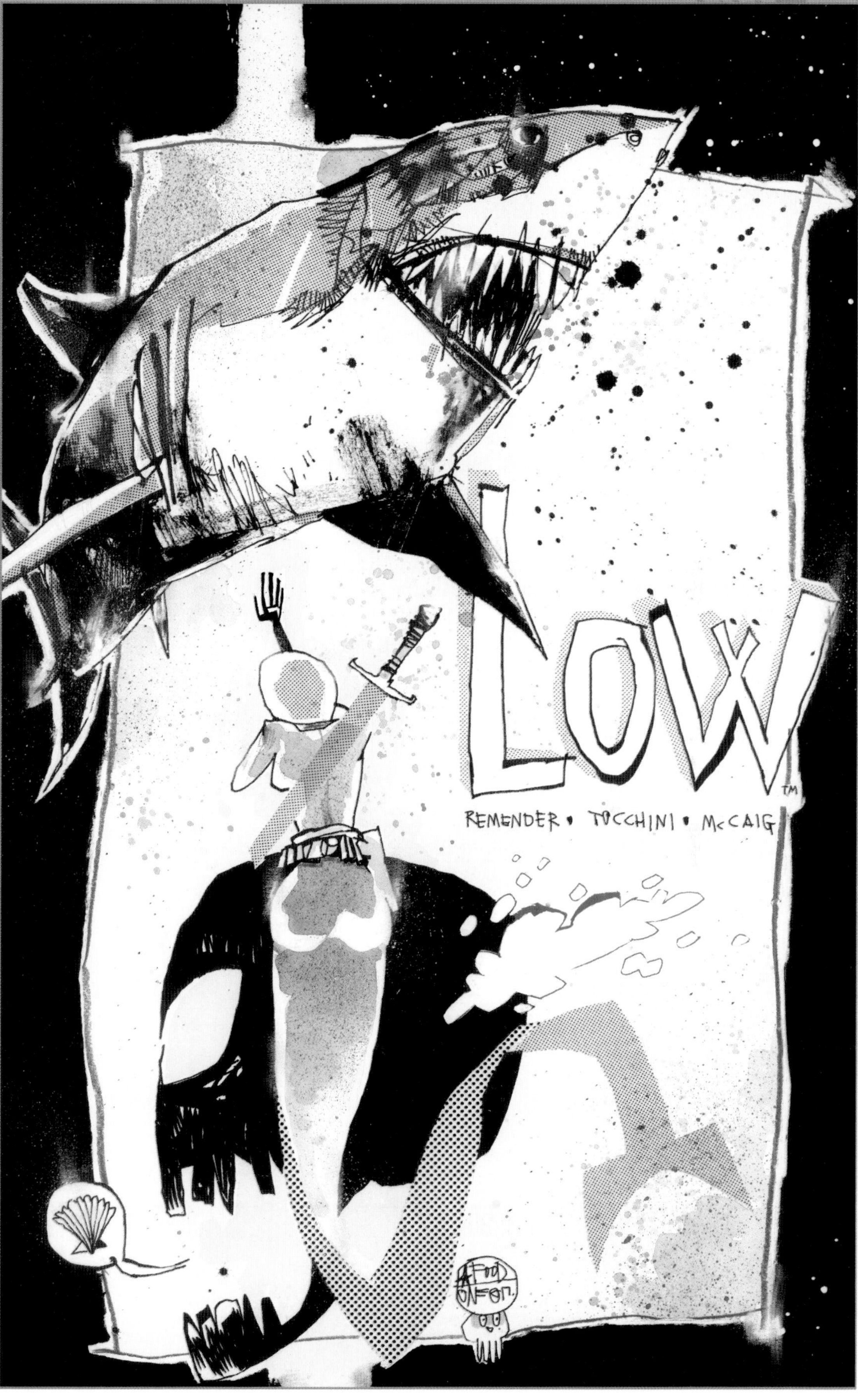
LOW™
REMENDER • TOCCHINI • McCAIG

#16 VARIANT BY JIM MAHFOOD

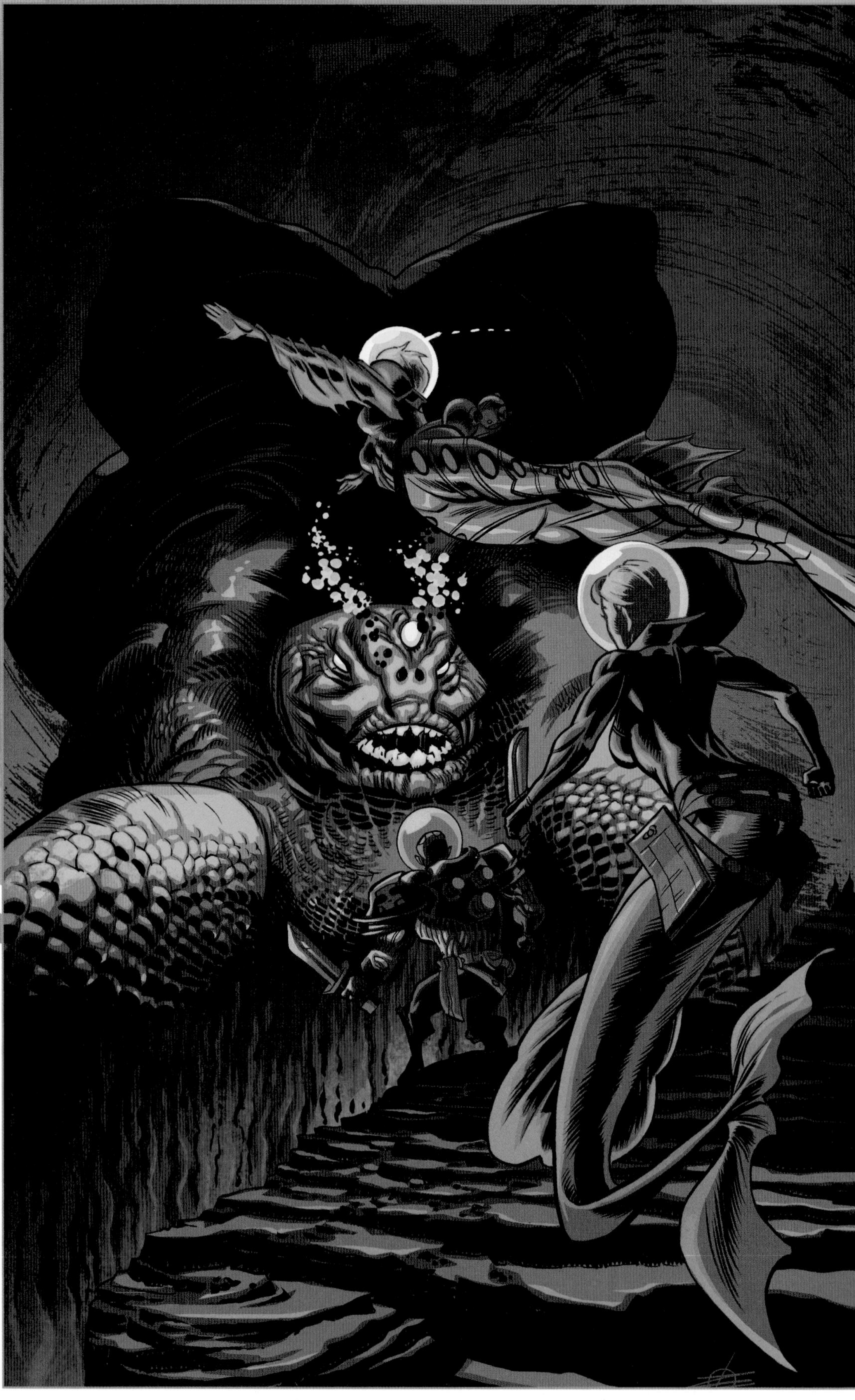

#16 VARIANT BY RICK REMENDER, INKS BY HILARY BARTA, COLORS BY DAVE McCAIG

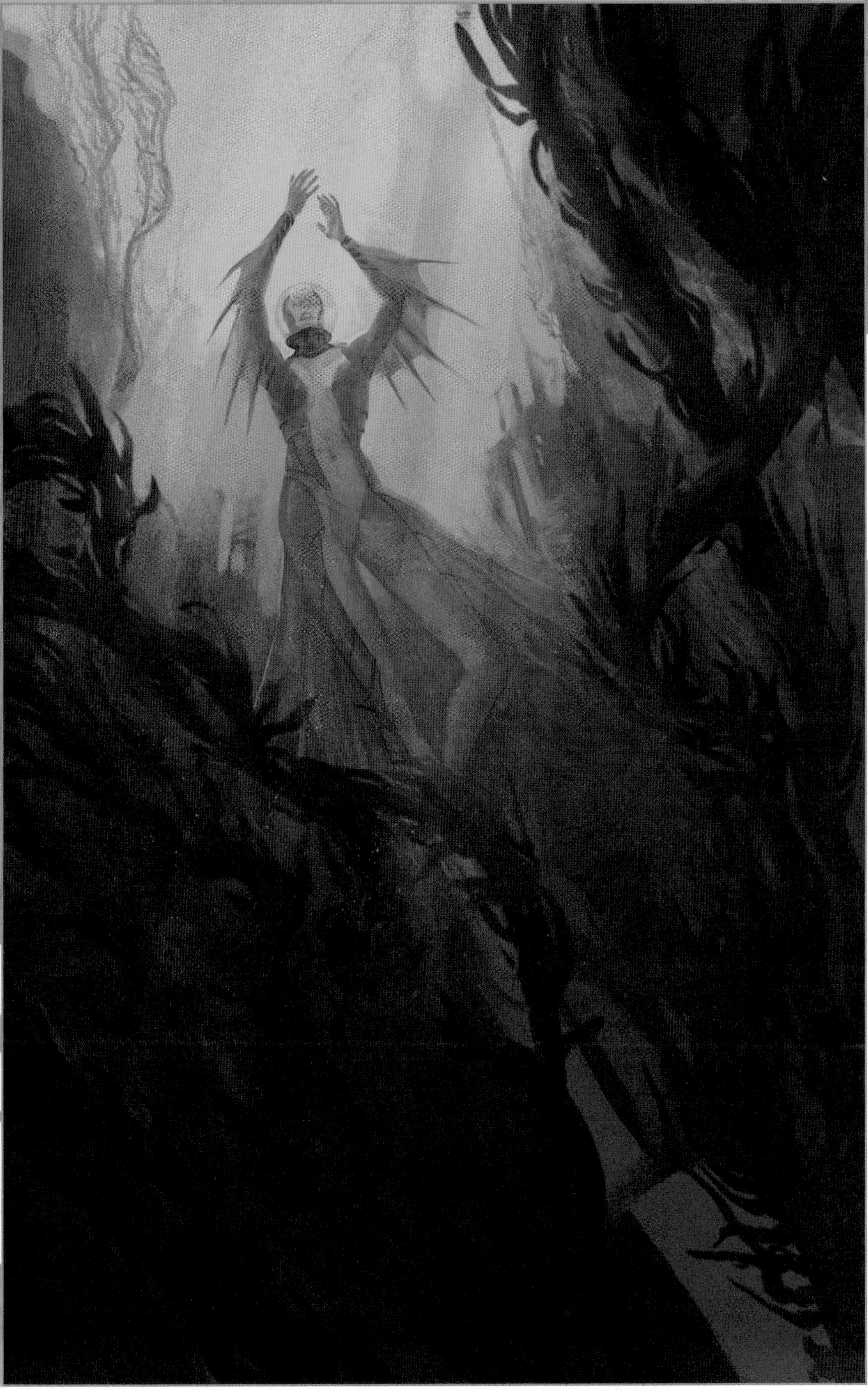

#16 WOMEN'S HISTORY MONTH VARIANT BY VANESA R. DEL REY

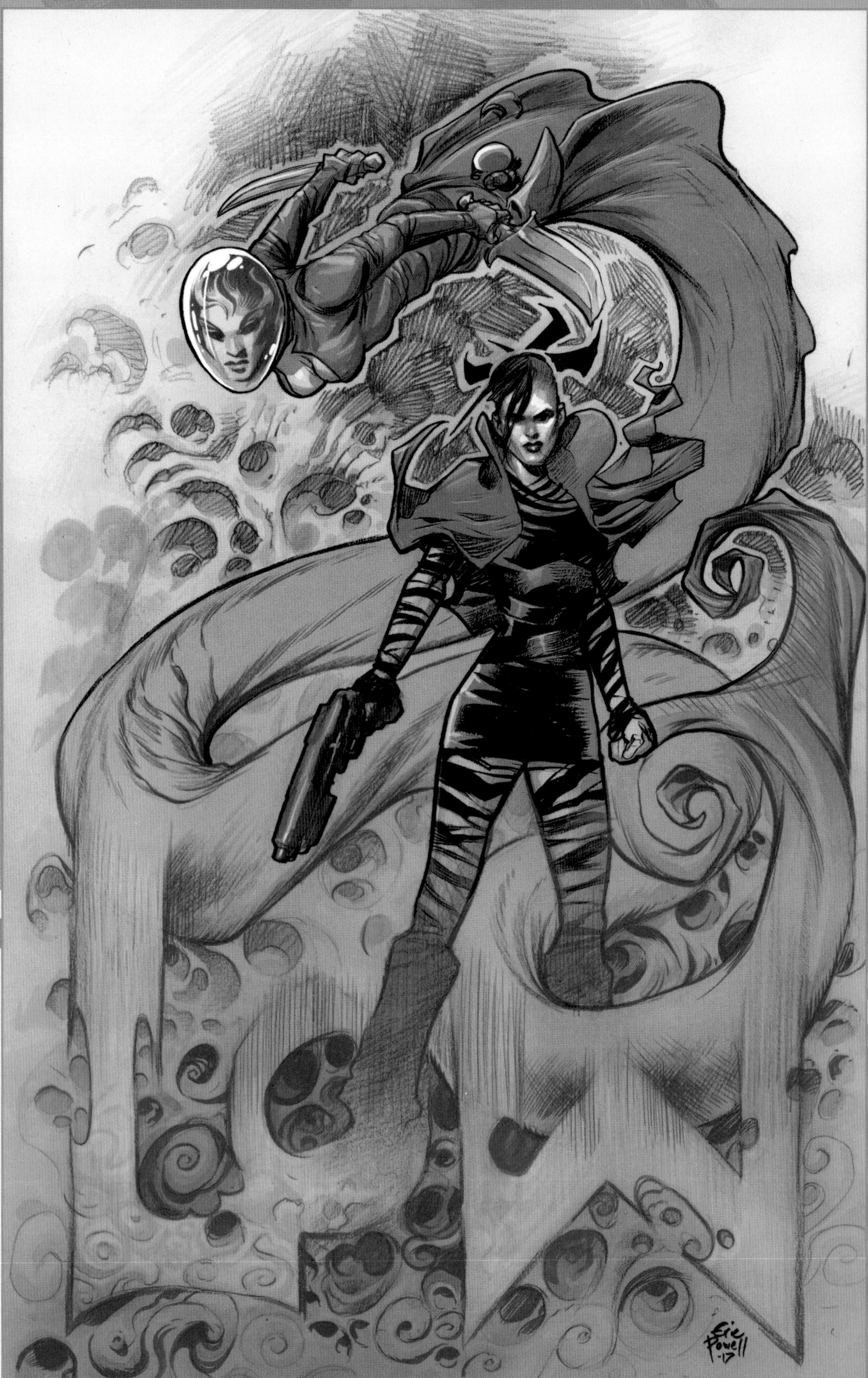
Eric Powell
'17

#17 VARIANT BY ERIC POWELL

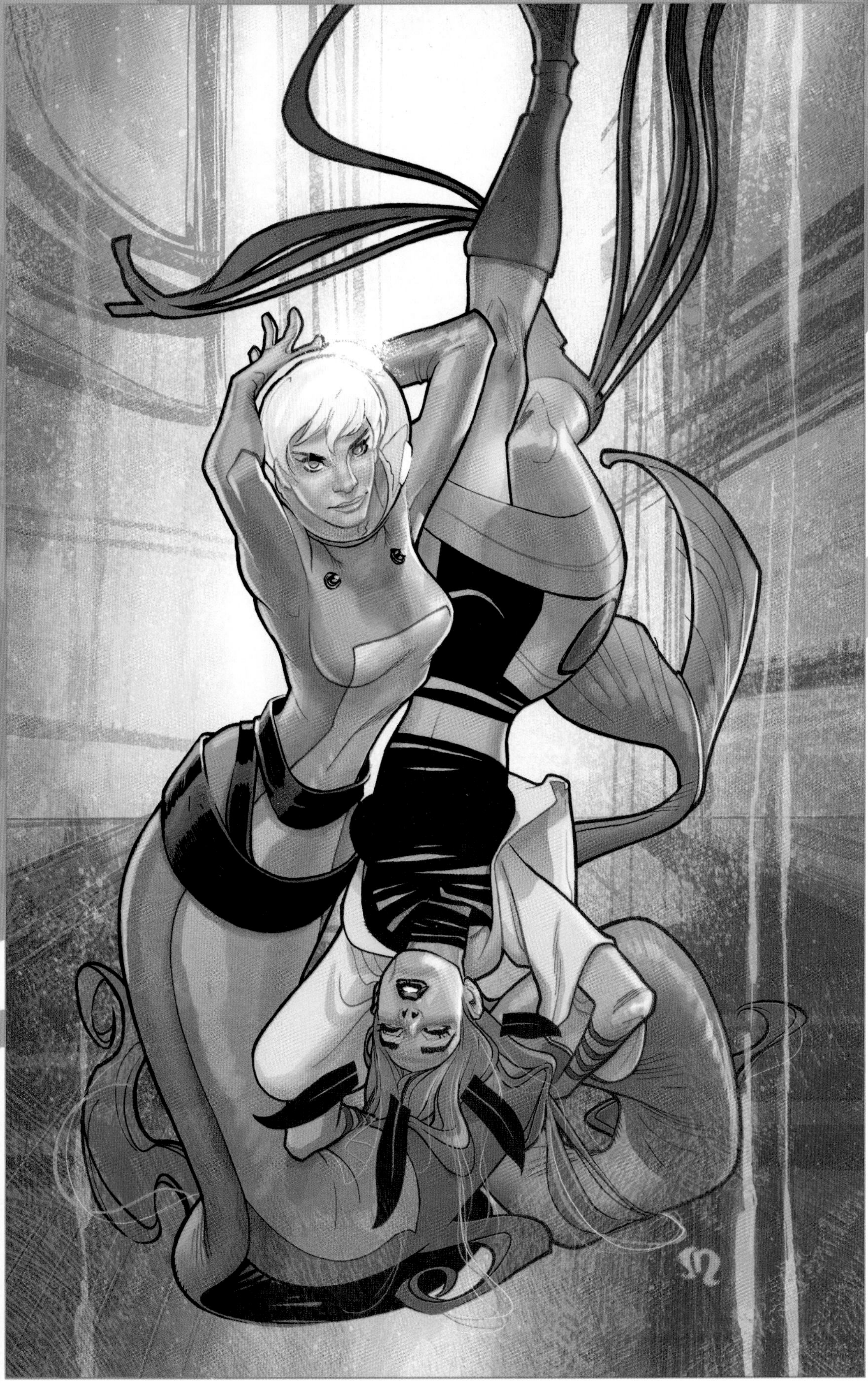

#18 VARIANT BY STÉPHANE ROUX

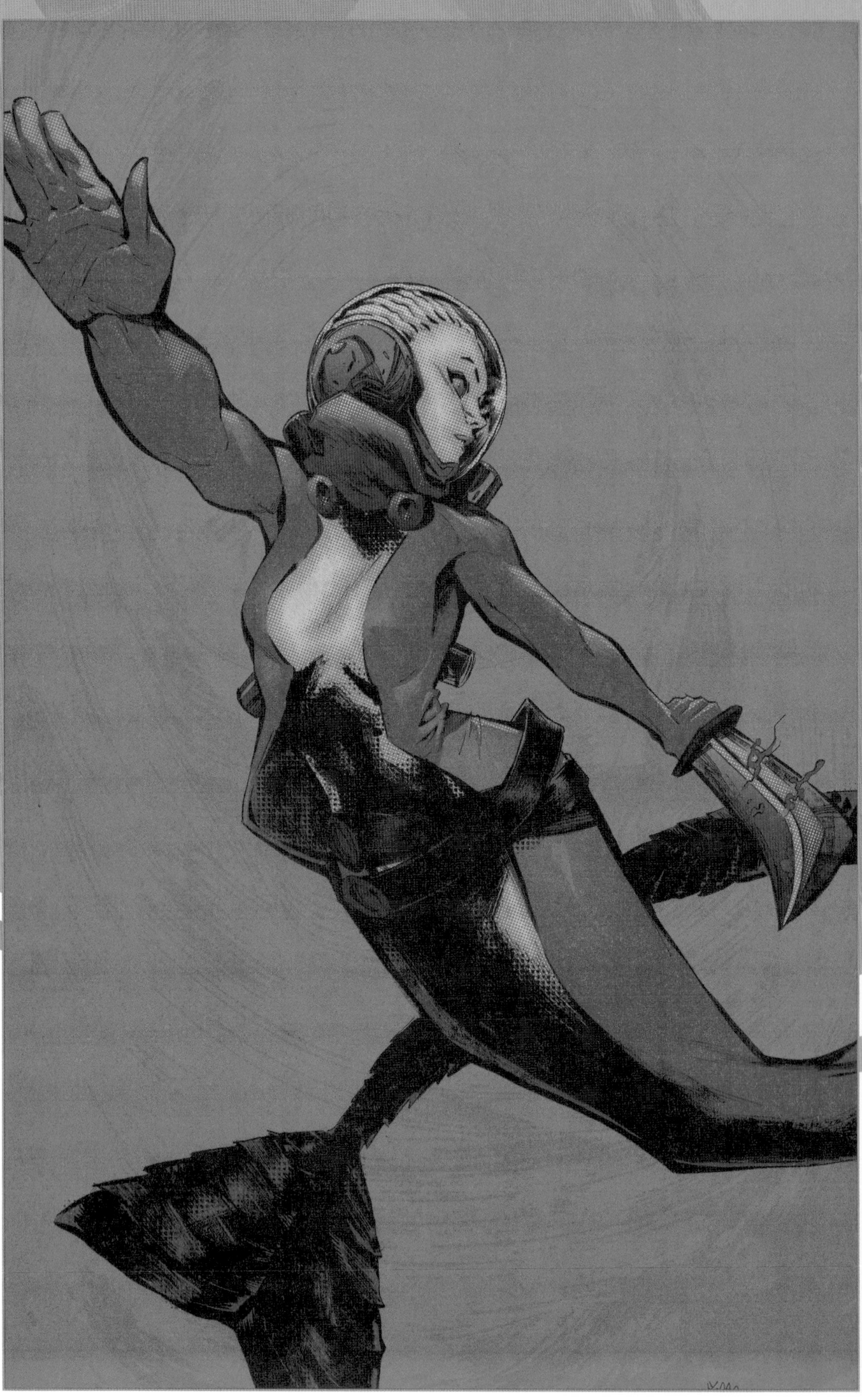

#19 VARIANT BY RYAN STEGMAN AND DAVE McCAIG

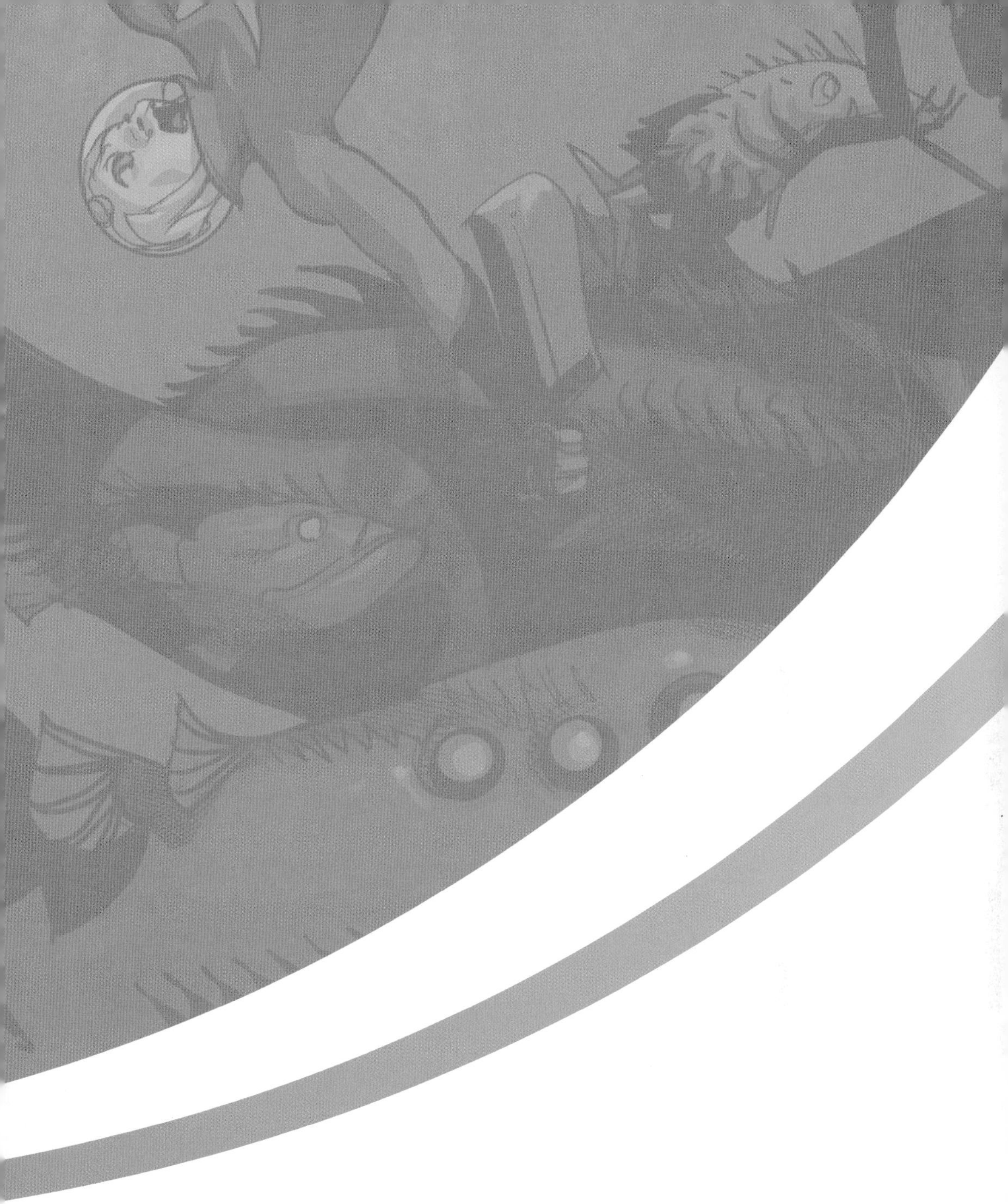

GREG TOCCHINI

SKETCHBOOK

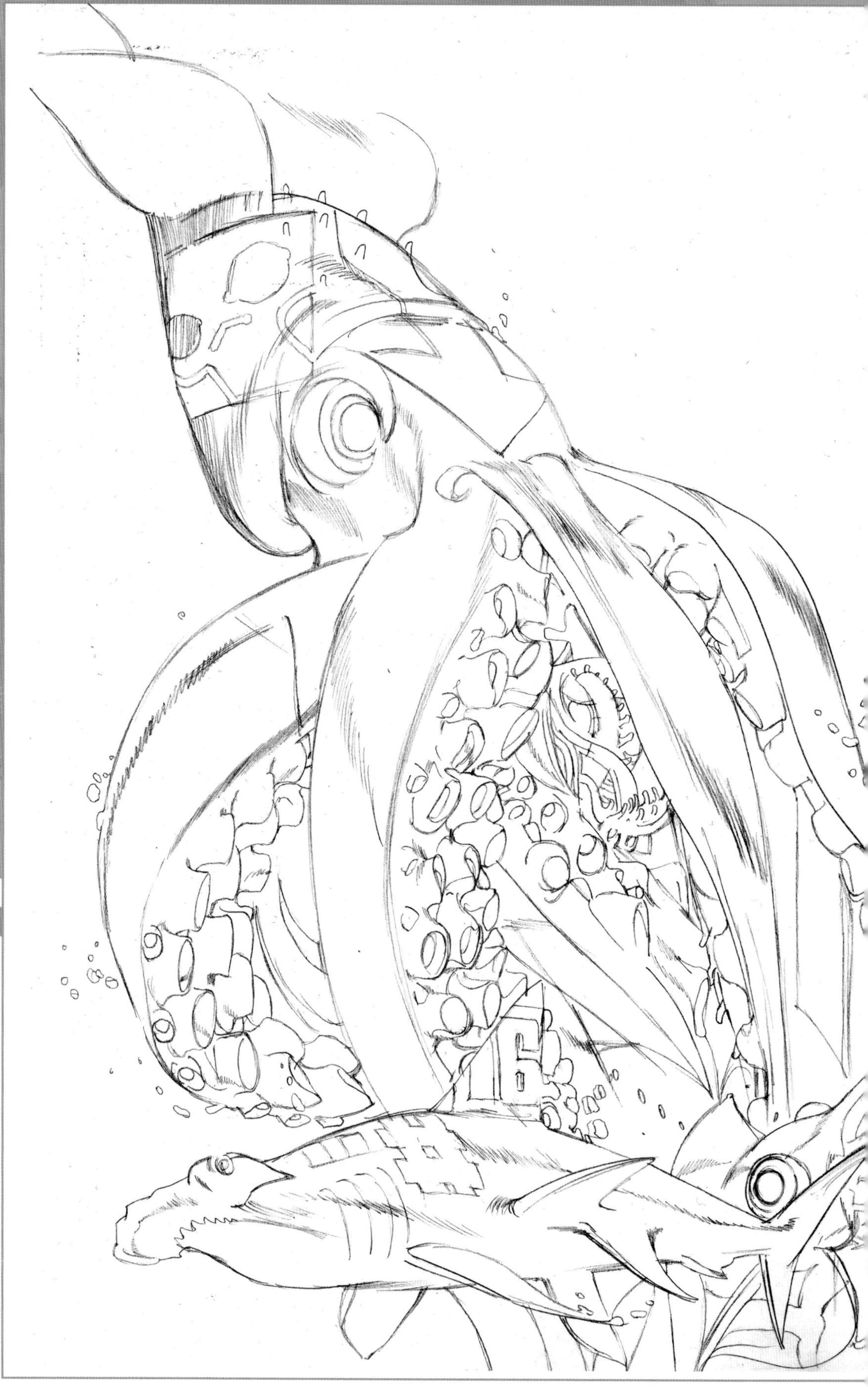
16

#16 COVER PENCILS

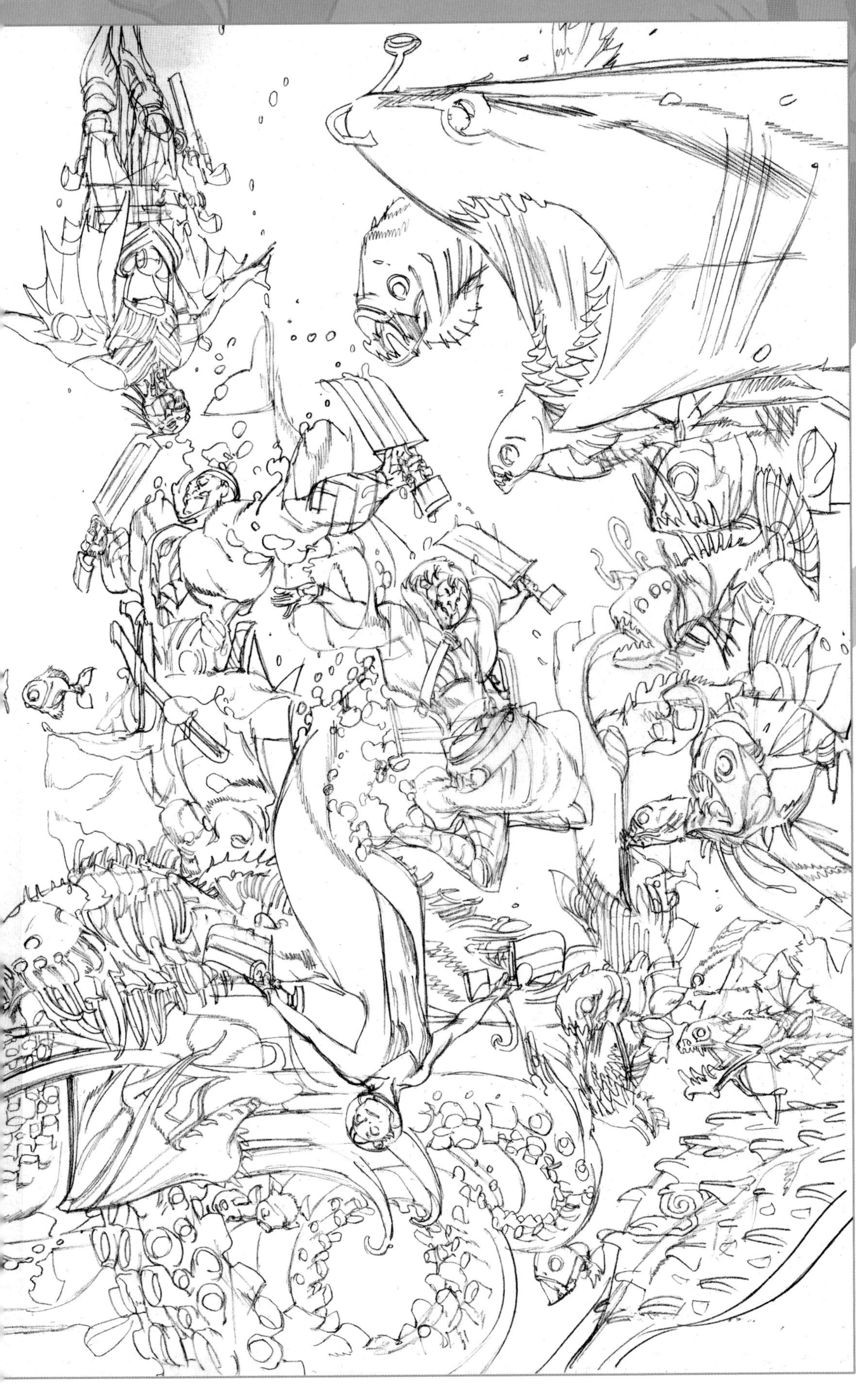

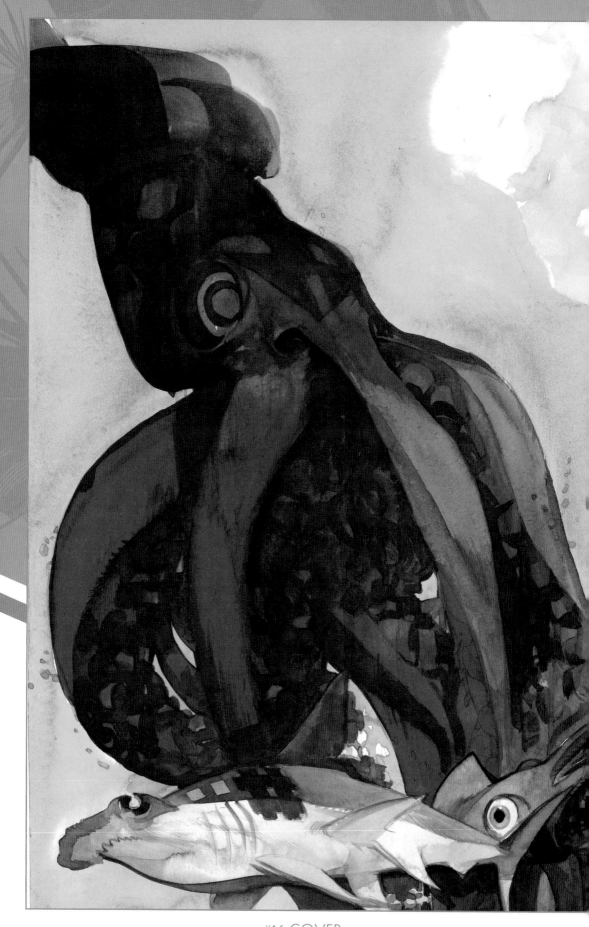

#16 COVER

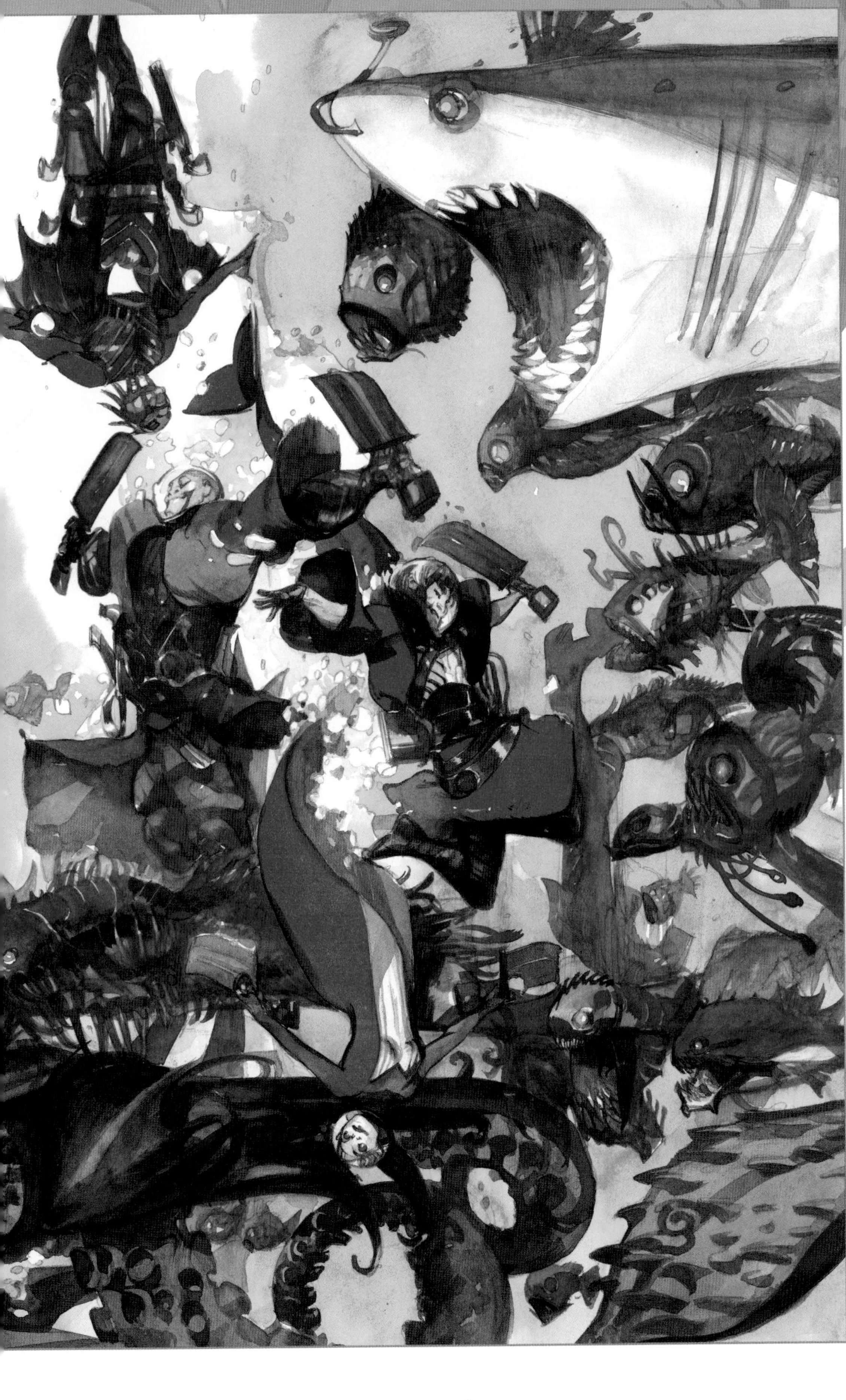

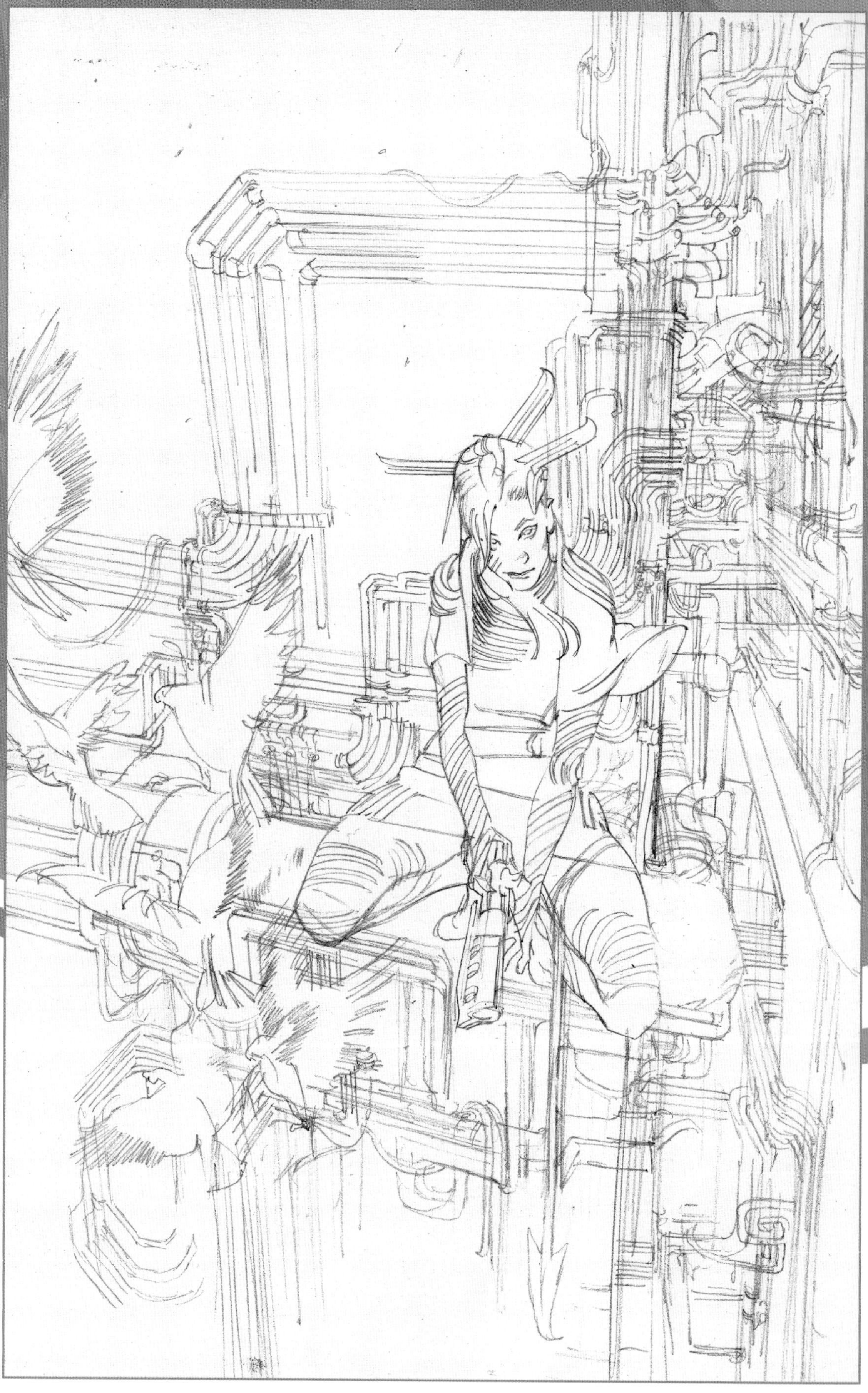

#17 COVER PENCILS

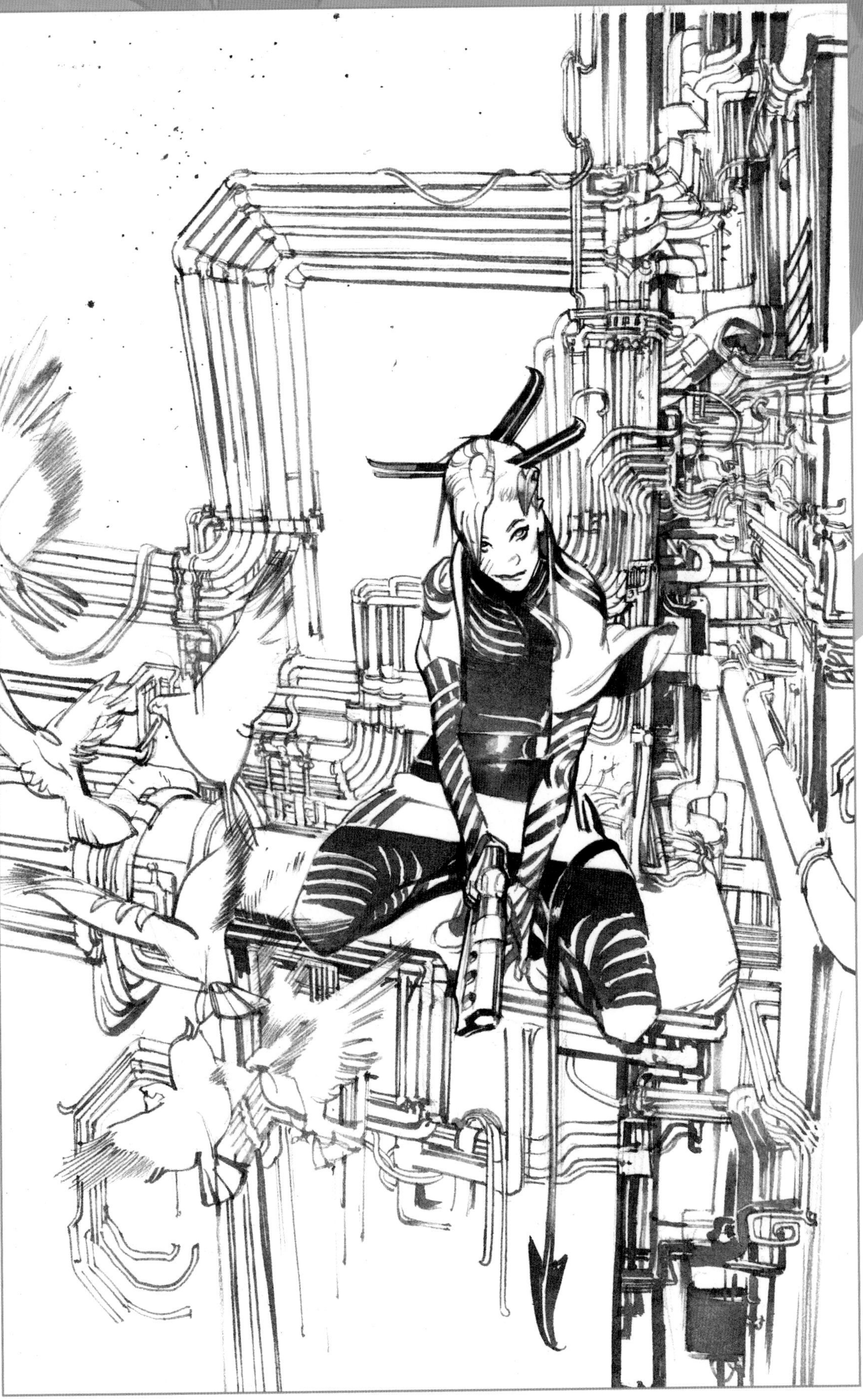

#17 COVER INKS

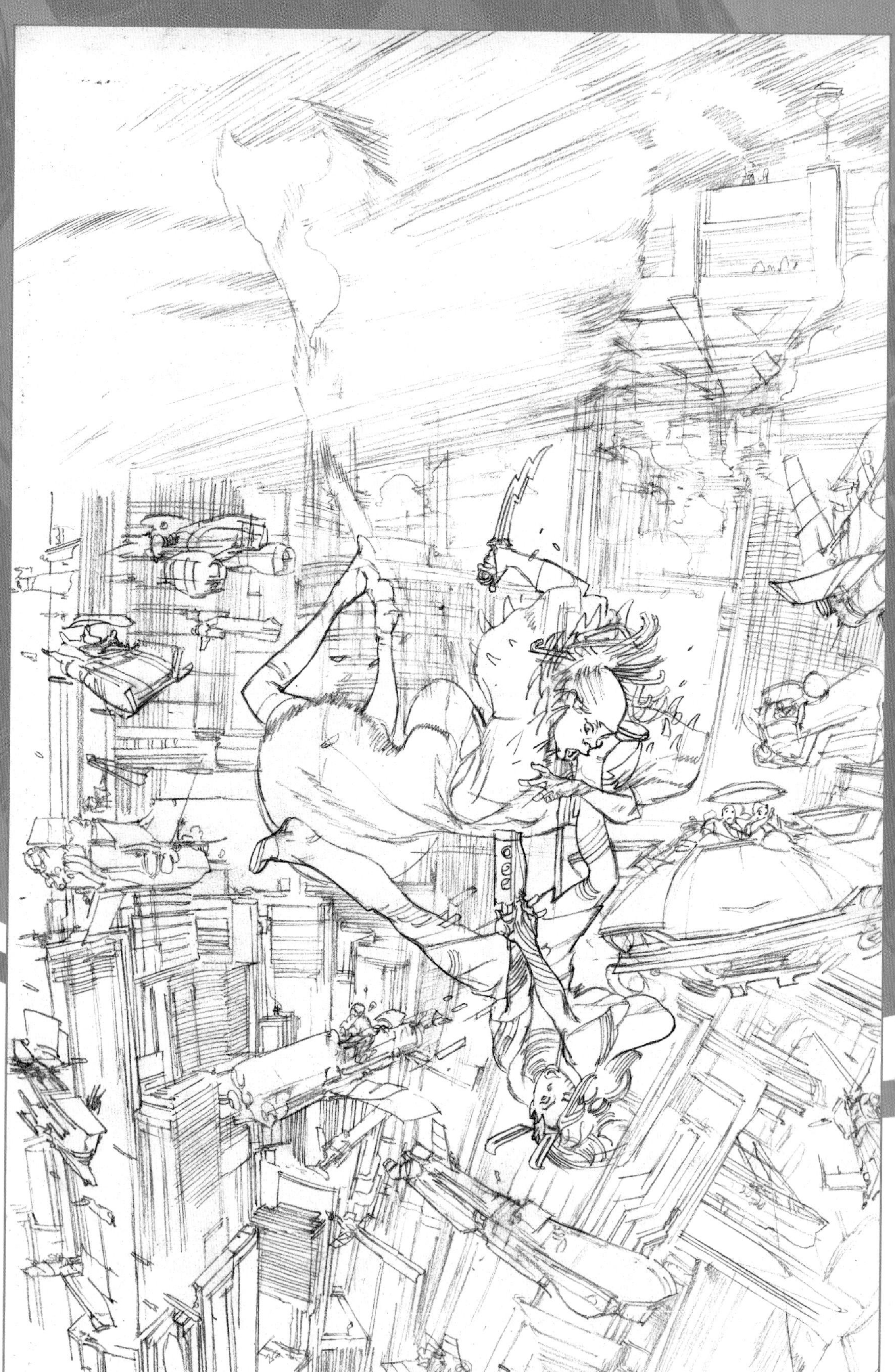

#18 COVER PENCILS

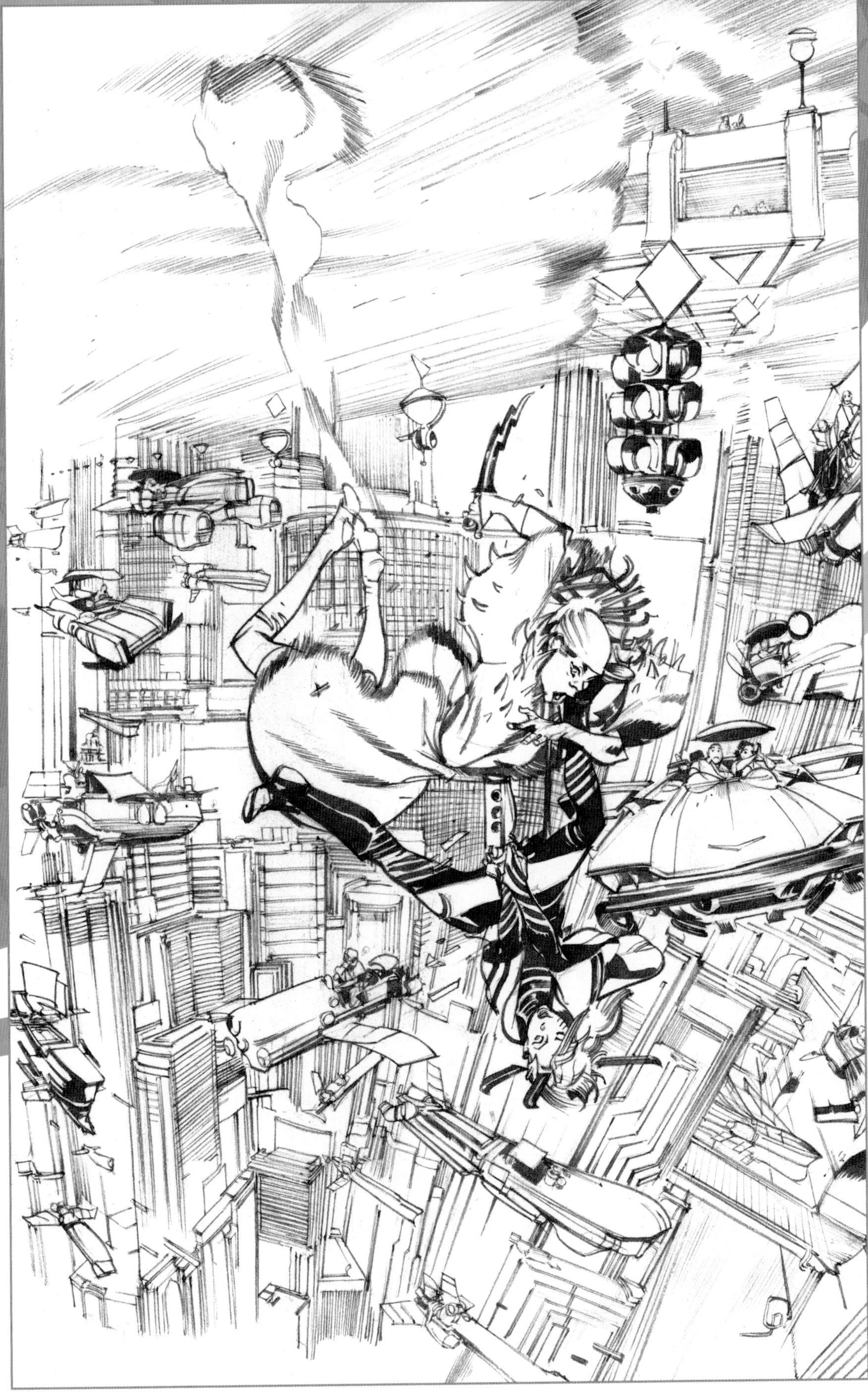

#18 COVER INKS

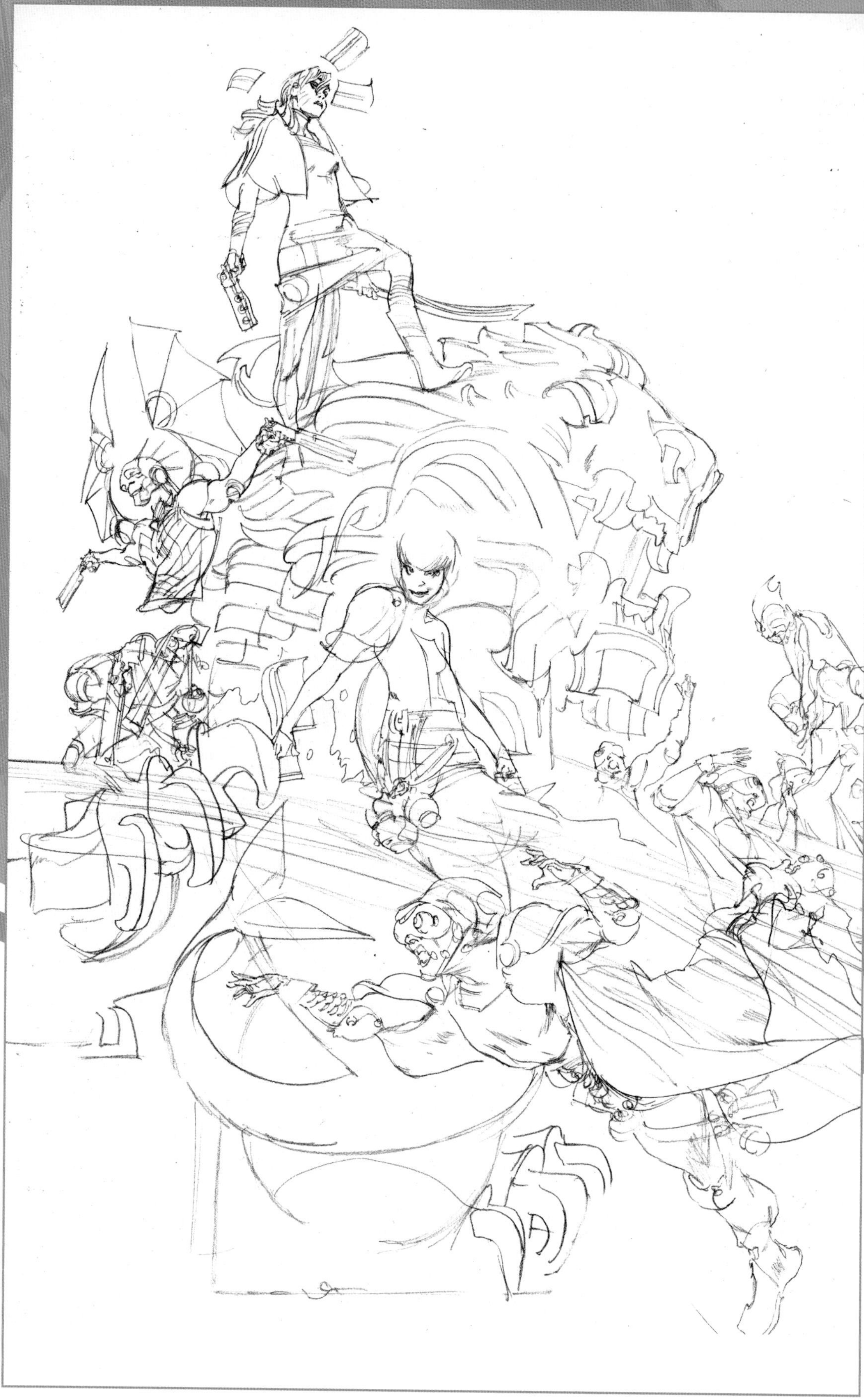

#19 COVER PENCILS

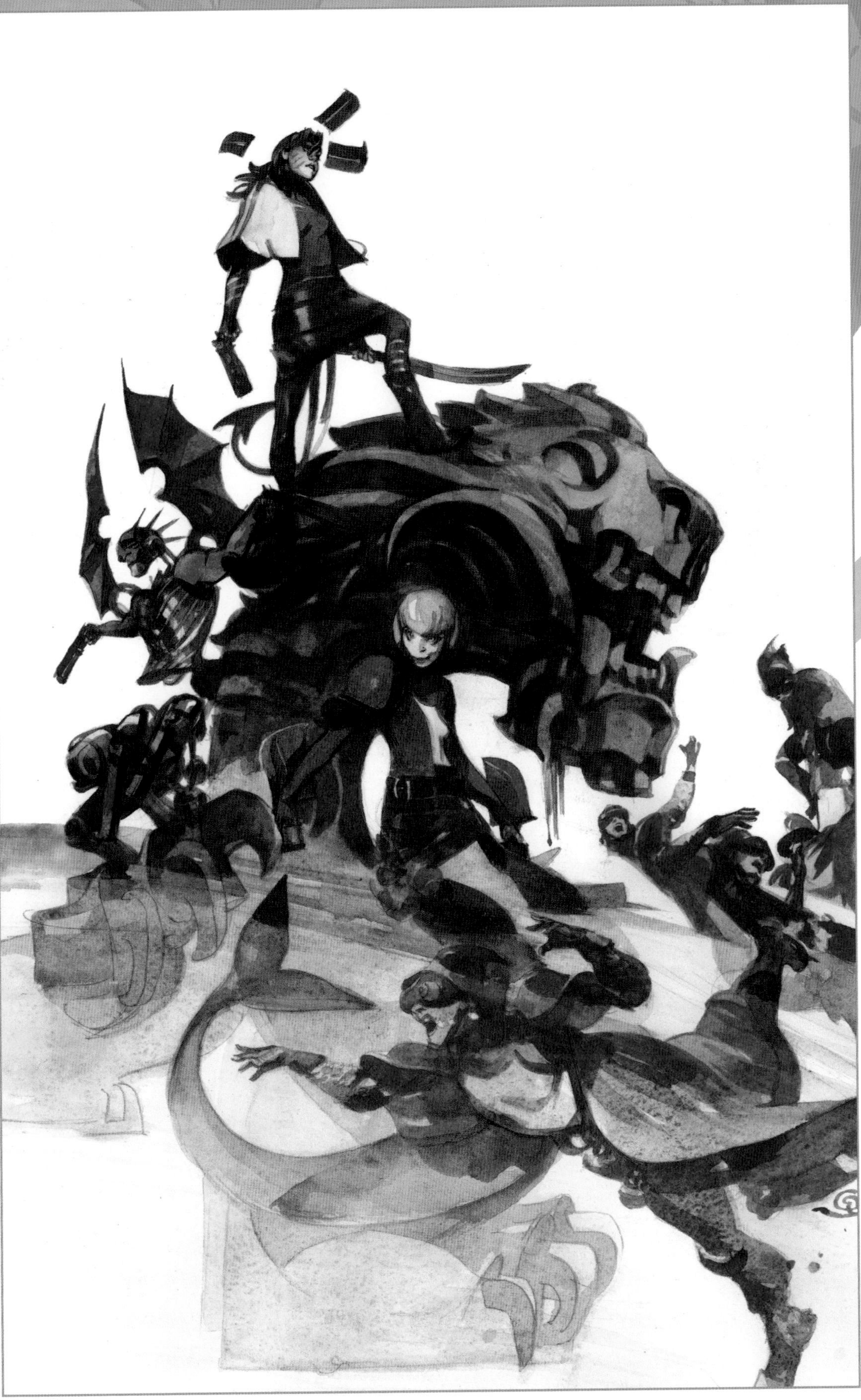

#19 COVER COLORS (ORIGINAL)

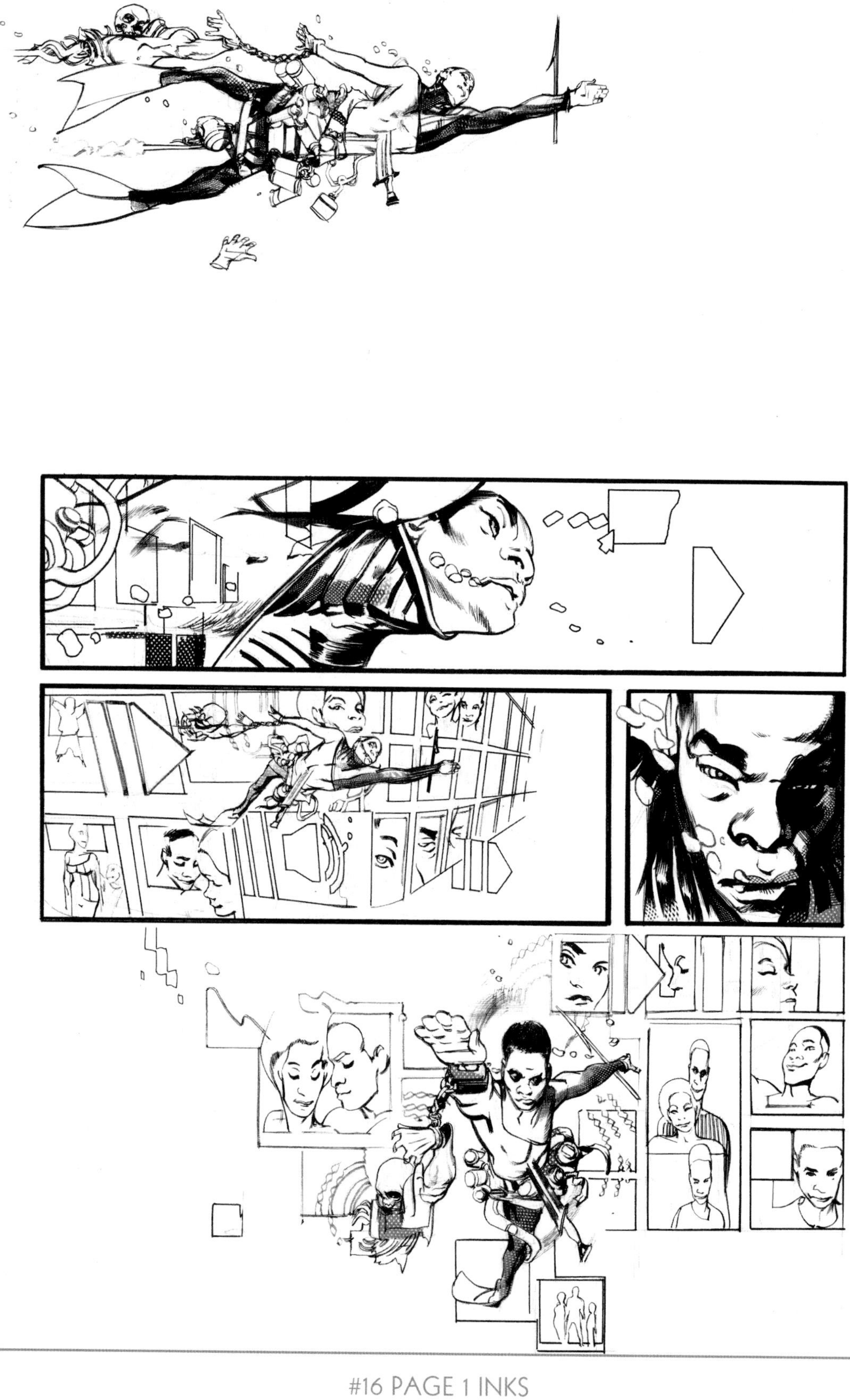

#16 PAGE 1 INKS

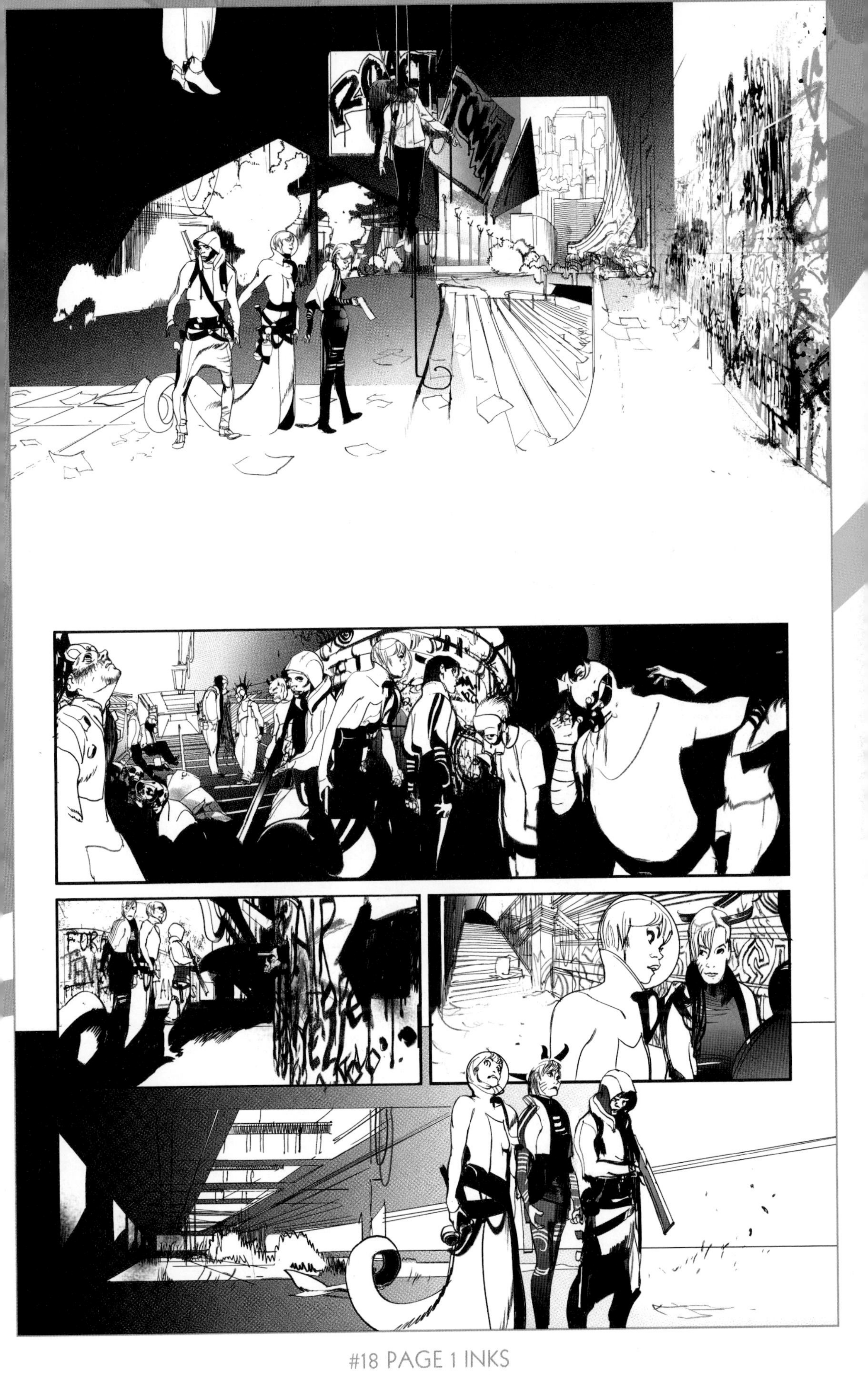

#18 PAGE 1 INKS

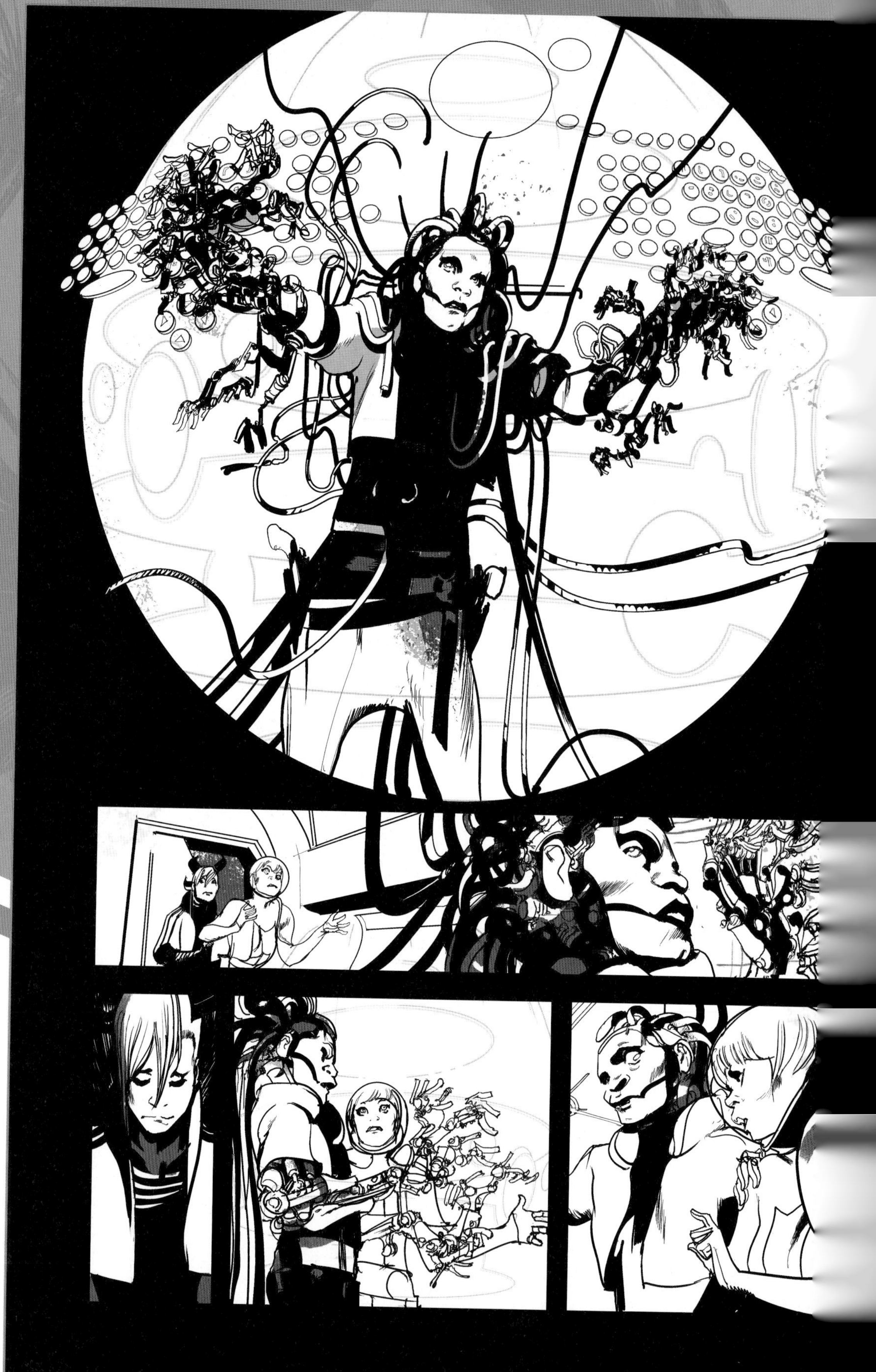

#19 PAGES 2-3 INKS

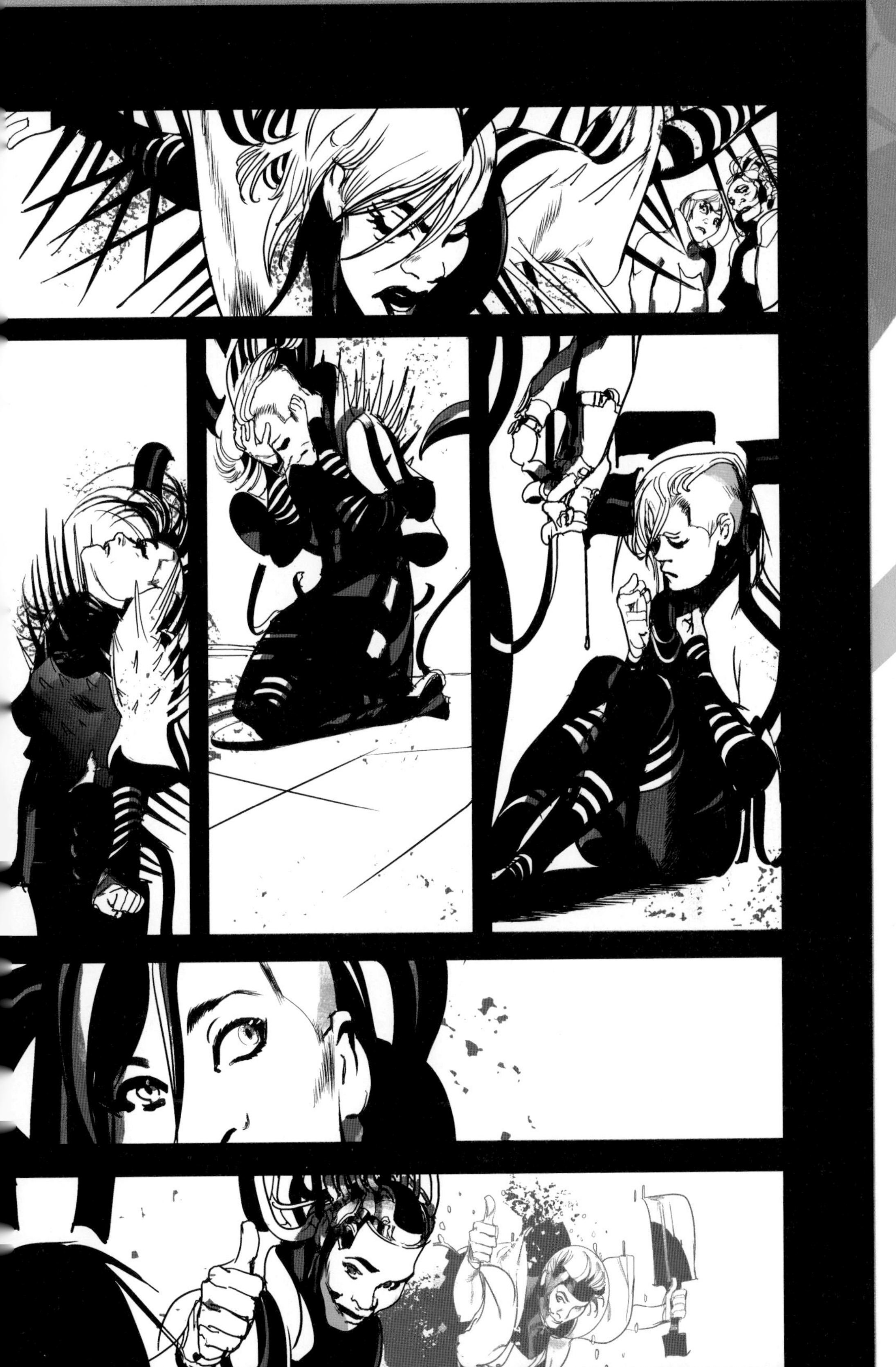

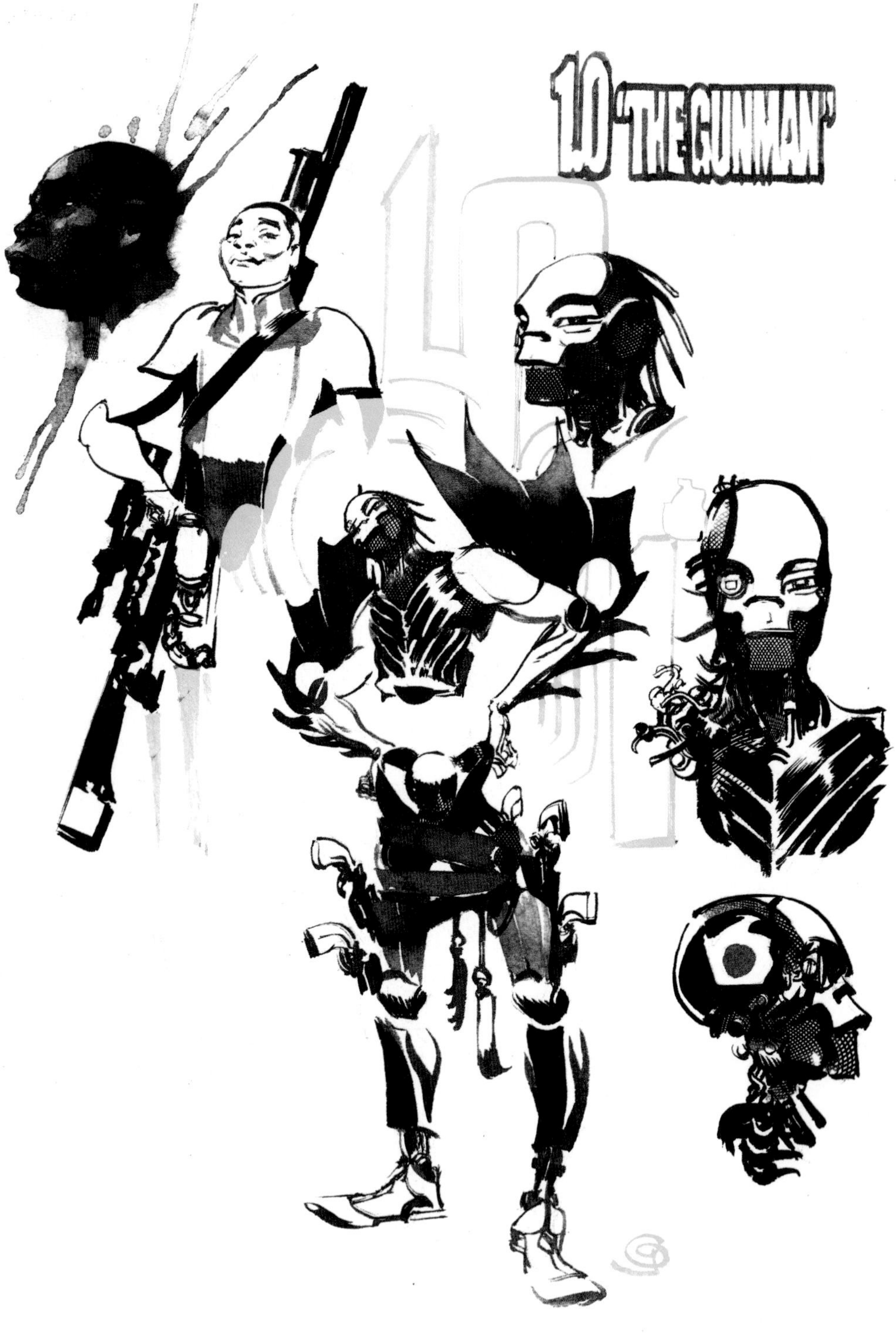
1.0 'THE GUNMAN'

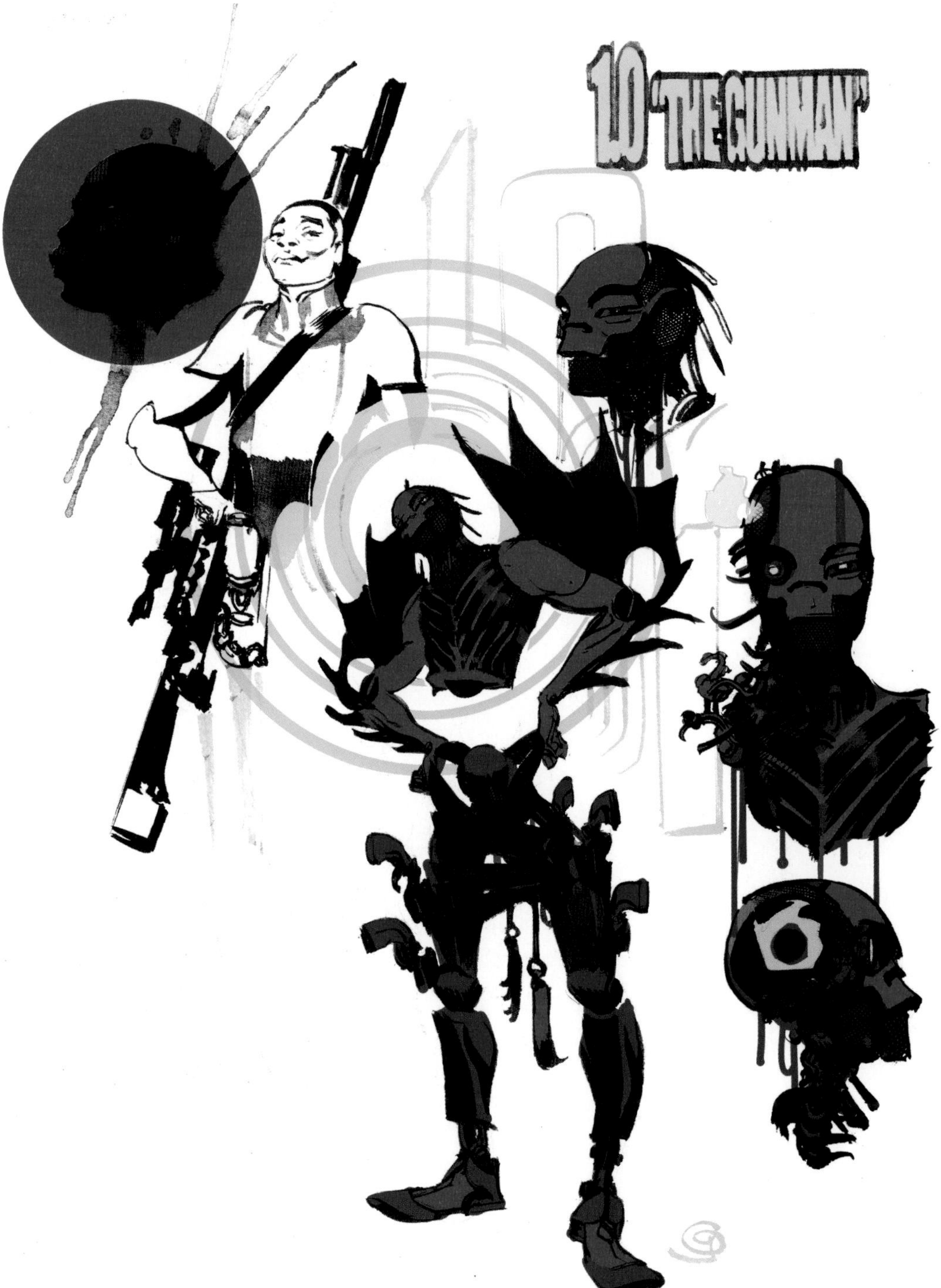
10 'THE GUNMAN'

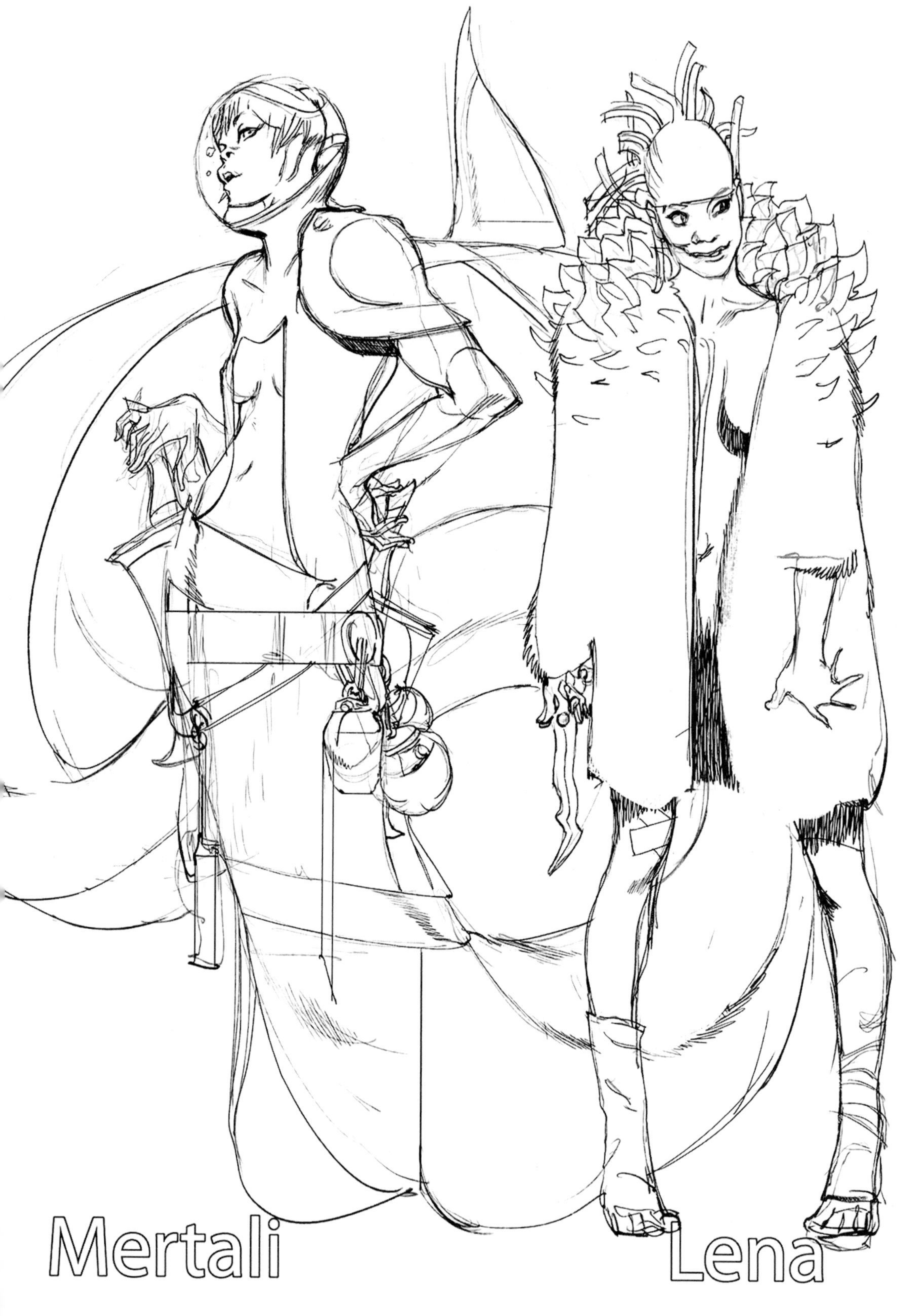
Mertali
Lena

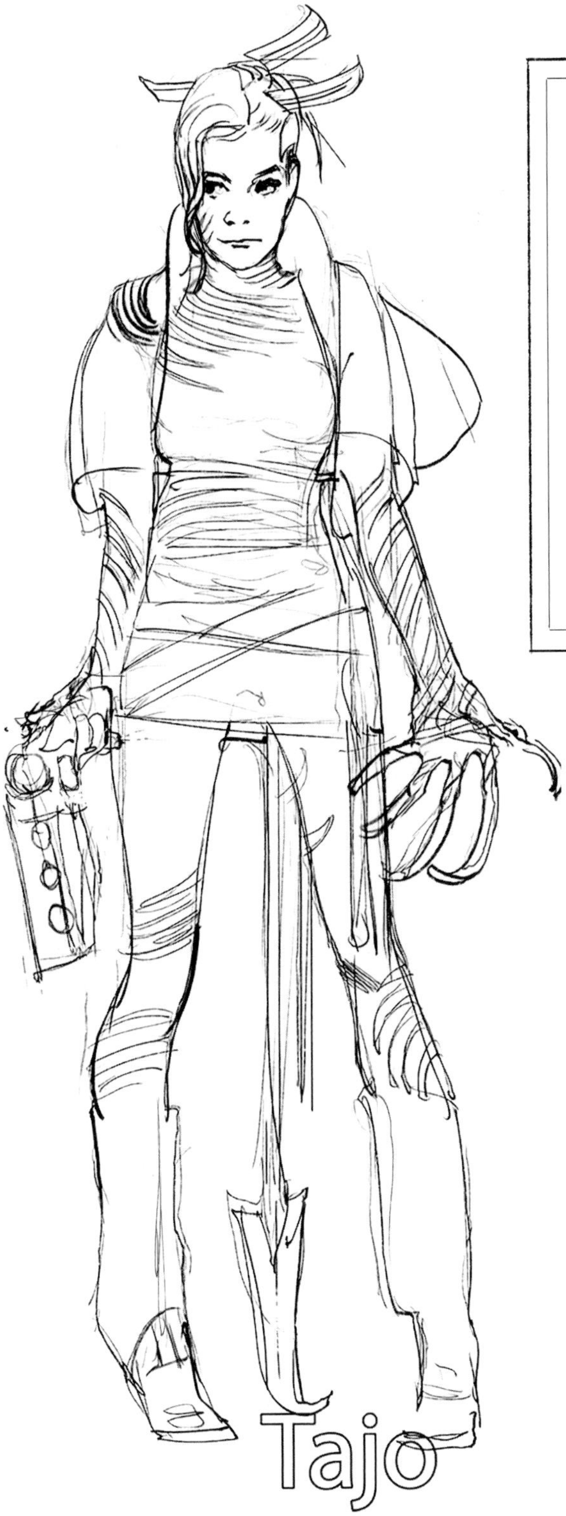

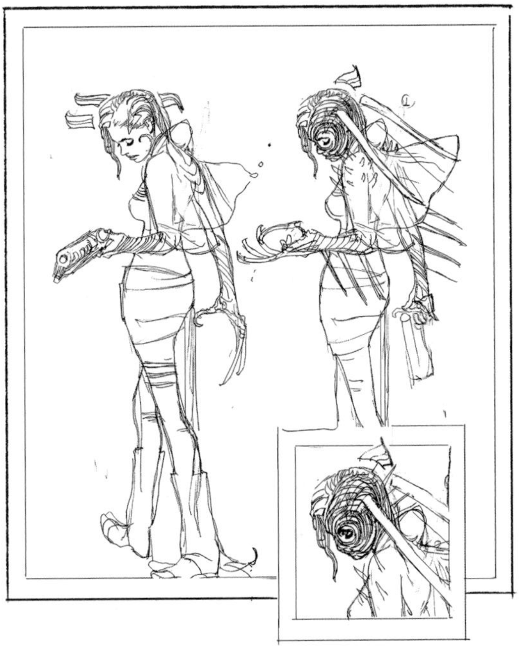

Tajo

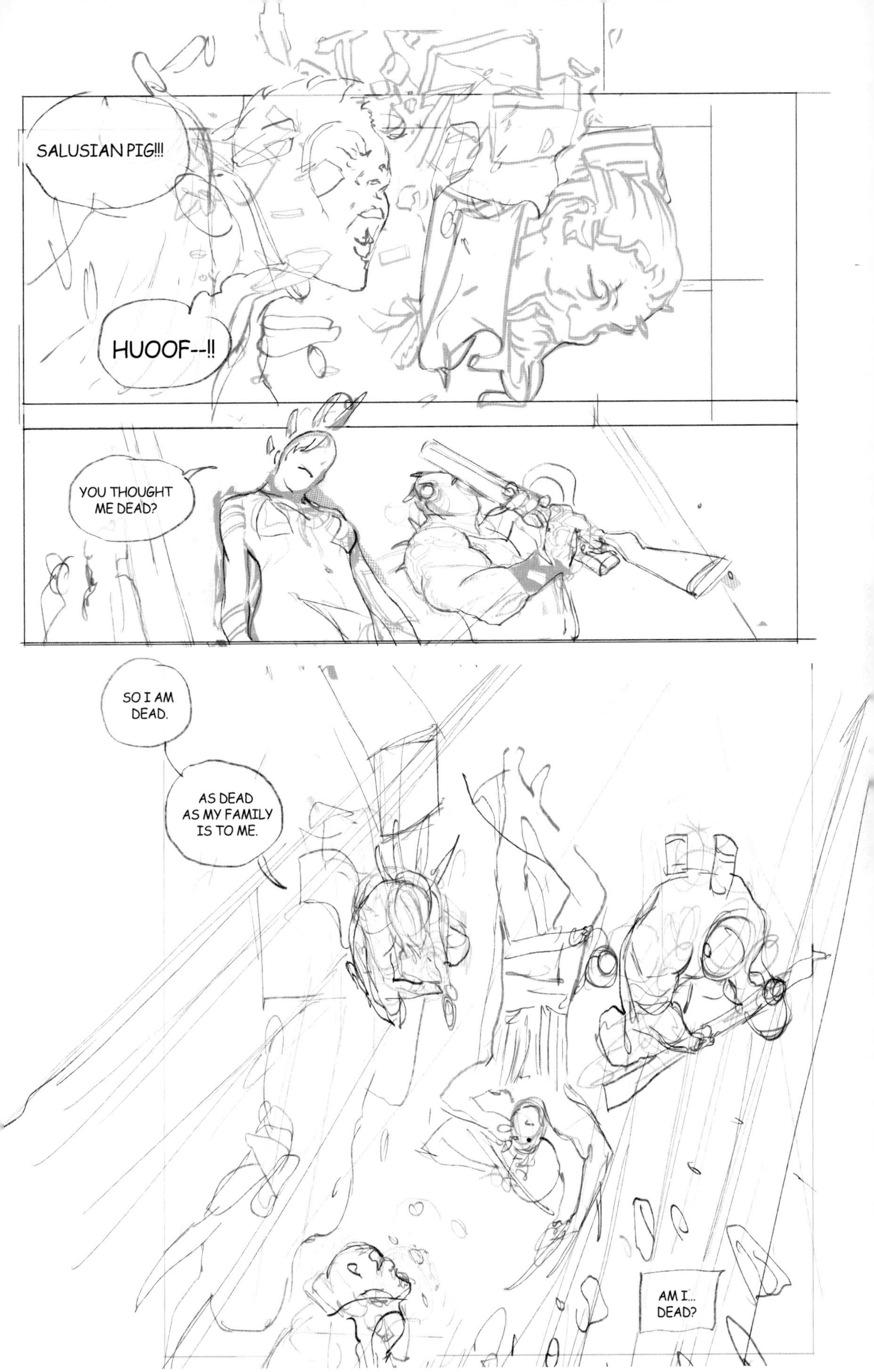
SALUSIAN PIG!!!
HUOOF--!!
YOU THOUGHT ME DEAD?
SO I AM DEAD.
AS DEAD AS MY FAMILY IS TO ME.
AM I... DEAD?

EARLY STORY CONCEPTS FOR LOW #16 BY GREG TOCCHINI

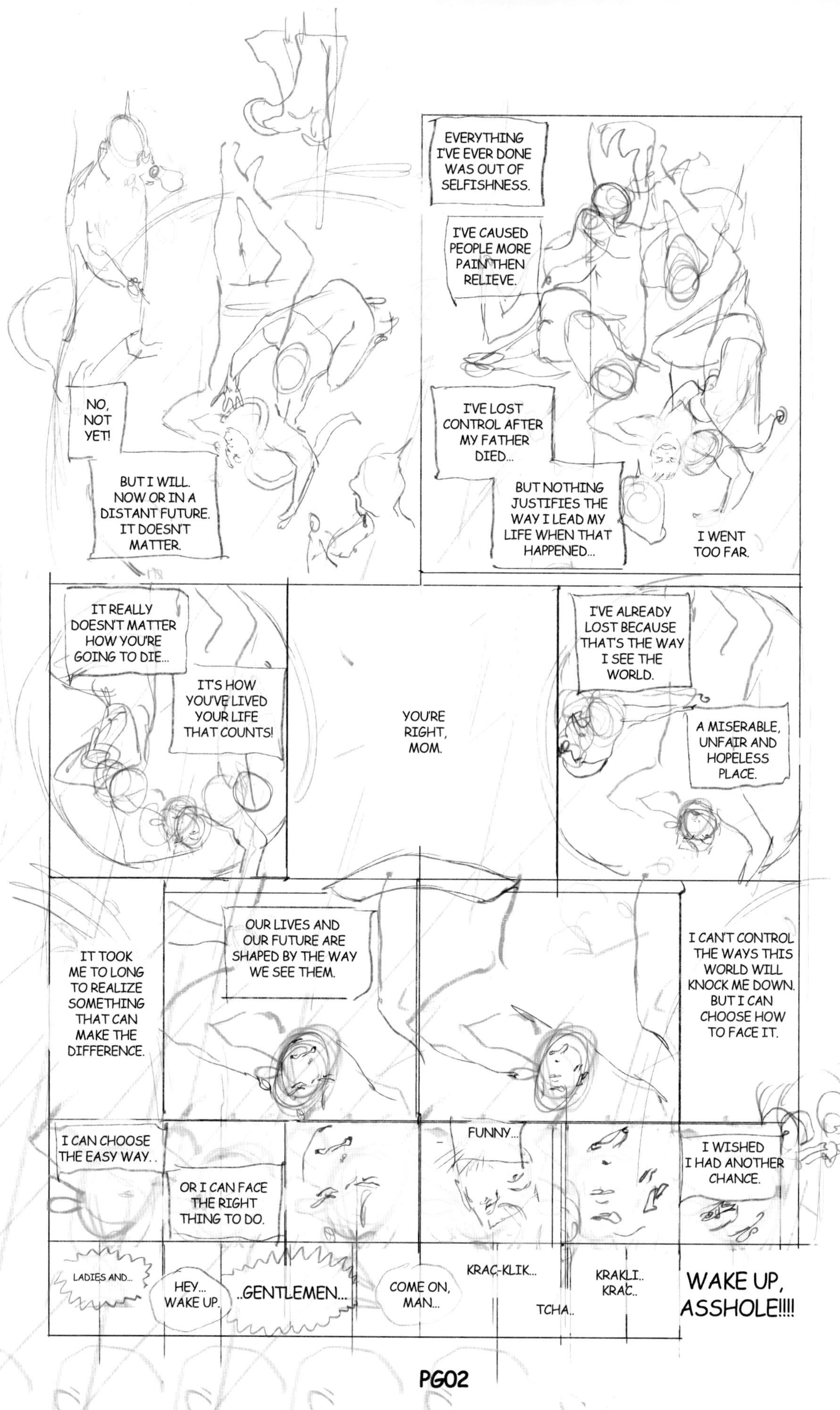

NO, NOT YET!
BUT I WILL. NOW OR IN A DISTANT FUTURE. IT DOESN'T MATTER.
EVERYTHING I'VE EVER DONE WAS OUT OF SELFISHNESS.
I'VE CAUSED PEOPLE MORE PAIN THEN RELIEVE.
I'VE LOST CONTROL AFTER MY FATHER DIED...
BUT NOTHING JUSTIFIES THE WAY I LEAD MY LIFE WHEN THAT HAPPENED...
I WENT TOO FAR.
IT REALLY DOESN'T MATTER HOW YOU'RE GOING TO DIE...
IT'S HOW YOU'VE LIVED YOUR LIFE THAT COUNTS!
YOU'RE RIGHT, MOM.
I'VE ALREADY LOST BECAUSE THAT'S THE WAY I SEE THE WORLD.
A MISERABLE, UNFAIR AND HOPELESS PLACE.
IT TOOK ME TO LONG TO REALIZE SOMETHING THAT CAN MAKE THE DIFFERENCE.
OUR LIVES AND OUR FUTURE ARE SHAPED BY THE WAY WE SEE THEM.
I CAN'T CONTROL THE WAYS THIS WORLD WILL KNOCK ME DOWN. BUT I CAN CHOOSE HOW TO FACE IT.
I CAN CHOOSE THE EASY WAY. .
OR I CAN FACE THE RIGHT THING TO DO.
FUNNY...
I WISHED I HAD ANOTHER CHANCE.
LADIES AND...
HEY... WAKE UP.
..GENTLEMEN...
COME ON, MAN...
KRAC-KLIK...
TCHA..
KRAKLI.. KRAC..
WAKE UP, ASSHOLE!!!!

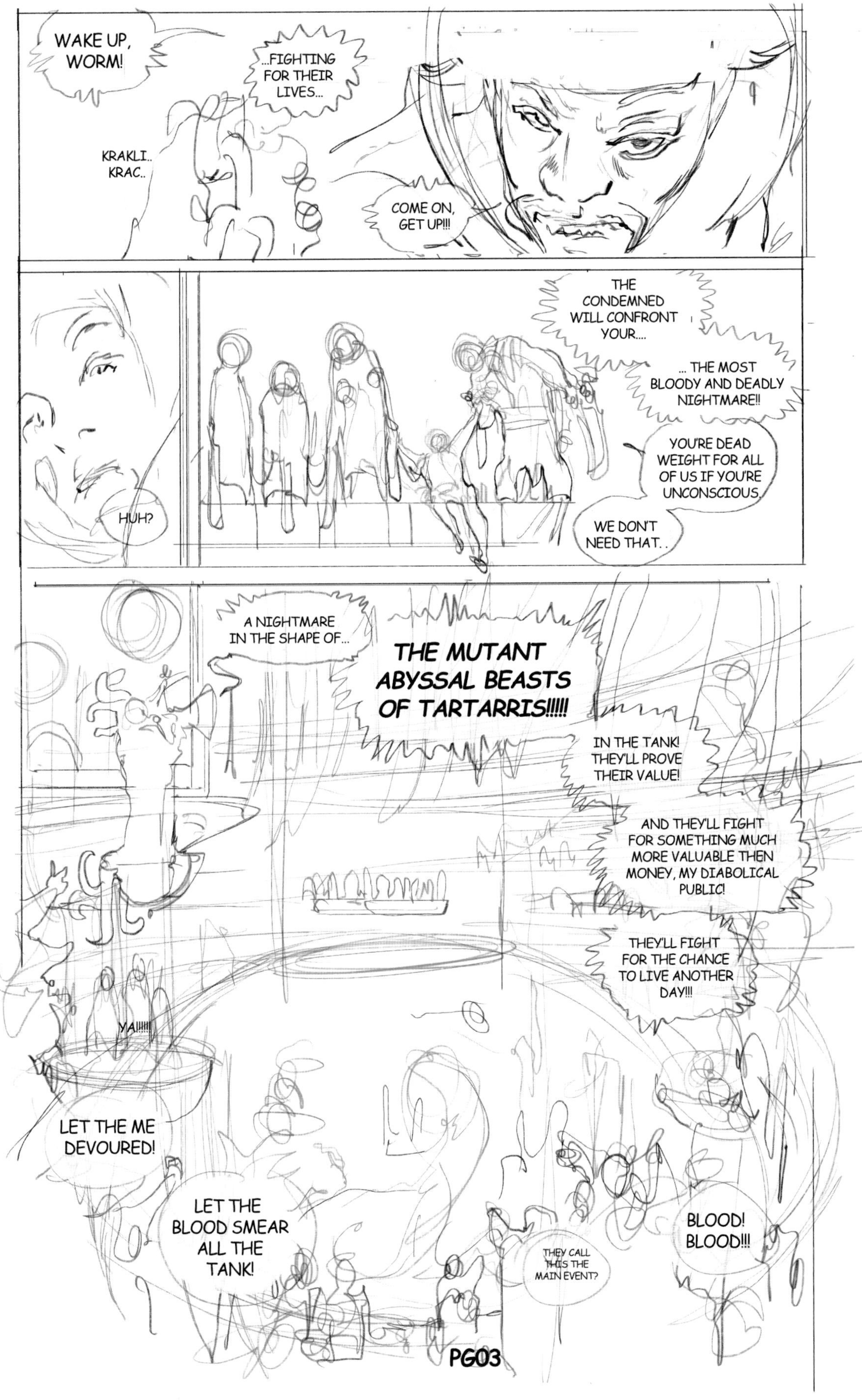
WAKE UP, WORM!
...FIGHTING FOR THEIR LIVES...
KRAKLI.. KRAC..
COME ON, GET UP!!!
THE CONDEMNED WILL CONFRONT YOUR....
... THE MOST BLOODY AND DEADLY NIGHTMARE!!
YOU'RE DEAD WEIGHT FOR ALL OF US IF YOU'RE UNCONSCIOUS.
HUH?
WE DON'T NEED THAT. .
A NIGHTMARE IN THE SHAPE OF...
THE MUTANT ABYSSAL BEASTS OF TARTARRIS!!!!!
IN THE TANK! THEY'LL PROVE THEIR VALUE!
AND THEY'LL FIGHT FOR SOMETHING MUCH MORE VALUABLE THEN MONEY, MY DIABOLICAL PUBLIC!
THEY'LL FIGHT FOR THE CHANCE TO LIVE ANOTHER DAY!!!
YA!!!!!
LET THE ME DEVOURED!
LET THE BLOOD SMEAR ALL THE TANK!
THEY CALL THIS THE MAIN EVENT?
BLOOD! BLOOD!!!

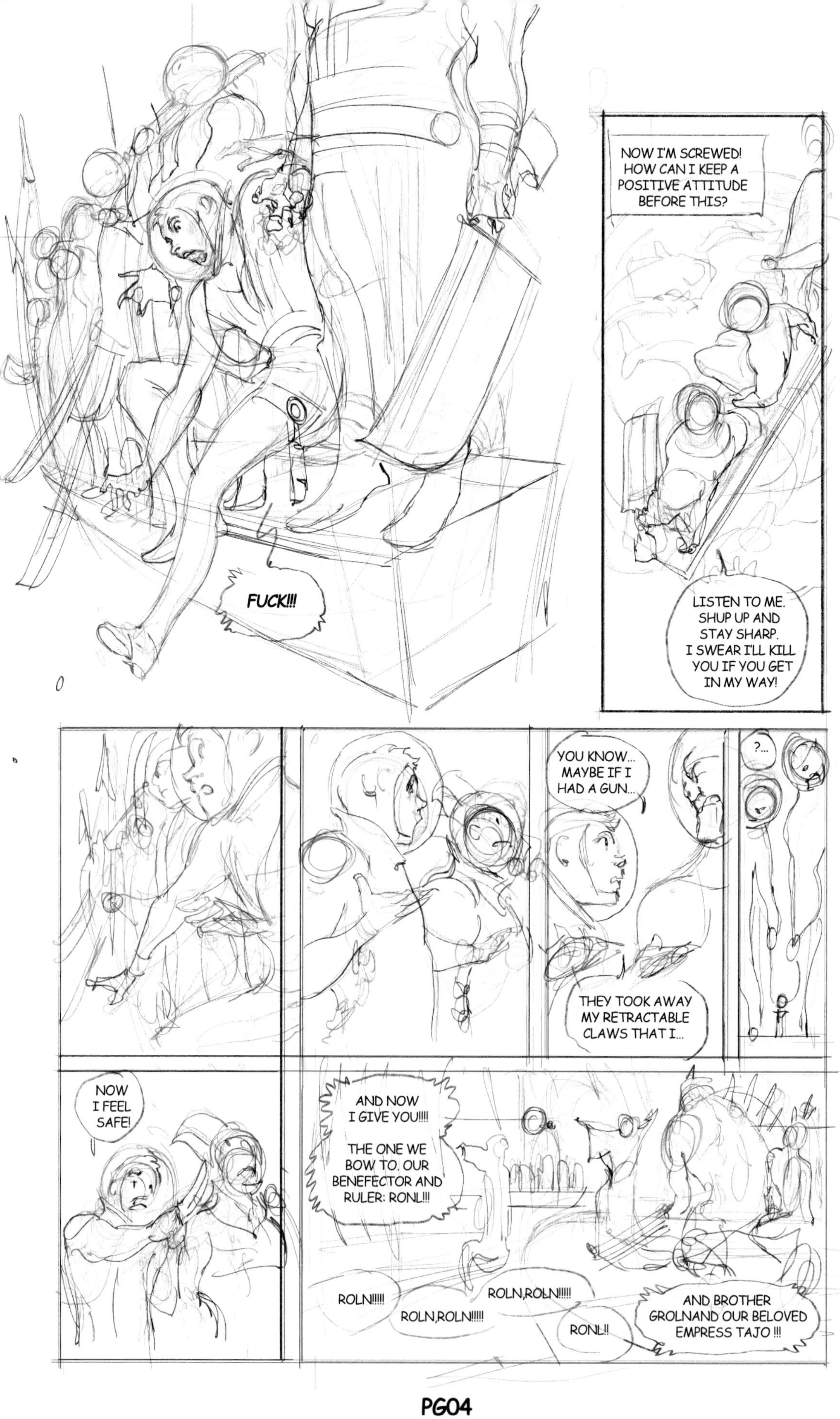
FUCK!!!
NOW I'M SCREWED! HOW CAN I KEEP A POSITIVE ATTITUDE BEFORE THIS?
LISTEN TO ME. SHUP UP AND STAY SHARP. I SWEAR I'LL KILL YOU IF YOU GET IN MY WAY!
YOU KNOW... MAYBE IF I HAD A GUN...
THEY TOOK AWAY MY RETRACTABLE CLAWS THAT I...
?...
NOW I FEEL SAFE!
AND NOW I GIVE YOU!!!!
THE ONE WE BOW TO. OUR BENEFECTOR AND RULER: RONL!!!
ROLN!!!!!
ROLN,ROLN!!!!!
ROLN,ROLN!!!!!
RONL!!
AND BROTHER GROLNAND OUR BELOVED EMPRESS TAJO !!!

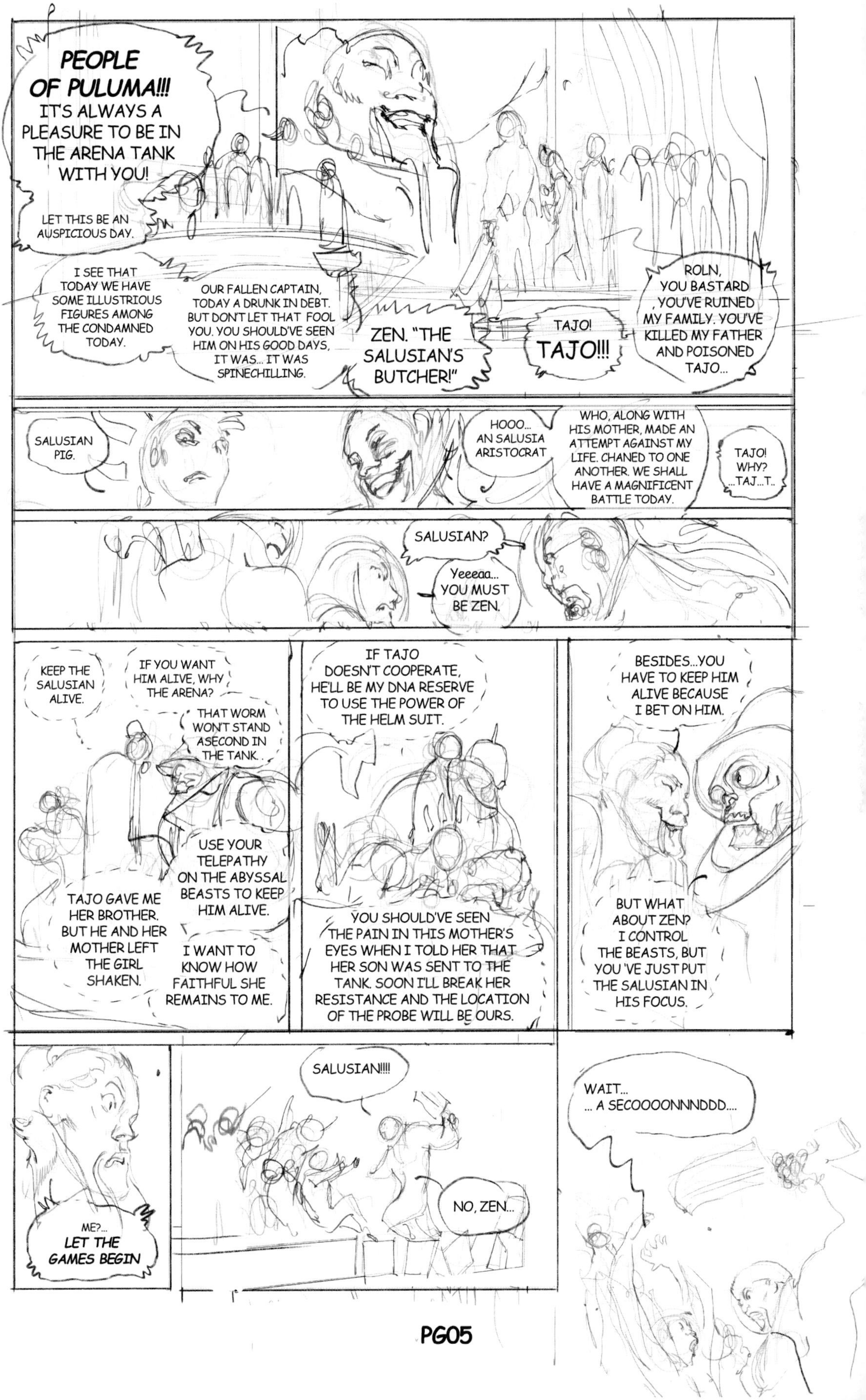
PEOPLE OF PULUMA!!! IT'S ALWAYS A PLEASURE TO BE IN THE ARENA TANK WITH YOU!
LET THIS BE AN AUSPICIOUS DAY.
I SEE THAT TODAY WE HAVE SOME ILLUSTRIOUS FIGURES AMONG THE CONDAMNED TODAY.
OUR FALLEN CAPTAIN, TODAY A DRUNK IN DEBT. BUT DON'T LET THAT FOOL YOU. YOU SHOULD'VE SEEN HIM ON HIS GOOD DAYS, IT WAS... IT WAS SPINECHILLING.
ZEN. "THE SALUSIAN'S BUTCHER!"
TAJO! TAJO!!!
ROLN, YOU BASTARD ,YOU'VE RUINED MY FAMILY. YOU'VE KILLED MY FATHER AND POISONED TAJO...
SALUSIAN PIG.
HOOO... AN SALUSIA ARISTOCRAT
WHO, ALONG WITH HIS MOTHER, MADE AN ATTEMPT AGAINST MY LIFE. CHANED TO ONE ANOTHER. WE SHALL HAVE A MAGNIFICENT BATTLE TODAY.
TAJO! WHY? ...TAJ...T..
SALUSIAN?
Yeeeaa... YOU MUST BE ZEN.
KEEP THE SALUSIAN ALIVE.
IF YOU WANT HIM ALIVE, WHY THE ARENA?
THAT WORM WON'T STAND ASECOND IN THE TANK..
USE YOUR TELEPATHY ON THE ABYSSAL BEASTS TO KEEP HIM ALIVE.
TAJO GAVE ME HER BROTHER. BUT HE AND HER MOTHER LEFT THE GIRL SHAKEN.
I WANT TO KNOW HOW FAITHFUL SHE REMAINS TO ME.
IF TAJO DOESN'T COOPERATE, HE'LL BE MY DNA RESERVE TO USE THE POWER OF THE HELM SUIT.
YOU SHOULD'VE SEEN THE PAIN IN THIS MOTHER'S EYES WHEN I TOLD HER THAT HER SON WAS SENT TO THE TANK. SOON I'LL BREAK HER RESISTANCE AND THE LOCATION OF THE PROBE WILL BE OURS.
BESIDES...YOU HAVE TO KEEP HIM ALIVE BECAUSE I BET ON HIM.
BUT WHAT ABOUT ZEN? I CONTROL THE BEASTS, BUT YOU 'VE JUST PUT THE SALUSIAN IN HIS FOCUS.
ME?... LET THE GAMES BEGIN
SALUSIAN!!!!
NO, ZEN...
WAIT... ... A SECOOOONNNDDD....

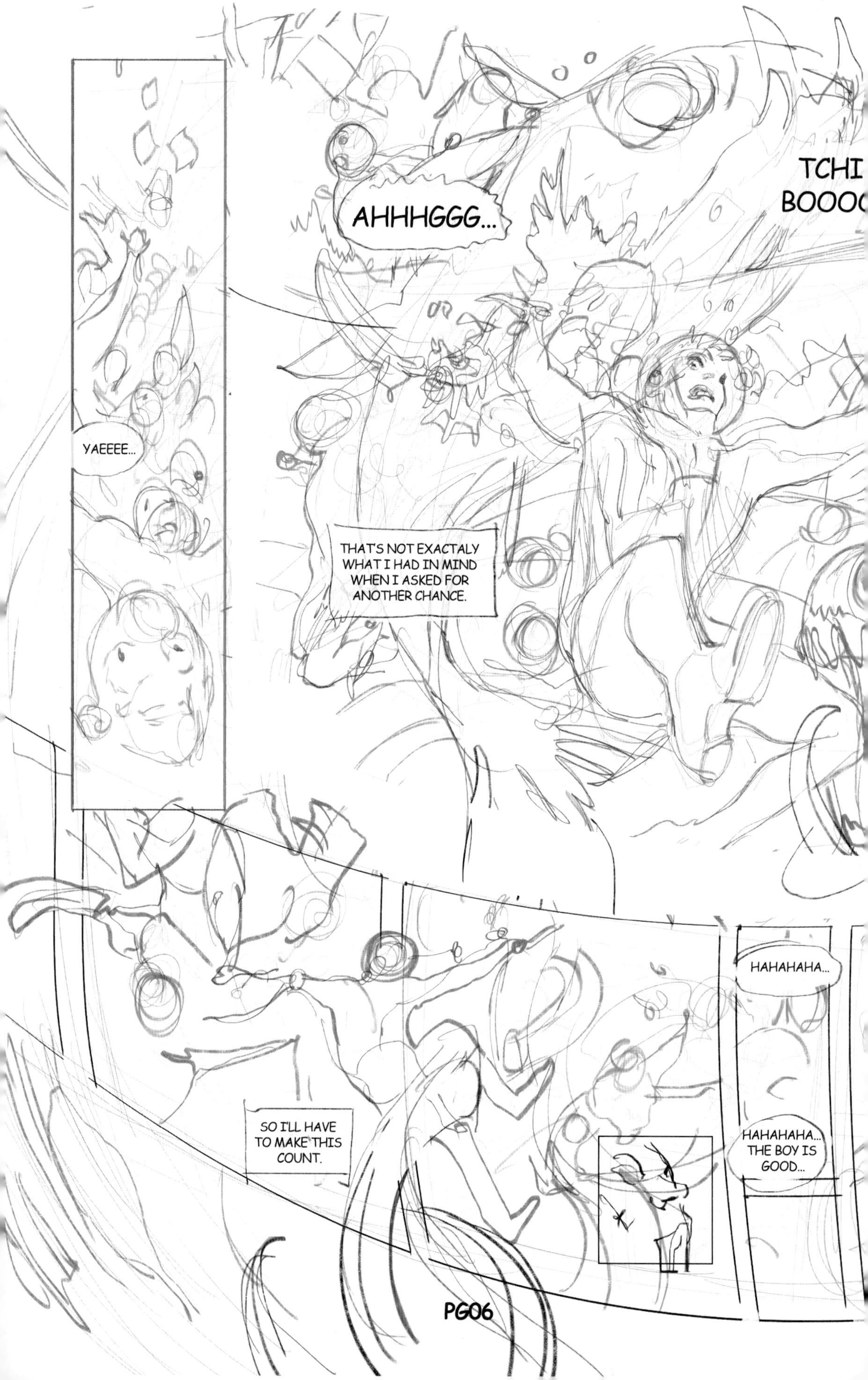
YAEEEE...
AHHHGGG...
TCHI
BOOOO
THAT'S NOT EXACTALY WHAT I HAD IN MIND WHEN I ASKED FOR ANOTHER CHANCE.
SO I'LL HAVE TO MAKE THIS COUNT.
HAHAHAHA...
HAHAHAHA... THE BOY IS GOOD...

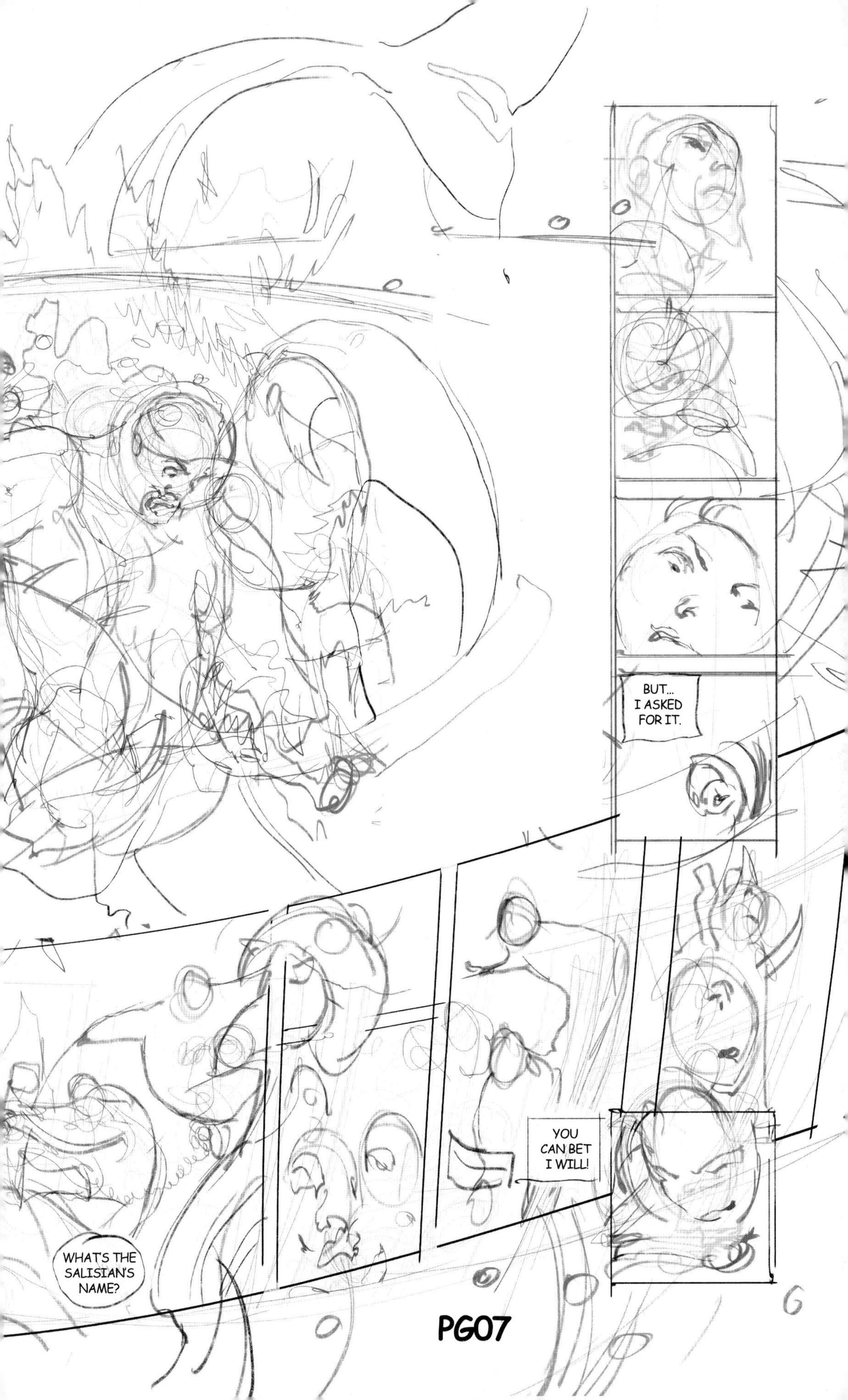
BUT... I ASKED FOR IT.
WHAT'S THE SALISIAN'S NAME?
YOU CAN BET I WILL!

PG07

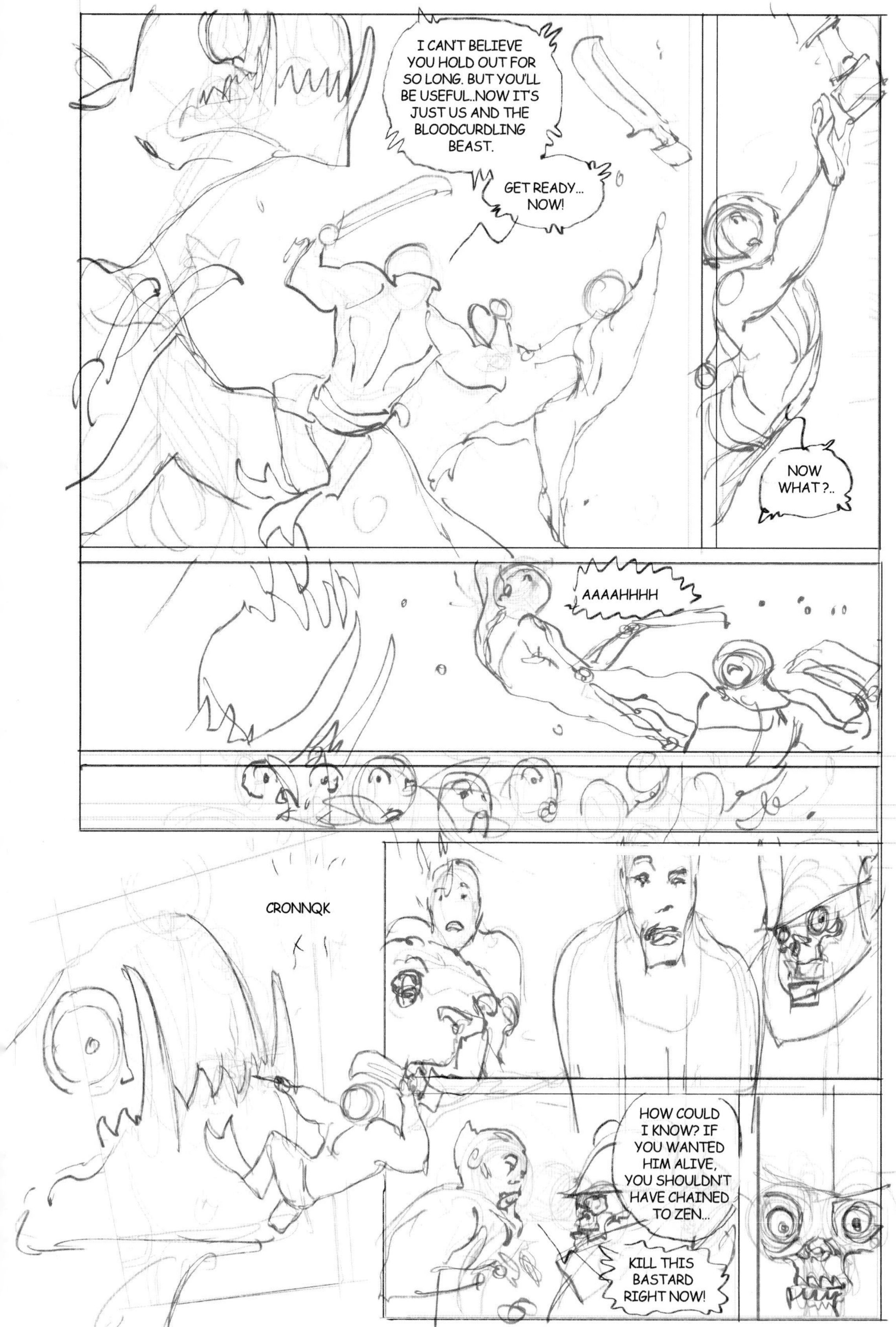
I CAN'T BELIEVE YOU HOLD OUT FOR SO LONG. BUT YOU'LL BE USEFUL..NOW IT'S JUST US AND THE BLOODCURDLING BEAST.
GET READY... NOW!
NOW WHAT?..
AAAAHHHH
CRONNQK
HOW COULD I KNOW? IF YOU WANTED HIM ALIVE, YOU SHOULDN'T HAVE CHAINED TO ZEN...
KILL THIS BASTARD RIGHT NOW!

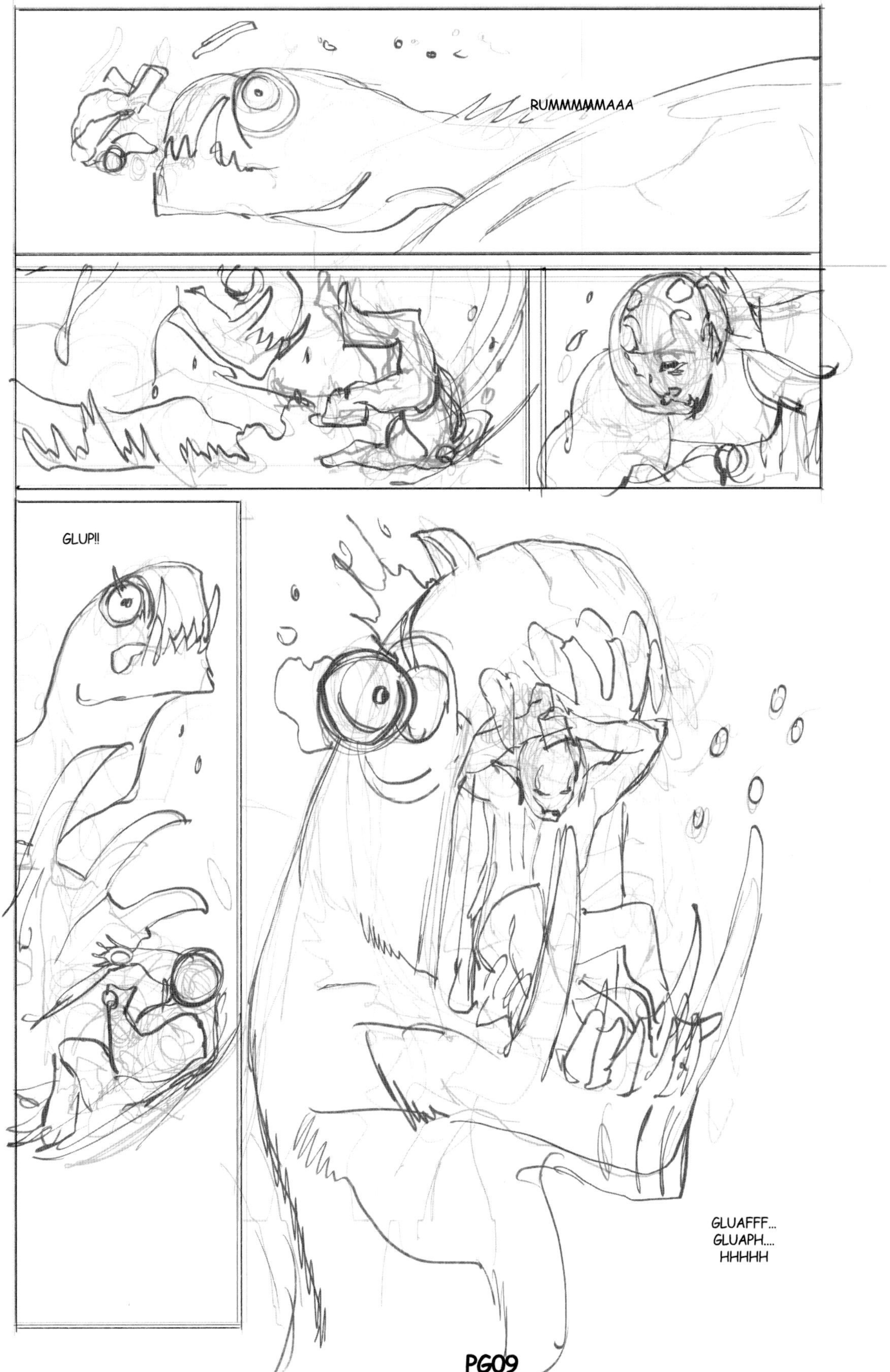
RUMMMMMAAA
GLUP!!
GLUAFFF...
GLUAPH....
HHHHH

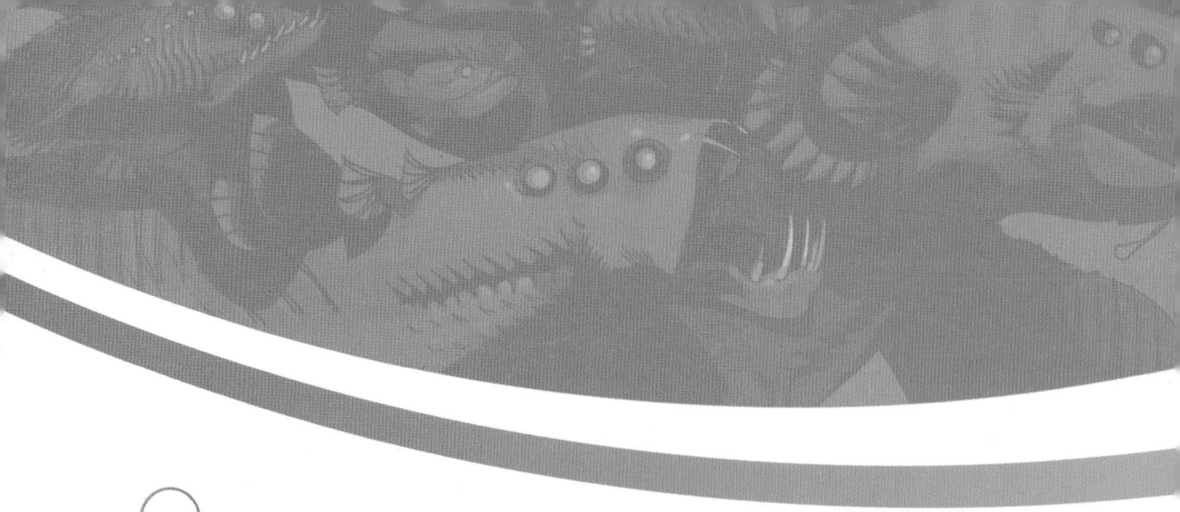

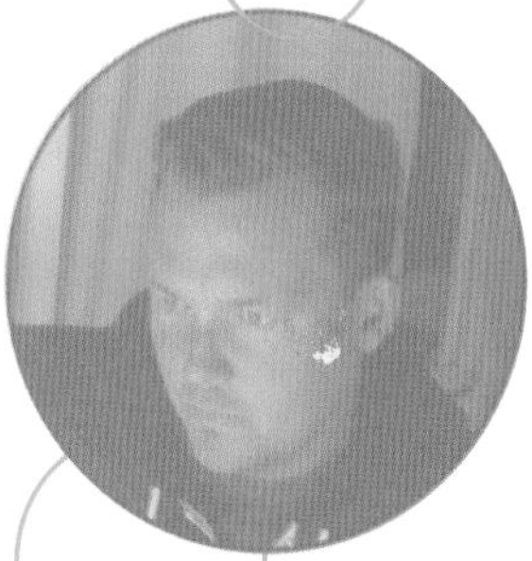

RICK REMENDER is the writer/co-creator of comics such as *Deadly Class, Fear Agent, Tokyo Ghost*, and *Black Science*. For Marvel he has written titles such as *Uncanny Avengers, Captain America, Uncanny X-Force,* and *Venom*. He's written video games such as *Bulletstorm* and *Dead Space*, and worked on films such as *The Iron Giant, Anastasia*, and *Titan A.E.* He and his tea-sipping wife, Danni, currently reside in Los Angeles raising two beautiful mischief monkeys.

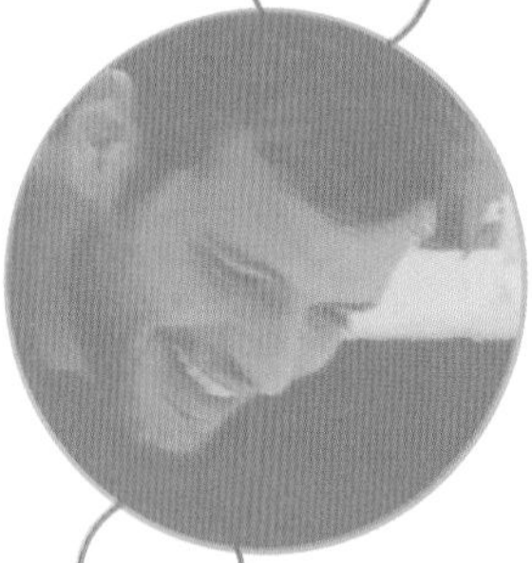

GREG TOCCHINI was born in 1979, in São Paulo, Brazil.

Since 2002 his work has been published internationally by companies such as Marvel and DC Comics (USA) and Le Lombard (France). Some titles include, *The Odyssey, Wolverine: Father, Fantastic Four, Thor: Son of Asgard, Captain America, Spider-Man, 1602: A New World, ION, Batman and Robin, Uncanny X-Force, Infinity Section*, and many others.

He was the artist on the mini-series *The Last Days of American Crime* written by Rick Remender, with whom he recently co-created the science fiction series *Low* currently being published by Image Comics. His independent label Dead Hamster Comics published his graphic novel *Sequence Shot* as well as works by various Brazilian artists.

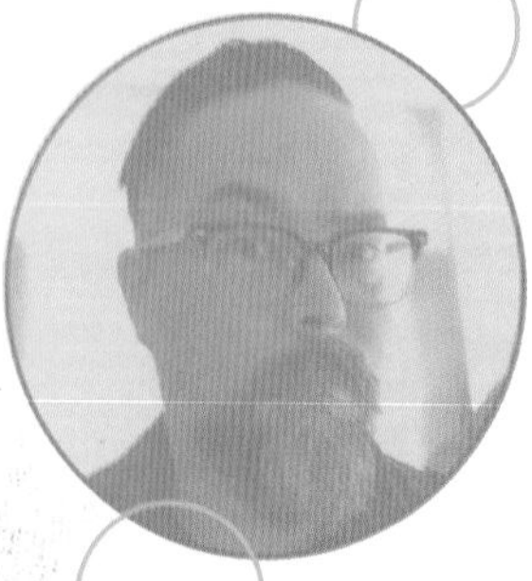

DAVE McCAIG is an Inkpot and Emmy award-winning colorist for comics and animation. He's known for coloring *Superman: Birthright, Nextwave, American Vampire, Northlanders*, and his work as lead color on *The Batman* animated series. He lives in New York with his two humans and two cats.